GUNPORT

John Corrigan

Copyright © 2023 John Corrigan

All rights reserved.

The characters and events portrayed in this book are fictitious. Any similarity to real persons, living or dead, is coincidental and not intended by the author.

No part of this book may be reproduced, or stored in a retrieval system, or transmitted in any form or by any means, electronic, mechanical, photocopying, recording, or otherwise, without express written permission of the publisher.

Contents

Prologue
Chapter 1: Welcome to Gunport
Chapter 2: Six Seconds Early
Chapter 3: The Visitor
Chapter 4: Line of the Dark
Chapter 5: Negotiations
Chapter 6: Spacewalk (Part 1)
Chapter 7: One More, One Less
Chapter 8: Renegotiations
Chapter 9: Kingdom of Bones
Chapter 10: Rotten in the Core
Chapter 11: Knowing is Nothing
Chapter 12: Counter-Offer
Chapter 13: Spacewalk (Part 2)
Chapter 14: Mors Machina
Chapter 15: Barrels of the Gun
Chapter 16: I'm Here to Talk
Epilogue (Part 1)
Epilogue (Part 2)

PROLOGUE

A lone spacesuit is floating across the Sea of Alacrity.

It drifts gently, simply, doggedly. Stars stab through the black of space and shine coldly. A metre below, the surface rolls by, a sea of grey that glitters like crushed glass.

It eases closer and closer to the lip of Anguta R-611's ancient canyon, the Vallis Adlivun. The suit's trajectory is unwavering, and it sags at its centre as it passes over the edge. Its arms hang loosely, its fingers curled, its head bowed, and its feet pointed towards each other. It passes alongside, the canyon's distant bottom miles below, where shimmering dust is slowly replace by the thick black of deep and toneless pits.

The canyon is left behind. The suit slows and dips, and as it touches the ground, it crumples at its knees. The toes scrape into the dirt, bending the feet at the ankles, and the suit gently collapses to the surface. For the first time in millions of years, this stretch of silvery dust on the surface is disturbed. Then, the suit rolls upward, rising out of the cloud of grit that has angrily risen. The surface of the Sea of Alacrity is scarred forever by trailing boots. The roll takes it up, before the thin thread of gravity tugs it down. The suit settles back into its path, a metre above the surface.

This circuit of the moon will be the same as all of the others. Where it scratches antique dust away it leaves a new streak of silver, another scar, stretching far behind, until it rejoins an earlier trail. The suit passes from scorching light to freezing dark and back again and continues on. Except for a slow bounce in a different place, or a toe catching a different rock, or the angle of its torso as it slides alongside another canyon, each circuit is the same.

It does not matter. The suit continues its journey. In time, plumes of gas emerge beyond. The texture of the moon has changed. There is a flicker of movement, blurry, but now sharpening into focus. There are ships, landing and launching. Vibrations in the ground rattle the dust, and as the suit gets closer, the grey dust has shaken away, revealing a solid floor of dull rock.

Perhaps this circuit will be different to the others.

CHAPTER 1: WELCOME TO GUNPORT

Anson Haig stared into the stars and searched for the right word to describe the inside of the shuttle. 'Tidy' was what he called seeing the floor in his son's room. 'Compact' didn't go far enough. 'Functional' was almost there, but missing something. It didn't express how in-your-face the shuttle's functionality was. How aggressive. Ah.

Aggressively functional.

Each and every flat surface housed some panel or switch or display. And often folded out to provide another. If it could float, it was strapped down. If it could move, it folded into an alcove. There were cupboards within cupboards. Windows created weak points, and so there were painfully few windows. Up front was a solitary permanent chair for a pilot, with two small portholes slightly above, so that sitting there and looking outside for too long made Haig's neck sore. There was a long monitor that could display the outside world, but it was unreal, somehow. It couldn't capture the life in the stars. Haig felt that if he crawled into one cupboard it would only lead to another cupboard, and another, and another; an infinite journey of cupboards. That, in fact, there was no outside. Only another cupboard.

Army ships he had served on were like this. Sparse, empty. But this was an Aphelion Systems shuttle. Longer range.

More complicated. But squashed into a smaller space meant the hostile usefulness. Do not touch, it seemed to say. But all of these gadgets made things heavier. More weight meant more fuel. More fuel meant more cost. Profit held ransom by kilograms. There was a short pre-flight briefing. Cursory medical. Everyone knew he was going, health conditions or not. They'd seemed pleased he only had one leg. Less weight, he assumed. Cheaper.

Still. He had begun his journey with brutal speed.

Victor Mangan called and loomed large on Haig's home screen. He loomed large in person too, an intimidating figure. Mangan was former military himself and ran IPRA, the Inter-Planetary Reconciliation Agency.

Haig's job now, post-Army negotiator, was to mediate corp-corp or corp-employee disputes. This was often peaceful, despite the empty hostility and shouting and threats of people involved, and in a post-lunar environment, it was almost always on a screen, and almost always over in less than a week.

His last job was a group of engineers who built cables in an orbital facility above the Moon for General Lunar Cable. 99.2% pure in zero-gravity, a pre-mediation packet assured him. Compared to 86.3% on Earth. That ten-odd percent must make all the difference, Haig supposed. GLC had been taking accommodation modules from the end of the facility each year until eventually there were ninety people in a space that should hold only thirty-two. One of their guys crashed a robot into a pylon in an oxygen-starved fugue and the company sacked him, then told him to make his own way home. How? With what?

After briefly rioting and breaking every piece of equipment there that wasn't bolted down, they realised that every piece of equipment there was designed to keep them alive. They'd rather be alive than angry. So they simply stopped working. GLC called in IPRA and Haig negotiated two brand-new modules out of them before making the engineers agree to start work again when the first one was fitted. Last he knew, everyone was – unhappily – back to it.

"I need someone with spacework," said Mangan. "Ex-military, ideally. Reliable. Guess who I thought of?"

"Spacework?" said Haig. "Don't need to go into space to talk to someone over a screen."

"This one's different," said Mangan. "I could order you to go, but you're a stubborn wanker sometimes and that'd probably make you say 'no' even quicker. At least hear me out."

"No harm in talking it through," Haig conceded. "Where?"

"The Anguta Rail Port," said Mangan.

Haig sighed. "Fucking Gunport."

"Gunport," said Mangan, nodding.

Gunport meant Aphelion, and Aphelion meant trouble. Ruthless and enormous, their aim, whether stated or not, was to dominate space. Which was absurd, thought Haig. Space was infinite. They were not.

"Reactor techs on strike about conditions," said Mangan. "Water, air, living space, food, medicine. You know how it goes. They're refusing to let supply ships land unless they're supplies for Gunport itself. WSA got involved. Aphelion's been ordered to get a third-party to talk the techs down. That's us."

Mangan took him through it. Haig had been in the Army, had fought in space. Had fought in enclosed spaces on the surface or in orbit, knew how to perform environmental restitution, the patching up of a moonbase after a gunfight punched bullets through walls and the air disappeared. He could operate a suit, fly a ship, drive a moon buggy. Didn't have any exotic implants to upkeep, so no replacement parts would be needed, no medications. Missing leg made no difference, in Mangan's eyes. Slap an imp on and away you go. Aphelion was

7

paying for travel and IPRA's fees, with the union's agreement. Six to eight months travel there, a month in negotiations, six to eight months back.

Nearly eighteen months in space, all told. Too long, thought Haig. Far too long.

"Why not do it over a screen, then? Why is it different?"

"We tried that briefly. Comms out there are too poor. Furthest point from Earth with settled people. No reliable connection for real-time work. Takes a week to send anything back, even with Aphelion's satellites and boosters."

"Aphelion are happy to wait that long?"

"They're under pressure," said Mangan. "Don't think they care about government pressure, weak as it is, but Triangle's got wind. Gunport's its own thing, but it relies on traffic to make its money. Triangle is blocking Aphelion's cargo flights from the North Point until a third-party sorts it out, and they want us. Means their supply chain is stuck. Techs are unionised through PAROU, the Power and Reactor Operator's Union, and they've agreed to talk through us. Aphelion tried to argue their strike was illegal because it affected the whole of Gunport and not just the Reactor techs, but PAROU argued back, said that because Gunport's on a moon and so concentrated, so isolated, Reactor techs not being able to keep the lights on affects the whole place."

"Let me put it another way," said Haig. "*Will* Aphelion wait that long? Normally they'd make this kind of problem disappear themselves. Normally they invoke the law to buy time to send a trigger squad in. Normally we'd be hearing about a moonbase full of bodies by now."

Mangan sighed. "This is different."

"Is it? Come on, Mangan."

"I agree. I was wary too. But I've done my diligence. They can't brute force this one. Everyone used to think Gunport was a big waste. An ego project. Maybe it was, but now Gunport's the crown jewel. The apple in their eye. Everyone knows Gunport. Everyone's watching. The guy who runs it has sway, too. John Sile. He's pushed the brass at Aphelion for a legal solution. He might be worried about them sending heavies in too. Aphelion makes trillions out of it every year. They've got plenty of enemies, just waiting for Gunport to fail, which means they can't afford any mistakes."

"Okay. Maybe there's scope with Aphelion then. What about the tech guys?"

"The tech unions know Aphelion pays pretty well. They want a solution too. The woman running the strike is Sunita Acaba. She's been there a long time. She's trying to look after her crew. She says there's been a slow decline in conditions and now it's unworkable."

"Why don't Aphelion just swap them out?"

"In the reactor industry, Gunport's is ancient. It's only been open for six years, but the reactor's been online for maybe eight? Installed for ten? Means none of the guys coming through can run a retro reactor. And it can't be updated because it can't be offline long enough. Gunport's got all the emergency batteries of a modern base but they don't have enough charge for two years to update their reactor to let the new guys run it. Allpower have been hoovering up Reactor techs too, so there's none out there. Aphelion's doing a training scheme to get the numbers up, but for Gunport, it'd mean two or three years without a crew. They have to do it properly this time."

"They've had years to train new techs. Not up to us to clean up their short-sightedness."

"You're right, it's poor planning, but this is where we are."

Haig rubbed at his beard. "And if IPRA can't find a resolution, they'll send the Army in, presumably."

"And you of all people know how that'll end."

"I thought you were trying to persuade me to go, not to stay at home."

Haig had been mentally rehearsing his 'no' since Mangan had said eighteen months, and nothing he had said since had changed his mind. Until –

Mangan leaned forward and looked at him carefully. "We know no-one wants this one, so IPRA's throwing in a sweetener. If you go, you get housing privileges."

Haig's 'no' stopped in his throat. Clever bastard.

Haig's house was not built for the knifing winds of his winters or the concrete-melting heat of his summers, but both inflicted themselves upon it. Whipped air clogged with thick dust. Rancid water burbling with streaked grease. Carbon Circles limiting travel to a carbon-neutral ring around your home. You can only go as far as is carbon neutral. If you've an old car or old house, you do not get to move.

And Tom, seven years old and up to fourteen near-fatal bouts of anaphylaxis. The last attack even with the mask on and the medications in him, a ten-minute walk to a filled-in rocket silo turning ugly when the wind came, defying all of the most reliable forecasts, the boy choking and wheezing and dying before him, and Haig had stabbed his son in the leg with adrenaline and held the oxygen mask so tightly to Tom's face that the bruises took weeks to fade, both weeping as he did, both terrified, the boy staring wide-eyed at his father and desperate for his help before the ambulance arrived. Olivia had blamed Haig and he had tried to explain that it had been fine before, but this was the one that their relationship couldn't recover from. I'm not going to watch him die, she had said. Haig came back from a hospital visit to find her and her things gone.

The boy was now sprawled out in front of him, oblivious to

Mangan and Haig's conversation, attacking his favourite toy, an over-loved rabbit that was once fluffy, now packed hard with dirt and grotty with exhaustion. The rabbit stayed in the house, and that was non-negotiable. Haig couldn't have it bringing the outside in, not given how much Tom put it on his face. Tom hadn't seem to connect the outside with his illness, forever upset at having to leave rabbit at home. Not that they really left the house anymore.

Haig prodded him with an outstretched foot, and Tom swatted wordlessly at him. Blond hair bounced in front of his eyes, and he tugged irritably at the mask over his nose. Most respiratory illnesses could be solved with implants in the throat, or in severe cases, replacing the lungs entirely. Haig thought about the doctors straddling Tom like they had straddled him when he had lost his leg, hacking parts out of him, carving away. At what point would the little boy on the table become a little robot? How many pieces would be replaced before Tom was no longer Tom?

And Haig remembered Tom's first vaccinations at age three. The kindest nurse gave him the faintest scratch when he flinched at the needle, and Tom had screamed for a day until bedtime, fell asleep for less than an hour before then having nightmares and ejecting Haig couchwards from his own bed, Olivia shrugging and smiling and comforting the sobbing boy. Haig couldn't even begin to think about how to tell him that they might take his lungs. Even just this imagined scenario, the thought of telling Tom what would happen, and then watching him be operated on, and the near-certain chance of the new lungs' allergic failure, filled Haig with a cold dread.

But privileges meant temperature-controlled housing. Breathable air. Reliable water. Travel permissions to beyond your Carbon Circle. Travel to newer hospitals. With better implants, anflams, and imsups, and allergy treatments. Gene therapies to remove his allergies. Successful treatments. A life for Tom.

Haig blinked and felt tears come and nodded at the screen, fearful to hope.

"What about – "

Mangan smiled and said, "We'll take Olivia on as an employee and pay both of you for the whole time you're away. Won't be much, but the bonus is in the package at the end. Will Olivia do it? When did you last speak to her?"

Bastard knew I'd say yes for housing, thought Haig. Didn't want to offer it but should have led with it.

"She'll break the Earth in half for housing," said Haig.

***

The transfer to the Moon was easy enough.

Firstly to the Triangle, the three-pronged spaceport that owned the Nevada desert. Every ship going from Earth that left this solar system went from here. There was a strong anti-corp feeling, the sense that the Triangle was neutral-but-not. We'll launch your ships, but we're not happy about it. Rumour was that Aphelion was building their own spaceport in West Africa, buying up tracts of land in Mali and building a brutalist city of concrete, but the Triangle owned the flight paths and exit lanes into orbit, so how the ships would leave Earth, nobody quite knew. Haig figured brute force. They'd build it anyway, and launch ships anyway, and risk crashes and the wrath of the WSA, and dare the Triangle or Blue High or Black Sand or anyone else to stop them. Fines? Bans? They'd push through them, cynically protest innocence, and do what they wanted.

Two hours on a moonbus with haggard journeymen had him more than ready to disembark. These were engineers, scientists, miners, pale-faced and solitary. Most in corp overalls. Some Black Sand Automation blue, the deep black-green of Blue High. And the smell was exactly as he remembered, a mix of concrete dust and tired air-conditioning and burned electronics and the stale, sour smell of warm humanity pushed up against each other.

He was scooped up before he'd gotten his bearings and corralled into an Aphelion holding area then marched straight through a series of concrete corridors until they gave way to a concertina walkway, and into the Alkonost-class shuttle Excalibur, his aggressively functional home for the next six to eight months.

A swarm of Aphelion engineers and technicians lay in wait. They strapped him into the Benaceraff-Davies Chamber onboard, and much like the doctors when he'd lost his leg, they had scurried around him in a controlled fury without telling him anything before disappearing all at once to leave him suddenly alone in silence. Only the B-D Chamber was new to him. Plastered in Aphelion logos – a blunt 'A', off-centre in a tilted oval – the chamber was just taller than him and just wider than him. Behind it were tanks of sloshing, gelatinous liquid. When he was in the Army, they used plasma engines. Haig understood them, to a point. Hot gas spewed the ship forth. An over-simplification, he knew, but that was all he needed to know. Aphelion had gone further. Vacuum Engines. They sucked their way through space. Haig had no idea how they worked, but they were fast, too fast for humans. Incredible forces that squashed blood into brains and drowned minds, and so, a little while later, Aphelion's scientists built the B-D Chamber. Benaceraff and Davies.

"If you're stood on Earth, you don't notice it flying through space, or how fast it spins. The B-DC is kind of like that," said a technician. "But, you know, more complicated."

The flurry was in part desperation. Haig would have been suspicious if they had been slow getting him there. When the big corps delayed IPRA, they were working on their own negotiations. And they were always less than friendly.

Aphelion wanted him at Gunport, and they wanted him there

now.

The activity faded. Hurry up and wait, he thought. He was in his isolation for hours before a tinned voice started muttering in his ear, then he felt the rumbling of the shuttle into orbit, the first lurch of the Vacuum Engines, and the pressure, building and building and building, incredible and relentless forces, his cheeks vibrating, his eyelids pushed over his eyes, and then a voice counted him down from ten, the B-D Chamber sealing with a shush.

He had the momentary amusement of hovering above himself and smelling what pink must smell like, before oblivion.

***

Haig awoke six months and a few days later.

The chamber must have immersed him in some liquid after he had become unconscious then drained it before he woke up, because his fingers stuck together and the hair around his chest and arms had matted. He could feel his ribs, now. Could feel his eyes moving in their sockets, would swear he heard a wet grinding in his skull.

A different tinned voice spoke to him.

"We're going to let you out," it said. "You won't like it, I'm afraid. You've lost a great deal of weight. You'll be weak and nauseous. It'll feel like you're deep underwater, a great weight on your shoulders and chest, and even though you'll be in zero gravity, it won't help. There will be pressure in your ears, and an unsettling feeling around your eyes. You might hear things. All of this is normal."

For days he ate and dozed, punctuated by vomiting of great violence. He allowed himself to float untethered in zero gravity because he did not have the strength to strap himself down. He vomited into air because he could not bear to travel the infinite distance of the shuttle's length for a waste tube.

When his head cleared, he realised that Aphelion must have

designed for this, because every disgraceful thing that came out of his body was sucked away and presumably – hopefully – deposited outside, polluting deep space. His vision tunnelled and he spent days staring through the cockpit's spaces at the stars.

Aphelion made itself known with shameless self-promotion.

The screens turned themselves on – unavoidable and unskippable, how he had tried, mid-migraine – that showed a tired-looking woman sat alone in an enormous living room.

Piano music started, ominous and insistent.

The woman would go outside, shield her eyes against an oppressive sun in a cloudless sky. Her house was empty of colour, the streets empty of people, the air empty of moisture. She would shuffle sadly through her neighbourhood, entirely alone.

But then the woman would then abruptly receive a ticket. She'd win it or be convinced to buy one or whatever, but she'd get one. Then she'd look up and smile with sudden vibrancy and colour in her face.

A ticket to Echion Alpha.

The music shifted in tone and became lighter and more hopeful. Suddenly the woman was carrying a bag to a spaceport with dozens of others, all smiling, relaxed. She boarded the shuttle – gleaming surfaces, curved lines, nothing at all like the Excalibur – and took her seat. Crew with brilliant teeth and flawless skin brought her a cold drink, condensation rolling down the side of the glass. She sipped it, sighed, then closed her eyes contentedly.

The shuttle landed smoothly on another planet, and she disembarked, full of wonder. Vibrant greenery surrounded her. She ran her hands over numerous leaves and branches, awe-inspired.

Then the video cut out and the Aphelion logo invaded the screen.

A list of dates appeared, each one screaming 'Sold out!' in red capital letters. Haig's post-flight fugue meant he didn't know if these dates were in three days or three years, and the more he thought about it, the more his head hurt.

Underneath, a caption said, 'Get your ticket now and be among the first to arrive on Echion Alpha. Share the adventure.'

***

The space outside shifted and transmogrified.

When he first began watching the stars beyond, they had moved so little that he checked the navigation computers once, twice, three times. A counter ticked down in lightyears. Earth was 14 lightyears from the Angutian system. The counter read 2 now.

His rehabilitation program offered no respite. AI flew the ship, but a person berated him for not following the program. Rarely kind, sometimes cruel, often cruelly distant – "Your circulatory system has been in a controlled crush for six months and what you're not doing right now is restarting it, so what you're doing is allowing your body to coagulate and it'll simply gunk up until you can no longer use it" – it was always a human voice.

But after overeating and oversleeping and the mysterious bruises and unexplained grazes that came with zero gravity and managing to make it now to the waste chutes before vomiting and the exercise bike that folded out and the resistance bands that snapped into their clasps on the roof and the desire finally to properly clean himself because he knew that he would not vomit into filth again and hazy briefings and fuzzy documents and cleaning every surface twice over with a very potent anti-bacterial spray –

Three weeks out of the Benaceraff-Davies Chamber, Domiyat Outer made itself known to Haig.

A subtle difference to begin with. The light from the cockpit seemed the same. The change was in the darkness, first of all. Changes in the shadows, softer shades of black shifting into something darker and impenetrable, doom-laden. Shadows from a different light. Something in the colour. The stars reorganised. That pale white burned, while that one pulsed. That orange throbbed. Another faded.

Haig pulled himself up the cockpit with ever-strengthening arms and gripped the portholes. Domiyat Outer loomed large, a dull orange. Ribbons of yellow pulsed from the surface before thinning and ripping and spraying drops of molten gas into the black space around. The surface itself exploded over and over, waves of fire catching each other and burning and burning.

There were dark pockets on the surface that were pre- or post- explosion, offering an illusion of calm. There were some shinier clumps, like glowing knots, that seem to suck in the surrounding light, making themselves brighter. The entire surface was shimmering and throbbing, like it was breathing.

All of a sudden, he realised that his mind was clearing. The murky thickness was gone, and he felt calm now, and safe, like he would be protected from everything outside. He was still prone to sudden sickness and dizziness, sudden exhaustion, but his mind was sharper.

He flicked on a screen and viewed messages first of all. Olivia's was terse, blunt, but not unkind. She didn't want him going and he didn't want to leave Tom, but they both wanted housing. However much they had rowed at the end, he knew that Olivia was on Tom's side. And Tom's message was ten minutes of Tom in monotone taking longer to recount the story of an episode of something animated than the episode lasted. The message cut out before Tom had finished, leaving his face frozen in wonder.

"And, Daddy, and, do you know why the slime monster wanted to devour his bones up? Well, it's because – " And Haig would never know why the slime monster wanted to devour his bones up.

The personnel files and mission packets made more sense but were less interesting. He skimmed them in his post-B-DC fugue but stopped when he found himself reading and re-reading, losing his place, forgetting the names of the major players. Perhaps his mind was not as clear as he would have liked.

Haig assimilated and summarised the broad strokes from Mangan's mission packet.

Officially designated the Anguta Rail Port, Gunport was three vast concrete cylinders alongside each other, just over half a mile deep. Ships landed in one cylinder and were rolled on a conveyor belt through a tunnel at the bottom to the middle cylinder. Gunport's staff lived and worked in this central cylinder, reloading and refuelling the ships. When the ships were ready again, they were shunted through into the third cylinder, and shot back into space using a railgun. A port using a gun. Gunport.

Aphelion was spreading miasma-like into the stars, desperate to be the first to properly colonise a planet. The ships that arrived from Earth came with supplies for colony projects. Gunport took them and aimed them at their next target. It was a balance between position, size, orbit, access, AI predictions of success. Colonisation was an intergalactic lottery. Which would work? Which ones could have real people sent to them? Only Echion Alpha looked viable so far, so Gunport sent ship after ship there, dumping supplies, machinery, robotics.

Gunport itself had been built in the same way, with trillions pumped into making it work. Robots had built it from nothing. Two gigantic drills landed first. Rockets with drillbits. They began work on the three holes that would be Gunport. Then the vast mining machines arrived and began blasting and ripping stone from the surface, creating pile upon pile of cubed rock. The next robots – enormous material printers – arrived, sucking up the cubes and churning them back out again as concrete. Melting and moulding. Finally they would be poured into the holes to shape it. Drones were sacrificed en masse to Anguta R-611 with razor-rock maimed exhaust ports and glitter-dust shredded vents and shingle-scoured sensors, a mess of metal collecting in the tubes, scraped out and resurrected, sent back to serve the project, drones cannibalising each other's broken carcasses to scrape out Gunport's tunnels, and later, to build finer robotics, to install circuitry and life support and gravity, and the all-mother, the AI called Galatea.

This took decades. And when it was all over, the exhausted machinery lay in ruin. Some of it could be reclaimed, and was. Husks now formed towers in a gleaming metallic graveyard a mile or so away from Gunport itself, designated the Mine. The empty spaces, the remnants of the mined cubes, were dug into the surface, the faintest of dust having formed back over the glittering razor-shingle, like steps that led down into some unknown cavern below the surface.

Construction started in 2045 and finished thirty-three years later, at least eight behind schedule.

Accusations of vanity, foolishness, tax-avoidance, legacy-building, and spacewashing were thrown at Aphelion. There was no hope for its success, said their competitors, said the markets. Every prediction was for a managed decline. That Aphelion would finish Gunport out of stubbornness, simply because it could. And then, it would be allowed to quietly, shamefully, drift out of the public consciousness. Likely replaced by another program first. Throw a dead space-program on the table and watch the heads turn.

John Sile changed that, the packet said.

The first Executive Officer of Gunport, still in position, six years later. Now Aphelion made trillions from Gunport, the number one profit machine in their corporate empire. The jewel in the crown.

No wonder they needed this dispute resolving, thought Haig.

It came down to conditions and pay. Gravity blips, water shortages, pressure failures, food anomalies. Whatever a food anomaly was. There was no single major issue to be resolved, thought Haig. Which made him wonder what had stopped Sile offering contract reductions or better pay or addressing the issues head-on. Or whether they had been offered, and rejected.

Sile represented Aphelion. The other side of the dispute was being led by Sunita Acaba, Gunport's Head of Reactor Operations. She wanted better water. Better food. Reliable gravity, air, pressure corridors. Increased AI safety protocols.

When the navigation computer ticked down below a lightyear, Haig strapped himself into a bed and the undulating light of Domiyat Outer had him asleep in minutes.

***

Gunport called the day before he was due to arrive.

"Courtesy call," said the voice. "I'm Matthew Barnes, the Space Traffic Controller. Galatea's picked you up and our AI is talking to yours. It'll guide you in. I'll be watching every step of the way."

"Good to hear another human voice," said Haig, surprised at how glad he was to be able to have a conversation with another living soul. Not some tinned telling off from a recording, but human interaction. "I'm Anson Haig, IPRA's representative."

"I'm pleased to make your acquaintance," said Barnes. "It isn't often we have new arrivals."

Haig reached for something to say, to draw out the

conversation just that little bit more. "How are things there, Barnes?"

"You're arriving at a most difficult time. Things have escalated. That's all I can really say at the moment. Our EO likes to speak to any new arrivals himself, in person, before anyone else does. He'll be most displeased if I take away such a privilege. Well. You've only a day to go. We're looking forward to meeting you. Most of us, at least. We will be looking to you, Anson. A pleasure to have spoken to you. If I can help you while you're here, please let me know. I do hope Gunport treats you well. Gunport out."

***

"Excalibur shuttle, this is Anguta Rail Port actual, respond please," said Barnes.

"Excalibur responding," said Haig, trying to adjust to the inside of his flight suit. Landing protocols dictated he wear it. He could smell himself in there, and he did not like it. "That you, Barnes?"

"It is, Anson. Our AI and yours are deep in conversation, Excalibur. Like young lovers, they only have eyes for each other, and they can't wait to meet for the first time. They shall consummate their budding relationship in three hours, Excalibur. Pre-landing checks, if you would."

Haig wondered if Barnes had an audience this time. Playing to the crowd. Perhaps he was heightened now, nervous. He might have done this thousands of times, but there were still myriad mistakes to be made. Plenty of them had happened in front of Haig.

"Go ahead, Anguta," said Haig.

"Passengers strapped in and secure?"

"Just me. Secure."

"Loose items are stowed, drawers closed, panels shut, modular gear folded away?"

"Everything secured."

"Look at the lights on the panels. Find the Emergency Systems panel and check each light. All lights should be on."

"They are."

"Are you aware of your Emergency Protocols in case of crash?"

"Yes."

"Tell me."

"Cockpit canopy ejection systems, activated by pulling a lever under my right hand. Airlock in the middle of the shuttle, also activated by pulling two levers. Come on, Barnes. You know as well as I do, if this landing goes that wrong, Emergency Protocols are as useful as an umbrella in a solar storm."

There was muttering at the other end, Barnes discussing something with someone else.

"I've got Dekker here," said Barnes.

"Anson Haig. Emilio Dekker here, Anguta Rail Port's Head of Security, former S-O-R-G."

"Dekker," said Haig. SORG was the Special Orbital Response Group, the Army's special forces for space work. Most of the big corps kept their own paramilitaries or employed mercenaries, so the Army's job on the moon was almost always peacekeeping, and SORG decided that proactive peacekeeping meant removing those that might not keep the peace before they ever broke it. Haig found that someone so keen to be recognised as one of their number was rarely a good sign.

He measured his tone carefully. "Good to speak to you."

"And you, Haig. Perhaps we'll have an opportunity to share stories. Yours about your talking, and mine about my real combat experience."

Didn't take long for him to prove himself a prick, thought Haig.

"I'm sorry if my talking denied you some combat experience, Dekker. But I'm always keen to hear more about collateral damage from an expert."

There was silence before Dekker sucked his teeth sharply. "I have questions about your flight."

"Go ahead, please."

"Have you any brought anything on board outside the manifests?"

"I've got my clothes, my kit, my weapon, some recording equipment for the negotiations. That's it."

"A weapon?"

"Sometimes being in the middle means *everybody's* shooting at you."

"Your weapon's in the manifest." He sounded disappointed. "Any contraband? Anything illegal? Any heavier weapons? Any controlled substances? Any chemistry? Gases? Nuclear material? I've known soldiers like you my entire career. What are you carrying?"

"I'm just here to help get things back on track," said Haig. "I've nothing you'd be interested in."

"Back on track," snorted Dekker. "Wait for Bethe."

"Have you anything *I'd* be interested in?" said the next voice.

"Who am I speaking to?" said Haig.

"Duncan Bethe. Surgeon, Biomechanist. The good doctor Prendrick is our Chief Medical Officer, but he is indisposed. Stomach illness, he says. I'm interested in biological material. Did you bring any plants, Haig? Or any food?"

"Food? No, nothing beyond what I was given when I boarded."

"Plants?"

"As I said, no."

"File says you've no implants?" said Bethe, clearly disbelieving.

Haig frowned. "No."

"A former military man, in space, and no implants? Not even a commstem? What about your leg?"

Haig said, "No, no commstem. Never had. Never had any implants. I have a prosthetic, and it's on the manifest."

Bethe said to someone at his end, "I hope he's not a pure-lifer, Acaba won't like it."

Barnes came back on and said, "Excalibur actual, you're entering the Angutian system. I'll call back when you're an hour away. Anguta Rail Port out."

Then silence. They left Haig with the sound of his own breathing, heavy against his helmet.

He tried to draw conclusions from this first set of people. Who away from Sile and Acaba might be able to support a resolution?

Barnes was a little eccentric, nervous even. There was a disconnect between the two times they had spoken. The first time, he had hinted at the difficulties Gunport had endured. Alluding to the hopes they had for Haig finding a resolution. The second time, there was an odd, frantic energy. Haig found it hard to reconcile, and wondered if he was feeling the pressure of his role or whether the landings invigorated him. Either way, it was something to watch.

Dekker was former military. Gunport's crew wouldn't like him. When he was a boy, before he lost his leg, Haig's father had been sent to run security on a small moonbase with a crew of miners, and everyone had hated him. The best SORG were terrifyingly competent but reserved and quiet. They understood that their presence was only in desperate circumstances. When Haig had worked with the best of them in the Army, they had escorted him in flimsy shuttles across barren stretches of open plains on Martian moons and they knew that if Haig's 'talking' failed, everyone on board would be ripped apart by some hostage-taker's make-shift mining-cannon turned shuttle-shredder.

Dekker was not one of the best. Haig knew it, even in these brief moments. And when he had last worked with the worst, it had made him leave the Army.

Bethe declined to give his Aphelion title, which felt to Haig as though he might be at least apathetic to the company. Clearly did not respect this Prendrick, either. And experienced, too. He was surprised that Haig didn't have a commstem or more significant implants. He'd treated soldiers before. Most of the Army had implants to function in space. Most of the Army did *not* have the medication to make the implants take to their bodies, and Haig wondered if they had that medication on Gunport. Without it, either the implants or the people would fail. If supply ships hadn't been landing, that would only get worse. Sudden Implant Rejection Syndrome was very real.

Bethe seemed to know Acaba, too. No doubt he'd be reporting back. They seemed to know about his past, about his military history. That meant that they had their own files. Aphelion's corp intelligence guys would have investigated him before IPRA even thought about sending him. He was a piece on the board, and he had been involved with them before. They thought they knew him, thought they knew what made him tick. Bethe's reaction could be genuine surprise, or a little reminder of what they knew. Those first shots across the bow.

Haig smiled. Negotiations had begun.

***

"Excalibur, this is Anguta Rail Port. I'm Leandar Sagar, the Flight Landing Supervisor up in the ARP Tower. I'll be taking you through landing today. I've got other colleagues with me, too, whose voices you may hear. Galatea has you locked into a smooth entry approach. No inclement weather today expected, Excalibur, so this should be as smooth as it comes.

Gravity here is incredibly weak, so you won't feel it pull at the shuttle until after landing. Alright. Landing gear will ease out momentarily, and you'll hear the machinery. Engine noise will change slightly. Perhaps a little more vibration, but you're unlikely to feel it without any air resistance here. There it is. Smooth as you like. I wanted to say smooth as butter, but butter's a myth here. You'll find out for yourself soon enough, I guess. Alright. I'm going to put us on your screen. Look carefully, and you'll see the solitary blinking light in roughly the middle of your display. That's the centre of your screen, but we're almost directly below you. Another moment, and you'll feel Excalibur's thrusters. They'll line you up and guide you in. You might feel like you're being jockeyed around. There's going to be the odd jerk here and there from now on as Galatea nudges you in the right direction. You're a thousand miles out now, Excalibur."

"Ah. Now, nothing to worry about, but we've got a shower of micro-meteors coming in. They're going to be close, Excalibur. Okay. Okay. They're closer than we thought. Excalibur, you'll see proximity alerts. The meteors are going to collide with your landing gear. You won't feel anything, Excalibur. They'll melt right through you. Perhaps a shuddering or a change to the vibrations of the ship. Sunita, we'll need more power. Here come the meteors. Alright, they've gone past. Tower, visual. Confirmed. The landing gear is gone. We'll need landing tube magnets up."

"Magnets are loaded."

"Brace for a Railgun Landing. Tobin, foam up."

"Ah, come on, Sagar. Pulling the trigger a little early, eh?"

"Tobin, it's Barnes. A reminder that every senior member of staff is listening in. *Every* member of staff, do you hear me? You take no chances. Release the foam, and do it now. Prepare for a rough landing. Have your men ready to breach."

"Alright your highness, it's done. Landing Tube is dum-

dummed. Here's to a pillowy landing."

"Sagar, my screen's flashing with warning signs now."

"Excalibur, some bad news. Those meteors have taken some of your landing gear away. The alerts will continue to flash, but we have them under control. You won't have felt anything. The meteors are too small and too fast. Nothing too much to worry about. Galatea confirms Tower visual. There are complete failures in two of your five landing stacks and malfunctions in the other three, so your landing will be rougher than we'd hoped. Thrusters are fine and working perfectly. We'll perform a Railgun Landing, which means you'll use thrusters to ease yourself into the tube and then we use the magnets in the gun to cushion your landing. We've used foam in the bottom of the tube to catch you. It'll be enough to rattle any implants free, but all you'll feel is a little discomfort. We're starting our countdown now. You won't hear my voice until you've touched down. See you soon, Excalibur."

***

"Excalibur is in the breach. Galatea has her."

"Ease down. She's in moon gravity."

"And magnets."

"And magnets, Sunita."

"Sunita, the magnets – "

"Surge, surge – "

"Fuck – "

***

Haig woke to a sea of faces staring at him in breathing gear, his own helmet visor smeared. He could feel dried blood in an eyebrow, pressure and throbbing.

"You passed out," said one. "Hit your head, looks like." Another said, "Good job you put that foam down, right Tobin?"

This man Tobin turned to Haig and smiled, said, "Tough lad like you can manage a bit of a bumpy landing, eh?"

"What happened?" said Haig, fighting to focus.

"Surge in the Reactor. Magnets caught you, then the Reactor jumped, magnets blipped out, dropped you. Shuttle fell about thirty feet, popped the nets, right into the foam. If you'd landed on the concrete, you'd be in bad shape. On fire, probably, flapping your limbs, crying for water. Or buffeted about so much every rib you have would have punched into your lungs. Better than your umbrella in a solar storm, eh? As it is, Excalibur is back in the stone and you're back on your feet."

"Not my worst flight," said Haig, wincing. "But definitely not my best. This happen often?"

Tobin grinned, slapped Haig's shoulder.

"Welcome to Gunport."

CHAPTER 2: SIX SECONDS EARLY

"Don't get too excited," said Tobin. "Security are on their way down, and your new home isn't much better than this one."

As much as Haig had been following his rehabilitation plans, the artificial gravity of Gunport flattened him. His knees buckled, his spine trembled.

"Alright, now," said Tobin, scooping him up, effectively dragging him across the gangway.

Haig let it happen. He was carried across a metal walkway that had projected into the Landing Tube. Excalibur had come to rest against the concrete of the tube in a bulbous head of foam that smothered the landing gear and pushed against the Vacuum Engines' rear arrays. They'd had to use a winch to haul him out.

"Everyone in? Right, punch it," said Tobin. One of his men operated a panel. The gangway retracted beneath them into the Airlock. Amber lights flashed. The Outer Airlock doors rolled smoothly across as the gangway tucked in, and the doors sealed with a thick metallic clunk. There was a moment as the pressure equalised before the Inner Airlock began to roll open, and Haig's home for the last six months was sealed behind billions of tonnes of concrete and magnets and foam.

"We've got him," said Tobin, pulling at the thick flesh on the heel of his hand to get his commstem working, then speaking into his palm. "Banged up, but otherwise well. Yes, flight suit intact. Yes, I understand. Kaneda, Excalibur's a fucking mess.

You ever repair Vacuum Engines before? Fucker's here for a while then, eh?"

Tobin and his men carried him through two thin plastic doors and into a control room, then placed him in a fold-down plastic chair.

"Okay," said Tobin, breathing gear discarded, hanging around his neck, "This is the Pit. Shuttles land like yours did – or didn't – and they roll across to be launched again. We came through a man-sized Airlock at the top, but if we need to get the whole shuttle in here, the whole thing opens out. You can see the conveyor even from up here. Now. Normally we'd greet you properly, but when the shit's hitting the fan, everyone waits upstairs until I say so. No air down here, you see. Means fire can't take hold. Carbon dioxide to create an atmosphere, but you need the masks to breathe. Me and the lads need to tidy this up. Need to make sure your shuttle's powered down, nothing on board that'll do any more mischief. You're going to sit here until Security and Medical arrive. Do not open your suit up, as much as you want to. You're going to be quarantined for a couple of days. It's standard, but it's important. If you're carrying any germs, viruses, whatever, you'll give it to us. Bethe reckons viruses love low humidity so keep that helmet on. Right, come on lads. Back in."

Tobin and his men pulled their breathing masks back up and marched into the Airlock, leaving Haig sagging in his chair.

The Pit was a smooth, featureless hangar, silent now in the aftermath of Haig's landing. Overlooking it, the Control Room was a series of tall plastic windows, flanked by a rack of oxygen masks and an array of crane and drone controls. It sat overseeing fifteen floors of empty space. Far below were two conveyor tracks that rolled ships and shuttles through. There was a calmness about the room now. Haig knew what it would have been like for Tobin and his men even an hour ago. Nervous tension, the unnecessary scratching at knuckles, the long silences. Gigantic concrete doors at both ends were firmly sealed, and the drones that organised cargo and repairs were still. Haig found it hard to believe that the shuttle he had thundered in with was half-broken, hardly any distance away at all, hidden from sight.

He didn't envy the dig-out, either. If a shuttle overshot, it would drown in dum-dum foam, kinetic energy booming through it, hardening into a tough shell. The foam suffocated fires, too, with the help of a zero-oxygen air mix. Haig's Vacuum Engines wouldn't explode – so said the little he had read of the manual – but if they weren't shut off properly, they would grind themselves into uselessness. The foam didn't care about any of that. There were solvents that could melt it in an hour, but they were on their own, trillions of miles from Earth, and the chemicals for that couldn't be wasted on foam. It might come down to Tobin and a pick-axe, and from what little he'd seen of Tobin, Tobin wouldn't be happy about it.

Pain rolled around Haig's skull and oscillated. Haig closed his eyes and tried to think it away. He was exhausted, suddenly, with a booming headache and fatigue in each and every one of his joints, his shoulders crushed down by gravity a touch weaker than Earth, a blood-smear across the visor of a claustrophobic helmet, and then nausea and cramps and dizziness took hold and he doubled over, face streaming in sweat, a giant's hand taking great delight in gripping and crushing and twisting his innards, pain pulsing into his throat, vomit surging, fingers stuck in gloves and flapping helplessly at the clasps of his helmet until it was too late, and he had splashed vomit all over the inside of his helmet.

It stank, and it greased his visor, and he had it in his beard, but he felt a whole lot better.

He realised that he was on the floor when he saw Dekker looming over him.

Dekker was the Head of Security, and Sile's personal

bodyguard. He had a sweep of lank hair crushed into a greasy wave and wore a grey t-shirt with a Gunport shield, sweat pooling at the armpits. Haig knew it was Dekker because he had a prosthetic arm that gleamed, high-grade military polymer with chrome flourishes, perfectly kept.

When Haig had left the army, he could have taken a similar one for his leg, but instead, he had given it back. He wanted nothing from them.

Dekker held his cybernetic hand up, then made it spin mechanically and gently at the wrist, rotating his hand in a hypnotic parody. Haig stared through it to the smile, Dekker displaying rows of glittering teeth behind his oxygen mask.

"Anson Haig," said Dekker, his voice smooth over the whirring of his shining wrist. His prosthetic arm shimmered like leaked oil. "As if this all-lifer shitstreak were ever a Colonel."

He stepped forward and held his rotating hand up to Haig's face. Haig blinked, weak beyond reacting.

"I have the negotiator," he spat into his commstem. "He'll need to put his guts back in if he's to be useful."

Haig was momentarily aware that he was being lifted up before passing out.

**

Quarantine was a room in the Medical Bay. Every new arrival spent two days in it undergoing every kind of viral, bacterial, psychological and nanological test available. They were months from Earth, so every test available on Gunport was a long way from every test available.

After hauling him out of his flight suit and spraying him liberally at arm's length with a mist that stank of chemical detergent, he was deposited in the bed, a series of sensors slapped to his chest and temples.

It was another of Aphelion's functional cells, this one squeezed into a concrete space. Lights were dim. Walls were white, one carrying a long screen that showed a thunderstorm raking across a booming sea. At first, Haig enjoyed the sea's cleanliness and movement and vigour. Now, however, the antiseptic medical stink and dry concrete waft was far between what the screen told him he *should* smell and what he *could* smell and the sea became more and more false. It was a pervasive reminder of where he was *not*.

Duncan Bethe was the first doctor to speak to him in person. He was an implant expert, surgeon, and gene-edited, standing an ungainly 7' tall. He carried himself with a smooth deliberation, delicately folding himself and his long limbs into spaces that he should not have been able fit into.

Bethe considered Haig for a moment, like a biologist studying a virus in a petri dish.

"I'm sure you wanted a different welcome to Gunport," he said, "But we don't always get what we want. Tobin reported balance and strength issues when he hauled you out of your shuttle. That's normal. Without my particular genetic gifts, it'll take a while to readjust. It might not feel like it, but you've managed well, given your lack of implants. Muscles atrophy, bones weaken. You'll be dizzy for a few days, nauseous, disorientated. B-DC chambers affect balance in particular. I'll prescribe medicine for all of that. Did you keep up with your rehabilitation?" Haig nodded weakly, and Bethe went on. "Well, I'll soon know from the scans. There's a tablet here, with various orientation videos. Your job is to read those over the next day or so. Wecht will be in to do memory and psychological testing when your physical comes back. Ah, yes, your equipment. It's being sterilised, and I imagine you'll want your prosthetic as soon as possible. I'll have it brought to you. Any questions? No? Good."

Haig did in fact have lots of questions, but Bethe was already gone.

***

Sarah Wecht was the Chief Wellbeing Officer, pale-faced but with lines around her eyes that said that she laughed and smiled often. Wecht had tied her hair up loosely using a rainbow of different lengths of copper wire, entirely mismatched with the bracelet that Haig guessed she must have made herself. The colour brought life in defiance of the clinical walls of Medical.

"I'm going to sign you off," she said. "Let you get to your task. You're fine. Mentally, certainly. Any questions, Anson?"

Bethe's medications had stood Haig up. He felt constantly nauseous and hungry, knowing that if he ate, he would see it again not long later, but this was the only real lingering after-effect. The orientation packets described how the B-DC affected different types of people. The gene-edited shrugged it off and started full duties an hour after leaving quarantine. At the other end of the spectrum, the sleep process had failed to wake up its passengers and left its inhabitant's brains fried, all-but-dead. It only occurred to Haig then that he didn't remember dreaming at all while he was in the chamber, but if your brain wasn't put into that fugue state, if the pink gas didn't work, then your mind would be a liquid mess. Bethe was right: for however awful he felt, he had managed well.

"Just two," said Haig. "Who's Anson? Where am I?"

"That's not funny. Maybe I shouldn't sign you off after all."

Haig laughed. "Come on, Sarah. It's been at least six months since someone made that joke. It's been over six months since I've made a joke at all."

"Making that joke once is once too much," she said. "What real questions do you have?"

He only had one, for now. What surprised him was that no-one had been to visit. It occurred to him that at the very least, he was new. They'd have been gossiping and chatting about him. It was the same when he was in the moonbases. A new addition to the team always sparked curiosity, especially when there was hardly any turnover of new people. Where was Sile? Acaba?

Haig said, "Have I had any visitors? While I've been asleep, maybe, or out of it on the medication?"

"No, no visitors."

"I thought Sile and Acaba might want to get a look at me."

"John doesn't want anyone to think you've been unduly influenced by him before the negotiations."

"What about Acaba?"

"I don't know what Acaba thinks," she said.

"You don't like her?"

"I don't know her."

"Then why don't you like her?"

Wecht sighed. "She's caused a lot of trouble."

"Is that what everyone thinks?"

"It doesn't matter what everyone thinks," said Wecht, standing up. "I've already said too much. Your six months in space have felt like a lot longer to us. John has asked that you have dinner with us in his offices tonight. You'll have the chance to meet all of the senior staff. In the meantime, you've been given a room to use. There are clean clothes and you'll be able to check messages. Your equipment's been sterilised and put in your room. And here, put this on."

She handed him an e-sleeve. It was a thin mesh that ran from wrist to elbow and mimicked a commstem. He let it synchronise. Heart-rate, breathing, temperature. All normal. It started to tell him to complete this round of employee engagement surveys, then started to ask him for post-flight feedback, so he swiped across it, frowning. Humidity was zero.

The AI had obviously turned water reclamation protocols to 'shrivel', thought Haig. It showed in the dry patches on his knuckles.

He'd absorbed pockets of conversation, gleaned information from between the sentences and the implied, the ulterior, the deep. He'd detected fear or reverence of the AI Galatea, but never apathy. The programmers in Galatea's Core would have said that Galatea has decided that more water is needed, and she is taking it, and you – you lesser mortal, lesser than the oceans of moondust that surround us – you are lucky to receive even as much as zero. Galatea was an AI, thought Haig. Nothing more, and nothing less. Certainly nothing to be revered. It was a computer that ran a moonbase, and while it would have been helpful to have one when he'd run moonbases of his own, it was not some binary miracle.

When he looked back up, Wecht had gone, replaced by a stocky man called Holden.

"I'm Dominic Holden," he said, "Security. Dekker sent me. I'll take you to your room. We don't think any of the crew would do anything silly, but sometimes the people in this place don't make sense."

Haig swung his leg out of the bed onto the cool linoleum and collected a sole full of concrete dust. He opened the case for his prosthetic. Nerve-endings told him the skin in both feet was puckering, losing its moisture. His eyes corrected them. He only had one foot now, only had one leg, the other taken off at the knee. Holden leaned against the door frame and watched him.

A few minutes later, he was dressed with the prosthetic on and he walked gingerly towards the Elevator.

***

He was funnelled along featureless concrete corridors by Holden and the occasional boldly coloured arrow, looking up when he saw the boots of someone else he was about to walk into. There were strips of screen at intervals, with the Echion Alpha advertisement on a banner on every piece of company software. Turn left? There she was, in the scorched town. To the Elevator? There she was, boarding the shuttle. It rolled onto the news. Today's news from Earth was the same as when he left. Six months old, arriving in the slowest bandwidths and beams.

And it was always good news. Some new discovery intended to draw awe. Aphelion wouldn't let it be anything less, thought Haig.

Each arrow pointed out a different facility or room, but everything on this floor led Haig to the single, central Elevator.

A low rumble disturbed concrete dust, sent it floating thinly into the air. Holden let Haig wonder what the rumble was for a moment too long before saying, "Reactor. Happens all the time."

Haig brushed it out of his hair as he joined a group of Gunport staff waiting for the elevator.

Hasan Choudhury, Leader of Developmental Science, was waiting for the same elevator. When he saw Haig, he eased through the small crowd towards him.

Choudhury wore a pair of small, opaque spectacles. Malfunctions in his eye implants made him sensitive to the harsh lights in the corridors. Body odour and chemical soap smells rose from him in waves. Haig thought he smelled great.

"Good morning," he said brightly. "You must be Anson, the negotiator. I'm Hasan, resident scientist."

"What do you want, Hasan?" said Holden.

"Morning, Hasan," said Haig.

"I have some wonderful news," said Choudhury. "Go ahead. Ask me what it is."

"What – "

"DIVA is in position."

Haig looked at different faces for guidance, wanting to match this man's enthusiasm but not knowing where to start.

"I've been in space for a while, Hasan," said Haig. "Who's a diva and why is it good that she's in position?"

Holden squashed a snort, and it was only briefly on his face, but Choudhury was crestfallen, his enthusiasm leaking like air from a hull breach.

"It's, well, my Deep Interrogatory Vehicular Activity experiment." He looked at Holden for permission to continue, who didn't tell him to stop, so he carried on. "It's, a, ah, a nuclear reactor with a drill attached, built to punch through the ice of Sedna R-8 to its subterranean oceans. Seven months, it has been," said Choudhury, pace quickening. "One of the last to launch before, err, everything. And a few hours and a couple of minutes and a smattering of seconds. Too long, too long."

The elevator arrived. The crowd shuffled in, found spaces.

Haig wanted idle conversation, wanted a conversation with a less-than-hostile face about something, anything. "It's all about the water, then, Hasan?"

Choudhury brightened, emboldened. "Mostly, and fuel. Hydrogen. Oxygen. There's a lot that I don't know, and I want to find out. If nothing else, when it hits the surface, it should be something to see. An explosion of ice, Haig. You should come and see when it crashes into the ice. The images will be astounding. You're invited to watch the landing. Everyone is."

"How thick do you think the ice will be?" said Holden.

Did Haig imagine a few of the others in the elevator quieten? A few ears leaning into their conversation?

Choudhury's eyes narrowed. "I'm not sure yet."

Haig caught the eye of someone else. Yes, they had been listening. They wanted to know too. "Come on. Rough estimate," said Holden.

"That vagabond Tobin has ensnared you too, has he?" said Choudhury. Haig couldn't decide what Choudhury's face was doing. The eyes were hidden behind the glasses. His eyebrows were up, open, but his lips curled into a sneer.

"DIVA is looking for miracles," said Choudhury. "It will find hydrogen, oxygen. You all want more water, more fuel, well, it's there. On Sedna. And without the volcanic churn of other planets and moons. Easy to collect. And not toxic." He was accelerating. "The potential, even, for life, perhaps microbial or bacterial. Medical applications. Food. Water. Solving hunger, drought."

"Yes, yes, that's all great, Hasan," said Holden, "But how thick is this ice?"

"I've bet ten seconds," said one of the staff. "Thirty seconds for me," said another. The Elevator drifted into easy conversation. They had sensed that Haig was someone safe to talk around.

Holden said, "Tobin's done a pool. You put your shower seconds in, and if you win, you get them all back."

"Shower?" said Haig.

"Forty-five seconds a week," said Holden. "The way Dekker talks, you won't be here long enough to have more than one."

"My shuttle needs repairs," said Haig. "I'll be here longer than a week."

Holden shrugged.

Choudhury made himself heard and said, "I can give you a small clue. It is thicker than my thumb," and then he grinned, "But thinner than Sile's ego."

And the easiness of the conversation died, almost instantly.

Holden balled a fist, looked at Haig, seemed to make a decision. He reached pressed the Elevator button.

The crew inside looked at Holden. Looked at the floor. They seemed to sense what was coming. Haig didn't. He looked at Choudhury, still pleased with his joke.

When the Elevator stopped, Holden said, "Get out, Hasan."

"We're still two floors from the Dining Hall – "

"Now," said Holden. Choudhury slipped out.

***

The Food Hall was a great concrete cavern on the 8th Floor. Benches stretched from one end to the other, striplights dangling down on metal chains. The arched ceiling had been painted in a powder-blue with white streaks, resembling clouds. Where the lights couldn't quite reach, high in the corners, deep in the alcoves, the darkness reminded Haig that this was only a pretence at a sky.

Haig joined Holden at the back of a shuffling queue. It recognised the newcomer, earned him some glances and whispers, but as soon as those glances took in Holden, they moved on. Conversation was at a minimum. A long rectangular screen announced breaking news, six months old. A banner said that Gunport had distributed a million tonnes of payload cargo towards Echion Alpha. "A remarkable achievement," said a disembodied voice. Another voice: "Everyone at the Anguta Rail Port should be delighted."

Haig scanned the queue, trying to garner some idea of Gunport's mood. They didn't react to this 'achievement'. The news was white noise to them by now, thought Haig, much as it was for me in the shuttle. Muttering in the queue ahead drifted his way, said, "Send as much as you fucking like. None of it gets there."

At the front of the queue, a dispenser growled before ejecting a tray and splatting his food into a cardboard bowl. A paper cup followed, full of water, then a paper sachet with a cocktail of vitamin powders. He sat down at a bench and held a scuffed cardboard spoon, then absent-mindedly started to move a thick glob of food-paste from one side of the bowl to the other. It was an off-white, stuck fast to the spoon. The entire glob moved as one squelching whole. The spoon buckled in the middle.

The sachet of vitamin powder glared at him from the tray. He forced himself to pick it up, then ripped it open and tipped it into his water. A murky cloud settled, stubbornly refusing to disappear. He stared hard at it, as if it might transform into something more palatable, spinning it gently in his hand. He frowned, watched it swirl, closed his eyes, then gulped it down. Licking the walls would taste better, he thought. His stomach churned while trying to decide whether to accept this not-quite-solid offering, and after mildly cramping, it approved, and some of Haig's hunger abated.

The bench creaked under his weight, despite how slight he was. Those six months on a B-DC diet had seen the weight slide off, until he could count each of his ribs. Printers had cut the edges of the tables to the bone. Sharp edges and parchment dry skin made for a bad combination.

Haig cut off a thin slice of food-paste and chewed it for much longer than he needed to, then took a deep breath and swallowed it, feeling it squelch all the way down and into his stomach.

He listened to snatches of conversation running through the hall. More than one person had said they weren't in Tobin's pool because Choudhury's DIVA probe was never getting there, dismissing his experiments as flimsier than one of Gunport's plastic toilets. More than once he heard, 'Why make one good one when you can make three shite ones?' sometimes in chorus, sometimes followed by derisive laughter, sometimes with real exasperation.

Gunport's crew kept glancing at him, meeting his eye, then glancing at Holden, then glancing away. He was clearly off-limits, so he stood up without telling Holden and walked over to the Reclaimer to get rid of his empty tray and bowls. He fed his tray in, watched it slot the paper to one side and the cardboard to the other and eat them greedily, crunching and ripping everything to be broken down for what little moisture was left behind.

As he turned to leave, Sunita Acaba stepped up behind him to use his Reclaimer. He recognised her from his mission packets. Three other Reclaimers were free.

"Kaneda's still not upgraded the food dispensers," she said, to no-one in particular.

The Head of Reactor Operations had hands that were pocked with the marks of thousands of repairs, her nails short and cracked nails with a thick crust of black under them. She had shaved the hair at the sides of her head and left a thick, tangled mat that reached down from her scalp to the back of neck.

A rectangular tattoo – a techtatt diagram of her breathing implant – was scored on tightly pulled skin just above her left ear. Haig had seen these techtatts before, intricate instructions on how to repair a person's implants in case of accident, injury, or failure: SIRS was a real problem for those with a significant number of implants.

Her sleeves were rolled up.

She was staring at him, expectant, so he said conversationally, "Upgraded them?"

Acaba said, "To dispense medicines."

"Have you been getting enough? During the dispute?"

"The dispute," she said, shaking her head. "That's what you're calling it. You know who I am?"

"I do," said Haig. "We're long overdue a meeting, I think."

"It won't do shit," said Acaba. "Stubborn bastard won't accept that this place punishes us. Thinks we should be delighted to endure this shit."

"You haven't been getting enough medicine?"

"What would you know about it? You're not one of us. You don't have imps. And you'll fuck off back to Earth as soon as your shuttle can take you, leaving us high and dry."

"My son has enough allergies that breathing can be enough to kill him. I know how difficult life can be without the right medication," he said quietly.

"So it's an accident that you know."

Haig felt the adrenaline prickle his face, the conflict unexpected. Was surprised that he was surprised. Willed himself calm. "It's hard to research them by accident. Hard to change your entire life by accident to keep a child alive."

"So we'll wait an hour for Wecht," said Acaba, as if Haig had never spoken. "Or wait four for fucking Prendrick. Then I have to make that time back up. Because Kaneda can't be bothered to upgrade a few machines."

Her voice had risen, a few eyes drifting her way, so she took a breath, calmed, took the volume down.

"It's not just me, Haig," she said. "Everyone with an implant. It would take nothing to put them in here. Then you can get them with your food. Make it easier for people with implants. Stop us having to go through hoops just to get medicine that they know we need."

"We can talk about this in our negotiations. You know that this isn't the place."

She said, "Ask about Jan de Wiart," rammed her tray into the Reclaimer, and marched away from him.

Haig turned to leave, and saw Felix Blatt staring at him, and then at the back of Acaba. He licked his lips.

Again, he recognised Blatt from the packets. Blatt was a 6'5" gene-edited tower of muscle, with a dull, blunt face. It was blemish-free, scarless and hairless, but he would never be called handsome. It was a functional face, built to speak and breathe and see, but nothing else.

Blatt caught up to him near the elevator. "I heard you talking about those drugs Acaba needs to take," he said smoothly. "It's just so much work to put them in."

Blatt was the Chief Programming Officer, creating software for Galatea, the AI. He reported to Alison Janulis, the Head of Artificial Intelligence. Galatea had its own floors, an enormous computer that controlled Gunport. The programming team were insular, widely hated, some gene-edited. Blatt made Haig twitch.

In the early years of the push for intergalactic travel, humans struggled to survive. Atrophy of the body, inability to sustain the concentration required of operating vast craft, the cloying loneliness of the journey. Knowing that your life had been given over to this one-way voyage, and that it could end only with death.

Various governments and companies and space programs noted that the failures were not in the machinery, but in the flesh. They agreed to fund experimentation. Humane, of course. Of course, Haig had thought. Aphelion is so very humane. And therefore a vanishingly small proportion of people had been gene-edited. Built, from the womb up, for the purpose of carrying humanity into the stars.

They were flawed geniuses to the last. They would have you believe they were superior. Space travel stalled before the B-DC was built, and so they were child prodigies who could never do what they were born for, became intellectual rockstars, the next billion-dollar tech Gods. Then, disaster. Always something borne of a misunderstanding. Crimes borne of arrogance. They were better than you, and they always had to prove it. Their files were littered with bitter fights with other researchers and colleagues. Failed ventures, unrepentant criminal behaviour. One, not on Gunport, had performed unsolicited surgery.

Gunport's crew was only made up of four gennies. Bethe he had already met, Blatt towered in front of him, while Janulis, Galatea's 'mother', and Attar, another programmer, were likely in Galatea's core.

"Whatever you think," said Haig, finally, "There's clearly a problem there."

"Perhaps they should just remove their implants," said Blatt.

Blatt looked at Haig evenly, but Haig saw a tell-tale glint in the eyes. Blatt was trying to provoke him. Haig very deliberately pressed the button for the elevator.

Blatt waited for him to respond. Waited another moment.

The glint faded when Haig said, "What's your name?" stepping into Blatt's space, looking up at him, and putting his hand out to be shaken.

Haig wasn't going to be drawn into squabbles between groups of people. Medicines and equipment wasn't up to him. If he took a side, maybe he'd be liked. Everybody liked to be liked. But he wanted to remain neutral. Acknowledge grievances without agreeing with them. Make people heard. Loved by none, hated by none, tolerated by all. Respected by most.

Blatt blinked and held his hand out, suddenly aware that he was being watched. The handshake carried unbridled power, fingers like steel cables, arms like hydraulic pistons. Gene-edited strength coming to bear. Haig saw Blatt concentrate and realised that it was because Blatt did not want to turn his hand to powder.

"Felix Blatt," said this hulking man.

"Let him go," said Holden, leaning against a Reclaimer. "I'll take you down to your room."

Haig released the hand and stepped into the elevator.

"Goodbye, Felix."

***

The room Haig had been given was a concrete box with fold-away plastic furniture slapped to its sides. A thin desk, a wobbly wardrobe. All plastic, all bolted to the walls, walls broken only by a door on one side and scuffs along others. The optimist saw scuffs on the concrete as a cascade of meteors, blazing across some other distant world. The pessimist saw the dangers lurking in the lack of light in space, and the abject, smothering emptiness. Even with both striplights on, shadows pooled in corners.

Haig sat in front of the desk, scratching at a dry knuckle, waiting for the screen to recognise him. He'd taped a picture of Tom to the corner. He was blonde, toothy, stood in some sand, seemed confused by his own toes. Haig's knuckle-skin flaked onto the desk and he brushed it away.

His equipment had been packed into a plastic crate, unceremoniously dumped in the centre of the room and scored with dozens of new scratches, dragged straight from the hold of Excalibur. He checked the locks first, and they were intact. When he'd packed it, he'd carefully held a scrap of cotton thread between the seals before locking it. The cotton was now gone. He imagined Dekker would have been delighted to find exactly what Haig had told him would be there. After an hour checking the equipment, he was satisfied. In particular, he opened the small gun case and spent forty minutes or so checking that his weapon hadn't been tampered with. It was unusual to allow non-Security staff to carry weapons in Gunport, but IPRA insisted. The middle-man was far too often caught in the middle.

Finally, there was a series of soft chimes. A huge company logo thrust itself into Haig's face. 'Aphelion Systems – Making the stars come to you.' Gunport's own logo came next, an octagon with 'Anguta Rail Port' printed along the bottom three edges, the railgun proudly splitting the centre. Eventually it displayed his messages.

Olivia and Tom sent Haig a picture of a birthday picture Tom had drawn for him. Some robots that Tom liked, and some animals that Tom liked. Of course, thought Haig. I've missed my own birthday.

Mangan offered something new. Sile had doubled down and had threatened to cancel Reactor tech contracts, leaving the techs stranded. No Aphelion shuttle home for you, he had said. Employees only, and you're not going to be employees anymore. The tech union would send a shuttle eventually, but it would be slow. Without a B-DC, it'd take them years to get home. And all that time, they'd be unpaid.

Acaba responded with escalation of her own. She could have relented and everyone could have gone back to work, or she could have had her entire team simply quit. And if they did, everyone on Gunport would die. No air circulation, no heat pumps, no gravity, nothing. She wouldn't go that far, thought Haig, based even on their brief meeting. All of her anger was reserved for the mistreatment of everyone in Gunport. Her techs were the priority, but the medicine dispensers would benefit everyone with implants. If Sile wasn't careful, the whole base would stop working.

In response, she refused to land anything at all. No shuttles, no cargo. No more payloads for Aphelion to report in the news. Haig's had been the only one for a week. There was still a stalemate, but things *had* escalated, thought Haig. Subtly working their way towards collapse. It was down to who blinked first, and Haig imagined it would be Sile. He had a lot more to lose.

He pinched his eyes at the bridge of his nose and sniffed, air like the dry stink of an overworked computer overlaid with sour, under-washed people. The connoisseur would detect hidden notes of concrete dust, of greasy hair. The self-aware critic would point to these smells coming from the only person in the room. Haig dry-coughed. His eyes watered, reacting to Galatea's carefully curated atmosphere.

No windows to open, obviously. A concrete cell to call home. Another day in Gunport for most.

All of a sudden, he desperately wanted a shower.

He left the prosthetic in a heap on the bed and swung into the bathroom. It was a shower cubicle, a sink laid into an alcove halfway up the wall. The shower was a glass booth with a single button inside, and a timer above. He hopped in, grabbed a rail, and decided to take an entire week, all forty-five seconds of it, in one long blast.

Deep breaths. In through the nose, out through the mouth. Brace for the heat. He took one long breath and held it, then stabbed the button with his finger.

The timer showed forty-five seconds and flashed, warning him that the shower would start in five seconds. He was pre-emptively jealous of the winner of the pool on DIVA's ice. They might count their shower in minutes, not seconds. Haig would never have done the pool – too unprofessional, too unpredictable – but the thought of a long shower made him shudder with pleasure.

There was a gurgle-rumble from piping behind the wall, then the water exploded out of the showerhead and the bathroom erupted in steam. He'd worked out a routine long ago where he could clean himself properly and make sure his leg was looked after. And a way of using the hard blocks of chemical soap that persisted in Army moonbases which took forever to lather. Haig scrubbed himself quickly with one hand, switching rapidly from one to the other, all the time wincing when a different part of his body went under the heat.

The shower clicked off before he was finished.

"For fuck's sake," he said. A thin layer of off-white bubbles dripped out of his hair, blocking his view of the timer, dripped into his eyes. He rubbed them, looked at the timer again.

Six seconds early.

CHAPTER 3: THE VISITOR

All of Gunport's timber was in John Sile's Boardroom.

The Boardroom was long, rectangular, narrow. There was a great table that occupied the entire length of the room, rich brown wood polished to a brilliant gleam. allowing barely enough space to around it. Murky and ambiguous reflections, like twisted oil paintings, moved on its surface. Haig saw himself being stretched into the distance along the sheen.

Tucked away in the corner was Sile's palm tree, the only plant he had seen since he had arrived, its vibrant emerald fronds hanging without a care, planted firmly in damp and healthy dirt. Haig wondered what it had done to earn so much water. Whether its showers had been cut short.

On the wall in the precise centre of the room was a painting. This was a real oil painting, impressionistic and distorted, of a man in a suit, a dark hole where his mouth should be, stood proudly in front of an old, intricate chair.

"Anson Haig," said John Sile brightly, striding into the room, extending his hand, "I'm John Sile, Executive Officer."

He was tall, hair cut closely to the skin and greying at the temples, with a fleshy plumpness in his face that reminded Haig of the palm tree. Haig shook his hand and Sile invited him to look back at the painting.

"It's a wonderful painting, isn't it? Full of power and mystery. Gunport was conceived almost forty years ago," said Sile, walking slowly around the table, "And that man, Jackson

Carlisle – " he said, jabbing a finger at the painting, " – drove it all. He was the one who had a singular vision. Do you know what that vision was, Anson?"

"What's your tagline? 'Making the stars come to you'?"

"Ah, yes. 'Taking you to the stars'."

"Everyone should be able to go to the stars, then," said Haig. "Affordable space travel, perhaps."

"Partly, yes. What you're describing is the end result," said Sile. "It was progress, Anson. Progress. That man should make progress. And when resources on Earth didn't match our ambition, he argued for going beyond, to defeat entropy. Not the first pioneer in space, not just to understand that an infinite universe provides infinite resources, but to act on it. To act. To seize hold of it."

Sile took his seat at the head of the table and motioned for Haig to sit, "Don't stand on ceremony for me."

Sile opened his hands expansively over his misshapen reflection in the gleaming table. "And man has made progress. We have acted. This place is the outermost home for humanity in the entire universe. We are the ones that hold others up. Like a scaffold for humanity. We fire them into the stars."

Rehearsed? thought Haig.

"When I first came here, this place was new. Six years ago, now. It smelled so much of concrete. Freshly set, with the dryness it has when you run your hand over it, like its taking moisture straight from you."

Sile made a slurping noise and squeezed his hands into two fists, then looked directly into Haig's eyes.

"Your fingers are slightly dusty when you're done. They have this faint grey dust to them. You immediately want to wash them."

Haig flexed his fingers involuntarily, and felt a dry creak at one knuckle.

"When I welcomed my first spacecraft, I went to the Cargo Bay to see it for myself. A gleaming block, it was. Ugly and squat and blunt, and not at all beautiful. I'd travelled here in a ship, of course, but you don't see your own ship, do you? You walk into it through corridors and gantries and everything else. But now I could see this ship. This hunk of metal to be shot to somewhere else. You and I don't know the science, do we? How the magnets and everything else works. So I began to think about what it had taken. What it had taken to make Gunport possible."

Sile's eyes shone.

"Ten years of planning and twenty three years of construction to build this, this, cathedral, to human endeavour. How much money? How many resources? How many people? How many people have come here and never gone back to Earth? People who started their journeys, planning to go back? Wanting to see loved ones, their homes? People who have given their lives for this place?"

"Far too many," said Haig.

"So many people forgotten. This place will be here long after you are gone, Anson. And there will be another Gunport. Here, or somewhere else. Another moon, another beacon. Another perfect place, mathematically perfect, all of the angles and trajectories and curvatures matching perfectly, like they do here. The perfect spot to receive and send ships on to the colonies. And then there will be another, and another. This place will be a monument to human progress, and we will either disappear into oblivion, or have our names carved in the concrete of the next Gunport. Named after us."

Sile leaned in conspiratorially. Haig had been waiting for this. Sile's pitch was coming.

"I hope that now you understand. Gunport is far too important for this dispute to continue. Your role in allowing us to continue our work is enormous, Anson. You are so important to us. All of these good people need to be able to perform their duties so that all of the people back on Earth can start to hope again."

Haig felt his defences rising. They'd be speaking for less than ten minutes, and Sile was as subtle as a rocket. He had expected it, this 'moment alone'. Acaba's had felt more like two people coming together by accident, time snatched. This was much more organised. Both of them would want his sympathy, which was only natural, but Sile had used his influence and power to his advantage – and Acaba's disadvantage.

"I want a positive resolution as much as you," said Haig, "Our goal is to end the dispute. But it's negotiation, conversation, dialogue. We can't have a reconciliation without the other party. And because she's not here, I'm loathe to talk about it. There are protocols to follow. And I know how keen Aphelion is to maintain neutrality."

"The progress of humanity is not neutral, Anson. It's littered with the deaths of trillions who died to teach the rest of us something. Isn't that what we're doing here? Explorers. Pathfinders. All of our sacrifices need to mean something."

Haig did not offer an opinion. Sile was turning something local into something galactic. Conditions and pay in a place only a mile high would become a battle for the very soul of humanity, if Sile had his way. Haig had to confine it to what was in the mission packet: bosses and staff falling out about pay and conditions. He was here to get them back on track, not debate for humanity's future.

He said, "I'm here to help you and your staff come to a resolution. That's all. It's better if we think about it in those terms. Have you arranged a venue for the negotiations?"

"We'll do it here."

The gleaming table, the leering painting, the gleaming plant. This was Sile's room, and he knew it.

Haig said, "Again, we need to ensure neutrality. I know you don't have many comfortable spaces here, but I believe the Viewing Gallery would work. It's a large, open space, and it's neutral. I don't want to take it away from the crew for any length of time but we can't do it here. This office is definitely *your* office, John. Again, I would hate anyone to accuse IPRA or Aphelion of bias."

Sile's smile changed. Or perhaps it was not the smile, but the eyes, thought Haig. Darker. Then his face refreshed partly, his smile recasting its brilliant wattage, but his eyes became black spaces and he said coldly, "Of course. Humanity has been waiting an entire year but what's another day? They're watching us, Haig, to see who will win. These things always have a winner. Which means someone has to lose."

He lifted his head and smiled and pressed his commstem and said, "I'm ready to eat. Emilio, would you bring everyone in please."

The first round of negotiations were over, thought Haig.

**

The table seated ten, and eight places were laid. Sile sat at the head of the table and spent a few minutes introducing everyone. Haig sat next to Sile. Tobin and Wecht sat on Haig's side. Dekker, Kaneda and Barnes sat opposite. Janulis faced Sile at the foot of the table. Sile's boardroom had real, comfortable chairs, but there was a sour smell of sweat ingrained into fabric. Haig caught the dark shadows behind some ears, dirt in the creases of pale faces.

They wore their Gunport overalls in different ways. Tobin rolled his sleeves up to reveal a scattering of tattoos, his left arm carrying icons from a sweeping history of flight, from pedal-power to propellers, jet engines to ion streamers.

Kaneda, the Head of Maintenance, had a plain, wrinkled face. His sleeves were down, and his hands were a deep brown, carrying odd textures, differently patterned skin from finger to knuckle to heel, wisps of hair that had grown in odd directions. A lifetime of chemical burns and heat burns and steam burns that had never quite healed.

Haig hadn't met Janulis before. Alison Janulis was the Head of Artificial Intelligence. Galatea's mother, as they called her. Her face was dry and composed, not a hair out of place, all hard lines and sharp edges, with grey eyes buried at the back of a tightly-skinned skull. Her overalls were far too big, hanging shapelessly around her.

Dekker wore a tight-fitting t-shirt with a Gunport logo on the sleeve. He seemed to be resisting any ostentatious display of wrist-spinning, at least for now. Having Dekker and Tobin sat near each other made Haig realise something about Tobin. He'd been struggling to work out what it was, but it was their hair. Dekker wore his hair swept back and it shone dimly with grease, even in the half-light of Sile's boardroom. Tobin's hair reflected the light and moved gently with his head. It was because, unlike everyone else, his hair was clean.

Holden brought trays of food-paste in and they started picking at it. When Haig looked up, Dekker was staring at him.

"How was your flight here, Anson?" said Sile.

"I don't remember any of it," said Haig. "I was under for most of it. The waking up was the hard work."

"The rehab isn't fun," said Wecht. "I remember mine. Even now I sometimes wake up with ringing in my ears, and I've been here for three years. No doubt Galatea will have some cardio lined up for you."

Janulis said, "Galatea will look after you, Haig. She will make you run, for your own good."

"Do you play squash?" said Sile. "We have some excellent

players."

"A long time ago," said Haig.

Janulis was already tapping something into a tablet. No doubt he would find himself ordered to play squash by the AI in no time at all.

"The exercise is vital," said Wecht. "Keep muscles strong, bones strong."

Tobin nodded. "I still have these spots in my eyes. In my peripheral vision."

"How long have you all been here for?" said Haig.

"Four years," said Tobin. "And six months, and two weeks, and three days. But who's counting, eh?"

"All of it in service of humanity," said Barnes, looking at Sile.

Haig looked at Barnes properly for the first time. The Space Traffic Controller had a gaunt head balanced on top of sharp shoulders. His eyes rolled. They were quick and hawkish, implants surrounding watery blue irises. Perpendicular red in them coiled and made his eyes look forever bloodshot.

Dekker shifted in his seat.

"I arrived first of all," said Sile. "Over six years ago. Only the fifth person to ever use a B-DC. Barnes is right, you see. This is only one stage in the journey. I was the first permanent resident here."

"And you took the best room," said Tobin.

Sile ignored him. "Robert, Alison and Emilio came next. More than five years together now."

"Robert is Doctor Prendrick? I haven't met him yet," said Haig. "And I thought Sunita Acaba might be here."

"He and Sunita send their apologies," said Sile. "But they cannot attend."

Unlikely, thought Haig. Acaba hasn't been invited or said 'no'.

Prendrick was another story.

"Any news from Earth?" said Wecht.

"Nothing you don't already know," said Haig. "I had to catch up myself when I got here."

"I hear they've installed a new AI network on Mars," said Janulis.

Kaneda nodded. "Talos-OGP."

"It'll control Aphelion's satellite network in orbit. Stop them from crashing into each other, I suppose," said Janulis.

"You don't sound too thrilled," said Barnes. "Anything that supports our work is marvellous, surely."

"Galatea does your work, Barnes," said Janulis.

Sile raised a conciliatory hand. "We know how important Galatea is, Alison."

"I met Hasan Choudhury in the elevator," said Haig. "He told me he's working on an experiment to find water on an ice moon."

"Choudhury's experiments are like our plastic toilets," Dekker said dismissively.

Tobin laughed and said, "Full of cracks and full of shit."

"What if he does find water?" said Wecht. "There's not a person here who wouldn't appreciate a longer shower."

Janulis shifted in her seat.

"Would they build another Gunport?" said Barnes.

Sile glared at him. "Another perhaps, but they could never replicate our success. Choudhury is Aphelion's concession to the scientists. They wanted a presence and I allowed one. Choudhury will get all that is coming to him. I just hope that his ego is thick enough to hold it."

Dekker smiled and stroked his mechanical wrist. So, thought

Haig. News travels fast.

"Besides," said Sile, "He has more value to you, Chris."

Tobin fidgeted slightly. "I'm with Wecht. I'd love a longer shower."

Sile stared at him and waited until he had eye contact. Then he said slowly, "How many takers are there in your pool?"

"I've got the same amount of water as everyone else," said Tobin. "Janulis knows, don't you? Same as my lads, same as you."

"Does it cut out often? The water? My shower ended early before I came up here," said Haig.

He looked across at the different faces.

Janulis looked warily at Sile. "Galatea decides," she said.

Kaneda said, "I understand you grew up on a moonbase, Anson. So you know how much of my time I spend repairing those things that others take for granted."

"Water was one," said Haig. "Gravity failing, that was always nasty. Like an upside down earthquake, nothing was ever the right way around afterwards, and we were finding things that had floated off and gotten stuck for months. Or sometimes, it'd be the next gravity failure that revealed things to you that you thought were lost. They'd float out of some alcove you never knew existed. Air pressure always had the engineers moving. Army moonbases were always leaking air somewhere. They used to say they were the puncture police, running around slapping repair patches on things."

Kaneda smiled, nodded. "Aphelion has a hydrogen plant on Deimos. Only tiny compared to Gunport and some of the bases on the Moon."

"Big Blue," said Haig. "The water farm."

"Ah, you know it then," said Kaneda. "I had a trolley full of glue and aluminium sheets, and my first job after graduating was wheeling it around sticking patches to things that hissed. What took you there?"

"Making holes for you to patch up," said Haig.

Haig didn't feel the need to tell Kaneda how those holes had gotten there.

He'd been embedded in a SORG team who had gone to negotiate with a hostile mercenary group that had taken over the plant. Haig later found out the mercenaries were Allpower-paid thugs, hired anonymously to take the plant offline and drive up fuel prices around Mars. Allpower's own plant would be ready a month later and they wanted demand to spike. Aphelion had the contract, but their in-house combat forces couldn't go in because Big Blue belonged to the Triangle, so SORG went in as a neutral party. They jammed all comms, sealed up the airlocks with hydraulic clamps, then blocked air filtration and recycling systems. The ammonia built up, carbon dioxide, monoxide. The mercenaries asked to negotiate two days before the end. SORG kept Haig away from comms, and every living soul inside choked and died.

Allpower took the contracts and a billion-dollar slap on the wrist, and Haig saw it as seventy-two civilians having died for no reason.

Sile hadn't stopped looking at Tobin. After a moment, he glanced at Dekker, and Dekker leaned forward, his mechanical fingers bending the wrong way and tapping the back of his hand in a clinking rhythm.

"Answer the question, Tobin," said Dekker. "How many takers in the pool?"

Tobin looked at Dekker, looked at the expectant Sile, then cleared his throat, said, "About half the crew."

"Explain," said Sile. "For Anson's benefit, at least."

"Choudhury's experiment will bore through the ice surface of Sedna B-8 using a drill strapped to a fission reactor. He's made a guess based on seismic activity and weather, and he started blathering on about layers, the daft twat. When he's pressed, he thinks maybe a mile or two. People trade shower time. Whoever is closest gets it all."

"Is anyone here in this pool?"

Silence thickened, curdled. He's reminding them who's in charge, thought Haig. A power play. Sile would keep him waiting for just a moment too long, make a show of flexing his authority. Haig had no doubt that Sile didn't care in the slightest about Tobin's pool. If anything, it helped Sile to distract from the real problems. Acaba would probably have said, 'why not just give everyone a shower instead of gambling for it', but it was that kind of question that meant Sile wanted her kept away. So it was performative, but not for Haig's benefit. If he hadn't been here, it would have happened anyway.

"Well," said Sile finally, "Conditions can't be so bad if our staff have access to more shower time, can they? At least his experiment will be useful for something."

"With any luck, I'll be too busy for any pools soon, eh Haig?" said Tobin. "And I'm sorry to say, you might be with us a bit longer than you thought. Arthur isn't pulling Excalibur out of this stone anytime soon."

"I knew the shuttle had been banged up. How long?"

Tobin nodded to Kaneda. "Vacuum engines are – interesting," said Kaneda. "The landing gear is perfectly doable. When Tobin has cleared out the foam, it will be a straightforward repair. I have no experience with Vacuum Engines beyond routine maintenance, however. Truthfully, Galatea guides most of the routine work with the drones. I'm waiting for some repair packets in the comms from Earth for guidance and to program the drones before I get started. They should arrive within the week."

Tobin looked at Haig and said, "You've gone white. Pale even for here. Well, you're here for at least month anyway. Come on. Let's see what you make of this. Have a drink."

The others watched with interest as Tobin held out a small paper cup. Haig sniffed it and recoiled. He caught a drone-fuel cocktail that singed his nose hair and smelled like oily rags.

"Alcohol?"

"Not just alcohol," said Kaneda. "Gunshine," said Tobin. "My own recipe. Sometimes we all need a little chemical stimulation."

Haig looked at them each in turn, all curious, all silently encouraging him, before he shrugged and drank it. The fumes hit the back of his throat and his nose ran before he coughed, but then felt the warmth reach his fingers and foot.

"Potent," he said weakly.

Tobin grinned. Kaneda smiled. Janulis and Barnes were unimpressed.

Dekker said, "There's a lot to be said for abstinence. Discipline. Too many drunken fights. One man complaining of dirt in his water. Or a shorter shower," he said, looking at Haig. "You know how it is. A small grievance plus a lot of alcohol becomes a large grievance."

Sile said, "We've talked about this before, Emilio. The only thing worse than everyone drinking is telling everyone they can't drink."

"Our first negotiation is scheduled for tomorrow," said Haig suddenly, the room moving without him, the gunshine taking hold. "I'm hoping for positivity and openness."

"It's a shame Acaba couldn't have seen sense," said Wecht.

"This is the process we must follow," said Sile, nodding to Haig. "I'm confident it will end in the right way."

That seemed to shut the conversation down. The others looked at each other and then at their food, and fell to eating, the gentle scratching of plastic and cardboard the only sound for a few minutes.

Haig reflected. They were in thrall to Sile, that much was clear, either his allies, or at least prepared to present as his allies. There were so many unspoken threads dangling in the air. Haig wasn't sure if they remained unspoken because of his presence or because they did not want to risk Sile turning Dekker's rotating wrist onto them. Dekker clearly didn't enjoy mopping up scufflers and brawlers but this behaviour was normally because conditions were difficult. His own experience on moonbases told him that when all of the small things were going wrong, it made life unbearable. The pool should have alerted Sile to the lack of water. It should have been resolved. And it definitely wouldn't help to that Sile had a comfortable office space and a plant, and they did not. Acaba would have more to say on this tomorrow, he was sure.

Barnes had been picking at his food-paste with a misplaced meticulousness. He'd sliced away at the blob and turned the gelatinous cube into something approaching a sphere, even easing away at the underside to give it curves.

He said, "We've a flightpath to Fujin-77 prepared and ready to go. We simply need the payloads to arrive to be redistributed."

Tobin pointed his fork at Barnes. "Not this shit again, Barnes."

Haig glanced around at Sile. He was holding his bowl up in front of his face and cutting small slices of the food-paste with his spoon. He looked between Barnes and Tobin, and then ate the slices slowly, sucking at them rather than chewing. He wants this to play out, thought Haig.

Haig lifted his own spoon and scowled at the glob. His hands felt swollen and tingled. His head was throbbing and he could feel pressure behind his eyes.

"It's the furthest we've ever sent anything," Barnes continued quietly, reverent.

"Solar winds are – problematic," said Kaneda.

"The winds?" said Haig, closing his eyes and putting the entire spoonful in his mouth, then started chewing doggedly.

"The good Cargo Master doesn't like to launch when there's but a little passing wind," said Barnes. "He needs to pull his trousers up and realise how inconvenient it is."

"Does he now?" said Tobin, offering Barnes such a stare that Barnes looked away, implants whirring, eyes glazed.

Haig swallowed the last thick glob of his own food-paste.

Haig thought Barnes had decided to let this go, but then Barnes surprised Tobin by saying, "These ships are full to bursting for the colonies. Everything a colony needs, except the colonists themselves. Robots that have started to build a decade before anyone thinks to arrive. And then colonists begin to land, and it simply will not do for them to arrive to a couple of waterproof matches and a half-hearted hut, with some abandoned mining robot left to shrug apologetically and say, 'Sorry you've come all this way, everyone, but Christopher Tobin decreed the wind was a little strong the day your supplies should have launched and so you'll need to starve, suffocate, boil, freeze, and die miserable, lonely deaths.'"

"At least they can only die once, eh?" said Tobin. Wecht tutted at him. Tobin shrugged.

"The future of humanity is worth more," said Barnes, far too earnestly. It felt forced. It felt like the Barnes who had spoken to him on landing, the Barnes playing the role of Barnes. Nervous, anxious, something behind the façade.

Dekker jabbed his spoon at Barnes and said, "Do you need arresting?"

Barnes huffed and rolled his eyes. "It thrills me to see how much you care about our work here."

Tobin smiled, then frowned, then smiled again, and said, "Look, Echion Alpha has got everything it needs. You're just talking about Fujin, now. One step at a time, eh? Besides, ninety-five percent of our turnarounds are within the SLA," said Tobin.

"Ninety-two-point-four," said Sile.

"Solar winds fucked up the last two. Fujin is like trying to shit through a hose," said Tobin.

Sile blinked. "Excuse me?"

"We can't launch them because of the solar winds. It isn't about me pulling my fucking trousers up. Radiation and other shit, same size as your fingernails, nearly at the speed of light, frying every electrical that isn't shielded. Kaneda knows. How many of your drones have been mangled by radiation?"

Kaneda looked up, considering, started to say "Tw-", then was cut off by Tobin saying, "There's a circle of drones we've never been able to get back, spread out around Gunport, just sort of floating about. You send supply ships out in those winds and you may as well let a toddler decorate a rock with tinfoil and call it a spacecraft. If I don't unpack and repack things properly, they get fried. I know it makes our numbers look shit, but what can we do?"

Sile leaned forward, said, "Firstly, Chris, you need to watch your tone. You need to watch your language."

Tobin belligerently shoved some food-paste into his mouth.

Sile said, "Ninety-five-percent in a rolling quarter is arguably the most important target we have, Chris. The Service Level Agreement is what we agreed to, and we must meet it. We must land and launch supply ships. When we are back on track, we will overcome this obstacle. What are solar winds against our ingenuity? We are the first step in the future history of mankind, Chris."

Tobin looked like he wanted to say something else, then Haig caught Kaneda raise his eyebrows in the gentlest of 'Don't say anything else' gestures. Tobin saw it, turned his words into a deep breath, taken up through his nose, then straightened his back. His tone softened.

"I understand," he said.

"All I want is for us to be ambitious," said Barnes petulantly.

There was a quietness. Tobin leaned over to Haig's cup with gunshine before Kaneda put his hand over it and shook his head gently, Tobin retreating with a shrug.

Haig coughed. The gunshine had faded, leaving a throb behind his eyes.

Kaneda said, "Chris is right. The solar winds do stop us from launching. The ship might well reach its destination, but we need it – and its cargo – to arrive intact."

"Choudhury is your scientist," said Haig. "Does he not have any ideas?"

"None that I can execute," said Kaneda. "But that isn't his fault."

Barnes and Dekker made noises, gestures.

"It's true, whatever you might think of him," continued Kaneda. "All of his suggestions and options would help, but I don't have the resources. There are three main options. One is avoiding the storm, which requires more fuel to fly a longer course. Fuel is expensive. Two is greater shielding. Either metal or something organic. Aphelion's OGRYN labs have had some success with a radiotropic fungus between layers of aluminium. Both are expensive, and the fungus is an unknown without a human being tending to it. Three is to make it into a numbers game. Send a lot more and hope for the best. Numbers are expensive."

Kaneda sipped his gunshine and shuddered.

"None of it is without risk," said Sile. "The first manned ship to Echion Alpha is due to leave in three years. When the Masamune launches, the colonists onboard won't know if our bases there will be finished when they arrive. They go into the unknown, the abyss."

"They're not just promises," said Wecht.

"You're going?" said Haig.

Wecht nodded, slightly embarrassed. "I've been offered an office to work from. It's a new field, really. Deep space psychology. It's fascinating."

"It seems we aren't quite far away enough from Earth for Sarah," said Sile.

"How long will it take to get there?" said Haig.

"Twelve years," said Wecht.

"Fucking hell."

"A year or two more or less."

"Not all in a B-DC, surely? You'd be soup."

"In and out, on rotation," said Wecht. "It'll be tough, sure, but I've been chosen because I've already got the experience."

Tobin said, "They've really built you an office?"

"It'll be ready when I get there," said Wecht, uncertainty betrayed in her voice.

"You can't trust something that isn't finished," said Tobin. "You can't trust them just because you want to believe it."

"We've been sending cargo payload for over three years," said Kaneda. "If it isn't ready, it won't be because they haven't tried. It isn't like Gunport. The atmosphere will support human life."

"Just about," said Tobin. "You think Earth's shite, you just fucking wait. Imagine the most inhospitable places on Earth but an entire fucking planet of it. That's your Echion Alpha."

"I think they're the bravest of all of us," said Barnes. "And you,

Sarah."

"Fucking stupid is what you are," said Tobin.

"Don't be so narrow-minded," snapped Janulis. "They have faith. As, in fact, do you, Chris, as do all of us. Not something spiritual or religious but faith in other people and faith in our machines. You're here, right? You chose to believe that these great brains, the granted gifts of the Advance, have provided transport. Transport built by the Machine Minds. You believed it would be so, and it was. A leap of faith. A chariot to blaze through the stars. So it was that the first engineers of this place believed. They believed that the robots had done their jobs, believed in the telemetry that they received that told them that it was safe. The first person to come here had faith. To believe they did not come simply to die. And that is the same for the colonists. They believe it will be ready when they come. A new kingdom. A chance to start new, and fresh. To escape this place and find themselves anew somewhere else. Rebirth. Resurrection."

"Would you go?" said Haig.

Janulis blinked. "No, of course not. I am needed here."

"Perhaps I could release you," said Sile, leaning back in his chair, his eyes black, pupils glinting, teeth bared.

Janulis was startled. "No, of course not. No, that's not what I want. I was simply explaining why some people would face years of treacherous space travel."

"Hope for something better," said Haig, nodding. "I wouldn't be able to do it. I admire those who can. I'm far away enough from home as it is."

"We have all sacrificed to be here," said Sile, leaning back into the light. "And I admire that about all of you. What we've accomplished so far. I have no doubt that soon we'll be back on track. And that we'll get you home as quickly as we can, Anson."

Dekker tilted his head to the side suddenly, listening to the earpiece of his commstem, then said, "Excuse me," before leaving the room.

"I'm sure it's nothing too serious," said Sile, sipping his water.

Tobin muttered, "Perhaps they've made a shinier prosthetic and they've just gone on sale."

Wecht tutted while Haig noticed Kaneda smile for the first time.

Dekker re-entered and spoke urgently into Sile's ear. Sile's eyes widened before he said, shaken, "Dinner is over." He stood up suddenly.

"There's somebody outside."

CHAPTER 4: LINE OF THE DARK

Silence.

"No-one's been outside for months," said Kaneda quietly. Sile looked at him, ashen-faced.

And then everyone spoke at once. Rumours began to circle almost immediately. Haig couldn't follow the voices. It must be Blue High. That's it. Someone from Blue High's research station has gotten lost. Came here to be rescued, died on the way. Don't mention that, said another. Not with *him* here. They don't know that we know they're there.

"He knows now," said Tobin, shrugging.

Blue High were one of Aphelion's major competitors. The WSA encouraged competing corps to build near each other, just to have a presence. Keep each other honest. Blue High had a listening post, and that was really all it was. A squat plastic dome that could house two people and an array of comms, but not manned. It simply tracked the landings and launches and sent packets of data back to Earth. Haig had set these listening posts up himself when he had joined Comms and Logistics. Set up your own, mess with others, stop them messing with ours. He had gone out in suits and bolted thudders into shingle on ridges, the vibrations simulating large-scale activity.

"Just go and fuck with 'em," said his CO. "Make 'em think we've got a thousand men hiding in those shadows."

Another rumour was that someone had tried to make a run for it. That makes no sense, said a different voice. Go where?

"Suicide?" said Kaneda. Wecht looked at her nails, nodded.

Sile seemed to reawaken, like he had reemerged from a long sleep in a B-DC chamber.

"I want this to be kept as contained as possible," he said. "Everyone in Traffic who knows is to be held there and away from comms until you speak to them, Emilio. You make sure they understand the consequences of speaking out of turn." And then, it seemed to Haig to be for his benefit, "Tensions are high, and I do not want people fearful. Scared people do unpredictable things."

Dekker stood up and marched out, his task clear.

Sile leaned back in his chair, finished. Haig looked from one to the other and found himself bridling at their inaction. Kaneda wanted to say something, so did Tobin and Wecht, but none of them did.

Haig shook his head and leaned forward, said, "What about the person?"

Sile blinked. "The person?"

"Are they in a suit?"

"A suit?"

Haig looked around the table, and only Kaneda looked back.

Haig thought, For fuck's sake, John, yes, the person outside. Haig said, "Are they in a suit? Could they be alive?"

"Yes," said Sile. "They're in a suit."

"Have we spoken to them?"

"Spoken to them?"

"No-one in their right mind goes out without a radio and a locator. Have we spoken to them?"

"Dekker didn't say."

"Barnes?"

Barnes looked at him blankly. "Yes?"

"Speak to whoever first saw the suit and find out if they've tried the radio."

Barnes took a breath and pulled at his hand, said, "Tower, this is Barnes. Who found the suit?"

Haig said, "We need to get them inside, as quickly as possible. How far is this Blue High listening post?"

"Two hours on foot," said Kaneda. "We send drones out every year. They can't be from there, though. Blue High haven't sent anyone. They don't even have B-DCs."

"You know that for certain?" said Haig.

"Well, I, er – "

"Army suits have up to four hours of air," said Haig. "I've dealt with Blue High before. If it's them, they use Army surplus. Bought it from us when it outlived us."

Barnes said, "No contact. Sagar saw it first, says he ran through the protocols. No radio, then no locator. They tried Morse from the landing lights – no ships out there now – but no response."

Tobin said, "Doesn't seem like there's much of a hurry, then."

"Prick," said Wecht, scowling.

Sile resurfaced, said, "Wait a moment, Haig. You want us to go outside and get them?"

"I've got experience with spacework. I've brought suits in before, in almost exactly this situation."

Sile gawped at him. Haig stared back. Waited for permission. Didn't get it. Decided –

"Kaneda, you're with me," continued Haig. "What suits have you got? Salvage equipment?"

"Everything we have is in the Ramp," said Kaneda. "Retallick's in charge. Suits and his buggy. The drones we use for maintenance are too lightweight to bring a suit in."

"Tell him we're coming and tell him what we need. Barnes, get up to Traffic. You've got cameras covering the ground around Traffic, yes?"

Barnes cleared his throat, surprised to be spoken to. "Yes," he said. "Yes, of course."

"Get up to Traffic and get a fix on the suit. Feed it back to Retallick and Kaneda."

"I don't want anyone else told," said Sile.

"It's too late for that," said Haig. "If there's even the faintest chance this person's alive, then we go out and we get them. Every WSA or Aphelion or Army or whatever protocol says, 'You don't leave people outside to die'."

"That's my choice to make," snapped Sile.

Haig pointed at him, angry. "It's not a choice. It's the only thing to do. You want to let everyone here think you left someone outside to die?"

Sile sneered, then waved his hand dismissively.

Haig went first, Barnes following without meeting Sile's glare, but Haig saw Kaneda's grim expression. Kaneda met Sile's glare, and glared back.

***

Haig clenched and unclenched his fists in the Elevator. He didn't want to be involved in this, but all of those old instincts took over. Sile didn't want to risk the equipment or spend the money or suffer further embarrassment or risk Gunport being closed for longer or whatever reason he had, but he had been paralysed with shock and surprise, thought Haig. He had instantly and subconsciously calculated all of the consequences of this body appearing and the only way for it to resolve how he wanted was to pretend it had never happened.

Haig followed Kaneda through Maintenance and into the Ramp, their footsteps echoing.

Maintenance's 3D printers clicked and buzzed, one making a keyboard, another making a desk. All cheap plastic.

"I should warn you," said Kaneda. "Retallick is difficult, and he will ask for something in return."

It was a glorified hangar, with Airlock doors big enough to drive a buggy out onto the surface. A rack of flimsy plastic drones lined one wall, with a chute for them to go outside. Conrad Retallick maintained the Ramp with a zealot's precision. There was a startling lack of clutter.

The buggy took centre stage under a gantry of spotlights and dangling chains. Shadows stretched into the corners of the hangar, making it hard to know how big the hangar actually was. Brilliant white lights bleached it from above, like it was waiting for an audience before it could perform.

Every excess component had been sliced away until this was all that was left. It was a bare chassis atop four wheels with hollow chainmail tyres. The tyres sagged heavily into the floor, like four flattened sieves, and above each was a small electrical motor. Each motor carried a thick cable to a small steering wheel at the centre of the buggy in front of a plastic seat.

Four concrete blocks had been slapped onto the four sides in metal baskets, the metal sagging slightly at the weight. They were the only thing that would keep the driver from hitting a bump too quickly and finding themselves floating in orbit, Anguta R-611 quickly becoming a grey marble against a black carpet.

"Conrad?" shouted Kaneda.

They stood in the semi-dark and listened to the low hum of air-conditioning, air-recycling, pipes and everything else.

"Retallick? Come on out, we need your help."

"From on high?"

Haig spun, the voice behind him. Kaneda turned slowly,

sighed.

Retallick was a long man, as if once regular but then taken and stretched out. His overalls were for a much wider man, puffing and bunching in all the wrong places.

He was leaning against the bulwark next to the door, and Haig realised that he had been watching him since he had walked in. Retallick pushed off and stepped into the light, long limbs striding into the centre of the room.

Haig realised that his gunhand was at his holster, and let it drop.

"There's a spacesuit outside," said Haig.

"I received your messages, Kaneda," said Retallick.

Kaneda held up his tablet. "Haig, look. Barnes has sent us images. Wearing a Z-series pack."

Retallick said, "Ah. The drones won't get that in. Old Army surplus is too bulky. I don't understand the urgency. No radio, no locator, no response to any signalling. There is no occupant or there is a dead occupant, yes?"

Haig said, "It's moving like it's got someone limp inside. Probably dead. A slim chance that they're alive, but slim enough to get out there."

Retallick gazed blankly at the floor and shuffled towards the buggy. No haste whatsoever.

"Not Blue High," said Kaneda. "Wrong colour. Wrong configuration. I need to look at it properly to confirm, but I think it's one of ours."

"Has it ever been used?" said Haig, pointing at the buggy.

"No," said Retallick, placing a hand against one of the chainmail tyres, prodding a finger in-between the links in the metal.

"Could she even do it?" said Haig, leaning in. "Looks like

you've worked hard to build her yourself. The Army always had these shiny metal vehicles. Teams of people to make them run." Humanise the buggy. Appeal to his vanity. Give him an opportunity to use it.

"Of course she could," said Retallick, his voice sharpening, taking the bait. "But it's dangerous work, Haig. You're here because you know you can't do it. Urgency is key, hm? You should know that my equipment needs refreshing. Angutian dust is like broken glass. It is just waiting to embrace even the gentlest of falls by shredding a suit. And I've nothing nearly as hardy as a Z-series to call on. We rarely go outside, and if we do, Kaneda's printers run the suits we use from the cardboard we eat our protein blocks from."

"It's dangerous, then."

Retallick stared at him for a moment.

He half-smiled, shook his head, and rolled a sleeve up, revealing perpendicular grey lines against black skin in a startling tattoo. His techtatts.

"This is a diagram of the electrical motor in my elbow," he said, pointing at various lines and symbols. "It failed, long ago. Not long after I came here, started working for Sile. Now, it convulses every few days, and my arm locks. My elbow is a knot rather than a hinge. I can't move it. And this tattoo reminds me of how I can't fix it."

"What do you want?" said Haig quietly.

"I want everything repaired. All of my implants. By Bethe. By the company. An end, finally, to those infernal drugs. To be clean again."

"Okay," said Haig. "You know who I am. You know I can't promise that. But I'll try to get it for you."

"If I get the suit in," said Retallick, staring at him.

They locked eyes. Retallick held the breath a moment

longer, scanning Haig, searching his face with brown eyes, the implants chittering and twitching. A moment more. Calculating. Gauging trust.

"Where is it?" he said finally.

"Come in, Barnes," Haig said into his e-sleeve.

"Barnes here."

"Retallick's going to go out and bring the suit in. He'll need precise co-ordinates and someone to talk him through it."

"I've never conducted this kind of operation before."

"I'll come up to you," said Haig. "I haven't got a commstem, so I'll need a headset."

"Very well," said Barnes. "Conrad, are you there? The suit is currently amusing itself a few kilometres north. Currently drifting outwards in a rough spiral around us. I'm sure it will be delighted to see you."

"Thank you, Barnes."

"Haig out," said Haig, cutting Barnes off.

"I shall need some time," said Retallick. "The surface is sharp and uneven. It will be slow. And if the suit drifts further, I may be unable to reach it."

"How long will you need?"

"An hour."

"That's a long time."

"Let's be blunt. Your visitor is most likely dead, Haig. I will recover them, but it must take time. And I will not endanger my equipment unnecessarily. My chariot will ride into battle, Anson Haig, but I will retreat without hesitation at the slightest hint of danger. I shan't risk myself for a corpse."

"You need to go as quickly as you can. Kaneda will help you. If there's even a chance they could be alive, we need to try."

"I shall prepare the equipment, plot co-ordinates, predict the suit's path. The buggy is methodical, not fast. I'll say it again. The entire surface is razor sharp, uneven. I must tether the suit properly. Then return it. Any kind of weather shall make the mission take longer."

"I get it, Conrad. It's going to be really hard. That's why I'm going to be asking for implants for you."

Retallick stared at Haig and rubbed his elbow.

"I am realistic," said Retallick, "Not cruel. Very well. I shall make the preparations. There is nothing for you to do now but wait. Wait, and to organise those implants."

Retallick walked towards a corner and was consumed by the dark.

Haig turned to leave.

"There is one other thing," said Retallick's displaced voice, booming from nowhere. "I'm more than a little ripe, Haig."

Haig pulled at the back of his t-shirt and nodded. They all were.

Retallick said, "My shower ended eight seconds early this morning. I want an extra minute every day until the day I leave."

***

Haig followed the coloured lines painted on the floors and made it back to the Elevator. He stood scratching at his beard and at his hairline, waiting for it to clank and whirr back to him. He was tapping his fingers against his thigh, starting shifting his weight from foot to metal foot.

Maintenance and the Ramp were at the top of Gunport, just below the Space Traffic Control Tower, and the Ramp opened out onto the surface. It meant Haig was right at the top, and he was stood above billions of tonnes of concrete and metal. The greatest thing humanity had ever done, the biggest project ever committed into space, on a moon the universe would register as a grain of sand in a desert wind.

And now Haig was all alone inside of it, trying to save a person in a suit. What he thought was a person. Because if that suit was empty, and the suit was a shell, there would be more than questions. Mangan would back him – IPRA followed WSA rules and expected their people to do the same. It would be Sile and how he perceived it. Repercussions for taking it out of his hands. And if the suit had a body inside, then he'd inserted himself into something he didn't want to be a part of. Get the suit in, let Dekker handle it – even if they had different ideas about what the word 'handle' meant – and resume negotiations.

"So is it true?" a voice behind him said, the words said so quickly as though a great swell of pressure had told and finally pushed them out.

A thin, pale woman stared at him across the corridor.

She was stood bolt upright, her back against the wall and one hand touching it with fingertips, her wide eyes glassy and shimmering. She carried raw, aggressive scales where the skin joined her ears to the sides of her head. The skin at her cheeks sunk and clung to her face, making her wet eyes throb in their sockets. Her left eye carried a black square around it, fading to a yellow-green as it rippled away from the centre. She had an implant around it, thought Haig. The skin was taut along the edges of it. Some polymer reinforcement after a head injury. There were messy scars spreading away from the corner of her mouth on the implant side, going away from her lips, claw marks or scratches.

"I'm sorry," she said. "I should introduce myself."

She didn't. She stared at him.

When the introduction didn't come, he said, "So should I. I'm Anson Haig."

"You're the negotiator from Earth," she said. "From IPRA. Is it true that you're not with the company? Not corp?"

"You're right," said Haig, extending a hand. "You *should* introduce yourself."

He was used to different reactions when he came to negotiate. Hostility was an obvious one, but nervousness and awkwardness were familiar too. He was an unknown, an outsider. He liked to let people lead the interactions and mirror them, make it easier for them to talk to him. Try to project a certain boring competence. Ah, they would think. He'll do a good job but what was his name again? Functional and forgettable. Aggressively functional.

She looked down at his hand and then back at his face. "I need your help," she said.

"What's your name?"

"I heard about the suit."

"Shake my hand and tell me your name," said Haig, his hand still extended. "I like to know who I'm speaking to. And then, if I can help you, I will."

"I know who's inside it," she said.

Haig dropped his hand. "I'm here to negotiate between Aphelion and the Reactor techs. That's my job. I'm neutral. If you know anything, you need to report it to Dekker or Holden. Security will investigate and they want any information anyone has."

"I can't," she said, sliding along the wall away from Haig.

The Elevator clunked and clanked as it arrived and Haig turned to watch it open.

When he looked back around, he saw the back of her disappearing around the corner at the end of the corridor.

※※※

Traffic was intensely quiet.

It stood atop a tower on the Upper 10th Floor at Gunport's peak, overlooking the top of Gunport's concrete cylinders. On the surface of Anguta R-611 below, between the vast openings for the ships and shuttles, were the Airlocks and Ramp, their guide lights blinking. Only the Communications Array was higher, perched outside on top of Traffic, a clump of antennae hanging over the side, nanomesh weave stretched over hollow shells, a single long rod jutting towards the stars above.

The Bottom Hub of Traffic was a circular concrete cell, desks and computers a hand-width apart. A raised platform – the Upper Ring – surrounded the workstations and provided the view out to space.

A black screen looped around and loomed above one side of Traffic entirely. Galatea conducted streams of spacebound traffic in and out, with human help. Some ships back to Earth, some to Echion Alpha, or beyond. Earth was prominently labelled but small on the left, Anguta R-611 a little way to the right, and an enormous empty space – the rest of the known galaxy – sweeping away beyond. Echion Alpha, bigger than Earth, hugged the far right of the screen. Sedna B-8 hadn't earned its dot yet.

A hundred squares represented company spacecraft, using varying flight plans, but all destined for Echion Alpha. A purple square, 'Stormthrower-3', was closest. Each square carried its distance from Echion Alpha below its name, steadily counting down. Each was in the billions.

Haig came out of the Elevator and was met with the backs of ten Traffic Controllers, clustered above on the platform. He saw stained armpits in company coveralls and caught the sour smell of the underwashed. Air filters hummed and cleaned the air, but not the people.

Barnes turned and saw him, then beckoned him over. His Traffic Controllers were staring out in the blackness, pointing, whispering, craning their necks. Then, without a word being spoken, they remembered that they were supposed to be working, shuffled away, still whispering.

Haig stood next to Barnes at the window on the Upper Ring, watching Anguta R-611's nothingness with a blank, wide-eyed glare, arms folded.

"He's coping rather well," said Barnes. "I did not think I could be impressed by a golf cart made of concrete, but I am."

They stood like this for thirty minutes. Forty. An hour. Near silence.

Haig turned away from the empty blackness and sagged against the sweeping window. He watched Barnes' Traffic Controllers idly, sat at their own consoles, quiet, focused. The black screen displayed a banner with more old news: Gunport staff boarding a shuttle, all beaming smiles, thumbs up, walking on gantries in flight suits.

Prickling heat, the itch just before sweating, rose up Haig's back. His face was damp, moisture easing into broken skin at his hairline. Perhaps Galatea was pumping water back into the air. Perhaps it was because he'd asked Retallick to go out. He wiped his face, then rubbed the moisture into his knuckles.

He turned idly back to the surface. The window took all of the texture out of the grey grit that stretched off to become the moon's horizon. The shimmer of the glittering sand was dulled and blank. Above it was a bar of black, punched through with white holes, stars billions of miles away. Haig was dazed, yawned, before –

Retallick's voice filled Traffic. "Direction check," he said breathlessly, voice echoing in his helmet, his head bouncing around.

Barnes went over to his console and sat down, his face shining under the bright lights. Dark patches had spread under his armpits. He tapped for a moment, and the screen changed.

A drone feed appeared, positioned above and behind Retallick's shoulder. His bulky gloves were far too big for the buggy's steering wheel and controls. He pinched at it with finger and thumb, prodded it occasionally to keep it straight. The buggy bobbed up and down, sometimes bouncing up, sometimes crashing down, but mostly bobbing, up, and down, and up.

There was a thick belt of grey under a block of black, and even with the up and down, it stayed consistent, like Retallick was traversing a photograph. A speedometer on the Traffic screen showed 4mph, and Haig thought it was the most violent 4mph he had ever seen.

Barnes blinked and turned back to his own screen.

Behind him, Haig heard the elevator doors hiss open, but didn't take his eyes from the screen.

Footsteps padded in behind him until Sile appeared and said, "Update please."

"Retallick is close," said Haig. "Barnes is guiding him using the locator on a drone we attached to the suit. Retallick will check to see if there is any sign of life, load the suit into the buggy, and we'll bring it – or them – back."

"Are there any? Any signs of life?"

Haig looked at Barnes. Barnes shook his head.

"No," said Haig. "No signs. Radio is down. Locator's down. There should have been some trace. Some ping. That suit could have been out there for ten minutes or ten years. There's no way to know without getting it in."

Sile waved Haig over to an alcove and spoke quietly, urgently.

"I allowed surprise to cloud my thinking, and for that I'm sorry," he said. "You've done everything correctly. I allowed too many variables to enter into my thinking and for a moment, I forgot about the person outside. You were right to remind me and right to speak to me as you did. I understand Retallick requested implant care?"

Haig nodded.

"And this work is dangerous?"

"Lethal, if you're complacent," said Haig.

"Then if Bethe can do it and he has the right inventory, any request will be granted."

Haig nodded warily.

On the screen, light flashed.

"Visual confirmation," said Retallick's voice, filling Traffic. "Thirty seconds."

Silence now. No-one spoke, or moved. Any muttering had ceased. Retallick's breathing rasped through their speakers.

"Ten seconds."

Then the spacesuit was upon them, looming large, filling the screen, just beyond Retallick. Retallick brought the buggy to a stop and the buggy sank into its tyres, the weight bearing down on the mesh-metal, until it settled. A thin cloud of dust drifted upwards.

"Contact," said Retallick.

The suit hung above the surface, floating gently away from him. One of the shoulders dipped below the other. The helmet was tipped forward, towards the dust, and the feet dangled obediently behind.

Haig and the others watched as Retallick's two thick gloved arms rose slowly and unclasped the seatbelt, then pushed up. The drone floated up with Retallick, its camera tilting.

For a moment, the screen was entirely black, punctured only with cold starlight.

Silence had smothered Traffic. Haig pulled his arms together tighter. The Traffic Controllers were in hypnotised awe. Barnes' mouth was slightly open. Sile had folded his arms too, his mouth set into a thin line. His eyes were bulging, even in the half-light.

Retallick's voice punched through, and Haig caught Sile flinching.

"If I try to catch it from this side, it'll move away," he said. "I shall manoeuvre around it to secure it."

"Be careful," said Haig. "It doesn't take much to crash in a suit."

"I have this under control," said Retallick, panting.

"Just grab it," said Sile.

"Quiet now," said Haig softly. "EVA packs in weak gravity can be lethal. There's a lot of power in those little puffs of air. If he misjudges this, he's in trouble. Too much power going up, and he's a satellite. Too much power coming down, and he's an asteroid."

Sile recoiled slightly.

The drone tilted down and re-centred itself behind Retallick.

"What can you tell about the suit?" said Sile. "Is the person alive?"

"Be quiet," hissed Haig.

Sile blinked, opened his mouth, closed it again.

The mystery suit's enormous backpack came into view, coated in a thin film of dust. Now that they had caught up to it, Haig thought the suit looked like it was simply resting, suspended in the air, the weak gravity acting as a hammock. It moved at a deceptive speed, even now far enough away that Retallick would need to hurry to catch it.

"Touch the stick like it's on fire," said Haig under his breath. "A small jump. Make sure its small."

Retallick had started to float upwards, almost unnoticed, having given himself a small puff from his jets, making him rise above the suit.

"Like it's on fire," said Haig, following Retallick's movements with muttered, unheard instructions.

Retallick fumbled behind his own suit before bringing forth a small joystick, attached to a thick cable. He set himself, aiming his entire body, making sure he was properly lined up.

Haig tensed.

Then Retallick shoved the stick with his finger – only a fraction – and deliberately moved his hand away. A brief spray of gas from the thrusters jerked him forward, and then he began to move towards the suit.

"Fuck," said Haig.

No-one else reacted.

"What?" said Barnes.

Haig jabbed at his e-sleeve, said, "Haig for Kaneda."

"What?" said Sile.

The drone behind Retallick held its position above. It righted itself and showed Anguta R-611's surface, stretching into the distance. Retallick and the suit became small figures in the centre of the screen, moving silently towards each other.

Haig heard himself swallow.

Retallick glided downwards towards pockets of razor-sharp rocks that glinted in the light of the stars, clumped around dust and craters. He began grunting and muttering.

"Barnes, prep another drone," said Haig. Into his e-sleeve again, "Haig for Kaneda."

Sile looked to Haig for understanding. Haig took an involuntary step forward and sucked in a breath.

"Why?" said Barnes, dumbfounded.

The surface accelerated towards the screen.

"Too fast," said Haig.

Retallick's arms came up and spread, their palms open, and his legs followed, straight out in front of him, bracing for landing. He shot over the suit, and they saw a plume of dust and grit shoot up seconds before they heard the audio of Retallick bouncing and skittering along Anguta R-611's surface.

Retallick gave a series of low and raw grunts of pain that rasped through the radio. Then Haig recognised the wet thud-crack of a skull bouncing off a visor and Retallick was silent.

"What's happened?" said Sile.

"Conrad," said Haig, "Conrad, come in, come in."

"Tell me what's happened," said Sile, stepping up to Haig.

Haig stepped around him. "Barnes, get that drone in there now. Kaneda, come in."

"Kaneda speaking."

"If it goes into that cloud – "

"I need a suit, Kaneda," said Haig. "You need to prep it now."

Kaneda's voice was small. "Retallick?"

"What will happen if it goes into that cloud?" said Sile.

"He's crashed," said Haig. "And he's not responding."

Barnes stood up. "Haig, if the drone enters the cloud – "

Haig spun to face him. "It's a fucking drone, Barnes. Do it." Haig stared at Barnes, shoving him with a glare, until he turned back to his console and started to operate it.

"I shall prepare a suit now," said Kaneda, clicking off.

Haig turned back to the screen. The others hung limply in place, looking back from Haig to the screen and back.

The dust cloud from Retallick's crash was beginning to fade, becoming ever wider and longer, and not settling, but continuing in a slow spatter from where he had hit the surface. The suit floated towards the cloud, and then was gone, subsumed into it. Somewhere in the cloud, with the suit, was

Retallick.

"Retallick? Conrad?" said Haig. He folded his arms and took a step towards the screen. The drone began to move towards the cloud. The image on the screen closed in.

"Make sure you go straight to him, Barnes," said Haig. "We won't have long."

"I'm not a schoolboy," said Barnes.

The drone entered the cloud, and their picture was swarmed by glittering shards and grey grit. The screen began to shudder momentarily, grey edges creeping in and then rushing into the centre, and then the shuddering consistently before it became violent shaking.

"I'm losing control," said Barnes.

"Land it," said Haig.

"I'm trying."

"Fucking land it, Barnes," said Haig, spinning to look at him.

Barnes didn't reply, his arms shaking as he tried to keep his hands steady. Haig turned back to see the surface suddenly appear out of the cloud. The drone crashed and rolled, spinning the image in vicious circles, flashing between black and grey, swirling together.

"What is happening?" said Sile, stepping towards Haig, leading with his head.

Haig leaned both hands onto a desk, dizzy, feeling his stomach roll.

When Haig didn't answer, Barnes said, "The drone's thrusters have sucked up too much dust, and given that their resilience is rather pathetic, it has done the dishonourable thing and crashed."

"You knew this would happen?" said Sile. "As soon as Retallick touched the stick, you knew."

"I've been in too many suits," said Haig. "He pressed too hard. As soon as you press too hard, the damage is done. Like standing in the path of bullet when you know it's going to hit you. All you can do is watch it happen. You're helpless, useless. Maybe the cold is getting into his suit, if they're as poor as he says. And he's definitely out of practise. But I need that drone to look at Retallick. See if we can help him."

They looked at Sile. All of Traffic. Waiting to see what Sile would do and full of doubt.

"Conrad Retallick is a valuable colleague," said Sile finally. He cleared his throat. Raised his voice. Made sure the room heard him. "A drone is expendable. Use whatever resources you need."

The drone had come to an abrupt stop on the surface, its camera broken. Traffic's screen showed a thick crack running from one corner, thin splinters poking into the opposite corner. Anguta's surface was angled diagonally.

"Where's my suit, Kaneda?"

"I'm preparing it now, but it will take time," said Kaneda. "How will you get there without the buggy?"

Then the image on the screen started to move, and the bars of black and grey centred, creating two parallel blocks.

"Barnes? Are you doing that? Is that you?" said Haig.

Barnes stared. "No," he said softly, making a show of not touching his console.

"Retallick?"

The drone was turned around, grasped in two gloved hands. Retallick held it, looking unsteady.

Haig sighed and caught Barnes' eye, and they both smiled, relieved.

Retallick spun the drone so that they could see his face. Haig saw a thick black clot through the sheen of the visor, a streak of blood oozing onto the inside of the helmet. Retallick took one hand away and made a thumbs up sign.

"I am injured," he said. The radio was distant, blurred. "But, I shall be able to complete the mission."

"Can you hear us?" said Barnes.

There was silence. Then, Retallick's breathing came through, much fainter than before, permeated with crackling.

"Kaneda, come in," said Haig.

"Your suit is as ready as it can be."

"Hold on that. Retallick's okay."

Kaneda's tone changed, pleased, and he said, "That stubborn old warrior would never let this place take him."

"His radio's out. Is there anything you can do?"

"Give me a moment."

On the screen, Retallick turned around with the drone in his arms, and his mission objective was a few metres away, hanging above the surface, a thin scatter of dust around it, its head bowed deferentially.

"Can you hear us?" said Barnes.

"I cannot hear anything," said Retallick. "My radio is damaged."

Barnes rolled his eyes.

The mystery suit had greyed, the once white suit now curdling. Retallick tapped the chest plate and none of the dials or gauges in the display registered any power, never mind oxygen or water. He eased his fingers around the edges of the plate and gripped it with both hands, then shook firmly, looking for any signs of life.

"I'm going to keep communications open, in case you can hear me, and explain what I'm doing. I shall deactivate the drone to prevent further damage, and then attach it and the suit to the buggy."

The screen in Traffic went black, and Retallick's breathing suddenly became louder, his suit radio still transmitting. It rose and fell, scratchy and laboured.

"This is an old suit," said Retallick, wheezing against the inside of his helmet. "Old military surplus. A Z-series. M-model. The fan assembly and oxygen inlet valves seem older, too. The shape of the backpack isn't one I recognise. I don't see any sign of a radio, but it'd need opening up to know with any certainty. I think this suit is one of ours. Patched together with different components. The shell is military shell, but this gauntlet's from a mining suit. Impossible to tell everything without getting it in."

"Is there anyone inside?" said Sile.

"I shall return in an hour." Retallick grunted. "The implant in my shoulder is frozen. The Angutian night-time is fast approaching. It'll drop to -390°. The suit will only take that for fifteen minutes, and I can see the line of the dark coming fast." Retallick swallowed. His voice shook. He said, "Tell Bethe to be ready."

"Can he see if there's someone inside?" said Sile.

Retallick said, "There's someone inside. She's dead."

Sile said, "She's dead. Negotiations begin now."

CHAPTER 5: NEGOTIATIONS

The Viewing Gallery was an anomaly.

This was an empty space dedicated to peace, calm. Like all of the smaller spaces in Gunport, it was four concrete walls with one wall carrying a long screen.

This room, however, displayed something different.

This screen oozed light. Domiyat Outer displayed in one corner as an enormous white ball. Flames and solar flares burst and swelled around it, firing brilliant white debris away, flicking blobs of molten gas across the blank blackness at the centre. Swirling colour blended and blurred, shades of heat swaying into and out of each other, like a living oil painting of a firescape. It reminded Haig of desert sands when a strong breeze collects the top layer of dust and moves it in odd, curving patterns. At the centre was a hole. A perfect black circle, the oily colour ebbing and flowing around it, like a belligerent stone cutting into the flow of a rushing stream. Haig imagined that if he could hear it, billions and billions of miles away, it would roar.

He sagged on a bench in the dark, light washing over him in waves. His prosthetic had grated his leg raw so he had removed it. When the cool air had reached it, he felt instant relief, felt like he could sit here and simply bask.

He'd set tables and chairs in a small square. Sile and Acaba would sit facing each other, and Haig would position himself between them. IPRA wanted everything recorded, so Haig had placed a device on the table to make it clearly visible.

Acaba entered first, and she said, "Is that recording?"

"Not yet."

"Did you ask about Jan de Wiart?"

"No."

"Why not?"

"A spacesuit was found outside."

"I heard."

"I was in the military."

"I know."

"I have experience."

"So?"

"I helped to bring it in."

"Who cares about a suit?"

"There was someone inside."

"Who?"

"I don't know."

"Who?"

"A woman."

Acaba reeled. Went pale. Wobbled on her feet. She said, "How old? How long?"

"I don't know."

"Why don't you fucking know? Tell me," she snapped.

Haig shifted on his bench. "Retallick's bringing her in."

"Now? Why are we doing this now?"

"Doing what?"

"This fucking nonsense."

"The negotiations?"

"Yes, the fucking negotiations."

"I thought this was what you wanted?"

"Of course it is, but – "

Sile and Dekker entered. Sile tutted and said, "Lights on, screen off."

One of the UV striplights above clattered and came on. Haig looked down and blinked through the sudden proliferation of bright spots. Acaba shielded her eyes with her hand.

"You're bringing a body in," Acaba said to Sile.

Dekker glanced at Sile who shrugged and nodded. Dekker cleared his throat, said, "A spacesuit was located on the surface by a member of the Traffic Control team. That suit is being recovered by our Engineering team after which it will be examined, and its appearance will be investigated by the Security team. Our current working theory is that the suit was released accidently during one of the last Airlock testing phases. Perhaps it was not secured properly."

Acaba said, "Why are you here, then? Not looking into this suit?"

Sile sat down and said, "For negotiations, Sunita. I thought that was obvious."

Dekker said, "Deployment of Security personnel is my domain."

"A security situation simply doesn't concern the Reactor," said Sile.

"The Reactor and the Reactor alone is your domain," said Dekker. "Where you should be."

"That's what we're hoping to achieve now," said Sile. "Anson has come such a long way. Let's not waste any more of his time."

Dekker glared at Acaba and rotated his hand, said, "Unless you know something that will help us."

"Perhaps you know something about the circumstances in which the suit came to be outside?" said Sile.

Acaba shrank. Haig watched her become smaller, somehow. She took her seat at the table. "No," she said quietly. "No, I don't know anything."

Haig thought, she knows who it is.

Sile nodded at Dekker, who promptly marched out.

"Now," said Sile. "Let's see if we can't get our Reactor team happy and working again."

***

Haig took them through his role and how he saw these negotiations. They were to be polite, cordial. They could express disappointment and criticism in calm and productive ways. He would record everything and mediate, referee, interject. They needed to remember the weight of this situation. Whatever was going on outside, however distracting – and Haig was struggling to do this himself – it needed compartmentalising. He reminded them that he had been sent from Earth at a massive cost to both Aphelion and the Reactor unions to find a solution that both of them could make work.

And he reminded them that if they made offers, or signed agreements, or reached accords, that IPRA and the WSA would hold them to it. That they should not make false promises or renege on agreements, or there would be consequences. Sile scoffed at this. Haig had said it for his benefit. He saw uneasiness in Acaba and wondered if it was this negotiation or that suit.

They'd been speaking for forty five minutes. Haig hadn't expected much progress to be made, and it hadn't.

"I believe less and less that you speak for your team," said Sile. "I wonder if I should speak to them instead."

"Choose one and send them up," said Acaba. "They'll say the same."

"Solidarity. Wonderful. Or instead, perhaps Aphelion should release all of you from your contracts. Treat you all as one. Let you stay until you can organise your own ride home. We'd be within our rights to withhold landing permissions until any levies are paid. Have you pay us for providing accommodation. Begin charging for water, air, food."

"And power, too? The power we provide? Heat, light, electricity for all of your filtration and pumping systems? Pressure? Galatea? Galatea dies without us."

Sile seethed. Acaba bristled. Haig watched and waited. They needed to blow through all of this residual hostility and pent-up resentment before solutions began to present themselves.

"Withhold gunshine, then. Withhold perks and privileges."

"You already have. These are empty threats. Gunshine's not a real perk. It's not in anyone's contract so you can't grant it or take it away. We'll get it from the Recycling guys or the Engineering guys or anywhere. Even if we wanted it, which we don't. We just want basic things fixing and protection for our guys. Medicine and water. That's it. I don't understand why you won't do it."

"We don't have the resources. We can't integrate the things you want."

"The things we want are the things we used to have. We used to have longer showers. Cleaner water. We used to have more medicine. Bethe could hand it out. More comfortable furniture. What's changed? Why can't we have what we had before?"

"If you want those things, you'll force me to send half of your technicians home."

"'Force' you?"

"Yes. You'd force me to make a choice. Gunport continues to exist because it continues to be profitable."

"It could still be profitable while looking after its people. Profit is still money Aphelion makes after costs. So you choose between more money and people."

"Profit is money *I* make for Aphelion. People here are very well compensated. We recognise the risks they take and expect them to accommodate for them."

"You can't send half of them away at a whim."

"Yes, I can. You rely on me not to do it but that doesn't mean it can't be done, if you force my hand."

"If you send half of my guys home, the Reactor would become unsafe."

"It can be automated."

Acaba scoffed. "With specialised equipment and staff from Earth, with a shutdown for a year, yes it can."

"There would be no shutdown. We'd make do."

"There'd be no power."

"Galatea has run the numbers. Janulis assures me that we could make do until a relief crew arrives."

Acaba hissed. "You're playing with people's lives."

"So are you," said Sile, jabbing a finger accusingly. "But you're not just playing with the people here. You're playing with the future of humanity. All of us. Forever."

"So that we can all live in fucked up versions of Gunport?"

"All of the early pioneers suffered, Sunita. Casualties on the first permanent moonbase are still being tolled. Tantalus Gate was our predecessor. And worse. We are lucky to have lessons to learn from them. Poor access to water, food, heat, light. Not just physical injuries and sickness, but mental. Depression, anxiety. Paranoia. All of it. Wecht is here because of it. Aphelion insists on a Wecht in every space facility we operate. And we still don't know the extent of it, even now. Families still on the Moon. The first batch of children in space. It is up to us to endure. To make it safe."

"Then why is it getting more dangerous here? *More* accidents. *More* gravity failures. I have the statistics here – "

"They do not account for – "

"How can you know, you haven't even – "

"They're wrong, their source is tainted, you have alternative evidence – "

Acaba hit the table. "These are good numbers, pulled from your – "

"Easy to misinterpret evidence when all you see is danger – "

"Tell that to Jan de Wiart."

Sile went pale. "Unfortunate. And ancient history. It doesn't help us now."

Kaneda's voice punched through. "Haig, I need your help. Retallick's due, but there's a problem."

Sile said, "Kaneda, this is John. Haig is committed to negotiations with me."

"Retallick hasn't responded on comms for ten minutes, but he's still heading towards us," said Kaneda.

Sile said, "We're not finished here."

"I'm on my way," said Haig.

***

Kaneda brought him into the Ramp, said, "Retallick is minutes away." He nodded over to the corner, where Wecht was pacing. She was next to a pair of automated stretchers on gurneys and a trolley full of medical supplies.

"Wecht is here for immediate first aid. Bethe is standing by in the Main Operating Theatre for the implants that Sile has agreed to."

Haig nodded. "What can I do?"

"I've never brought a buggy in under these circumstances."

"You want me to take over?"

"Yes," said Kaneda. "Please."

"Update me then."

"Retallick doesn't respond and his course has been erratic. I've tried sending a drone out but he doesn't signal it or respond to it."

"Your suits aren't built for any period of time outside," said Haig.

"The Angutian night has been following him too."

Haig scratched his beard. "Have you anything for hypothermia? Frostbite?" said Haig.

"Yes," said Wecht.

"Get it ready," said Haig. "And he took a blow to the head. Concussion may make him woozy, unfocused."

"Right," said Wecht.

"We'll open the outer Airlock door. The buggy may crash into the Airlock doors or into the side of the Airlock," said Haig. "We'll need to close the doors as soon as he's in. We have to assume he won't be able to help us. Have we got masks?"

Kaneda swallowed, nodded.

"Get them," he said, and Kaneda scurried out.

"How long, Barnes?" said Haig into his e-sleeve.

"Haig?" said Barnes. "Five minutes. What are you doing?"

"Lending some expertise," said Haig. "I want you to tell me when we have two minutes."

"Understood," said Barnes.

Haig turned to Wecht. "What will happen if there's a body in the suit?"

"I conducted the last autopsy because Prendrick was, er, indisposed," said Wecht. "Assuming she's there and she's dead, Sile wants Prendrick to conduct an autopsy. He is our Chief Medical Officer. I know you would want to see company regulations followed."

"I'm here to help with negotiations," said Haig. "Once this suit is in, it's up to you to deal with it."

Kaneda re-entered, giving a mask to Haig, who strapped it on. Wecht and Kaneda both looked at Haig, wide-eyed, nervous.

Haig stood in front of the Airlock glass, peering through, seeing only the black of space. He could hear Wecht shuffling behind him. He turned and looked, then offered what he hoped was a reassuring smile. Kaneda was staring at him.

"Two minutes," echoed Barnes' voice, startling Kaneda.

Haig nodded to him, and Kaneda opened the panel that operated the Airlock. Haig moved to the opposite side so that they flanked the entrance, and then he opened his panel. Kaneda's breathing was exaggerated, too long, too slow.

"Ready?" said Haig. "Relax. I've done this a thousand times."

"Yes," said Kaneda, wiping sweat out of his eyebrows.

"Yes," said Wecht, tapping her foot.

Haig felt the buggy before he saw it. A low rumble in the concrete announced it, then a gentle easing of concrete dust from the ceiling. He leaned and peered through the glass of the Airlock door. After the first few metres of guide lights, the darkness of the surface was thick and total.

Then the buggy eased into the light, rolling towards the outer door, bouncing and juddering.

"He's here," said Haig. "In three – two – one – now," and they pressed the buttons for the Outer Door at the same time.

The Outer Door opened silently. Kaneda's face shone with sweat. Haig prepared to close the door. Wecht had stopped shuffling.

The buggy rolled into the Airlock between the Outer and Inner Doors. As it crossed the threshold, amber warning lights flashed, round and round. The lines around Kaneda's eyes disappeared but the shadows underneath grew, drowning out his eyes. A klaxon blared, over and over, 'Warning. Breach. Warning.'

Haig could see Retallick now. He was sagged in his chair, his head lolling as the buggy bumped into the Airlock Bay. There was a red-brown stain spattered on the inside of the visor.

"He's in," said Haig.

"He's not stopping," said Kaneda.

"Close the Outer Door," said Haig. "Three – two – one – now," and they pressed together, the Outer Door starting a torturous slide down.

The buggy banged into the Inner Door.

The door groaned as the buggy pushed against it, then started a metallic roar. The chainmail tyres began to eat into the concrete floor, a plume of concrete dust spewing into the Airlock.

Retallick jerked forward, sliding across the buggy's control panel.

"Sarah, stretcher," said Haig.

The Outer Door finally closed, and air was injected into the Airlock.

Air hit the tyres and sparks fired into the concrete-cloud. They began to glow in ragged and uneven shapes. The buggy's engine finally burned out and smoke poured up until the engine ceased grinding. After a moment it settled heavily into the scored concrete.

Haig heard it crackle, then fade.

"This is much too quickly," said Wecht, staring at Haig. "If you take the helmet off now, the pressure change will make him sick."

"One thing at a time," said Haig.

"The buggy will be unusable," said Kaneda.

"I don't care about the fucking buggy," said Haig. "Concentrate on your button. Is your pressure light up?"

"No."

They stared at the lights on their consoles. They willed them to light up. Haig's finger hovered over his. Kaneda the same.

"Now?"

"No."

They looked at each other. They looked at their buttons. Has the other one lit up and mine hasn't? Then –

"Mine's up."

"Mine too."

They pressed at their consoles and the Inner Door began to clank upwards, wrenching it free of the buggy. The lip of the door slid up and the buggy slid down it, then crashed into the floor.

Haig moved away from his console and pulled his mask up, took a long gulp of air, waited for a gap, listening to the gears of the door grinding. When it was waist high, he rolled under and leapt up alongside the buggy.

The motors were making erratic grinding noises. Haig clambered into the buggy and switched everything off. The mask did nothing against a mouthful of burned metal stench. Retallick was lying prone amongst the recovered suit and the drones. Haig heaved him up and used his weight to slide him off the buggy and onto the floor. He clattered down and his suit scraped in the newly roughened concrete until he sagged, uneven.

Haig jumped down. He crouched and grabbed Retallick's backpack with both hands and dragged him out of the Airlock, limp arms sliding behind a lolling head. The door was fully open now. Haig sucked in a breath and yanked the backpack up and over the lip of the Airlock. His arms were shaking.

Wecht steered one of the stretchers alongside Retallick. She lowered it down and Haig lined Retallick up, wrestled him on, strapped him down. Wecht pressed a button. The stretcher motors raised Retallick up.

He's on, I'm done –

Haig staggered backwards, wheezing, his face dripping. He threw the mask on the floor. The room was spinning. He leaned on his knees, drew great breaths of disgusting recycled glorious concrete-clean air.

Wecht looked at him, concern in her eyes.

"I'm fine," he said, raising a trembling hand. "Look to him."

Wecht snapped her focus to Retallick instead.

"Kaneda, get the helmet," she said, taking a breathing mask and small tank from the trolley.

Kaneda blinked at her, uncomprehending, hanging there like the chains above him.

She glared at him, snapped, "Kaneda."

Kaneda jolted, rushed over to her.

Retallick was flopped across the stretcher. Kaneda grabbed a shoulder and twisted it up, then reached behind and pulled out the clamps from the neck of Retallick's suit. When he heard the thick snap, he twisted the helmet away, letting it drop with a heavy, hollow thud, and let Retallick back down. Next were the air and water tubes that went into the backpack. Kaneda's hands were shaking, slippery. He'd taken off a suit a thousand times but was now reduced to looking like an amateur.

Haig moved up next to him and eased him away, offered a nod, breathing heavily. Kaneda backed away, letting Haig take the tubes from him. Haig detached each of them with calm, firm hands. The last one popped, dribbling water, and then Haig pulled the helmet off.

Retallick's eyelids were flickering, his eyes rolling around their sockets. His head was spattered with blood, thick and crusted. The skull cap he wore had slipped, also bloody. Haig took hold of it and peeled it away, feeling it stick, revealing matted and bloody hair.

Wecht shoved Haig aside and got the mask strapped to Retallick. His breathing became regular. The eyelids stopped flickering.

"Get his gloves off," she said.

Haig took one side, and Kaneda took the other. Kaneda's hands were steady now. He was smooth, calm, did it perfectly, a moment before Haig.

"Is he alright?" said Kaneda.

"Let's have a look at his fingers," said Wecht.

She clicked off the outer glove carefully, then let it fall to the floor. Underneath was an insulating glove, encased in ice crystals. She gripped it, winced at the cold, but held on, rolled it off. There was a crackle as Retallick's skin stuck to the glove. She pulled until it was off, and Haig winced at swollen, blue-tinged fingertips.

Retallick started mumbling and slurring under the mask. Haig offered a hand, trying to offer comfort. It was sharply cold, leathery hard. Retallick gripped it and squeezed it, pressing his rough hands into Haig's, before he moaned, released it.

"He's got hypothermia and frostbite," said Wecht. "Pressure in his suit must have been low. We'll watch out for pressure sickness too."

"Will he be well?" said Kaneda again.

"Too early to tell," said Wecht. "Wecht for Bethe."

"Yes," said Bethe.

She lifted and prodded, gentle touches, examining Retallick. "We'll need fingers. Wrists. Forearms. Elbows okay. Eyes borderline. We'll need a lung. Maybe lungs."

"Understood. I'll be waiting," said Bethe, clicking off.

Kaneda looked at her with growing horror.

"Take him," said Haig. "We've work to do here."

Wecht nodded and spun the stretcher around with the panel, then guided Retallick into the elevator. She offered a pained, sympathetic grimace, and they were gone.

Haig took a sharp, pained breath as he climbed into the back of the buggy. The excitement of Retallick's return had spiked his adrenaline and pushed him through, but it was fading, and he could feel a sharp ache in his leg, his hip.

"Kaneda," he said. "We need to get the buggy out of the Airlock. Now, before it causes a problem."

Haig went back into the Airlock.

The mystery suit was on its back in the centre of the buggy. The backpack pushed it up, the arms and legs hanging limply, giving the illusion that it floated. Looking at it now, Haig saw that it was old. The material across it was furred. There were gentle scuffs and plucked fibres, and the chest plate was all scratched metal and dull lights.

He looked into the helmet.

The head was wearing a paper-thin layer of skin, wrapped tightly around a skull. The lips had receded, leaving prominent rows of white teeth, defiantly healthy. The eyes were still there, opaque and dulled and thickened. The head was topped with a thin frizz of hair, and underneath the faded holes of her ears were tattoos, like the scratched ink of ancient parchment. Haig wasn't sure how Retallick had been able to tell that this was a woman.

He looked up and swallowed and slid the glare screen over the visor to cover her face, a parody of dignity.

***

The Elevator opened at the Medical Bay and Kaneda pushed the stretcher with the mystery suit out. Dekker and Holden lay in wait.

"We've come to assist," said Dekker, smiling.

"I'll take her in," said Holden, easing Kaneda to one side.

Dekker's smile was unwavering. His hand started to spin. "This is a Security matter now. John has asked us to look after this. To make sure that all of the rules are followed."

"Lead the way, then," said Haig.

"You'll be comfortable right here," said Dekker, closing the distance.

Dekker was especially sour and acrid. His sweat mingled with the grease in his hair and another tinge – electrical burning. Holden's eyes flicked from Haig to Dekker and back. Haig kept his back straight while his stomach rotated and broiled.

He nodded at Haig's prosthetic. "You've had a busy day. You must be very tired."

Dekker stepped away, finally. Haig was grateful for a lungful of reconditioned metallic air.

Prendrick emerged from a side-room and said, "Put it there."

Haig said, "There's a person in there. Not an *it*."

Robert Prendrick was tall, thin, and had a glazed look about him. He was looking through Haig when he entered, like the more interesting thing was behind him, like the spacesuit on the stretcher was unimportant, like this was his hundredth mystery body-in-a-suit and he was bored. He had wispy blonde hair that spilled out from his scalp, covering a bald spot towards the front of his head. The cheeks were ruddy, the nose pocked and red.

Prendrick looked at him with wet and glazed eyes, then shrugged.

"I need the suit intact," said Kaneda. "It's evidence."

"Evidence of what?" said Dekker.

Prendrick slow-blinked and ran a fat dry tongue over cracked lips.

"Did you hear him?" said Haig, gripping Prendrick's shoulder and shaking him. "Prendrick?"

Prendrick came to life and muttered, "Intact, yes."

Haig shook his head, turned to Dekker, said, "Where's Wecht?"

"Operating on Retallick," said Dekker. "Your job's done, Haig. Sile wants you back in the negotiations."

Dekker nodded at Holden, who nodded back, then wheeled the stretcher into Prendrick's side-room. Haig stood limply for a moment, staring at Prendrick. This half-aware doctor was was about to chop and slice and snap his way through the suit.

Haig said, "If he's not careful with that suit, he'll damage the body, and you'll never know where they've come from."

Dekker said, "The Doctor knows what he's doing."

"Negotiations are your priority," said Holden. "We all want things to return to normal. You need to get us back on track."

"I'm on my way back. I just want to check in on Retallick first."

Dekker shrugged. Holden nodded.

Haig went next door. Retallick was lying unconscious on the

Operating Table.

A sheet covered his lower half, and an assortment of wires were clipped to different parts of his arms and shoulders. Even in the half-light, Haig could see that there were fewer implants lined up than before. He winced, knowing how they would be used. Retallick's hands were inside two white plastic gauntlets that also covered them entirely, thickly wrapped, resting on his legs. An untidy square of hair had been shaved back above the crack on his skull, and the rest of his hair combed away. A small bandage, prickled with red, covered the wound.

"My ministrations have been successful thus far," said Bethe, standing with his back to Haig, tapping at a tablet. "The gauntlets will prepare his hands for new fingers, and I have a polymer crown to slide into his skull."

"How is he?"

"Ah, but he shall live. He will receive new fingers, and his x-rays will be forever different, but he shall make a full recovery."

"He'll have no fingers and a new skull," said Haig. "That's not a full recovery."

"Only the fingers have succumbed to frostbite, and I have saved his hands and arms. The skull was cracked, and only his absurd refusal to die has kept him alive long enough for me to operate."

"You'd do the same to me, then. In those circumstances. To keep me alive."

"We're talking about different things, here. The ones he'll get are to help him live."

"Not live a better life?"

"A better life?"

"He should be getting new implants."

"New?"

"Sile him to have full repairs, at cost to Aphelion."

"I've had no such instructions. In fact, I was very clearly told to make sure he has exactly what he had before."

Haig's eyes flashed. Sile, you prick –

He said, "Even the ones that don't work?"

"I'm only replacing the organic components that don't work," said Bethe.

"You're not swapping the defective implants for new ones? Or at least repairing the old ones?"

Bethe took a step backwards. "Relax, Haig. I'm following instructions. I've been told not to."

"This is why I don't have fucking implants," said Haig, marching out. He stopped in the corridor, breathing deeply, balling and unballing his fists.

Sile had been caught by surprise when the suit first appeared, thought Haig. This was a man who wanted full and absolute control at all times, and always on his terms. He'd let it slip for just a moment, but was now over-correcting. Make sure he controlled the narrative around the suit. Force Wecht and Bethe out. Make sure Retallick was in thrall to him for implants. He couldn't help but feel that the suit's origin had already been decided. That whatever this Doctor Prendrick found, it was irrelevant. If he even found anything, thought Haig. He had been taking his own medicines, thought Haig. Glazed over, permanently detached, forever somewhere else. Sile wanted this to go away. And he had chosen Prendrick as the man to make it disappear.

He reminded himself why he was here, what his job was. Get the Reactor techs back to work. Get back to Earth. Save Tom.

Save Tom –

He started moving. Dekker was stood in front of the side-room, flanked by Holden, his arms crossed. He looked at Haig in the way that someone does when they cannot quite tell if something is a smear of dirt, or a faint shadow. Haig met his look with one of his own until Dekker looked away, entirely disinterested, like he had never been looking at Haig to begin with.

Haig said, "Any news on our mystery body?"

Dekker said, "Body?"

Holden said, "What body?"

Haig blinked, swallowed, said, "The body inside the suit?"

Dekker said, "Inside the suit?"

Holden said, "The suit was empty."

"Prendrick didn't find anything."

"His report says there's nothing in it."

Dekker said, "There is no body."

CHAPTER 6: SPACEWALK (PART 1)

Haig sat alone at a table in the corner of the Spacewalk bar, nursing a cup of Tobin's simultaneously rancid and irresistible gunshine.

The Spacewalk was a rough box with a low concrete ceiling. The bar itself was made from repurposed spaceship metal that was saturated with stress fractures. No good for spaceflight, but perfect for a glorified table. Every second striplight had been taken out, creating pools of darkness. Everything had been painted black. There was a loose scattering of furniture scavenged from other places, the metal brackets that once bolted them somewhere else twisted and snapped. Benches and the Bar reflected some light, capturing oily glimmers, exaggerated shapes.

Haig had spent too long wrestling with the idea of the body existing and not existing and everything else, so he decided to think on it. That didn't work, so he'd decided to drink on it. Now he was letting these ideas lap at him like waves on a shore, gently insistent, but not the swirling and unmanageable typhoon of shite he'd been exposed to.

His job was very simple, he thought. Or at least, the goal could be simply defined. But since he had been here, he had rescued a mummified corpse from the surface – not just a suit, but a body, he had seen it with his own eyes – and seen the man who had rescued it hospitalised. The promises made to him were broken, and the body denied. The suit itself would be ripped apart in the autopsy by the hapless Prendrick, any clues as to where they came from obliterated, and the body likely incinerated.

Whoever it was, they were about to be scrubbed from existence.

Sile had moved the next round of negotiations back to allow him time to deal with the arrival of the suit. Haig couldn't help but think about the people the mystery body would have left behind. Where had it come from? Did anyone know they had gone missing?

Haig scanned the room and saw pale grey hands and faces in the murk. Some rested on their tables, some sipped at gunshine. Dark sweat patches on light uniforms were magnified in the dim light, and the black paint made a hot room tropical. They were animated but wary, sneaking glances at Haig with glinting eyes. Haig raised his cup to them, nodded, then looked away. He sensed them resume their conversation out of the corner of his eye. Implants whirred and settled.

One table had a tank of something in the centre, unclear in the dark, some ethyl alcohol mixture in a worn-out oxygen tank. This table regarded him coldly. He recognised Janulis and Blatt, sat closely together, regarding him coldly, her hand in his lap, scanning the room together, eyes glinting, in search of something. Their table seemed frozen, like a flotilla of military bots assessing a threat. Unerringly still. No obvious social interaction. Dry, sweatless faces. They stared brazenly at Haig. When he stared back and raised his cup, they became bored and looked at other things.

He swallowed his drink and felt it burn all the way to his stomach. The fuel stink made his eyes water.

Janulis was still looking at him, her head cocked. He sat and swayed gently for a moment, then took a breath, hoped he was walking more coherently then he felt, and went to the bar.

Tobin saw him coming and prepared a cup. He tapped Haig's old cup against the vat, rescuing those precious last drops of gunshine, and placed it in a stack with a dozen others. The alcohol burned too quickly through the paper cups for a refill. Haig rested heavily on the bar.

"On the house," said Tobin. He leaned in. "I'm hearing its three miles thick."

"Prendrick's skull or the chip on Janulis' shoulder?" said Haig. His vision was furry at the edges.

"Well," said Tobin grinning, "Someone's acquainted themselves with the local liquor."

"It's disgusting."

"It is. Another?"

"Absolutely."

Tobin pushed the cup towards Haig. "You've had an exciting start to life here."

Haig felt the heat and the alcohol and reeled. He blinked, gripped the bar. Pushed the gunshine cup back. "I'd better not," he said.

Tobin smiled, then poured it back into his vat. "When I first brewed it, I had a night of colour and vomit. The headache made me want to die. And now look at me, eh?"

"What can you tell me about those two?" said Haig, cocking a head at Janulis and Blatt. "I can still feel her eyes boring into my skull."

"Don't worry. You're not her type. Neither's Blatt, though. Janulis has a thing for imps," he said. "She'll be taking some unlucky devil back to her quarters later, and it won't be someone sat at her table."

"She seemed very focused on Galatea."

"Yes. She won't be away from the Core for long. She doesn't

drink, either. Blatt does. They get two cups and he has both. Gunshine does nothing to him. Well, just makes him more him. Some of us like to drink. Some of us fight. Janulis is sex. Blatt is a nasty piece of work. Ask Wecht tomorrow if she's seen anyone with a broken dick. She's like a fucking sex vampire."

"She intimidates you?"

"She's fucking terrifying," said Tobin, laughing. Then he leaned in and said, "The ice, Haig. Choudhury's ice. Come on. What do you know?"

Haig smiled and turned the cup in his hands. "I'm a neutral observer."

"Okay, fine. If you had to play, then. Or for fun."

Then he whispered, drawing out each word, each syllable.

"There's a lot to be won. Six. Whole. Fucking. Minutes."

Haig wasn't sure if it was the drink or the idea of a six minute shower, but he felt light-headed and gripped the bar.

"Yes," said Tobin, watching Haig regain himself. "Imagine it. Instead of that juddering of pressure behind the wall being like a starter's gun, urging you to hurry up and fuck off, now you can rest. Lather and luxuriate. Knock one out. Have a dalliance with Chernyshov in Recycling or Evans in the Reactor and rub them up the right way. Then, in this fucking place, the wrong way. Add the time on to other showers. Pass it on for all kind of favours. Take it all at once. Who fucking cares. Do what you want."

Haig imagined himself drowning in thick, soapy bubbles.

Tobin ran his hand through his hair. The screen behind him began to play a shortened version of the Echion Prime video. Haig saw the woman boarding the space shuttle and the sun gleamed through her hair, blonde and brown and black and always shimmering, taking all of the life around it and throwing it at the screen.

"What do you say?" said Tobin.

"How is it," said Haig, "That you can be so filthy and so clean at the same time?"

"What do you mean?"

Haig ran his hand through his lightly greased hair, then wiped it on his sleeve.

"Look around this room. Dark armpits. Matted hair. Shadows under eyes and around necks. But you," he said, pointing a finger at him, "Your uniform. Your hair. You're pristine."

Tobin's smile hardened. "I keep myself tidy."

"Tell me again what you get for winning the pool. Minus your cut," said Haig.

Tobin leaned away from the bar. His mood had cooled. "You either need another drink, or you've had enough."

"Another, then."

Tobin placed it down warily. "I'm able to help people with things."

Haig looked into his drink. Swirled the gunshine around. Watched the alcohol burr the paper cup. Make sure the drink doesn't speak for him again. Of course this is why Tobin runs the fucking bar. Everyone tells him everything.

Haig said, "Soap?"

Tobin smiled. "A trade. If you play the pool, it's yours. The wager's the same for everyone. Twenty seconds."

Haig swallowed. He scratched the knot of dried soap in the back of his hair. That shower was only short by six seconds. Twenty seconds was enough time to get wet, and that was it.

"No," said Haig finally, painfully. "It's unprofessional."

Tobin shrugged. "Alright. Suit yourself. But if you had to?"

"Who knows? Six miles? Seven?"

"Only one person has gone higher. Mihalik. She went with ten. No way it's ten miles thick, says Choudhury. I think he's fucked if it's thicker than seven."

"Let's hope that he remains unfucked," said Haig, raising his cup to Tobin. "Seven."

Tobin raised a cup of his own and said, "Seven it would have been, then. I hope, for your sake, that your guess is entirely wrong."

Haig finished his drink in one gulp and immediately regretted it.

***

The concrete swirled and moved. Haig planted himself against the wall in the corridor and fought hard not to vomit. He'd underestimated the gunshine, and badly. His head throbbed and he wanted to itch the surface of his eyeballs. His mind felt sharpened, racing, but far too quickly, thoughts jumbling, colliding, coalescing, breaking, forming patterns and then new patterns, never settling long enough, shattering and kaleidoscoping and rotating and reversing and –

Haig doubled over and vomited in the corridor, a stream of liquid bile. He stood up and gasped and burped wetly.

She was watching him. The woman who had said that she knew who was in the suit.

"I wouldn't drink any more of that," she said. "It makes people forget themselves."

"Isn't that the point?" said Haig.

She was unkempt, her hair straggling and clumped. Across the bridge of her nose was a ragged cut, clotted blood black in the weak light. Her implanted eye was as before, but her other was swollen shut, purple and yellow and black and blue and colours that skin should not be.

"What happened?"

"I have a black eye," she said. "My wrist hurts."

"It looks painful."

"It is. This is because I spoke to you."

"What do you mean?"

"I was visited. While I was asleep. He had an override for my door."

Haig sobered. "Who did?"

"What would you do if I told you? Would you report them? Confront them?"

"What do you want me to do?"

"It was because I spoke to you. Are you neutral? Are you corp?"

"I don't even know who you are."

"I know who's in the suit."

"Who?"

"Are you corp?"

"No. I told you before. I'm neutral."

"You told me to report it before."

"You clearly want to tell me. So tell me."

She had wet eyes now. "I'm scared. While he was – in my room – he told me not to speak to anyone. That I didn't know what I thought I knew."

"Who told you? What do you know?"

Haig heard footsteps filtering along the corridor. She heard them too, wiped her eyes, sniffed. The Spacewalk door opened, and she spun around, suddenly walked away.

Two of Gunport's crew emerged from the bar and looked at Haig, looked at the wet slap of vomit. He groaned, watching this woman walk away behind them, affected his best embarrassed face. He pointed at the wet stain on the floor, drew their attention, covering for the woman without knowing why.

He said, "Strong stuff."

**

The Food Hall was nearly empty. Haig wondered if the crew had retreated to their rooms when they were off-duty. Tensions between the Reactor crew and Gunport's management were still high. News of the suit was filtering out. This mystery woman had been attacked. It wouldn't be a surprise if they felt more comfortable out of the way.

A group of three sat eating across from him in sullen silence. One said, "At least it was empty." Another said, "Waste of a good suit."

Haig said, across the Hall, "I heard it had a body in it."

They looked at each other. Then one said, "Nah." Another looked up. "You weren't there."

Haig frowned. "Anyone put out an official story?"

"You don't get messages? Sile sends out them out all the time."

I'm being kept out of the loop, thought Haig. "I'm external," he said. "Not on your networks."

"Here, have a look," said another, drawing a small tablet out of a uniform pocket.

Haig walked over and took the tablet. He read the Gunport-wide message from Sile, summarised it. A spacesuit was found outside, it said. What a terrible fright for those working hard in the Tower! Fortunately, it was empty. Security are investigating, but early indications are that it was stored improperly during an Airlock test. It named Retallick as the guilty party. An egregious error. Consequences inbound. Nothing to worry about for everyone else.

An excuse not to give him what he was promised.

"Do either of you know a woman with a head implant?" he said, "Maybe around her eye? She's got some scars around her mouth."

"That's Mihalik," said one. "Reactor tech. One of Acaba's," said another, disregard for Acaba obvious. "What do you want to know about her for?"

Haig deflected. "You don't like them?"

Conversation turned sour.

"She's caused a lot of trouble," said one. "Trouble you're supposed to be fixing," said another, pointing a finger.

"We're all working on it," said Haig, scratching his beard. "You don't like the strikes?"

"We're in outer fucking space," said one. "You can dress a pig in golden robes but it's still a fucking pig." The others looked at him. He sighed and said, "Some jobs are going to be awful, right? Regardless of the perks."

"It's Aphelion," said another. "We get paid a lot for this. And I mean, a lot. We knew it'd be shit before we came. But them being on strike means our bonuses don't get paid."

"You all work together?" said Haig.

Nods. "Chemical Line's not so bad," the other said, and the first nodded agreement. "Mostly automated. Nothing dangerous by itself. We monitor the scrubbers and make sure the oxygen recycling gear is doing its bit. Easy work."

"Straightforward, not easy," said another. "We get paid well because when things go wrong, they go really wrong. Especially when we have to change one thing to another on the fly."

"You guys make Reactor fuel?" said Haig.

They wore serious looks. More nods. Haig said, "I worked with guys who made Reactor fuel. One guy in particular, but I can't remember his name. He made tritium for the last base I worked on. Old-school alchemist, we always thought. Turned dust into power. He sent out a massive tractor to scrape the rego for lithium, all automated."

"Lithium farmers are an interesting breed," said one.

Haig nodded. "Heat pipes above him ruptured. Blew half his face off. Then the steam caught the lithium and blew the other half off."

"Dangerous business," said one.

"We don't use lithium," said another. "We take hydrogen from water. Safer."

"Not by much."

"Where does the water come from? It isn't in my shower," said Haig, making a show of sniffing an armpit.

"You won't notice that in a while." "You get used to it." "Water's in the tanks. We get hydrogen and oxygen. Shipments top us up with oxygen and the scrubbers pull a lot from the carbon dioxide. Hydrogen's in the clouds. There's a massive cloud of it somewhere between here and Earth. Fuck knows where. One of the supply ships runs a scoop into it and processes it before bringing it to us."

"Why are your showers so short then? If you can make as much water as you want?"

One sighed. "If only." Another said, "Hydrogen's fuel, too. For the guns."

"Guns aren't running, though. You all could have enough water to drown in."

They looked at each other. They shrugged.

"What happened to Jan de Wiart?" Haig said suddenly.

They looked at each other nervously. "Who?" "I don't know who that is." "I don't know him."

Except all of you do, thought Haig.

Throats were cleared. "Oxygen won't measure itself," said one, and cocked her head to the others. They got up and left, quickly and silently, and Haig found himself alone, staring at the false sky's blue hues.

The food paste stuck to the roof of his mouth and he picked at it with the blunt knife.

The suit occupied his thoughts. An un-named body. Retallick's resulting hospitalisation. The brazen pretence that the suit was empty. This Mihalik knowing who it was. Offering to tell. And then being silenced. Contempt for Acaba. The fear that Jan de Wiart's name struck.

His commstem pinged and he checked the message: *Negotiations now. Sile.*

***

Negotiations continued much as before. They stared at each other across the Viewing Gallery's tables and neither gave ground. Sile referenced profit margins and made empty threats. Acaba was more agitated than last time, more distracted. Still she kept up with the question: why are things worse now than before? What's changed? Haig watched this with a practised indifference. He wanted them both to recognise that solutions might need to come from an external place. Eventually they would turn to him. He had begun to form possible solutions even during the first few minutes of their first meeting, and nothing had changed.

Some measure of goodwill was needed from Sile. He would need to agree to the medicine, at least. Haig had read from incoming cargo manifests and Gunport's own manufacturing logs that it was perfectly possible to provide enough. Sile would need to cede control of the medicine to satisfy Acaba. To Bethe, most likely. Sile had his hooks in Prendrick and so Bethe would be an acceptable third party.

Water was a problem. Chemical Line were saying they could

make more, so it was likely a management choice. Perhaps keeping resources back, either punitively or in preparation for the strike to be over. Sile would need to surrender some. Efficiency was likely an answer. Tobin's pools wouldn't help either. It was no good Tobin skimming from his pools and leaving some of the crew unable to clean themselves properly. Tobin wouldn't like it, but rationing would have to be recalibrated.

Acaba might need to accept a reduction in crew numbers and some automation to provide better conditions for those left. Sile would need to agree to a transitional period of transporting some crew home, and Acaba would need to agree to train and certify any replacement techs.

Acaba clearly didn't feel safe here, that much was clear. Haig felt it for himself. There was dishonesty at the core of Gunport. He put it down to corp fear of embarrassment, or fear of shrinking profit margins, but neither explained it adequately. Why not tell the truth about the suit? They were billions of miles from Earth. Bad things happened in space. No-one expected anything less. These were hardened campaigners and they would accept it. Retallick had lost parts of his body in a straightforward task gone wrong. Why lie about it? And why not tell the truth about Jan de Wiart?

There was a lull.

Haig said lightly, "Both of you are unhappy with the current situation. Both of you have heard each other's grievances and concerns. You've both been repeating yourselves for hours. Now we need to move past that and offer solutions."

Sile said, "I've been offering solutions for nine months."

"They're not solutions," said Acaba. "They're demands and ultimatums and threats."

"Let me try to summarise," said Haig. "John, your primary concern is the lack of power needed for what you see as

Gunport's primary function. You want the Reactor techs to produce more power because you want to land and launch more ships. This upsets you and angers you because people on Earth are depending on you. One, for the money that Gunport makes for Aphelion. Two, you see Gunport as important to how human beings progress into space. You think that both of these things are being threatened by Sunita's actions. You want the Reactor techs to return to work so that Gunport can resume its mission. Is that fair?"

"They *are* being threatened by – "

"We're just talking about you," said Haig. "Is that fair?"

Sile said, "Yes. More or less."

"Sunita, your primary concern is the health and wellbeing of your techs. You have decided to withhold your labour because you feel that Gunport's leadership has not taken the necessary steps to keep you all safe and healthy. Conditions have deteriorated over time so that things that you used to rely on are no longer available. You want better conditions before you return you and your crew to full operation of the Reactor. You've said that you don't want increased pay but you do want better conditions. And you're confident that you speak for everyone in your team. Is that fair?"

"That's fair," said Acaba.

"This is a stalemate," said Haig. "You can't sack them, John, because replacing them isn't viable. You've got a real problem with a lack of expertise. And because you can't sack them, you've been threatening them instead. Legal, yes, but threats nonetheless. You can't strongarm them because you've not got the manpower."

"You've taken sides, then," said Sile, crossing his arms. "IPRA will need to be informed. What a waste of a trip."

"No," said Haig. "I'm simply laying it out. I'm trying to help you to recognise where we are. Sunita, you know that this can't last. My understanding of Gunport's finances is that Aphelion won't let these kind of losses go much longer. Another six months or so. Is that right, John?"

Sile said, "We have the capacity to last well beyond – "

"Fine," said Haig. "But they'll shut it all down. All of it. And bring everyone back to Earth. And almost certainly blacklist all of you. No jobs at Aphelion would make things difficult. Not many corps run your Reactor, so there's not many jobs out there. It's all in the packets I've had. Phobos have a station that uses this Reactor, but believe me, space station conditions will make Gunport seem like a tropical paradise. So if you persist, the whole place will be shut down. Now, the senior staff will be redeployed. The same jobs in different places. Your reputation will take a hit, John, and you'll never be allowed on Earth again. You might make it to a palladium mine somewhere, but no more prestige projects. That's how corps work, isn't it?"

Sile stared at him. Angry but quiet. More accommodating. Haig saw it. He'd hit some nerve somewhere. Something he had said resonated.

"You need each other," said Haig. "You both need to give something. Something realistic and something plausible. Something achievable. I've sent you some suggestions and some proposals. Things that I think you could both do. You can't think of this as backing down or losing. You have to be magnanimous and forward-thinking. You'll both surrender something to gain something. And then this will be over."

Sile said, "I won't surrender to this woman – "

"Just look at the proposals," said Haig. "Remember that your only goal is getting the Reactor back online."

Acaba was staring into the middle distance, offered a slight nod.

"That's it for now, then," said Haig. "We'll reconvene tomorrow." He turned his recording equipment off and stood up. Sile stood up too, but Acaba stayed in her seat. She was shaking her head, eyes wide, disbelieving.

"Just like that?" Acaba said. "And what about the people who have been churned out?"

Sile looked at her coldly. "They give their lives for the future."

"Spare me this future-of-the-human-race bullshit. It's all about you. You look like an asshole because you can't keep all the little worker bees under control. Body appears outside and the blame gets dumped on a guy in a hospital bed."

"He was so desperate to recover his mistake that he did not take prudent measures," said Sile. "Besides, there is no body."

"Are you joking? Are you fucking joking?"

"Sunita – " said Haig –

"You can fuck off," said Acaba. "I know she came to see you – "

"Who?"

"Mihalik," she said, then jabbed a finger at Sile, "And one of *your* lapdogs let himself into her room – "

Sile hissed, "Be careful what you insinuate now, Sunita. We've come so far today, we don't want to undo that good work with baseless accusations."

"We haven't come anywhere when you use words like 'surrender' – "

"I've agreed to consider the proposals."

"What are you doing about it?"

"If you believe something untoward has happened, you need to log a report with Dekker."

"I said, what are you doing about it?" She was pacing now.

"What's happened?" said Haig.

"That's not your concern," said Sile.

"He's fucking bragging," said Acaba, speaking to Haig now.

"Nothing's been done."

"Who's bragging?" said Haig.

"This doesn't involve you," said Sile.

"Maybe if you had implants, like us," spat Acaba. "Maybe if you got a proper leg instead of that lump."

Haig rubbed at the join between prosthetic and leg. His tone hardened. "Sunita, I don't know what you're talking about. Has something happened to Mihalik?"

"Why haven't you? Why haven't you got an implant?"

"I don't know what's happened, so I can't help you until you tell us."

Sile raised his voice. "That is not for you to deal with."

"That doesn't answer my question," she said. "Anyone else loses a leg like you, and they just get an implant."

"What has this got to do with my leg?"

Acaba flicked her hand dismissively at his arm and his ear. "Everyone has at least a commstem in their ears. You don't. Why not? What have you got against implants?"

Haig was silent. Whatever had happened to Mihalik was clearly serious, clearly important, but she was enraged. He needed calm and information, not anger and recriminations. His choice of implants – or not – was irrelevant.

Finally, Acaba said, "Maybe you should explain it to her yourself."

Haig leaned forward. "Where is she now?"

"She thought they were going to kill her, Haig."

Sile almost shouted, "Enough." Calmed. Brought the volume down. "I will review your suggestions. But you need to remember your place here, Anson. I need to make certain facts very clear. The suit outside was empty. Regardless of what Conrad believed he saw or what you might believe you saw, it was empty. I have witness reports. The Chief of Security, the Chief Medical Officer. The suit is ancient history now. It is in Gunport's past, and so can begin to be forgotten. The crew's excitement for novelty has waned. The suit is gone. Kaneda will repurpose it and it will be gone. You would do well to remember that. Mihalik's promiscuity has been reported. Dekker will deal with it as with any other frivolous claim."

Acaba seethed, pointed her finger in his face –

Kaneda on Haig's commstem, panicked –

"Mihalik's in the Airlock and she's locked herself in. She said your name."

***

Haig ran through Maintenance and into the Ramp, past the recovered buggy. Yellow lights flashed a warning: the Airlock's opening procedures have been triggered. The doors were battered and scraped, but firmly closed. A tablet was hanging from the door panel, swaying, the screen glitching. Its casing lay on the floor, insides cannibalised, wiring mutated to fit the control panel. Haig sprinted to the porthole and looked in.

Mihalik was sat on the floor inside, cross legged, looking out into space. Haig hammered on the glass, thudding and thudding.

No reaction. The glass was too thick. He spun to Kaneda was working on the door from the control panels on his side. He wiped the sweat from his top lip, looked at Haig, shook his head.

Haig hit the button for the tannoy inside the Airlock. It crackled and sputtered.

"It's Mihalik, right? We've met before, haven't we? You wanted to talk to me. Well, I'm here now. Come on, Mihalik. Come out of there and come and talk to me."

She seemed to sense them then, and turned, wide-eyed,

dreamy, like she wasn't fully there. She stood up and a cardboard tube fell to the floor, the last few of the tablets inside skittering across the airlock floor.

Haig stared. We need to get her in, get to Medical –

Mihalik wandered over to the tannoy panel and switched it off.

"Shit. Kaneda, come on."

"She's locked us out," said Kaneda, wide-eyed, showing him the broken tablet. "She's rewritten the locking program."

Then –

Yellow flashing became solid red. Haig hammered uselessly on the glass –

"Mihalik, no – "

The Outer Door opened –

Her tablets and concrete lumps lurched forward, yanked at by the escaping air, rattling along the floor, stopping suddenly –

Mihalik hung there and nothing happened.

And nothing happened.

And –

And after a moment, after a few wretched seconds that felt like years, years for Haig to hammer on the glass and know that she was going to die, she came to. Eased out of her fugue, like she had finally raised her head out of a warm bath into the cold air above.

She blinked, and blinked, and blinked. Something in her eye –

Then she started scraping at her tongue, panic-stricken, her saliva starting to bubble and froth. Angutian grit pricking her bare feet as she stumbled out of the Airlock and onto the surface, barbed between her splayed toes. She was unconscious before she could go beyond the lights outside the Airlock, sagging in the weak gravity. She began to fall. The momentum carried her forward and away from the Airlock and beyond the guide lights.

Then the darkness swallowed her.

CHAPTER 7: ONE MORE, ONE LESS

SARD was three concrete walls dominated by a screen on the fourth. Another Gunport room.

A white sphere dominated the screen, its watery light washing the room. This was Choudhury's moon, Sedna R-8. Light sheared across its surface and reflected cleanly. The surface like scar tissue pulled tightly over a large marble. Black slashes icy canyons. The moon's North Pole was a scattering of pock marks, small craters. Steam exploded sporadically and boomed from cones of heat under the ice, flash-freezing into ice towers and resealing this hostile surface. On the screen, they showed as puffs fading into the black surrounding.

Choudhury was hunched in front of the screen, the half-light reflecting in his glasses and exaggerating the thin lines around his mouth. A row of data at the bottom of the screen gave him a library of indecipherable readings that sometimes made him happy and sometimes made him frown.

Haig was squeezed into a gap between piles of computer carcasses and worn out tablets. Wire pressed into his hip. Choudhury had invited everyone in Gunport to watch DIVA's dive but had no space to seat them. They wouldn't come, didn't care, or Choudhury was making a point about how much space he had – or did not have – to work in. Haig didn't care which.

Choudhury didn't look up, said quietly, "I'm glad someone decided to watch. There is some time before I can crash her through the ice and into the Third Ocean."

"I like how peaceful it is," said Haig. "I never understood it in the Army, when you'd go out to somewhere like this, and get to see something like this, and all of the lads would go and sleep or read or whatever. I always wanted to see what we came for."

Choudhury turned around and smiled, said, "When it was launched, Tobin filled some glasses with that drone-fire he serves, and we watched it roll out of the Pit and into the gun. I didn't drink it and neither did Hiro, so Retallick and Tobin had two glasses each. Retallick became morose and Tobin became louder, but he launched it safely before he had another drink."

"Where did he find the glasses from?"

"Where does he ever find anything?"

They sat in silence for a long time, the silvery sphere turning on the screen. The pockmarks at its pole turned and became smooth. The slash marks disappeared.

Haig held his e-sleeve up and checked his messages.

Tom had sent him a collage of pictures of plastic animals – all faded, chipped, discoloured – in a row, while he pointed sternly at them. He was the Zoo Keeper? thought Haig. Some of the pictures had Olivia in them, looking tired or bored, while Tom's finger covered a lens. In more than one picture, Tom's breathing mask was being reset by Olivia. She was looking after him, thought Haig. As she always did.

Wecht's message was less friendly. *All new staff need a full mental health evaluation when they get here. I need to see you faster than ASAP.* I'm not staff, thought Haig, and I'm fairly certain I've done it already, but who am I to disobey a doctor?

The silence became comfortable. Choudhury checking readings. Haig watching the screens.

The faint canyons had been scored in the surface by the heat underneath splintering and cracking, then resealing, trapping the water down there forever. Forever until humanity forced itself through, a nuclear drill wrenching the surface apart.

Haig watched the gentle rotation and saw three canyons that fed into and through each other, like cables laid carelessly over each other.

"Alright," said Choudhury, bringing Haig out of his trance. "Do you see the group of craters at the north, there?"

Haig looked at the screens and shrugged. Choudhury stood up and started pointing at a group of dark circles that turned into view.

"Here, right here," said Choudhury, jabbing a finger at a circle, "Is where a cluster of something smashed into it, sometime in the last million years. The ice is weaker there, so I'm going to aim DIVA at it, let it batter through, and see what happens."

"Just like that?"

"Well, not just like that, there's some months-long trajectory calculations and equipment calibrations, but more or less. There's a fission reactor and some thermal drilling involved, but if it helps, yes. Just like that."

Haig watched the slow rotations and Choudhury's tapping in silence for an hour, and he started to feel the muscles in his neck and shoulders soften and become more obedient. The join between his leg and prosthetic was still raw but the throbbing was insistent rather than outright painful.

"We're ready," said Choudhury.

Haig blinked and sat upright. Choudhury's finger hovered over his tablet for a moment before he deliberately, firmly pressed it. A countdown timer emerged on one of Choudhury's screens.

The images on the screens began to move. Gently, at first, heading towards the dark circle Choudhury had pointed out. It began to accelerate, and then the screen was suddenly white, ice craters clarifying. Haig could see spray from exploding geysers hanging lazily in the air, miles above the surface. DIVA's camera became dotted with snowflakes. Their edges thawed as they touched the camera.

"Alien water," said Choudhury, grinning, then pressed a button and the screens changed to a different camera. This view showed DIVA's sides, lined with caterpillar tracks to push it through the ice. It was effectively a giant corkscrew wrapped around a metal barrel.

Choudhury pressed buttons and DIVA began to slow down, only a faint movement in the screens as it righted itself with thrusters, puffs of air ghosting into the corners of the image.

He said, "Look," leaning into his screens, the light flickering across his face.

Haig pushed himself upright.

A plume of steam was rising from the surface, easing outwards and slowing before it reached DIVA. The steam turned to droplets, then froze back into snow.

"She's lined up. Time to punch through," said Choudhury. He took a breath before entering another set of commands on the keyboard, then leaned back and breathed out.

It was slow at first, then quicker, accelerating, faster, the screen beginning to shudder. It dropped into the crater, the image dissolving in glitch-ridden blocks before it came back. Then, there was a moment when they could see the surface covered in slick, freshly thawing ice, water, and steam, bubbling and sloshing together, before DIVA crashed through and the screen went black.

Choudhury exhaled, and Haig realised that he had been leaning forward.

"What happened?" said Haig.

"Don't worry," said Choudhury. "It's the impact. It's landed and has begun drilling. We should see soon."

Tobin burst in, grinning, waving a small flask. "Has it landed?" he said. "How thick?"

"It has," said Choudhury, nodding, smiling. "I won't know until it clears the bottom."

"Well," said Tobin, "That calls for a drink."

"Come to check on your pool?" said Haig.

Tobin grinned, tutted.

"I must defend Chris here," said Choudhury. "He's supported DIVA since the beginning."

"I'm only late because of your shuttle. Landing gear is proving to be difficult. It's wedged its weight into the concrete below the magnets. When we've gotten it into the Pit, Kaneda can carry on with repairs. Anyway. You're still stuck with us. Drink?"

Choudhury swallowed and looked at Haig and said, "I might stick to water."

"What happened the last time you drank my concoction, Hasan?" said Tobin, winked at Haig.

Choudhury said, "Well, I refused the first drink at least. I remember you wanted to break a bottle over it before it launched."

"If it makes you feel any better," said Tobin, "Haig did a technicolour yawn in the corridor. Fucking vile."

"I wasn't proud of myself," said Haig.

"Well, I'll have a drink. Ancient ships called for broken bottles," said Tobin. "And I don't have any bottles."

"Hiro crafted a pair of hatchets," said Choudhury. "With the faintest silver edge. Even more impressive when you consider where we are."

"They're for the ghosts," said Tobin. "And they were axes. You brought a fucking coconut."

"It wasn't a coconut. It was a cannonball."

"Fuck off," said Tobin. "It was neither."

"It was neither *and* it was both," said Choudhury.

"Hiro made a plastic sphere, and we broke it with his axe in the Pit. We couldn't smash a bottle against your beloved DIVA, could we?"

Choudhury tutted. "You don't hit spacecraft with bottles. And certainly not an axe."

"Axes are for smashing against people's skulls, aren't they Haig, eh?"

"Did you say a coconut?" said Haig. "You're supposed to launch ships with bottles."

"Yes, for good luck. A coconut for a puja ceremony – sort of – and a cannonball for old artillery."

"It fucking made it, didn't it?" said Tobin, waving a hand at the screen.

"Hiro's axes are for good luck too," said Choudhury. "Ward off the spirits that bring bad luck."

"Perhaps all of our good luck went with DIVA," said Tobin.

They looked at each other, sudden and temporary silence stretching out, becoming a longer silence, until it had been an hour. Choudhury was becoming more and more agitated. Occasionally they leaned forward at a non-existent flicker, leaning back when there was nothing to be seen.

Choudhury muttered again and again. Variations on, "Why isn't it there?"

Haig sagged forward, rubbed his eyes, opened them wide, blinked, woke himself up with a start. Choudhury's face was full of exaggerated lines, the light from the screens creating dark parts, separating his face up.

Haig sat back and promised himself he'd pay attention. Tobin caught his eye and offered him the flash. Haig refused instantly, and Tobin laughed.

When the screens spluttered back to life, flooding the room with a different kind of blackness, a different kind of dark, he woke again out of a doze. Tobin was leaning forward, rubbing his hands together.

"That's it, finally," said Choudhury. "We're through." His face oozed relief.

Haig looked from Choudhury to the screen and back, and it took a moment for him to realise that the black was in fact an incredibly dark, rich navy, the blue tint bleeding through the black. DIVA had hit the water.

"How thick?" said Tobin.

Choudhury pressed a button and waited, then DIVA's lights came on. There was nothing to be seen, but it was clear that it was submerged and had cleared the ice.

"We need to see whether or not it's immediately viable for human consumption," said Choudhury, almost to himself. "And even if it isn't, if it's full of hydrogen and oxygen. Fuel, air and water. Just what we need."

"How thick?" said Haig. More interested than he thought he would be.

Choudhury was staring at his hands. "I only built it for four," he said quietly. "All the data said it would be less than four miles thick. Every risk assessment. Every probability. Between one and three. Seven? Seven is so much. I just needed a few hours of data. But – "

DIVA listed in the water and turned, its lights reflecting back from the bottom of the ice surface above, and it began to sink. A lump of metal, sheared off and twisted, sank through the screen and disappeared. The image glitched and the signal was lost, unrecoverable.

Choudhury slumped in his chair. DIVA was out of range, drowned and gone.

The cameras began to lose their connection and the pictures faded. After another moment, the screens were black.

Choudhury had aged years in moments. He wallowed in his disappointment. He said in a low voice, "Seven."

"Seven? Seven miles?" said Haig. "You're sure?"

Choudhury nodded. Haig's stomach tightened. Tobin looked at the floor.

Mihalik would have won the pool.

"Mihalik would have won the pool," said Tobin quietly.

***

Wecht brought Haig into her room and closed the door firmly behind him.

It was a smaller room than Bethe's treatment room. The polished metal walls had mostly been covered. A khaki rug had been fashioned out of exhausted overalls. She'd draped some cream sheets along two of the walls, and in the centre of both, she'd painted terracotta suns above navy skies. One was slightly bigger, the other not quite a circle, more a squashed oval.

The third wall carried a screen like the one in Haig's quarters, with a block of brilliant blue ocean above a beach so clean it was a bar of white sand. The fourth wall was mostly clear plastic, looking back out into the corridor, and Wecht had used a black sheet to cover the window, fluorescent shapes scattered about it, chopped into rough stars.

She pointed to the chair and he sat.

When she didn't say anything, he said, "I thought I'd been signed off."

"You have," she said. "This isn't that."

He scratched his beard and waited.

"Mihalik was my patient," she began. "She came to see me after she was attacked. Until this happened, I thought the work we had done together meant that she was on the right track."

"I spoke to her in the corridor," said Haig.

"What did she say?"

"She wasn't making a lot of sense."

Wecht nodded. "Will you watch something? A recording?"

"What is it?"

"Will you watch it?"

Haig shrugged, nodded.

Wecht tapped her screen on. The Aphelion logos faded and she loaded a video.

It was a blurry, blocky recording of a session between Wecht and Mihalik. Mihalik sat upright in her chair, ramrod, tense.

In the recording, Wecht said, "Can you tell me what happened?"

Mihalik looked at her hands. "I was having a drink. We're getting squeezed in the Reactor – always 'more power, more power' from higher up – so for the first time in weeks I thought, 'fuck it, I'll have a drink'."

She was more comfortable with Wecht, thought Haig. Spoke much more at length. Angry, at least in this recording, but more coherent.

"I'm at the bar when he comes close. Really close. He touches my shoulder, then touches my back. It happens all the time. Everyone knows everyone, sometimes they're too familiar, and sometimes they've had a drink. But you just sort of go with it. I wanted to rip my own shoulder off, but I can't do that, and I can't say anything. Do anything. You know what happens when they think you're trouble."

Mihalik looked away and scratched her arm, red streaks angry on her arm.

"Maybe I should have flirted a bit, let him down gently."

"This isn't your fault," said Wecht.

Mihalik looked at her, her eyes raw with challenge. "It was Blatt," she continued. "He's not said anything, just kind of sidled up to me. I shrugged him off and moved down the bar. He comes along too. No eye contact or anything. Just reappears next to me."

"What happened next, Alice?" said Wecht. She'd adopted a neutral tone.

"I mean, I'd had a rough day, right? Always more. Today there's some outages in the water purification systems, and that needs more power, they said. More fucking power. 'Where from?' we said. There's finite power here, right? No water, no hydrogen. Some lithium maybe, but not now, not right now."

She sighed.

"Normally I might have had a drink in the end. Even if he'd been like that. Just to keep things even. But I told him to 'fuck off', then he looked, well, sort of pleased, like there was a thrill in it for him."

"Do you think he was looking for a fight?" said Wecht.

"I don't know. I probably shouldn't have said it. I didn't want to get into it, so I finished my drink and left. I was walking away when he whistled behind me. He started saying something. I didn't hear every word properly, but it was stuff about my implants."

"What can you remember?"

"Something about having implants in 'intimate areas'," she said. "So I lost my temper and turned around. Which is when he hit me."

"Try to be exact," said Wecht. "Don't ignore it. Let's work through it. What did he say?"

She let the words tumble out of her mouth. "That I was a whore like a broken airlock. Wide-open. Sucked on everything. Easy to get to the other side. That I needed implants to tighten up. To stop being such a slut."

Haig winced. Wecht said to him, "He's a real charmer."

Haig said, "I know. We've met."

Mihalik continued, "Maybe not that exactly, but you get what I mean." She sat back in her chair and her head lolled around her shoulders. Talking to Wecht was taking its toll, thought Haig. She looked exhausted. He couldn't see clearly on this recording, but he knew that she would have been carrying fresh bruises.

"He hit me like he was slotting a hard-drive back into a server, you know? Like it was no effort at all. There was nothing on his face. I don't remember it even hurting. It was like he punched me and my body kind of switched off for a second. I don't remember anything after that. I woke up here, in the Med Bay, and you were pouring something onto my face a couple of rooms down, and I had a black eye and bruises all over."

Wecht paused the recording. Haig looked at her for a moment, rubbing at his beard. "Do you think he might have chosen her deliberately?"

"I don't know."

"If she'd had a drink with him, would he have left her alone?"

"You know he wouldn't."

"She had an eye implant."

"Yes. A reactor pipe burst, eight years ago. Not here. The Moon. It crushed part of her skull. A med-pod pulled all of the slivers of bone out while she was in a coma. It took three months. Her 'plastic head', she called it."

"Blatt know that?"

"Everyone knows everyone here," said Wecht. "Even if you're missing techtatts, just being friendly with someone who's printed makes you an imp."

"Who was she friendly with?"

"Her team. The Reactor crew."

"You think she was targeted for being friendly with Acaba?"

"There's always some tension between the Reactor and the Core. You must have seen it, right? You're always watching, always listening. You stop before you speak and you ask a lot of questions."

Haig said, "Why are you showing me this, Sarah?"

"Let's get to the end."

She pressed play. In the recording, Mihalik leaned forward and whispered urgently. "I can go back to work now, though? Right?"

"Are you sure you're ready? You could take some time. I can authorise it," said Wecht.

"No, no, I want to go back," she said. "I want to be busy."

"Okay," said Wecht.

Mihalik stood up and looked at the floor, bowing her head low, unable to make eye contact, so he looked at the top of her head, a 'goodbye' feeling uncomfortable.

Wecht turned it off.

"Sunita took her back to the Reactor," said Wecht. She fiddled with the bracelet around her wrist. "She was always someone Mihalik could go to."

"She'll be angry. Mihalik being attacked was almost enough to derail the negotiations. I don't know what this will do."

"Yes," said Wecht. "Blatt's got a lot to answer for."

"This is why you asked me to come?" said Haig.

She said, "I'm going to tell you some stuff about her. And I trust you not to say anything to anyone. Not to Sile, not to Bethe, not to anyone. Certainly not to Dekker and Holden."

Haig nodded.

"She was in therapy with me because she went to work one day, then woke up the next with implants in her face. She feels like part of her was taken, feels like part of her is missing every day. She wakes some days and tries to rip them out. You've seen her scars."

"Psychosis?"

Wecht blinked, surprised. "Yes."

"I've seen it before."

"The Army?"

"Yes. Most of the time, before I was a negotiator, we'd be sent to break something or threaten something. Comms, mining gear, whatever. Breaking resource chains, breaking up logistics. Fighting in space isn't about actually fighting, it's about air and water and food. Any kind of stand up fight and everybody dies. And even if you live though them, suddenly, you're full of implants. Implants post-trauma don't always take. And that's assuming there's no SIRS."

Wecht nodded. "She smells cooking meat. Smelled. She thinks it's her. Thought." Wecht rubbed her eyes. "She *thought* 'someone' was burning away her skin to replace everything inside her with plastic and wires. Sometimes it was her mother. Sometimes she couldn't tell. This 'someone' controlled her, drove her around. She felt like she was watching herself. Like a robot. Voices sometimes warned her about certain rooms and places. Told her that if she went into those rooms, she'd never come out whole."

Haig frowned, exhaled. "And she was still working in the Reactor?"

"She was on some very strong medication, Anson. And before the body arrived, and before she was attacked, she was doing brilliantly."

"Does Sile know?"

"I'm not sure. He makes little comments, speaks in a way that makes me think he does. He's not entitled to see her medical records. All her file shows is an accident and some recovery time. Perfect record afterwards."

Haig scratched his beard. "She was sent here so that she was out of the way."

Wecht nodded. "It took a long time for her to trust me. We had to do a lot on her terms first. Sometimes on paper, having her write letters. No tablets, no video. And it is hard to get paper here."

"Could you have reassigned her?"

"Where would she have gone? What could I have said that would have gotten her out of here without putting her in a company institution? And her contract would have run – while she had been institutionalised – until she was 'better', which she wouldn't ever have been, not by their definition. Doing her job well enough to pass Sile's performance management reviews, that's what they call better."

Haig opened his mouth –

Wecht continued –

"She was here because even though her face was shattered, and even though her mental health was blown, and even though gene-edit pricks like Blatt and that wanker Tobin see her as a piece of meat, those bloody arseholes at the company would never release her from her contract. They gave her that face. A face she never wanted."

Wecht jabbed her finger into Haig's face. Haig blinked. He hadn't been ready for her sudden anger.

"She had no choice. She's a lot braver than you or me or anyone else in this wankering place, and I'll step up for her if I need to, and if you're not going to go after Blatt, then I bloody well will."

"Alright. Alright, Sarah. Let me get this clear. She came to see me. In the corridor. After the suit arrived. She wanted to tell me who it was, but couldn't quite trust me. She gets seen speaking to me, so Blatt is sent to warn her off."

"Call it what is it. He raped her."

Haig nodded. "He raped her to what? Show her what happens when people speak out of line? So then she tries to speak to me again. I was vomiting in a corridor on gunshine."

"She told me that after she got out of Medical, she sat in her shower for nearly an hour," said Wecht, "Just sat on the floor and stared at the back of the door."

"She would have won the pool," said Haig.

"That's not the point. She shouldn't have to win the pool."

Haig scratched his beard furiously. "It's one thing to pretend a suit is empty. I understand that. Sile wants Gunport back to normal, and it's another distraction after this strike. But it's another to drive someone to suicide."

This is a bad idea, Haig. But –

"Alright. Alright, fine. I'll help. But we have no proof of anything, so don't speak to anyone else. It feels all wrong, but anything could have happened. It could have been an accident after all. We need to prove that there was a body in that suit, first of all. I think I can get Kaneda to help with the suit. And we need to find out who she was. If we find out her connection to Mihalik, we'll find out who she was. But carefully. That means you don't go near Blatt. You don't speak to him and you don't ask about him. He'll crush you."

"I'll check Mihalik's sessions. If she knew who was in the suit, perhaps they were important to her. What will you do?"

Haig said, "Where's her room?"

Wecht took his e-sleeve, recorded it for him.

"Is that really what you think?"

"What?"

"That it could have been an accident?"

"I don't know, Sarah. Guessing doesn't help."

"But you know it's not right."

"I'm amazed at how brazen they are."

"Welcome to Gunport."

***

Mihalik's room was as full as Haig's was empty. Rubber mats were laid across the floor, with some crude drawings of relaxation poses taped to the wall next to them. Stick figures contorted into impossible angles. The mats were pretending to be organised, running misaligned to the bed, so he eased them straight with his boot. Dirty clothes were tossed in the corner.

He sat at the desk. Half-finished bracelets and necklaces made from fragments of contraband copper wire were strewn across it. She had taken the plastic insulation from the wiring, used the colours to make vibrant bands, and in some cases used a soldering iron to create small icons, tags, charms to hang from them. Wecht must have got hers from Mihalik.

He brushed them neatly to one side and sat at her screen. Wecht knew her password. Most of her history was relaxation music, gentle exercise, jewellery tutorials. A range of messages from Wecht that prescribed behaviour therapy. There was no suicide note. Haig watched the first few minutes of the therapy video. A woman was talking about reframing sexual assault. 'It is only ever the attacker's fault, and never your own,' she said.

Something else on the desk caught his eye. A piece of an implant, held in a plastic vice. He unscrewed it, held it up.

The screen reacted, blinked back to life, said, 'Your mood seems low. Perhaps some exercise will help?' It showed an image of a bright sun over a gleaming ocean.

Haig put the implant piece down with exaggerated care and re-opened the screen, re-examined what she'd been working on. He read the most recent files and found one linked to her own projects. Haig read carefully, interpreted jargon, flicked between documents. She'd built a program that could detect changes in her hormones, blood pressure, heart rate, and it warned her when her mood was changing. She'd loaded her baseline in, and it thought Haig was her, detected how he was feeling.

Shelves above the desk carried pieces of wire, bolts, other assorted electrical bric-a-brac. He left the desk and went through her wardrobe, finding clean uniforms worn thin at the knees.

Under her bed was dust, concrete, and a hard plastic case. He slid it out and opened it. There were some trinkets. An old ticket for a flight to Mars. An empty pill bottle, prescription label worn thin. A lump of glass offering first prize in a biomechanical programming competition. A weighty instruction manual for her myriad implants, both consensual and not, personalised with her name. A small ceremonial knife, engraved with her initials. Another prize, a sheet-metal certificate showing an electronic brain, given by Black Sand Automation. And there was a picture of her with Acaba, somewhere on Earth, holding hands, smiling. He closed it and placed it on the bed.

Her covers had been discarded, sweat marks in the pillows and sheets. He took some time to make her bed, whipping the sheets up, rearranging them, tightening them into blemishless rectangles. When he'd finished, the corners were sharp.

He sat on the bed and leaned against the wall, looking around.

Her body had gone. Acaba had wanted it recovered, but Sile had said no. She would be a block of ice, thought Haig. She could be anywhere on Anguta R-611 now. One day she would crash into Traffic and shatter into a billion pieces. Or sink into the

Harwell Basins and shatter. Or the Vassal Canyons and shatter. Or the –

At least she would have been unconscious after fifteen, twenty seconds. If she'd stayed in the Airlock, they might have saved her. Kaneda had broken through her programs nearly five minutes later. The Airlock door creaked and groaned as it raised up, still bruised from Retallick's buggy. The slimmest of chances, but a chance all the same. There was nothing left of her in the Airlock. There was no suicide note.

Haig tilted his head back and looked at the ceiling. Patterns in the concrete, if he looked for them. Imperfections creating swirls. Small spikes hanging down, stalactites in these musty concrete caves. Implausible lines betraying the joins between one block of concrete having been bonded to another. The work of decades of robots and great thinkers. Scientists and engineers. Haig knew that Sile would argue he continued their work, however many people were churned up. What was the point in taking humanity to the stars if all they took the worst of themselves too? When all they wanted to do when they got there was escape from it?

He turned his head lazily to the furniture, the rest of the room. The door was grey, the walls bare. The mats covered part of the floor. The wardrobe a thin collection of plastic sheeting clumsily joined to make the shape of furniture. Holding lightweight uniforms and barely containing them. A gap between the back of the wardrobe and the wall. Too wide. The wardrobe almost being pushed away from the wall. Something there. The wardrobe –

When he stood in front of it and pulled it towards him, the plastic crackled and buckled, and then he heard something fall down behind it. He clambered over the freshly made bed, slid his hand down between the wall and wardrobe.

It was a sheet of plastic, run through a 3D printer, grooves and contours making it map-like. This was a photograph, once, thought Haig. She's had it turned into a keepsake. It was important to her. Enough to hide it away and keep it safe. If Dekker and Holden had anything about them, they should have found it. They clearly hadn't been here.

The image was the same grey colour as the rest of the plastic on Gunport. It showed Mihalik, Acaba, and another woman. They held raised glasses or cups. The 3D rendering and lack of colour made the background vague. A handful of dots and bumps, then a scored line, could have been a bar. Their smiles were easy to find. Haig ran his fingers over their faces and felt the bumps of their smiles and looked at the unknown woman. He stared at it for minutes and became certain. He knew.

This was the woman in the suit.

CHAPTER 8: RENEGOTIATIONS

The Farm was the largest single room in Gunport.

An enormous field in a concrete box. Grains and wheats grew to the height of people and were all too still. They should have been swaying in some breeze, but were silent, noiselessly siphoning dioxides and processing monoxides and absorbing nitrogen. Precious oxygen was returned and then pumped upwards. Vents opened for air and heat pumped up from the Reactor. Four thick concrete pillars punctuated the crops, one in each quarter, the elevator perfectly central. Each pillar in its own quarter. Each quarter sharing a wall with the edge of Gunport. And behind each wall, infinite amounts of rock. The Moon itself. Dangling above, glowing a dim orange, were hundreds of UV lamps. Shadows crept into untouched corners.

Haig walked out of the Elevator. Chiaki was waiting for him.

"The next harvest is due soon," said Chiaki, eyes glinting. "I do hope you're not here to negotiate me into an early grave."

Agnes Chiaki – Chief of Food Production – had long, crackling hair. There was no weight in her cheeks or chin, and the hair looked like it should be too heavy for her head, that it should be forever pulled backwards by the weight. She smiled and ran her hands through her hair. It was dry, far too dry, and it crackled static, a few strands sticking to her hands and floating outwards, charged.

"Is that what everyone's saying?" said Haig.

"They think you're bad luck," said Chiaki.

"Bad luck was already here."

"And if they don't think you're bad luck, they don't like you. Dekker's been more talkative than usual, and he really doesn't like you. Wecht does, though."

"He's not a difficult man to read. What did Wecht say?"

"Help you, if I can."

"And?"

"If I can, I will. Sarah's helped a lot of people here."

"I need to see Acaba. Wecht says she comes here sometimes."

She narrowed her eyes, the humour gone. "She doesn't want to see you."

"Look at these," he said, taking out the 3D image. "Do you recognise these people?"

"That's Acaba, obviously. This one's Mihalik." Her tone softened. "I heard about her, Haig. That you were there. When she pressed the button."

"It was exactly as bad as you think," he said. "What about this third person?"

"She worked upstairs. Programmer. Left on a shuttle a while ago. Why do you want to know?"

Haig thought, Because I want to put a name to a corpse.

Haig said, "Mihalik left some effects behind. I wanted the right people to have them."

"I think she knew the Recyclers. Maseko? Ask him."

"Anything else?"

"Well. Programmers and Reactor Techs have always had this sort of weirdness, right? It happens in Briefing. These looks that Attar gives Acaba. They hate her, Haig. She's clever, outspoken, and she's got implants. But these two look like they're getting along, right?"

"So you remember her arguing?"

"Yeah," said Chiaki. "But with her own team. Janulis and Blatt would have been her bosses. Especially when they'd had a few drinks. I do remember, actually, that these three would drink gunshine together. Janulis and Blatt *really* didn't like that. Neither did Attar."

"I'm hoping Acaba knows more."

"I'll take you to her, but I want to show you something first."

She pointed to the back of a small tractor and Haig climbed on to the back. It was electrical, quiet. She got into the driver's seat and turned the switch and it jerked forward at speed, slapping and rustling, beating its way through the crops. After a minute in the crops, Haig could barely tell where he was, only the concrete walls looming at each end to navigate by.

"The UV lamps, tractors, whatever, are doing their jobs," Chiaki shouted. "One of the lights is out. That's normal. That's fine." She shifted in her seat. "There's a bigger problem, though."

"What's that?"

"Sometimes idiots joyride the tractors," said Chiaki, laughing and slaloming.

They arrived abruptly into a clearing.

Dead crops crackled beneath his feet. They were sand-coloured and brittle, and the few that still stood fell away at Haig's touch, their roots too weak to grip anything. Haig turned slowly and realised that he was in a perfect square of golden tinder. He walked to the edge of the dead crops, felt the healthy ones gripping plasticated soil.

"It's not just the Reactor crew who have problems."

"Water?" he said.

"None. The field is in grids, and for whatever reason, this grid's not getting its water."

"Why?"

"It happens sometimes. A block in the pipes, most of the time. A day or two, then we're back up. All of this stuff will go into the food processors anyway."

"This isn't food. It's dust."

"Kindling, not crops. Won't take more than a spark. And we're fucked if there's a fire. It'd get suffocated quickly enough, but not before scorching this place. The Farm is food, it cycles air, people come down here for walks, to be closer to nature. It's important."

Haig felt that in the pit of his stomach. Fire in a tight space likes this was doom for all of them, despite suffocating it with carbon dioxide or drowning it with sand or whatever else. Fire guzzled precious oxygen and destroyed metal and melted plastic and that was if it was brought under control quickly. A fire that escaped them would kill everyone on Gunport, either immediately or in the aftermath.

"Is this enough? To feed everyone?"

"These are modified crops. Higher fibre and carbs than any synthetic stuff. With some of the synthetic stuff for proteins from the Chem guys, Galatea says its enough."

"What do you say?"

"It calculates it just right. Scraped down to the bones. There's no room for error."

"You don't sound convinced."

"Portions are smaller. People are thinner."

"Why is it giving people less food?"

"Ask the programmers in the Core. They set the parameters, tell Galatea's what's what."

"Are you producing less here?"

"Overall, no."

"Why, then?"

"Galatea's like any other AI. You have to tell it what a person is. You have to teach it that a human needs oxygen, needs food, needs exercise, what a human can and can't do. Then the AI computates, or whatever. The programmers mythologise it. They say, 'Mother knows what you need'. That's bullshit. They decide what you need with their programs and algorithms and the information they feed in or leave out. Galatea is a top-of-the-line scheduler, and that's it. Tells you how much food, air, water, exercise, everything you can have, tells you when to have it."

"How does Galatea know how many people are here?"

She took her glasses off and pinched the bridge of her nose. "It's the air mix. There's sensors all over the air recycling." She pointed to the line of giant fans flanking the Farm, high up in the concrete walls. "It extrapolates from there and calculates how many people we've got."

"It doesn't just use that, though? Everyone's logged in and out, right? When I arrived, I was entered into the system."

"Just because it *can* be done, doesn't mean it *is* being done," she said. "The company hates this place. It's a vanity project turned black hole. All the proprietary tech has been sent somewhere else. Galatea has been reproduced and sent to Echion Alpha. The railguns can be automated. But the company can't let this place die. It can't. It's a massive fuck-you to everyone else. Shaped like two massive dicks because it's all alpha-male posturing bullshit."

"So Galatea doesn't really know who's here and who's not?"

She pushed her glasses up and sniffed.

"It needs to be told. Say the average person gets through maybe 600 litres of oxygen in a day. You have to *tell* Galatea that. It doesn't know what a human is unless you specifically tell it. But if you tell Galatea that a human only uses 400 litres in a day

– "

"It thinks we have extra people. Or it thinks we need less oxygen. So it tells you to produce less."

"Right. It looks at the logs and the crops and everything else and makes a decision. Then it tells us what we should be producing, what we should be able to produce."

"Everyone breathes."

Chiaki said quietly, "Until the numbers don't add up."

"Does that happen often?"

"More than it should."

"What are you saying? Galatea's broken?"

"You felt faint? Drowsy? Dizzy?"

"Pretty much ever since I got out of the B-DC – "

"Should've worn off by now. But it wouldn't if the oxygen mix is wrong. Food mix is wrong."

Haig stared at the dead crops, row upon row of fallen grains, roots dried and dead, puncturing the brittle soil.

Haig rubbed his beard. "Do you really think Galatea's broken?"

"Gravity's failing more often," she said. "Showers are shorter. Food portions are less. Crops are dying."

"Deliberate? Malicious?"

She moved her feet nervously. "That's a step too far, maybe."

"No it isn't. You brought me here, to these crops. You wanted to show me. That it's not working. You're saying that if you wanted to, you could tell Galatea that a human being was a hamster and it wouldn't know the difference. Conditions have worsened. And not because there are less resources to go around, but because someone has decided it that way. But if you're making the same amount and getting less, the rest must be going somewhere. Could it be that inefficient?"

"No. The opposite should happen. That it becomes so efficient that *everything* can be counted." She shrugged, said, "I know. I know it sounds stupid. But it doesn't add up."

"But if Galatea's wrong it means someone either made it that way or allowed it to drift. Why would someone do that?"

"Look, I'm just saying something's wrong that can't be properly explained."

"So if we disappeared, Galatea should know, right?"

"An offer I cannot refuse," she snorted and laughed.

Haig smiled. "There's a resort just a few billion miles from here. Called Earth. Lots of sunshine and water. Give yourself a holiday."

She smiled, said, "Every day on Gunport is a holiday."

"We all came for the bright lights and clean air," said Haig. "Every day an adventure, every paycheck a fortune."

"Came because the company sent us," she said, grimacing.

"IPRA sent me," said Haig.

"But you're here for the company," said Chiaki. "To help the company get their workers back in line. That's your aim, right? To make everyone work again."

"The aim is to find a compromise. Reactor techs wanted me here too."

"This strike'll be over soon. One way or another."

Haig stared at the dead crops and scratched at the join between ear and skull, feeling the scaly skin come away.

They climbed back aboard the tractor and slapped through the crops to one of the concrete pillars. Wrapped around it was a metal staircase that led up to a web of gantries that held the UV lights. Hidden above, beyond the brightness, were walkways used to make repairs, access vents, replace valves.

Through the holes in the metal, at least six flights up, Haig could see the shape of Acaba.

"She could have chosen somewhere easier to get to," said Haig, tapping his prosthetic.

"Being hard to get to is the point," said Chiaki, then the tractor lurched forward and she disappeared into the fields. Haig watched her go, the crops parting for her and shuddering in her wake.

Even looking at the steps made Haig tired. He took a deep breath, steeled himself for the inevitable rawness between his leg and prosthetic, and started the climb to Acaba.

He hadn't heard from Sile about restarting negotiations. Haig figured he was busy trying to control how the spacesuit and Mihalik were perceived by the crew. Acaba was at the top of a gantry in a different place entirely, so she wasn't negotiating either. He hadn't thought too much about people other than the Reactor crew when he'd arrived, but Chiaki had made it clear. Conditions were regressing. Less water and shorter showers. Less food and hungrier stomachs. Less medicine and sicker people. Everything being sliced away at. Chiaki claimed resources were the same as before, so why weren't they getting the same as before? If they were getting less, but Gunport was making the same, there should be extra. Some surplus. Then where was the surplus going?

When he made it to Acaba, he was sweating, panting. A great stain had oozed across his back.

Acaba was looking at him as he came up the last few steps. Had been watching him for a while. She was sat in a plastic sheet serving as a hammock, one leg dangling lazily out of the side.

She shifted to look at him properly, the plastic crackling.

She said, "You need a new leg."

He leaned against the railing and took a few deep breaths, wiped sweat away from his eyes, nodded.

He said, "I liked my old one."

She regarded him coldly. "I've nothing to say to you. I told Chiaki to send you away."

"She knows a lot. For a farmer."

"She's clever and she pays attention."

"I need your help."

"After all your talk of being neutral?" she said. "Fuck you, Haig. You're the worst of them. You know we get treated like shit. You know it, in your bones. But you're somewhere between them and us. You still come and tell me not to cause trouble, you want me to get my guys back to work, but you know exactly why trouble needs to be caused. You act like them but they treat you like us. They fucking hate you, Haig, because you're supposed to be on their side. Except you're not, not really. You're a token gesture. A tickbox. We fucking hate you, Haig, because you do their bidding. You do it, even though you know it's not right."

"It's not about the negotiations."

"Then what?"

"The woman in the suit."

Acaba sat up, fists balled. "Don't mock me, Haig."

"I think Mihalik knew who was in the suit."

"Sile says there was no-one in the suit."

"A lot of people believe him. Gunport staff believe it. But I saw it myself. Enough people have told me I didn't see it that I doubted myself. But I know what I saw. Repeat a lie often enough and it becomes self-perpetuating. Unless you've seen the original. Or you know the facts. Sile's created a culture here where nothing's true. And if you don't know what's true you can't feel anything about it. You don't know how to feel about it, so you won't do anything about it. You're sort of paralysed. If you *know* something's wrong, you do something. But if you're not sure, it creates that layer of doubt. And keeping you separated helps. I wouldn't be surprised if he feeds that animosity between you and the Programmers. That's how he keeps control. Its sensory overload via an overwhelming pummelling with bullshit. Sometimes even stating the obvious universal facts seems like rebellion. That's why he hates you, Sunita. Because you've pushed back."

"What did she say?"

"Mihalik didn't say anything."

"Sile hasn't said anything about it yet."

"I think she was murdered. On the face of it, suicide, but I think whoever did it gave her a push to walk out of that Airlock. She wanted to tell me but couldn't quite do it. Whoever killed her thought she was going to tell me something."

Acaba said quietly, "No-one's used the word murder."

"No, of course not. Because they say there's no body. But I'm almost certain of it. Proving it and working out why are another thing."

Acaba relaxed her hands. "Why talk to me now?"

"Someone killed a woman and threw her out outside, like so much rubbish. They thought she was worthless. People aren't supposed to be thrown away. I don't care if we're billions of miles away from Earth. People don't just get to do whatever they want. There has to be some fairness. Some justice."

Acaba looked away from him, gazed at the concrete walls and the blocks of crops.

Haig's chest ached. The sweat on his t-shirt had begun to dry, and the remaining patch was warm and itchy. He scratched at his back and looked over at the view. It was some drop to the field and the crops below, but it was quiet and still.

Tom would like this, thought Haig. Watching the machines at work, trimming crops and feeding them. They could watch the sprays working from Chiaki's booth near the elevator, or watch Kaneda climb up to repair a light. Or they could just run through the crops together, playing hide and seek. Or commandeering a tractor and racing it at speed, Tom giggling at first until finally it was far too fast and he felt his hands slipping and he squealed and cried until they stopped, and Haig, laughing despite himself, would have to comfort a crying boy.

And then, that horrible inevitable flash of reality: these crops and that much crying would kill Tom. Haig sighed. A place like Gunport could be perfect for Tom. Controlled conditions, always. The problem was the controller.

An e-sleeve message from Sile: *Extraneous issues resolved. Negotiations ASAP.*

Over to his left, far below, unwatered and brittle, was the perfect square of dead crops.

Acaba said, "How do you think I can help?"

Haig took out the 3D-printed image. "It's you and Mihalik. Who's the third?"

When she looked, tears came instantly. She wiped them away angrily. "You've ruined this view for me," she said, snatching the image, snapping a corner off it.

She started down the stairs, said, "Her name is Petra Komarov."

***

The Elevator clanked and rumbled, Haig the sole passenger.

"Two years ago, Petra Komarov left Gunport," said Wecht over Haig's e-sleeve. "Mihalik talked about her in our sessions. They were in a relationship. Mihalik talked about her a lot. She was a programmer in the Core, working on water algorithms. Then one day, all of a sudden, Mihalik said, Komarov left Gunport."

"Just like that?"

"Komarov didn't tell her anything. She just disappeared. When she asked, Mihalik was told that Komarov had left on a shuttle back to Earth. I can't see the logs without asking Barnes for an override but Mihalik was convinced there was no shuttle. Said there were no launches then. She was so confused. Komarov didn't tell her she was going, hasn't contacted her since. I've got my session notes here. I didn't believe her, Haig. And she didn't trust her own memory, so between us, we convinced her that Komarov had left on a shuttle."

"Who told her that Komarov had gotten on a shuttle?"

"She didn't say. 'They' is all she said."

"Barnes has the shuttle logs?"

"Barnes and Tobin. Barnes for the flight plans. Tobin does the cargo manifests."

"That tracks. Komarov's killed and dumped outside, then it's covered up. Send me the dates. I'll find a way into the logs."

"How?"

"I don't know. I'm making this up as I go along."

"Why was she killed?"

"I don't know that either. She was a programmer?"

"Yes. In the Core."

"Slle's called negotiations back. He says everything else has been resolved."

"Like hell it has."

"Acaba should be there. I'll try to find out what I can when I see her."

"How was she?"

"Upset. Angry."

"Help her, if you can."

"I will."

"I'll track through the rest of Mihalik's sessions."

"Be careful."

"I will. Wecht out."

***

Sile had clearly been sat alone in the Viewing Gallery for some time when Haig arrived.

His fingers were interlinked, his hands in his lap. He watched Haig as he came out of the Elevator, watched Haig as he pulled his chair from under the table, watched Haig as he sat down and sighed, watched Haig as he rubbed the tight skin at his prosthetic, watched Haig lift the leg with a grunt, watched Haig slide his negotiation packet in front of him, watched Haig sip at the water in front of him.

Being watched was fine with Haig. He figured it as another of Sile's power plays. The chasm of silence. Who would fill it first?

Haig basked in the silence. Listened to the gentle thrum of Gunport. Thudding of air pumps. Spinning of filtration systems. Smell of old concrete, thin soap masking the dry human stink of people sweating and drying and tolling and drying and stinking all over again, and their showers never enough to clean them. A slow, progressive stink. Haig barely noticed it unless he stopped to find it.

He took the moment to think. Compartmentalise. There was a body in the suit. The body was Komarov. She was a programmer. She was friendly with Mihalik and Acaba, but her bosses weren't. Janulis and Blatt hated those working in the Reactor. And Blatt had previous. He'd threatened Haig when he first arrived. He had attacked Mihalik. He had raped her. He was top of the suspect list.

"Sunita Acaba will not be joining us," said Sile.

"We can't proceed without her," said Haig.

"This isn't quite what you think."

"We need Acaba to continue. IPRA guidelines, WSA

expectations. Your company as well. This needs to be done properly."

"I agree entirely."

"Then why is Acaba not here?"

"It disappoints me greatly to have needed to do this, Anson. But I feel as though you have left me no choice."

"No choice?"

"Kaneda tells me that the suit was missing a vital component. A locator. Unfortunately, it seems that Retallick has carelessly forgotten to bring this suit in after using the Airlock to store it, and it could not be retrieved sooner simply because it could not be found. You will know from your experience in space that finding something outside is near impossible. And there was no body in the suit, despite your assertions to the contrary. Despite your insistence on it. Despite your telling my staff that a dead woman was inside it. Despite your telling my doctor that there was a body. My Reactor controller. These are my people, Anson. Mine. I tell them the truth and I expect them to accept it."

"There *was* a body in that suit. Her name was Petra Komarov."

Haig leaned back. Watched Sile's blood come to the front of his face. Watched his cheeks shudder, his eyes shake in their sockets, saw him tremble with a rage that surprised Haig.

Sile tried to bring it under control. He was at a tipping point. Embarrassed not because he was angry, but because Haig had seen how angry Haig himself had made Sile become. He sipped water with difficulty, the cup juddering in his hand. He closed his eyes. He willed himself calm.

Poke the bear, thought Haig. Don't let up –

He said, "Her name was Petra Komarov. Mihalik knew her – "

"She was an excellent member of the Reactor team," said Sile. Composed now. "But not without her issues."

"That doesn't matter. What matters is – "

"Acaba is a difficult woman," said Sile. "I'm told Mihalik had many arguments with her. Made her working life very difficult. Especially hard for her Gunport family when her work in the Reactor meant so much for so many. When it still does, and she refuses to do it."

"We all argue. Especially family. We all disagree. It's how you respond that matters."

The skin around Sile's eyes tightened. The smile changed.

"It seems clear to me that Sunita Acaba made life more difficult for Alice Mihalik than it should have been. It seems clear to Doctor Prendrick also."

"Prendrick didn't know her."

"I didn't realise you had become such an expert on my staff's medical history in such a short time," said Sile, smirking. "Prendrick has conducted a full review of Doctor Wecht's notes on Mihalik's wellbeing, and found that she was a mental health risk."

"Her health was established long before she arrived here. The company sent her here."

"The Doctor disagrees. He notes a deterioration in her wellbeing since arriving here."

"She was attacked and you did nothing about it," said Haig. "You ignored it, and now she's dead."

Sile recoiled as if slapped.

"She had every procedural protection," said Sile. "An incident was never reported. She was the aggressor, becoming injured because of actions Blatt took in self-defence."

"Self-defence?"

"I should not even be discussing this with you. I have seen the video feeds. Mihalik is clearly the aggressor."

"Blatt knows she couldn't hurt him. It'd be like punching a cliff."

"And yet she attacked him."

"He followed her and provoked her. Did she hit him? Or shout at him? Who struck who?"

"I'm starting to question your judgement, Anson."

Haig thought, Deflect all you like. He said, "Where's the video?"

"You're not seeing it."

"Who else has seen it?"

"That's irrelevant. She did not make a complaint and so I was well within my rights to ignore it. I had Dekker investigate as a courtesy to Acaba because I believed it might aid us in finding common ground in these negotiations. In fact, I did not share this with her because she would not have liked the outcome."

"Then tell her that yourself. Show her the video."

"You know that isn't protocol. I'll confess, Anson, that I do not like the way you are speaking. Let us be clear. There is no report. Verbal or written. From anyone. I would expect Sunita to have filed one after her outburst. It's beginning to look like you have an agenda against poor Blatt. Perhaps because he is gene-edited?"

Haig frowned, balled a fist. He has a gift for muddying the waters, for creating noise somewhere off to the side of the issue, thought Haig. And right now, Sile is the one shouting the loudest. He took a moment. Breathed deliberately. Fought the irritation he felt flushing his face.

"That's not true."

"A number of our staff cannot understand why you haven't taken a different prosthetic. Or a commstem. Or, frankly, any implants at all. Bethe's good work in his clinics would surely be of a benefit to you."

"This one works just fine."

"So you're not biased, Anson, simply heavy-handed and reckless. It was a knee-jerk reaction."

"My choosing not to have implants has nothing to do with it. It's real, report or not. It contributed directly to her death. And I want to know why she was attacked."

"She was hurt because she attacked a respected programmer who defended himself."

"She was attacked because she knew who was in the suit."

"Let me tell you what I think." Sile's tone hardened. "A man who is responsible for keeping our project alive is now, perhaps, feeling somewhat less responsible. Less inclined to maintain his impeccable standards. For some person in the Reactor. Something for people to gossip about. A grain of sand in the wind."

"Bullshit," said Haig.

"You'll mind your language," said Sile darkly. "I'm not saying it. A respected doctor is. The Chief Medical Officer of Gunport. He is saying that she killed herself because she has a history of arguments with her colleagues. She was isolated and alone. She had difficulty accepting that she had been tainted by her implants. All painstakingly noted by Sarah."

Did Sile emphasise 'Sarah'? Haig sniffed, hid a snarl, said, "She killed herself because of Blatt."

"Again, given that no incident was reported, it means that your bias against the gene-edited members of Gunport – those who keep Galatea, and thus us, alive – is still burning. Doctor Prendrick's investigation into Alice Mihalik's death has concluded that she was a perpetual suicide risk, and that all reasonable steps had been taken to assist her. He commends the work undertaken by Sarah in helping her to maintain her excellent work for as long as she did, and he commends Hiro Kaneda in attempting to stop her in her final moments.

Unfortunately, suicides happen here, and in this case, we are saying that no-one could have done more to prevent it."

Haig gently shook his head, disbelieving.

"Perhaps you're upset, Anson. Perhaps you and I have crossed wires. Well, let me rectify that. Let me be clear. In order to move forward, Anson, this kind of thing must be put behind us. In the past. You're making things more complicated."

Sile jabbed an accusing finger. "Blatt is being persecuted. You only seem concerned with dredging up the past. Making the past into the present. Making the past into our future. Dwelling on insignificant things. Your paradoxical thinking concerns me, Anson. Blatt is our second-most programmer. A brilliant man. Brilliant. Galatea's keeper. He and Janulis do more for us in a day what you could hope to do in a lifetime. What would it mean if you had offended him?" He waved a hand dismissively, snorted.

Haig said, "You need to conduct a proper investigation into both Komarov and Mihalik but you won't because you're terrified it'll mean another six months where no shuttles launch or land. And you talk to me about bias."

Sile's fist slammed into the table, screaming, "There is no fucking body!"

There was a moment's pause as his face trembled in rage and became a violent scarlet colour before his hair thrashed and the whites of his eyes pushed from his face as he slammed and slammed and screamed, "There is no fucking body!"

He ran his hands through his hair, made fists, unmade fists, pressed his fingers into his temples until they turned white.

"There is no fucking body!"

He slammed his fists into the table again and again and again until it buckled and the plastic legs finally cracked and the tabletop listed and fell away.

He lurched up from his seat and started jabbing a finger at Haig.

"Enough with your fucking lies," said Sile. "Enough. At one point, I thought I might reason with you. I thought that IPRA's most vaunted negotiator might be able to help me to convince a treasonous malcontent to get back in her box and do her job so that the future of humanity isn't threatened because some woman with a stick up her ass is feeling a little uncomfortable. 'Oh, I don't have enough water. Oh, I don't have enough food. Oh, my implants hurt.' She's in space, Haig. We all are. Nobody has enough of anything. We all make sacrifices for everyone else, but she doesn't want to and the whole fucking universe wants to help her to shut me down. Well she won't. I won't have it. I won't have that fucking bitch beat me, Haig. I fucking won't. I thought you understood. I thought offering you some housing through IPRA would help you to make good choices. But you haven't. You're walking around my facility telling people that someone has been murdered. Well. That's over now. I see you, Haig. You're another of those malcontents. Bitter and resentful and trying to take what's mine. Well, let me tell you. If you don't do exactly as I say from now on, I'm going to advise Aphelion that you haven't been attending negotiation meetings. That you've been stirring up trouble amongst my staff. That your neutrality is compromised. Galatea calculates that we can cope for long enough. Acaba and her cronies will be fired. If she's very lucky, her union will send a shuttle. She can rot in the Tank for all I care. Two weeks later that you'll be relieved of your duties and I'll finally be given permission to deal with this as I see fit."

He sighed, suddenly exhausted. "Gunport will finally be back on track," he said. "Humanity will be on track."

"Gunport isn't on track," Haig spat. "It's a shuttle with a broken fuel gauge. It's out of control. It's about to crash and explode and you can't see it. They deserve better than this. Than you. They're dead because they came here."

Sile's eyes glazed over and he yawned and said, "Who's dead?"

CHAPTER 9:
KINGDOM OF BONES

Haig sat at the desk of the room he had been given.

Arms folded. Breathing deeply. Thinking harder. Not getting anywhere. His face throbbed. He could feel how angry it must look. He was sweating. Gritty salt had collected in his eyebrows.

He started to think about a shower. He would scour himself clean with blistering hot water and enjoy being clean and pink for a while. He could sit on the bed and feel his skin throbbing and close his eyes and just be. Unless it cut out. Unless it ended six or ten or forty seconds early –

Things had unravelled. Sile wasn't simply a passive presence, but a hostile one, Haig realised. Not a murderer, perhaps, but he'd encouraged and empowered one by inaction alone. You don't need to solve a crime if you change the law so that it was never a crime in the first place. It's not murder, it's an industrial accident. It's not rape, it's self-defence.

Acaba was the obvious next link in his chain. He'd worked out who the woman was. Acaba could probably point him in the right direction, but Acaba was off-limits now. If he wanted to continue negotiating. If he wanted to let Sile and Aphelion strip Gunport's staff into units of value and run that value down until they were worthless husks of people, their value at zero, their lives over because Gunport had taken everything from them.

Haig still didn't know why. Couldn't work it out.

And Haig didn't like the idea that IPRA wasn't independent. He bristled. Didn't like the idea that Aphelion had tried to use him to get what they wanted. The WSA wouldn't like it either. He'd sent word to Mangan immediately after Sile's rant. Clarification. Housing was everything. But housing that others had died for was nothing.

He had seen Sile's temper. Sile had lost control. Pressure was building.

***

Everything that went into a chute or hole in Gunport ended up in the Recycler. Plastic was melted down and sent in blocks up to Kaneda. Food – and what used to be food – was sterilised, sent up to be pressed into protein blocks. Water was treated – barely – and pumped back out. Just enough to skim the top layer of soap scum.

The Recycler was effectively a series of conveyor belts housed in a long corridor with a low, oppressive ceiling. Everything on the belts was obliterated by crushers and blades and spears. The noise was incredible. Haig got off the elevator and reached for the rack of ear-defenders, then felt much better. The invasive clanking calmed to a persistent rumbling, and Haig took a breath, waiting for his eyes to adapt to the dark.

Lesedi Maseko greeted him with a genuine grin, two rows of gleaming teeth. He was naked from the waist up, body slick with sweat, the arms of his coveralls tied around his waist. His techtatts covered one side of his chest, a sweeping diagram of an ear canal. Old burn scars had been transformed with the addition of a tattoo; a small woman was cupping her hands and shouting into the diagram of the ear, her body made of the scars, her arms and legs with ink.

"Welcome to the realm of the abandoned and the discarded," he said, shouting over the noise, gripping Haig's hands. Then he cackled: "If you are here, you are either lost or I am in trouble. Which is it today? Or – blessed Machine, be not so – it cannot be both!"

"I need your help," said Haig, smiling despite himself, gripping Maseko's hands in return.

His face became serious, and he beckoned Haig away from the elevator. There was a small booth that overlooked the food conveyor, and Haig saw Chiaki's golden, barren crops shudder along, waiting to be obliterated.

Maseko ushered him in, closed the door to the booth and sealed it. He tapped his own ear-defenders, and they both took them off.

"Ah, much quieter," he said. "Speak of your trouble."

"What's that?" said Haig, pointing at the crops.

"Dead crops," said Maseko, shrugging. "No water."

"Chiaki showed me," said Haig.

"We receive our water here, and we return it clean and true. It is like they do not drink, like the soil is bad. I think that someone has a finger on a button," he said, pointing upwards, "And the finger does not press the button. Does not send the water to the crops."

"Have you said anything?" said Haig.

Maseko grinned, humour in his eyes. He held a long finger up, looked at it with mock-reverence. "The will of the finger is that the finger shall not press the button."

"You think they know?"

Maseko laughed. "The only department in Gunport not to be invited to briefings is Recycling. We are nothing to everyone else. But Gunport is an ecosystem, yes? Every part plays its part. More here than anywhere else. Everything here is needed. Always. We shall always do our part. And if Chiaki cannot do hers, we shall trust in the leopard to do his."

Haig stared at him. "The leopard?"

"Sile is the leopard, yes? Smiles and violence. When you feel as though you will all live together, it will pull its claws through your throat, and on the floor, your blood soaking the soil, you shall curse your incompetence."

"Chiaki's in trouble?"

"Sile leads us and we shall follow, but there is violence for those that do not follow."

Haig was starting to feel lost. "Violence?"

"This is an unforgiving place," said Maseko, "For those who do not do as they should. And it looks after those that contribute. Acaba should know this."

Haig decided to deflect. He said, "I came to ask you about this woman," showing Maseko the image.

Maseko took it and pinched the corner, holding it up, examining it, overly careful.

"Ancient relics," he said. "This is Mihalik, who we will see again, her soul making it further into the stars in its next time. This is Komarov, who we will see again also. Both have come so far, and will go again. But you are not a policeman, Anson Haig. Why do you show this to me?"

Why *am* I here? thought Haig. "Chiaki thought you might know her," he said. "Mihalik came to me before she died. I'm trying to understand why."

"There is only one reason to keep this artefact. The two of them were more than friends, perhaps," said Mascko. "The hand on her back is protective, not dominant. We knew her, here. She was troubled, but she was good. Komarov I think was not so good."

Haig scratched his chin, considered. He caught the stink of hot, obliterated plastic.

"Not so good?"

"She challenged and pushed."

"How?"

"She forgot why we are here. You are a man of faith, Anson Haig?"

"They were religious?"

"Children of the Machine Mind and Children of the Next Advance, fighting for which master is better."

"No," said Haig.

"Oh, we all are, Anson. You are here, yes? You have faith."

"That's not faith, Lesedi. That's trust. Neither will get me home."

Maseko smiled, shrugged. "You believe that the shuttle will work, yes?"

Haig ran a hand through his beard. Scratched at it.

"There is something," said Maseko, handing the photograph back. "Komarov was uneasy. She came to me. I listened to her troubles. Chiaki's farm is Chiaki's domain. If she cannot grow her crops, the leopard shall intervene. Komarov did not agree. She wanted more water in more places. She believed that one malfunction was everyone's malfunction."

"She thought it was a problem across the whole of Gunport?"

"There is nothing to be done here but endure. Like muscles that are used again and again in different contortions, our minds grow in hardship, become stronger but uglier. I offered her what advice I could but sensed she had more to tell. I did not press. I thought she might come to me again, in time. When she did not, I thought little of it. It is not unusual for someone to simply leave if a shuttle arrives. Even those that we know well are only known well while we are here. They are false friends. We help each other, yes, but it is because we are thrown together. We do not speak to each other of real things here, Haig. We are our own asteroids. You are learning this, I think."

"Yes," said Haig, nodding.

Yellow lights began to spin and flash, and the conveyors died. The silence was unnerving. Haig's ears throbbed, the roaring of the conveyors refusing to depart. Maseko pinched his nose and puffed his cheeks and tried to force pressure through his ears. The Recyclers moved to their positions.

Maseko smiled and put a hand on Haig's shoulder, then replaced his ear-defenders.

"Would Komarov have gone to Sile?" said Haig.

"Does a leopard wait for the gazelle?"

***

Haig had been sat in the Viewing Gallery for ten minutes before he realised that he wasn't alone.

The screen showed an explosion in the centre, a clump of white light, its edges furred and oily. The oil in the colour became less greasy and the oily brilliance reddened, still stretching from one corner to the other, but pocked with black gaps, spaces without light. An absence of colour or movement, dead zones, devoid of anything. The explosion had absorbed all of the image's energy, pressing it forward.

A clunk. A dropped gunshine cup, a distinctive, hollow sound.

Haig spun, hand at his holster. Paused. Waited. Heard faint breathing in the dark. The silhouette of a man solidified. He squinted at it until his eyes adjusted and he realised it was Choudhury, hiding in the dark.

"Zoom out," said Choudhury. His tone was flat, lethargic. The image changed and the perfect hole doubled, two small holes near each other.

"Zoom out," said Choudhury, irritable. The colour still held, now more like a sash of oily brilliance stretching from one corner to the other.

"Zoom out," said Choudhury.

"A million years ago, two black holes smashed into each other," said Choudhury, slurring. "Caused a shockwave more than hundreds of millions of times the size of the Sun. Means it's more than a million billion times the size of Earth."

Choudhury's tone was aggressive, confrontational. Like he was accusing Haig of pushing the black holes into each other himself.

"Supermassive black holes?" said Haig carefully.

"Yes. No. I don't know. Who fucking cares," said Choudhury. "We're so fucking little." Even in the dark, Haig could tell that he was measuring humanity between his finger and thumb. "We're tiny, Haig. We're tiny. We shouldn't be out here. It's so empty. It's so fucking empty. And we'll do what? Fill it up?" He spread his arms wide and said, "Whoosh!"

"What's going on, Hasan? What happened?"

"This place is some shit, Haig," said Choudhury. "Some shit. I've got a cupboard. A fucking cupboard. 'Hasan, find us some water, it's all up to you, now here's your intergalactic stick and a compass that always points at your arse, fuck off and find us some water, there's a good chap'."

Choudhury groaned and put his head between his knees, survived a dry heave, outlasted a series of wet burps, breathed deeply.

"You're drunk," said Haig.

"There's no water," said Choudhury.

"That's why the showers run short."

"Not here." Choudhury burped, stomach gurgled, contents roiled.

"What do you mean?"

"There isn't any."

"On Sedna? On your moon? But it's all ice."

"It's too deep. It's too heavy. We can't drink it. We can't mine it. It's too dense, too cold."

"You'll find a way, Hasan."

"There's no water, Haig. There is no water. Gunport is folly."

"Come on now. Who gave you that gunshine, Hasan? Was it Tobin?"

"The ice is too thick. Far too thick. I have been waiting years for DIVA to explore, Haig. And now it is dead. You saw the feeds. That place killed it in mere minutes. Even when you are looking for life. For the things that keep us alive. If we want to survive out here, we need water, but even the fucking water is hostile, Anson. It mocked me. It fucking mocked me. It showed me just a sliver of itself, taunting. 'Come to me,' it said. A moon-sized siren. Singing to me. Whispering sweetnesses in my ear that I could not resist." Choudhury sighed, chuckled, whimpered.

"There'll be another DIVA, Hasan," said Haig, putting an arm around him. "You'll find what you're looking for. You just need some time and – " then he muttered, " – sobriety."

"No, I won't. It isn't there," said Choudhury, and Haig heard him sob.

"Surely now you know what's there, you can send another craft," said Haig. "DIVA's latest model. She's moving up in the world. The WIFE."

Choudhury sniffed. "That's absurd, Haig."

"DIVA was absurd. You scientists and your acronyms. The WIFE, Hasan. What about 'The Water Investigatory Functional Extractor'."

Haig heard the smile in Choudhury's voice. "That is a terrible acronym."

"It's dreadful. They'd all think it was yours."

"Water Infiltration and Fermentation Engine," said

Choudhury, despite himself.

"Sounds faintly alcoholic."

"Tobin would enjoy it."

"So would you, apparently," said Haig, pointing at the discarded cup.

"I have never had a drink like that before."

Choudhury's guts gurgled and he groaned, then slumped to the floor and fell asleep.

Haig snorted. "Welcome to Gunport, Hasan."

"Haig," said his e-sleeve. "It's Kaneda. I have the suit."

***

When Choudhury was propped up and as comfortable as a concrete floor would allow, Haig took the Elevator, marched into Kaneda's Workshop, ignored the pain in his leg.

The tables now carried the drones Retallick had used, with wiring spilling from it, dust collected under it. Pieces of them were scattered about the table like an unfinished mosaic, brittle chips of metal and circuit board coated in thin Angutian dust. Haig picked up a shard of the dust and ran it across his fingers, marvelling at the flinty sharpness of it. A circuit board had a soldering kit laid out in front of it, and the strips of solder were laid out in parallel lines.

Haig went past Kaneda's small quarters in the Workshop, beyond a screen flickering with a clash of cyclists mid-race, past another table that was empty, gleamed, freshly polished.

The mystery suit lay severed into uneven pieces on a long table of its own. Prendrick had sawed and chopped and hacked his way through, maliciously negligent. Haig sighed. It had been laid out like a hollow skeleton. The EVA backpack was on a separate table. Dotted around it were tools and tablets. Haig picked up one of the gloves. The hard plastic at the fingertips was cool to the touch. He lifted the glove closer to his face and smelled inside. It was a cold, sweet smell, faint. Death and sickness.

He recoiled. He put the glove down. He didn't smell the rest of the suit.

"Don't smell any of it," said Kaneda, emerging from his quarters. He collected a toolkit from a drawer under one of the Workshop's tables and stood in front of the suit.

Haig pointed towards Kaneda's quarters, said, "You were a keirin racer?"

"My father," said Kaneda, surprised, smiling, nodding at the screen. "He was not a good keirin racer, but he was disciplined. He knew how he must behave."

"It's a tough sport. Did he ever win?"

"He won two," said Kaneda, "One in a yellow jersey, and one in a pale blue. You know the races?"

"Only the virtual ones."

"Ah," sighed Hiro. "They have no soul, Haig. My father would not have approved. There is no roar of people. No adrenaline. No nervous clenching of muscles in the openings, when you are part of the horde, waiting to make your move. No strategy. Too many second chances."

"You didn't want to race?"

"My mother always chastised me for not being ruthless enough when I raced. For not coming across and shunting others out of the way. I always liked the bikes better. Everyone's bike was the same. Always checked and rechecked. They had to be identical for each rider. There was precision in the bikes. Precision and conformity. Everything always conformed to the specifications. There was an ideal bike, and it was achievable. And so I would build and repair my father's bike."

"And now you're here."

Kaneda looked at the floor, nodded, cleared his throat. "It has been outside for a long time," he said, nodding at the suit. "It is intact. Lots of scuffing and scraping, but no puncturing or tearing. These are the kind of marks I would expect to see on a suit that has been used normally, regularly. I would say that it has been outside for twelve months."

"How does it stay outside for year? And no-one knows?"

"All of our comms equipment, radar, everything points up," said Kaneda. "It's all to help us spot things coming in. We know nothing else is on the surface because we were here first and nothing else has arrived."

The suit bore a number of labels and badges. Gunport's corporate logos had varied over the years, from an octagonal crest – Anguta Rail Port printed along the bottom three edges, the railgun proudly splitting the centre – to the current, Sile-approved shield.

The labels on the suit were curling slightly at the corners, having endured the moon's disparate temperatures. The main badge on the suit was a simple rectangle with the letters 'ARP' embroidered into it. It was set into a darker square beneath it where the old military labels had been replaced.

Above the letters was a grey circle – Anguta R-611 itself, Haig presumed – with a rocket launching from it, leaving a curving white jetstream behind. He tutted. Railgunned ships never left any gas or wake or tail behind, so some company designer with a pencil had been left alone for too long. He presumed it was an old Gunport badge. Below that were a series of badges that Haig couldn't even begin to place.

"You recognise any of these?" said Haig.

"Yes," said Kaneda, pointing to different badges as he spoke. "Aphelion, obviously. ARP is us, the Angutian Rail Port. Gunport. This one below tells us that the suit can perform surface work. This one for orbital work. This one – the fortress below the shuttles – is an Army Engineer badge. The sash stitched over the fortress tells us that it is no longer an Army suit. All of these badges are what I would expect to find. This suit is one of ours."

"I served with teams of Engineers. They got us through Airlock doors. Took control of different base systems. How old is the suit?"

"Hold the arm up," said Kaneda.

Haig pulled the arm up and let it rest on his shoulder. Kaneda brushed some Angutian dust away from the seals on the glove and revealed a serial number, then typed it into a tablet.

"Four years old. Repaired and refurbished on six separate occasions by Army technicians." Kaneda frowned. "This is odd. The serial number shows it leaving the Moon, but never arriving here."

"Well, it's clearly here," said Haig, nodding at it. "How does that happen?"

"If it's not put into the inventory when it's unpacked," said Kaneda.

"Who does suit inventory?"

"Conrad."

Haig looked at Kaneda for a long moment. Kaneda seemed to sense Haig's question and deliberately fixed his stare on the suit.

When he finally looked up, Haig said, "Why wasn't this suit put into Retallick's inventory?"

"I don't know."

"I'd take a Corporal's pudding if they didn't know where their suits were."

"Pudding?"

"No use putting them in a tank or a cell or confining them to their quarters on a moonbase. Take what they want. Amazing how quickly an armoury can be organised properly when a sticky toffee pudding is on the line."

Kaneda licked his lips. "Pudding," he said wistfully. "I maintain the suits, but I don't operate them. Retallick does. Suits are checked out for all number of reasons. Tobin climbs up the shafts on occasion, I believe. He may well need one to repair the guns after your landing. Barnes and his guys do maintenance on the transmitters above Control. We are still reliant on a person physically inputting a serial number. It's long and tedious, so it is not always done."

Haig grabbed the hips and Kaneda the shoulders, then they wrenched the suit up and over. It thudded down and the backpack faced them.

"There is something missing," said Kaneda.

He pulled at straps and catches until the material of the backpack fell away. He used a pistol-grip screwdriver to take out a range of plastic panels until they were left with a carbon-tubed carcass, a thin frame of plastic with a tangle of wiring inside.

Haig's eyes were drawn to a gap within it, a square of conspicuous emptiness.

"Here," said Kaneda. "This should be packed with electrical equipment. A radio, and a navigation device, the locator."

"So this is why she couldn't contact anyone. Why she couldn't be found. I thought it might be broken or installed badly, but for it to be gone… I don't like it, Hiro."

"She wouldn't have been able to find her way back."

"Deliberate then?"

"It hasn't been broken or ripped out. It simply isn't there. Yes. This is deliberate. After Prendrick conducted an autopsy, I re-checked our suits and equipment. There was an additional locator. I didn't think anything of it. We often have equipment unaccounted for or sent to us in error. But this should have been in the suit, and wasn't."

"How much air would this suit give her? Allowing for her weight, height, scrubbers and reclaimers in the suit, everything?" said Haig.

"The suit has a Black Box," said Kaneda. "I'll show you the primary data."

Kaneda took a cord from his tablet and plugged it into a slot on the hard-drive inside the backpack. He brought up graphs, charts, percentages.

Kaneda said, "The oxygen was full to begin with, and entirely depleted four hours later. She breathed it all or – "

"Or she decomposed. Or both." Haig scratched his beard. Stared at Kaneda. Kaneda stared back.

"Could this have been an accident of some kind? Of any kind?"

"There are no signs of malfunction, error, or tampering of any suit system. Everything worked like it should until it was exhausted. And I can see that even with Prendrick's methods of opening it up. The missing equipment means I have incomplete data from the Black Box. No locator means we cannot trace its path. No radio means no communications history."

"She wouldn't have gone out without a radio and locator. Not unless there was a damned good reason."

Kaneda nodded.

"One of two things happened," said Haig. "She died here, was put in the suit, and ejected out of the airlock." Haig rubbed his eyes, looked at the floor, felt his stomach turn.

"Or?" said Kaneda.

"Or," Haig said, "She was alive when she went out."

Kaneda's, voice was low, his eyes shimmering. He met Haig's

eyes with uncomfortable intensity. "Perhaps she was placed unwillingly into this spacesuit. She would awaken later on. Her air slowly running out. The alarm sounding to tell her that she had an hour left. She would suffocate, fight an overwhelming desire to open her visor, for air not there. The panic consuming her oxygen faster. She would not open the visor because, of all things, she would hope. Even without a radio or a locator. In her last moments, she would hope that someone was coming to help her, without knowing if anyone knew she was out there. She would hope."

Ah, shite, thought Haig. Don't know exactly when the suit got here. Don't know who used it. Don't know how long she's been out there for. A full tank of air but no locator. No radio. The locator turning up in the Ramp. It was deliberate, malicious. Murderous. If she was dead, she could simply have been tipped outside. No missing suit, no additional locator. No evidence. In time, perhaps, she would still have hit the tower, but she would have frozen entirely before that, pieces of her coming away as she scraped along the surface until finally there was nothing left.

"Send all of that to me."

Kaneda tapped his tablet, said, "Done."

***

The Elevator ride down to the Reactor was just long enough for Haig to stop sweating.

The suit confirmed it for him. Komarov had been murdered. Who and why escaped him but Acaba could tell him more, and that was where he had to go. Despite Sile's protestations.

The Reactor was a cavernous chamber, dimly lit.

Haig could feel a delicate hum in the back of his teeth. The wall and ceiling blurred into one long arch, creating a vast tunnel. Technicians operated in hushed silence, kneeling at panels, taking readings, adjusting valves. Some murmured faintly to each other before their voices faded away. The floor was thousands of small hexagonal tiles, slotted alongside each other but separate. Each had a small brass dome in its centre the size of a fist. The Technicians walked softly through the chamber, stepping carefully over each hexagon.

A hundred metres away, at the other end of the Reactor tunnel, Acaba stood over a control panel, illuminated by a range of screens. She was talking in reverent tones to a Reactor Technician with a tablet.

Before he could step out of the elevator, he was ambushed by another Technician with paper slippers who shoved them roughly – silently – into Haig's arms. The Technician stared at him until he raised a hand to acknowledge her, then she pointed at his boots. He sat on the floor, took them off, put them in a rack.

A hexagon began to rattle.

Haig looked at his Technician, and her face was blank. Then he looked from Technician to Technician, his stomach tightening.

The shaking became more violent until three more hexagons, randomly scattered, began to shake. Finally, one Technician stopped, looked blankly at the vibrating floor, then continued walking.

His Technician met his eye with a wry smile, held her hand up and counted down on her fingers, from five. Four. Three. Two. One. Zero. The shaking immediately and entirely ceased. The Technician arched her eyebrows at him, smiled, shaking her head. He looked around, searching for eye contact, but no-one looked up.

"We know what we're doing," she said, then pointed to the other end of the Reactor. "All visitors need to speak to Sunita."

Haig padded through the Reactor and could feel vibrations through the slippers, ebbing and flowing, and the hum circulated, sweeping around the tunnel.

An occasional Technician looked up from their work to see who was walking through, before they turned back to their task.

Haig picked his way across the tiles to Acaba's plinth of Reactor controls, and said, "We need to talk."

Acaba said, "I had a message from my union. Another from IPRA. They're disappointed in the progress that's been made. Or not made. They're talking about removing you. And if they do that, Sile will have all the power he needs to fire me. You were the last resort. WSA will back IPRA, and we'll all be on the next shuttle to the Moon."

"I'm sorry, Sunita. I really am. But – "

"It's alright. Really. I won't let them do that." She sighed.

She looks tired, thought Haig. The aggression and fight had gone from her, and a deflated husk of a woman stood in front of him. Her eyes were darkened hollows, her shoulders pressed down and sagging.

She said, "I thought I could make Gunport better by forcing Sile to confront his mistakes. He's the one it hinges on. Aphelion think he's some sort of interstellar magician. Even here, where we live through what he does, when it affects every slice of your life, people here still think of him as some sort of wizard. He lies and equivocates and ignores and twists and bends every truth and obfuscates and pretends and dismisses and does it so well and so often that you begin to wonder what's true anymore. I've got my own Techs coming to me asking what my problem with him is. These are people who have no water, no air, who break their bones on failing gravity, who are starving two or three days out of ten, and they don't connect that to him. It's *my* fault for risking the little he deems we are worth."

"What are you – "

"When you showed me that image of Komarov, I realised that he and Aphelion don't want to solve problems or find solutions. If it's a small problem, they ignore it. If it's a big one, they obliterate it."

"You're going to end – "

"I've brought a few of the Techs back. We're at about ten, maybe twelve percent. We're priming for a return to seventy in the next few days. Fuel reserves will bring us up."

"You're calling the strike off?"

"It was always a bluff, Haig. Conditions needed to improve so we took a chance. A big one. But when the other side pushes your friends out of Airlocks, it's time to give it up."

"You think they were both murdered?"

"Don't you?"

"I do."

Acaba blinked.

Haig said, "Komarov was. Nobody goes outside without a locator or radio. I'd need the autopsy to be absolutely certain, but I think someone killed her and put her in a suit to hide the body."

"Why not just throw her outside?"

"I don't know, Sunita. That's something else that doesn't make sense."

"Someone tossed her away. Like so much trash. That's what happens to big problems."

"Komarov was a big problem?"

"Why are you doing this, Haig? The strike will be over. You're going home."

"I watched one woman die trying to tell me about another dead woman, while these negotiations are being used as a smokescreen for her killer to hide behind. It's wrong."

Acaba stared at him. Made up her mind.

"Fine," she said. "Komarov's job was writing water algorithms. She programmed in the Core. Before she disappeared, she had been arguing with Janulis about what she had written. She couldn't make her algorithms work and she had no idea why. She ran tests, diagnostics, used a mirror of Galatea to check for bugs, glitches, did everything. It still wouldn't work. And then, one day, she was really worried. Scared, almost. When she disappeared and we were told she got on a shuttle, Mihalik couldn't make sense of it. Komarov didn't tell Mihalik about it, not really. She thought she'd do something – well, something like she did. I figured she'd found something she shouldn't and convinced myself she'd gotten out."

"Who told you she got on a shuttle?" said Haig.

"Barnes."

"Either Barnes lied to you or someone lied to him. Let's find out which."

"Let me do it. You said you need the autopsy to make sure? Go and see Prendrick."

**

Gunport's Chief Medical Officer had an office at the back of the Medical Bay. It was much smaller than Wecht's room. Wecht had told Haig what Prendrick's daily schedule looked like. Five minutes into his shift, he would go in there. Five minutes before it ended, he would reappear. Some days, she said, he would be wobbling slightly. Other days, his hand would be shaking violently, and he would be pale, sweating.

Haig's plan was to ask him about everything except the autopsy and see if there was a way in. Some comment that might lead naturally to asking about it. Some way of sliding into it that Prendrick didn't think worth reporting to Sile. Haig was starting to feel like he was on increasingly thin ice – definitely less than seven miles thick – and that Dekker would at any moment be released on him.

Haig knocked on the door and waited. There was no response, no sound of any movement. He put his ear to the door. He heard the sound of a plastic chair crackling, and the shuffling of feet, a deep intake of breath, then a drowsy voice said, "What is it?"

"It's Haig."

"A moment," said Prendrick, muffled.

A long moment.

Then, Prendrick opened the door and let it swing, looked Haig up and down, rubbed his bloodshot eyes, and shuffled back to his chair, sitting heavily.

He'd aged even since the last time Haig saw him, looked like he'd collected weariness in the crinkled skin around the corners of his eyes, deep shadows etched in. He'd lost some weight, too, was paler than Haig remembered.

On a plastic shelf behind him was a tablet and a cardboard cup. On his desk were dark spots from spilled liquid, and a sharp, acidic smell in the air. Gunshine.

"Well," said Prendrick, yawning. "What is it?"

"I'm negotiating between Aphelion and the Reactor unions," said Haig. "I thought you might have some insight. I've spoken to almost everyone else. I wondered what you thought about conditions here, from a doctor's perspective."

Prendrick shook his head slowly, blinked, held his forehead in a pale hand.

"I *was* a doctor. A surgeon, in fact. I was very good. Very, very good. Incredible, perhaps. Neurosurgeon. Manipulating the limbic system. Shortening the connections with the accumbens, getting dopamine released for slightly different reasons. Short-circuiting the brain to release it in the wrong moments. Complicated, dense. I would rearrange pieces of the brain. Decision making would become more about the need for reward and pleasure than the fear of failure, or death. Programming the brain to reward it for dangerous situations, stressful situations. Making difficult work into pleasurable, chemically-rewarded activity. The difficulties of space removed."

Prendrick poked his own eyes. He was sweating. Haig let the silence spread out. He'd been here before. He didn't know Prendrick, and Prendrick didn't know him, but they were sat in that momentary pause before it all came tumbling out. The desperate explanation of motive and actions that needed someone to understand.

Prendrick balled his fists, pressed them onto the desk. "I made people braver."

Haig pulled his hand through his beard.

"I had been operating for two days," said Prendrick, sagging back in the chair, eyes focusing nowhere in particular. "No breaks. Our friends in the Core know nothing about the complexity of a human brain. How delicate, how fragile. How complicated. Galatea is a remarkable machine, certainly, but it is a poor copy of the brilliance of a human mind. It is remarkable that I was able to improve so many minds, so many brains."

His eyes glazed over.

"Two days, then. I had slipped into a zone, Haig, a sort of wonderful place where everything became so simple, every decision presented itself to me with ease, with a minimum of fuss. Neurovascular surgery as symphony, conducted through these hands, with my mind."

He looked down at his hands until they began to shake, then he held them together tightly and put them under the desk.

"I had taken just about every stimulant I could find. All kinds of exciting names. I worked in an Aphelion hospital, so every few hours, a nurse would come in with a trolley. 'I have an interesting duraphetamine if you'd like that, doctor?' they'd say. And I would like that, Haig, I would like it very much. Thank you so much, nurse. Your mind would slip into the stream. And then when the shakes started, some fadeazepam. Or diazepam. Or whatever. Uppers and downers. Warpers, you Army lot call them?"

Haig nodded.

"I had blood tests afterwards, like everyone else, but I was in charge. So many blood samples were, ah, lost. Or sometimes, one of us would go without and give blood for ten people at once. Cramped in the toilets, like furtive mice, scurrying about, mislabelling and equivocating and lying, always lying. Head of Behavioural Realignment Surgery, that was my title."

Prendrick sighed, swallowed. Haig leaned forward.

"I'd performed three operations. Each taking ten, twelve hours. Precision and concentration. The first two were tedious, with a few sharp edges. The third was a triumph, Haig. Perfection. Every stroke of our lasers could be measured in genius. The entries in the journals had started to come to me, and the plaudits that followed, the words racing through my mind. Writing themselves. I saw myself finally recognised by others in my field, standing and applauding, clapping me on the back, or shaking my hand with a rough delight. And then I moved on to the fourth."

Prendrick grew quieter.

"I took direct control. I was shivering and sweating, and pale, said the other doctors afterwards. I had convinced them it was the only thing to do, but I don't remember what I said. I don't remember the operation at all, Haig, honestly. I had been awake for nearly two days. I had enough uppers in my body to launch one shuttle, and enough downers to land another."

"Your patient died?"

"Oh," said Prendrick contemptuously, "Oh, much worse. It took a day for us to realise the mistake I had made. He had an unusual brain. A genetic defect that had caused his limbic system to be arranged differently. I did not see it on the preliminary scans, did not see it on the confirmation scans, did not see it when we began to operate, did not heed my colleague's warnings when they had noticed something odd in post-op."

"What happened?"

"I took away his ability to make new memories."

Prendrick looked at the floor. "And Sile – " Prendrick stopped himself.

Haig nodded. "That's why you're here. Sile found out."

"He covered it up. I don't know the details. He ran some of the company hospitals. He should never have been there, but his mother knew the Director of Aphelion Medical. She was a doctor, and his father an engineer. Sile was sent there to be out of the way, but he took an interest in spacebound medicine. He found out. He covered it up."

"Just like that."

"I had shakes, headaches, everything. I was not in my right mind. Sile told me that it would all be fine. Come with me, he said. A fresh start."

There was no fresh start here, thought Haig. Only fresh gunshine.

Haig said, "So you owe him."

Prendrick's head flicked up, a flash of anger in his eyes. "A prison of my own making. There are worse places than this to send a person, Haig. The universe is growing. Echion Alpha, Haig. If that woman in the fucking video knows what's good for her she'll stay where she is and burn alive. Allow hellfire to burn through her and be glad of it. Echion Alpha scares me more than this place ever could."

He opened a desk draw and pulled out a plain plastic bottle, then flicked the top off with practised ease. The gunshine smell surged.

"You judgmental prick. You don't care about Komarov or Mihalik or anyone else. You want to know what Sile told me to write in Komarov's autopsy."

"Sile said there wasn't a body."

"Even after a gallon of rocket fuel, I'm not going to autopsy an empty bed." He giggled. "'Nurse, this patient seems to have died from a bad case of piss-poor paperwork!'"

"What killed her?"

"She was hit in the back of the head with something blunt and heavy. A tool of some kind. Wrench, most likely. Then she was put in the suit. Body shows decomposition consistent with limited oxygen and having been sealed for a long time."

"She was murdered?" said Haig quietly.

"Yes she was fucking murdered, you moron." Prendrick picked his nose. Flicked something black onto his desk. "She was alive when she went into that suit and she died while she was in it. Now, you know where the door is," he said, sipping from the bottle.

Haig stood up slowly, looking Prendrick up and down.

"All that knowledge, up there," said Haig, tapping at his temple. "All wasted."

Prendrick sneered, put the bottle down, watched it wobble, groped pathetically at it, stopped the wobbling with the exaggerated care that drunkenness brought.

"Have you ever stopped to think about your role here, Haig? Your purpose?" He made a sweeping motion with his arm. "These people, all so caught up in whether he's got a fake eye or she was made with perfect vision, all forget. They forget that we're all the same. An expensively implanted eye gives you perfect vision. A genetically engineered eye gives you perfect vision. All the fucking same."

Prendrick picked the bottle back up. Took another sip.

"They all want the same things. Need the same things. When all of the other shit is stripped away, they'll realise that. This person's got implants and they make power? That person's got engineered genetics and they keep the air flowing? We can keep each other alive? Perhaps we are the same, after all. But you, Anson? You're here because some Sile clone is sat in some office, billions of miles away, and it makes them feel better that someone is trying to keep the peace. You're the most useless man in Gunport."

Haig stared.

"And yet," said Prendrick, pointing a shivering finger at Haig. "And yet, you're the only one that matters. The only one who will keep us alive. Don't you see? Your responsibility? These gene-edits will kill everyone with implants before they admit they need them. The implants will tear the gene-edits apart for the same reason. You're the peacekeeper. The man in the middle. If you fail, Haig," he said, rolling his head back, searching the concrete ceiling for his next sentence.

"If you fail, we will all sit here, in the fucking flames, in a concrete kingdom full of bones and fire, and realise how foolish we were. How much we need each other. You know who did this. Who is responsible. Who did everything. You know it. In your bones. Everybody knows it. Everybody has always known it. From the moment you saw her. We all know."

Prendrick's eyes were wet. He pushed his fingers into them, far too deep. Haig watched until he worried that Prendrick was going to hurt himself, so he stepped forward to pull his hands out, before Prendrick took his hands away himself.

"Who?" said Haig quietly.

"Who do you think?"

Underneath Prendrick's fingers were bloodshot eyes, raw and twitching. He looked at the tears on the ends of his fingers, his eyes wide. He rolled one around his finger and onto his fingernail, then flicked the tears at Haig in a slow, deliberate way. Haig stood and watched them hit the desk and then his shirt, dark stains fading on landing.

Prendrick licked his fingers. "Not a drop wasted."

CHAPTER 10: ROTTEN IN THE CORE

The Core was a hub of cables and electronics, Galatea's skin peeled back, the pulse and machinery of Galatea opened up to be served by Janulis and her team.

Haig strode out, limping, and was hit with a wall of heat.

This much circuitry spinning in one place meant vast, sickly warmth. He stood for a moment, adjusting. He felt the sweat roll down his back. He ran a hand across his forehead then wiped it on his trousers. Cramped cylindrical corridors ran off in different directions.

Janulis would have had you believe that there was order in the Core, thought Haig. He'd met people like her before. She believed that every wire and cable and hard-drive fulfilled a great purpose in service of some divine being. Haig thought it looked like a computer had exploded and expelled wires instead of flame. He tried not to stand on anything important.

In the next room, a man hunched around a cable on the floor was snipping wire and soldering. He was damp and grimy, his hair matted at the back.

"Where's Felix Blatt?"

"Blatt's working on something for Janulis," the man said carefully, without turning around. "At the end of this corridor. If I thought you'd understand, I'd explain it to you."

Haig stopped himself from saying something unhelpful and moved down the corridor.

There were thick tangles of cable spilling out of panels in the walls, all falling around his feet. He had to pick his way carefully, using his hands to lean against the wall, balancing. As he reached the end of the corridor, the first man he saw skipped past, dancing effortlessly around the tangles of cables.

Haig emerged into a low, rounded room. The walls were no longer concrete, but a brushed, shining metal, pocked with dents and scuffs. A server stretched from his feet to high above, a tower that blinked and whirred and clicked. The thick wires around his feet were Galatea's roots, embedded into the concrete. Footsteps clanged on gantries above.

Janulis and Blatt were deep in conversation, their arms folded. They stood in front of a large tank that glugged with thick bubbles, the liquid within sloshing gently. Blatt jabbed a finger at a screen on the side of the tank, to which Janulis shrugged.

"Felix told me why you're here, Anson Haig," said Janulis suddenly, echoing. She didn't turn around. She muttered something else to Blatt. Haig's stomach tightened. He felt dizzy.

"We don't have time for you," she said.

Haig stared at the back of her head. "I need to speak to him," said Haig, pointing at Blatt's back.

She huffed loudly and turned around. Haig rubbed his damp face.

Blatt turned, and met Janulis' eye briefly with a glinting smile. His eyes were dull and unfriendly and his lips curved artificially, mechanically.

"There should be a flow of very cold liquid being pumped around Galatea's mechanistry," said Janulis, as if to a child, "And there currently isn't. Soon, she will begin to overheat. When a human nervous system has a seizure, Anson, do you know what happens?" She raised her eyebrows at him, aggressive, demanding. "The brain sends all manner of contradictory signals. Constrict this muscle. Relax that muscle. Do it again, faster, then slower. The patient writhes and flops."

Yes, yes, thought Haig. The AI was having a cardiac arrest, and Janulis was the vital restorative electric shock. Or Galatea was suffering a stroke, and only she could root out the clot of code in the brain.

Haig folded his arms and shifted his weight. He was tired of their condescension. He knew what coolant was. Had sent it as a gesture of goodwill in more than one negotiation. Hostage takers in space always forgot that they had to maintain the facility they were in to keep themselves alive, never mind hostages.

Janulis said, "When Galatea is sick, she will have a seizure. Open this valve. Close that hatch. Vent that pipe. But there's air in that valve. And water in that pipe. So now, we are all dead."

And then she opened her hands out, palms towards Haig, and her voice softened. "She is more important than some girl getting herself into trouble. Perhaps John will remind you later."

"I've come here in good faith," said Haig. "I want to give Blatt every opportunity to explain himself."

"Explain myself?" Blatt sneered. "To you?"

Janulis raised her hand. "Explain what?"

"You attacked Mihalik," said Haig.

Janulis said, "Dekker and Holden investigated. Mihalik was troubled, a known manipulator and inventor of convincing fictions. If she told you that Felix was responsible, you are not to be blamed for believing her."

"I defended myself," said Blatt.

"She was obviously a threat to you," said Haig.

Blatt bristled. He brought himself up to his full height,

towering over Haig.

"She killed herself not long after," said Haig.

Blatt opened his mouth before a glare from Janulis silenced him.

"She was unwell," said Janulis. "Unfortunate, but hardly Felix's fault."

Haig willed himself neutral. Wanted to say, and that makes it alright to rape her? Instead, he said, "What did she say?"

"I've no more to say about this," she said. "You've stepped well out of your area of responsibility. You should be dealing with Acaba. When will the strikes end?"

Haig glared at the hulking Blatt. Blatt looked through him, his face tight and calm, his eyes indifferent, two black marbles glinting in the half-dark. Haig reeled against the contempt. The arrogance. He wouldn't have it.

"I think you're a murderer," said Haig. "I think you raped Mihalik to stop her telling me who was in the suit. You might not have actually put her in the Airlock, but you did everything else. I think she would've told me that Komarov was in the suit. Your old colleague, Petra Komarov. A programmer, like you. I came here to ask about her, but I think I already know. You argued. About something. It doesn't matter. Water algorithms. Maybe you didn't like them. Maybe they were better than yours. She was killed with a single powerful blow to the back of the head. That's you, Blatt. You hit her and killed her, then put the body in a suit and dumped her outside and hoped that no-one would ever notice."

Janulis stared at Haig and cocked her head to speak to Blatt. "Don't worry, dear. I'll straighten this out for you. He's going to get himself in trouble if he carries on."

Haig's hand was suddenly on his gun. He did not put it there consciously, but there it was. He forced it away before it could take the gun out. Blatt made him want to shoot something.

"There is no need, Alison," said Blatt softly. His irises were surrounded by the whites of his eyes, open and unblinking. "I understand. A small, impotent man is threatened by a large, intelligent one. Implants could not make him whole, so he tries to take me down."

"This conversation is finished," said Janulis, "I shall tell Sile everything you have said."

Janulis and Blatt turned back to their coolant problem. They started to swirl, melting together. They turned and looked at him together, then turned back. Continued urgent whispers. Haig wiped his forehead, hand shaking, and stumbled out. He was pouring with sweat when he got back to the Elevator. It started its descent.

Haig slapped his greasy hands against the walls and bent double and inhaled deeply over his knees.

He hadn't regained his breath before Blatt leaned down and came up next to him and whispered, "My quarters. Late. Come alone. I was told to attack her."

Blatt stood and said loudly and made sure he was heard, "I'll break your hands to powder if you come here again."

**

Dekker was in front of Haig in the Food Hall. He received a tray of food, held it in one hand, pressed his wrist against the machine's scanner, used his override, received a second tray of food.

He looked up, saw Haig watching him. He said, "Eat when you can, right? You're an Army guy, you get it." Then, very slowly, meeting Haig's eye, Dekker said, "You never know when you'll next have the chance. This might be the last meal you ever have."

Dekker sat down, carefully combined the contents of both trays into one, and stabbed his first over-sized mouthful onto a plastic fork.

Fucking prick, thought Haig. He spied Choudhury and sat across from him.

"Thank you, for your advice," said Choudhury.

"What advice is that?" said Haig, poking the gruel, his appetite now nil.

"To try something new," said Choudhury, his eyes shining. "I thought about the problem as purely physical, the ice as a barrier to be destroyed. I thought of the water, the flowing, unfrozen water, as the key, but there is enough in the ice for what we need. Harder to collect, certainly, but I have ideas, again. Ideas that might generate enthusiasm, funding."

"You're welcome." Haig went to pick up the protein block, studied its texture, felt an involuntary twitch in his stomach, and put the block down again.

Choudhury leaned forward, conspiratorial. "Why has a Briefing been called?"

"What Briefing?" He had no idea what Choudhury was talking about. "What have you heard?"

"Sile has called an additional briefing," said Choudhury. "I don't know what for. I hear nothing. I'm very much outside of the circle. I thought perhaps that you might have succeeded in your mission. That the strike might be over."

If it was, it simply proved how far out of the loop he was. Haig shook his head. "I don't know, Hasan."

"A lot has happened," said Choudhury. Then, whispering, "I have been asked what I think would happen if the leadership of certain other departments changed, if Galatea could run itself, whether my expertise ran to fusion reactors. Theoretical, I am assured, but with the kind of specific detail that strayed dangerously close to practical."

Haig put his spoon down and pushed the tray away.

"It's finely balanced," said Haig. "Programmers and Reactor

techs. Implants and gene-edits. Management and staff. Each side looking for allies and support. I thought it would be a personal grudge between Sile and Acaba and I'd only have to settle between them, but it runs much deeper. There's a rot here, Hasan. A lot could be lost. You're neutral, more or less. Both sides will want you for what you can do."

Choudhury stared at his food. A few heads raised, glanced over, looked away again.

"See you after Briefing, I suppose," said Choudhury, and left.

Haig was unsettled. Blatt had admitted that he set out to attack Mihalik under orders. Now Haig wanted to know who it was. And why.

He sighed, waited a moment, then tipped the tray into the Recycler. His e-sleeve started to vibrate. Messages, from Earth. From Olivia. From Mangan.

He went to the Elevator, double speed. Offered those he walked past a curt nod, pained smile. Got to his quarters. Locked the door, opened the screen. It took a great deal of willpower not to break it when the unskippable Echion Alpha video started. Haig breathed. In, and out. And in.

Finally, he opened the first message. A short video message from Olivia.

"Mangan called me," she said. "They're going to pull the money unless you fall back into line. He says you've breached your contract. You've been fighting Aphelion. That's all they would tell me. They wouldn't answer any more questions. Makes me think there's more to it. Makes me think you might say something different. Tom and I will make do. We have done so far. You've always been stubborn, Anson. Do the right thing by Tom and I'm there with you."

The message ended and the second started.

"Haig, it's Mangan. Complaints have been made against you. The EO there says you're not neutral. It's the only thing you had to be. What happened to you? You've gone native? I'll bridge the gap for Liv and Tom until you're back, but there's no housing. You're done. You're coming home, Anson. Whether the strike breaks or not."

Both messages sent a few days ago. Acaba was ending the strike imminently. That had to be what Sile's briefing would be about. He would victoriously declare an end to the strike, no doubt through his own Herculean efforts, and announce a redoubling of effort to land ships and shuttles. Barnes and Tobin would be able to stop doing busywork and prepare for real work. No doubt you will be delighted, Sile would say.

So. Lines were being drawn. Punitive, vindictive. Sile, reminding Haig what he stood to lose.

Haig sagged over his knees and felt exhaustion reach into his neck and back, and he wallowed in it, allowed it to ooze through his bones and into his legs, and felt it seep into fingers and toes, and wanted to let it consume him.

He felt so tired, suddenly. The kind of tiredness that would be so very easy to surrender to. Perhaps Sile would take him back, after all. A warm embrace. Rejoin us, he might say. All is forgotten. Come back to ignoring bad things. Prendrick might have been right. Perhaps he knew exactly who. Leave your soul at the door and come on in.

But Komarov had been murdered. And so.

He had no proof. Everything was circumstantial. How didn't you see it? No-one remembers her leaving? Ah, well, we have records of her arriving on the Moon. Where is she now? We don't know where she is now. But those records were falsified, because we have her body here. Falsified? Mistakenly entered, perhaps. Falsified? No, we don't think so. Falsified? Human error. Falsified? Computer error. Falsified? Differing interpretations. Falsified? Alternative perspectives. And on and on –

These ridiculous retorts, so calm and logical, so convincingly delivered, so thoroughly absurd. She might have faked the records herself, they would say, chasing this hare-brained theory about water algorithms. Her superiors report that she was difficult to work with. Yes, that must be it. And she was careless. She didn't check that the suit had a radio and locator. She went outside because? She was joy-riding. They would open their faces into the most brazen of lies and repeat it until they themselves believed it could be true, and with each passing repetition, another person would feel the doubt cast by the heaviness of a thousand lies until finally, she *was* joy-riding and the only question was *why*.

You're being negligent, Anson, they would say. Consider the safety of people in your care. They're not important? Wait a moment: now that you are finally responding to your primary duty, you've over-reacted? Disproportionate time and resources taken away from negotiations to accuse a vital member of our team? And it seems there are personal, aggravating factors. You haven't got any implants, have you? You've got something against a gene-edited person, haven't you?

Perhaps you too are difficult to work with.

Perhaps you too will find yourself floating outside in a spacesuit, without a locator.

Haig stood up, his teeth grinding, and he roared, and he crashed his prosthetic foot raggedly through the plastic stool again and again and again until it was obliterated. The room was showered in slivers of plastic. He spent a minute kicking it uselessly around the room until his breath heaved and every stumbling step brought crunches of ground plastic underfoot.

So. Jump in feet first. Let's see Blatt.

***

The corridor outside of Blatt's room was empty.

There was a spatter of concrete dust and a brief shudder, the lights clanked off, flickered, then returned. Shadows rolled through the corridor.

Haig looked at the door for a moment, then pulled his pistol, slid the clip out, reloaded it, reholstered it.

Haig knocked.

Blatt opened the door and loomed in it, looking down at Haig. His face was blank, hard. His hair was wet, his face clean. Faint smells of meat and mint. There was an electronic whine, undulating, masquerading as music.

Haig saw a twitch at the corner of Blatt's mouth. His eyes brightened, curious.

Blatt said, "Come in."

Blatt switched the screens and music off, then took a folding chair – thin, plastic, buckled – and placed it in the centre of the room, watching Haig the entire time. He unfolded it and hit it down, eyes on Haig's, slow and deliberate. He sat on the stool in front of the desk and faced Haig, never turning his back.

Haig pointed at the chair. "You have a lot of guests?"

"More than some, less than others."

Haig picked up the chair. He wanted distance between them. Didn't want Blatt controlling the space. He placed its back against the wall, then sat down.

For someone who had been invited, Haig felt especially unwelcome. He hadn't expected Blatt to pour information forth, but was unsettled by this naked hostility. Something wasn't right.

"You said you were told to attack Mihalik," said Haig. "Told to rape her?"

"Yes," said Blatt.

Silence. Silence. Stretching out –

"Why? Who by?"

"That poor girl," said Blatt, the corners of his mouth twitching. The prick's hiding a smile, thought Haig. "I did not think that she would feel so guilty about what happened as to kill herself. I didn't realise she cared so much for me."

Oh, this fucker –

Wait. Calm. Haig realised he was being manipulated. Blatt had been told to find out who Haig had been working with. Haig took a moment. Breathed. Wouldn't let Blatt get under his skin. Thought about how he could get under Blatt's skin. Let's throw some names out. See if he bites.

"I know you feel guilty about what happened," said Haig. "But please don't. She had a lot of other things going on in her life and you were one of a long list. You shouldn't feel guilty for her taking her own life. How could you have known that would happen?"

It felt like ash in his mouth to say, but Haig was prodding at Blatt's vanity. Of course he knew it would happen that way. It was whether he could accept the insult to his intellect –

"Alison Janulis is the Head of Artificial Intelligence and the single most important person at Gunport."

"Such a tragedy. Perhaps she felt like she had taken some control over what was happening."

Blatt blinked.

"You have no idea what I am to this place," said Blatt. "What I do for Gunport every single day."

Pivot, thought Haig –

"Petra Komarov," said Haig. "She was a programmer, just like you. What do you remember about her?"

Blatt blinked. "Just like me?" said Blatt, sneering. "She was not like me."

"You were both Programmers."

"She was blunt, careless. Inefficient."

"How?"

"Her code leaked. Her algorithms were like lace, letting everything slip through."

"She wasn't good at her job?"

"She was not right for Galatea."

"That's not an answer."

"No, she was not good at her job."

"Does Alison agree?"

"Yes."

"So you and Komarov disagreed. You argued."

"There were no arguments. She was told what to do. Then she either did it to an acceptable standard, or she did it again."

"Did you have to tell her what to do a lot?"

"Implants fray the mind. She tried to do things beyond her."

"What things?"

"Algorithms of her own design. Flimsy."

"So you didn't like it when she took initiative?"

"Galatea works because everyone completes their tasks."

"She didn't complete them?"

"Not well."

"But you don't judge that. Janulis does. There's nothing in Komarov's file about poor quality of work. Perhaps Alison doesn't agree with you after all."

Blatt adjusted his legs in the chair and tilted his head back, looking at Haig down his nose.

"You know a lot about Mihalik. How did you find out?"

"That doesn't matter. You said you were told to attack her. Are you good at doing what you're told?"

"It depends who asks."

"Did Komarov go to Dekker? Janulis? Sile? about you?"

"It wouldn't have mattered if she had."

"Maybe Sile would think twice. Makes it seem like you have some problem with implants. That's most of the Reactor."

Blatt narrowed his eyes. "We have an understanding."

"Understands what? That you felt so threatened by a small woman with implants that you punched her, or that you've got a pattern of violent behaviour? Which is it?"

"You don't know what you're talking about. Perhaps you should go back to following orders like a good little lapdog."

"Perhaps you should go back to following your own. Until Sile starts to think you're useless and casts you aside."

Blatt's cheeks reddened. The half-smirk fell away. His nostrils flared, his eyebrows tightened. Haig slid a hand discretely towards his pistol.

Blatt rocked on his stool and blinked at Haig, the rest of his face stony and cold, a bead of sweat forming above his top lip.

"He wouldn't."

"Sile's special little employee. Did he tell you how important you were?"

"Be quiet."

"How vital you were to the success of Gunport? How you're all in it together? Except you're not, are you? Follow the rules and succeed, and you'll do well. That's what Sile tells everyone. There are perks in it for you. Extra water. But when Sile doesn't like the rules, he just changes them. Changes his mind. Ignores them when it suits him. Ignores you. Casts you aside."

"That's not true."

"As soon as he thinks you've made a mistake, as soon as he thinks you can't help him, you're done. You're finished. You're not special, Blatt. You're jealous. So insecure you had to attack a woman because she was friends with someone who made you feel weak."

Blatt gripped the bottom of the stool, tight, his knuckles whitening.

Haig pushed on. "He doesn't care about you. He cares about Gunport and his project. You're expendable. Just like me. Just like everything else."

Blatt shattered his stool with bare hands and took a giant step forward, scooping Haig up with one shovel-hand, holding him in the air by his throat.

Haig started to gargle and choke, hanging from Blatt's hand, thrashing his feet in the air, fists crashing uselessly against Blatt's arms.

Blatt's voice was calm, curious. He seemed faintly surprised to find himself strangling someone.

"You had to keep pushing, didn't you?" he said. "For five minutes, perhaps more, I have been thinking about killing you. Methods and consequences. Of snapping your neck, and thinking about what would happen next. Nothing so wasteful as the use of an entire spacesuit. Perhaps taking you apart and feeding you into the Recycler. Melt you in the Chemical Line. Perhaps I could pull at each knuckle and joint and limb until they pop apart. You'd be missed, of course. Komarov and Mihalik will be forgotten, but your IPRA simply would not accept your disappearance. I would fake your departure, I think. And leave with the same shuttle. Perhaps I would alter your biometric profiles and *become* you. Arrive on the moon as Anson Haig, the disgraced former soldier, washed up and useless, but slightly taller than anyone remembered. Perhaps visit your ex-wife and son and remind them just how tall you are. How tall you were."

He licked his lips. "And now that you flop here, your life is forfeit. If only you hadn't pressed. I wasn't asked to kill you. Other plans are in place. But, it will accomplish the same purpose."

Haig's eyes were bulging, his hands slapping and groping at Blatt's face, at his hands.

Blatt sighed, bored of his own threats. He poked Haig's head with his other hand, a firm, hard finger. Haig's tongue was stuck out, swollen.

"Inside here is a small mind, struggling to understand what it can do, what it knows. This is nothing compared to what I have done."

Haig tried to breathe, failed, snorted, a spatter of snot shooting from his nose, thick strings across Blatt's arm.

Reach –

"Of course I knew that Mihalik would kill herself. And I think you know that. You're cleverer than I allowed for, Haig. Sometimes it is brought home to us how proud or vain we are. An assault such as that to dredge up her trauma and insecurity. A few words spoken softly into her ear while I had her bent over. And then watch her go. Doing exactly as I knew she would."

Just reach the –

"In time, my work on Galatea will be understood. I will be recognised for what I am. And you will be forgotten. Like a grain of sand in the wind."

Haig's air was nearly gone. His eyes rolled up in his head.

So close, reach the *fucking* –

Haig gurgled, "Who?"

Blatt laughed. "Sile. Of course, Sile."

Reached –

There was a loud pop. Blatt's face contorted. His hand twitched. Then he dropped Haig. Looked at him. Haig sprawled to the floor, gasped, sucking in glorious, painful, recycled air.

Blatt put a hand to his throat, then regarded it with dull wonder, red and slick. His throat bleeding a steady stream onto his shirt. He clasped one hand to it and pointed the other at Haig. There was no pain on his face, only anger and disbelief.

Haig held his own throat with one hand, massaging the bruises. His pistol in the other.

He moved a hand from his throat to cover his face. Gene-edit skulls were notoriously tough. Haig expected bullets to bounce back.

Blatt regained his composure and snarled, gouts of blood gushing, took a step forward.

Haig calculated the risk. Blatt managed another step, hands outstretched, leading with his thumbs, looking for Haig's eyes.

Haig looked away and emptied the pistol into Blatt's face.

A handful of bullets bounced off his skull into the ceiling, sheared off into the desk behind, shattering plastic. Shards of porcelain and plastic sprayed around the room.

Haig winced at the ricochets and when he turned back, Blatt had stopped in the middle of the room, raising a shaking hand to his obliterated face, trying to push a piece of his cheek back up, the bare skull beneath scorched but intact. Both of his eyes were gone.

Blatt gargled, then toppled forward, landing with a dull boom, concrete dust thrown into the air.

He gurgled and wheezed and then he died.

CHAPTER 11: KNOWING IS NOTHING

"Congratulations are in order," said Sile.

"I know that we have had our disagreements. That things have not always gone as smoothly as they could have, but you didn't travel billions of miles to get here because things were going well, did you?"

Staring up at the ceiling in the smallest room of the Medical Bay had been his only view for a day. Wecht found him unconscious in Blatt's blood, so she and Kaneda hauled him in and made Bethe tend to his injuries.

Haig's neck had thick, ugly bruises along it, Blatt's hand imprinted into his throat. He struggled to breathe enough to stay awake for very long, ragged breaths followed by a slow hiss, like air escaping a broken valve. Bethe had slapped a chemical bandage to his neck to accelerate his healing. Haig remembered how annoyed he was about using it.

Now Sile was here, sat next to Haig's bed, barely containing his glee. Haig swallowed and felt like he was forcing a squash ball down his throat. He couldn't bring himself to speak. It was him. Sile had killed Komarov. Or ordered it.

"I'm delighted," said Sile. "I am. You are to be congratulated. We have already begun our preparations to receive the next supply shuttle, which is due to arrive well ahead of schedule. Weeks, rather than months. The faith that IPRA and Aphelion have placed in you to achieve success. It was as if Aphelion knew that you would be the difference, Haig. You deserve your housing. After everything you've been through. I was premature in contacting IPRA, and I've contacted them again to let them know that. Whatever you said to Acaba certainly worked. You missed the Briefing, I'm afraid, but the whole of Gunport knows."

When Haig coughed, his eyes pulsed and his brain throbbed and his throat roared. He glared. Sile was oblivious. Sile was lost in the sound of his own voice.

"I can see you're not comfortable speaking yet. Well, let me tell you something Anson." His voice lowered. "Of course you were right about Blatt and Komarov and Mihalik. Of course you were. But you must understand that I have an entire facility full of people to protect. I could not in good conscience have my staff believing that there were dead bodies appearing all over the place. Suicide has happened before, so I wasn't concerned with that, but the idea of someone having been killed and put outside, well. That's just too much for some to bear. People wouldn't understand. How distracted everyone would be from our purpose here. I'm delighted that you've put this to bed, Anson. Broken a strike up and brought justice to a murderer! It's a shame that it was Blatt. He was a good programmer. He always did what was asked. Now that he's dead, perhaps everyone can settle down. See that justice has been done. Dekker and Holden found evidence that he was planning to take implants from other women. It seems that he had some contraband surgical tools. They are investigating, but I'm sure that will be complete soon."

How convenient, thought Haig. Wrapped up so very neatly. All roads lead to Blatt. Especially the ones that were built after he was dead. Sile's putting all of this at Blatt's feet. He thinks it's going to go away.

"I've submitted my reports," continued Sile. "IPRA doesn't

deserve you. Be careful. Aphelion might try to poach you all for themselves."

Sile leaned down. "Let me be clear, Anson. I know we had our difficulties, but I'm delighted that everything is resolved. Everything. No holdovers. No lingering desire to do anything more. No little threads for you to pull on. None. Reopening old wounds would lead to significant new ones. And I won't be responsible for what happens to those who open old wounds, Anson."

Sile slapped his thighs and got up. "Well," he said. "I'll see you when you're back on your feet. You'll be with us for a while longer until your shuttle's fixed. Onwards, Anson. I have so much to prepare for!"

Haig seethed thick-throated.

***

He drifted in and out of sleep. Wecht had visited, Dekker too. Wecht spoke, Dekker glared. He sensed urgent whispers, harsh tones, people pointing at him.

When he was lucid, he thought about Blatt. Blatt had been engaged by Sile to attack Mihalik. This much was true. A hook on which to hang other facts. An anchor in the swirl of bullshit that Sile was bound to vomit forth.

With Blatt dead, Sile had had a number of lies available with which to suck Haig into. He whittled it down to two. Haig could be the man who captured a terrifying rapist and murderer that had driven innocent women to suicide, or he could have brutally and mercilessly assassinated a programmer – in his own home – who had worked so tirelessly to keep the good people of Gunport alive. He could be hero or villain. Both embarrassed Haig.

Sile had chosen to make him a hero. At least for now. He'd shown he could burn narratives and build new ones without any care for honesty. He was a moral gymnast, gold medal in brazen and shameless reversals. Haig was now a hero, but Sile could have easily made him a villain.

Wecht visited. She prodded his bruises and winced before he did.

"Looks painful," she said.

He groaned, nodded. Of course it is.

"The swelling's reduced," she said. "You'll be fine in a day or two."

She leaned in, whispering. "You got lucky."

Haig closed his eyes and breathed her in. Gunport soap, skin, sweat. Different smells for different things. Arms and hands of chemical soap. Armpits of something warmer, sour. He thought she smelled fantastic.

She sat up and cleared her throat, wiped her eyes, laughed nervously.

"I get the feeling you wanted to have done things differently," she said. "But I'm grateful that you risked your life to do something for them." She frowned suddenly, her voice dropping, looking for Bethe. "Every time I walk past one of them – they're all taller than me, and look at what just one of them did to you – every time, I feel nervous. Stomach all bunched up. People I could say hello to, who knew me, now won't say anything. Lots of sneers, people looking away. People are taking sides, Anson."

"No compromise left," said Haig, rasping. He swallowed, tilted his head back to get the lump past the bruising.

"Yeah," she said. He noticed then the deep lines across her face.

***

He woke to a gentle, metallic chittering a day – maybe two – later, and his throat ached but didn't roar. He massaged it from chin to collar bone and found it suppler, malleable, happier to let him breathe. His leg had been removed, placed on a stool to the side of the bed.

"Haig," said Retallick, stood beside him.

"Conrad," said Haig, smiling. "You're awake."

"I am," said Retallick. "I've been waiting for you."

Retallick had aged. Skin around his eyes was flaccid, wrinkled, hanging around the sockets. New lines had formed at the corners of his eyes, the edges of his mouth. He looked like he was wearing a mask made of his own face.

The rail of the bed clanked. Retallick's new metallic hands, skeletal and hollow, metal fingertips chittering against metal palms.

Haig stared at them, tried to swallow, moved his eyes to Retallick's face before he was caught staring, then said, "How are you feeling?"

"Bethe says I can't put them under water yet," said Retallick, rolling the fingers the wrong way, double-jointed but beyond, touching the back of his wrist. "Not that there's enough water here. You can see the joins here, and here," he said, pointing at angry welts that sealed his new hands to his arms. "There will be no swimming in the sea." He snorted bitterly. "Sile has made a fool of you, Anson. He waited until you were in this bed and made a fool of you."

One of Retallick's fingers whirred, then began to jerk monotonously. Retallick stared at it, trying to bend it to his will, until sweat popped across his forehead. He gripped his wrist with his other hand, wrestling with his own arm.

Haig looked out into the corridor, shouted, "Bethe."

"No," snarled Retallick. "No, no," and the finger was still.

A moment.

A beat.

Retallick exhaled. Released the hand. Looked at Haig and

smiled, relieved. Haig smiled back.

Then they watched the whole hand lurch out of control. The fingers twisted backwards and chittered at right angles against the back of his hand, then snapped forward, like they wanted to launch from his hands, twisted back again.

Retallick slumped to the floor, staring helplessly at the whirling mess of fingers, the chittering getting ever more violent –

"Bethe," shouted Haig, louder, trying to get up, head swimming, panting, throat roaring, dizzy dizzy dizzy –

Bethe slid in with a syringe. Retallick flapped at him, trying to push him away, while Bethe tutted, effortlessly wrapped an arm around Retallick's chest to hold him down, then injected him in the neck. Retallick went limp, the fingers hung from his hands like lengths of string, and Bethe guided him to the floor.

"Relax, Conrad," said Bethe. He collected a plastic stretcher – a board, really – from the wall. Bethe bent down and slid this enormous man with his metal limbs smoothly onto the stretcher, effort minimal, then pushed through his knees, lifted the entire weight to his chest, Retallick and all, then hauled him out.

"Bethe," he rasped. "Duncan, for fuck's sake."

Bethe re-entered smoothly, the effort of single-handedly carrying a man in a stretched having never registered. He placed Haig carefully back onto the bed.

"The shouting suggests that you're feeling better."

"What happened?"

"The implants have been difficult to integrate. Imsups are at a premium. They are slow to make, too, so Conrad has a choice. Or, I have made the choice for him. He'll be in moderate pain for a long time instead of no pain for a short time then agonising pain all of the time."

"Fucking hell, Duncan," said Haig. "Give him painkillers. Ambro, manzo. And I know you've got some other combat stuff for the heavy industrial accidents."

"I don't have the energy for this again."

"Again?"

"I've danced to this tune with Sile, Prendrick. Unauthorised. Always unauthorised. 'We may need them in the future, Duncan.' A myriad of what-ifs. What if this happens? What if that? I have a sick man here, and my experience will heal him. I will repair him, body certainly, the mind if it is willing. And they don't care. They ignore my expertise. Why prevent a doctor from using medicine?"

"We must be able to do something."

"Let me tell you a story, Anson. When I first arrived, this place was lethal. And I do not exaggerate. The masks in the Pit did not fit correctly. Men suffocated in there. The Chemical Line spilled and splashed and cost limbs. Acids and alkalis there are potent, Anson. Lack of water. Lack of food. Gravity failures. Imagine, if you will, the gravity failing while you work in the Pit. Before you know what is happening, you are three floors up. And then you go down. Not into a cushion but into concrete. Bones pulped. Faces unknown. And so I asked for a new surgeryI argued that a new theatre would help me to improve the people working there. Provide implants, repair broken bones, frozen hands, crushed legs. Did you ever stop to think why Tobin, who spends every moment in the Pit, would create his own toxic liquor?"

He looked hard at Haig, his tone harsh, and Haig didn't answer.

"Yes, well," Bethe continued. "A year or two here would cost a lifetime. Atrophied bones and muscles were the least of Aphelion's concerns. You know the risks, they said. And for me, the risks were minimal. Denser bones, thicker muscles, and so on. But spending years here for you means going back to Earth would be like living underwater for the rest of your life. How did you feel when you came out of the B-DC? Imagine that that became your life. I wanted my patients to have lives beyond this place. I fought for it, and was granted it. Sile's bosses granted it. It took a year to build, a slice at a time, the very surface of this hideous place being mined for Hiro's printers, working and working, combined with equipment and resources shipped from Earth."

"You got what you wanted?" said Haig.

"A victory," said Bethe, smiling.

The smile became a grimace. "But be careful what you wish for. I was told that I should be excited to use this new theatre. That I should enjoy it for a longer time, given how forcefully I had asked. For another two years, in fact. And so Sile gleefully extended my contract. 'What is Gunport', he said, 'without talented people? Without people who want to make things better.' He offered it as – " Bethe shook his head, searching for a word, " – a reward."

"Two years is a long time."

Bethe shrugged. "I endure. And I prioritise pain, Anson. I choose who suffers and for how long. And it should be up to me when to relieve it, when not to. Prendrick understands this, too. He is the worst because he understands it but does as Sile tells him."

Haig shook a hand at the pill bottles on the other side of the room. "What did he authorise for me?"

"For you?" Bethe's eyes were fierce, shining. "Just me. A doctor of my expertise shouldn't be anywhere near you. On Earth, you wouldn't even have needed a nurse. Rest."

"He nearly fucking killed me, Duncan."

"And you certainly killed him."

"Mihalik killed herself because of him. Would you have given *him* manzo? Ambro? Would Sile have authorised it for *him*? You know he would have. Tick a different box on an inventory form. That's all it would take."

"If he was lying in a bed in my Medical Bay then I would use all of my considerable talent to help him. Even if that meant him walking out whole and you lying in wait to shoot him all over again."

"Use all of your considerable talent and help Conrad."

Bethe sighed, looked at him, considering. Then he went to the pill bottles, swept them into his pockets, and left without looking back.

Haig eased back into his bed. This was the least he could do. Haig had encouraged Retallick to help him, made him promises, and now he needed to do something to make it right. The drugs were the very least he could do. He rubbed at the swelling on his neck.

He lay back, was grateful for thinking time. He'd spent far too much time reacting, moving around things, not focusing on the problem.

There was one question that came back again and again, that he couldn't address. A thought that had taken root in his mind, and however much he wrestled with it, or convinced himself he was thinking too much, or tried to rationalise it, it came back. A problem with an irresistible pull, like a black hole. An idea at the event horizon, that to grasp it and understand it would mean racing to the centre of the black hole and never allowing the solution to it to emerge. He thought about how to articulate it. How to investigate it.

He was convinced. Galatea was broken.

***

Bethe wheeled a sharper Retallick in the next day. He was tired, but lucid. Reasonable. One of his hands had been detached. We need his room, said Bethe. A fight gone bad. Another one. Bethe looked expectant. You'll be out of here soon, he said. You need to be out of here.

Retallick lay there, gently and rhythmically breathing, relaxed, hypnotic. Haig watched him, hoped he might turn and make eye contact.

"I'm sorry about all of this," said Haig.

"You have nothing to answer for, Anson."

Haig said nothing. Retallick breathed like he was drifting into a sleep. After a moment of silence, Retallick spoke.

"Sile visited me when I was awake. I was brave, he said. Heroic, even."

"What did he say?"

"He itemised it. How can we argue with a list of statistics, Anson?"

"Itemised what?"

"My service. My repairs. The time spent by my doctors."

"That's what we agreed."

"We did."

"But?"

"One year, now added on to my contract. My heroics have earned me my new implants, Sile says. The high costs of medical care."

"Fucking hell."

"He had the good grace to seem remorseful," said Retallick, staring glass-eyed at the ceiling, "But he reminded me that you asked. Next time, I'm staying put. Doing the right thing costs too much."

Haig didn't say, you did it for the year, not Komarov. I've given up my pain medication for you. I'd give you more if I could.

"I know who killed your mystery woman," said Retallick.

"She has a name now," said Haig. "Komarov. And everyone knows who killed her. It was Blatt."

"My contract should have run much longer," said Retallick. "Another year at least. I was given twelve months back for 'extraordinary services'. Do you know what those services were? When I found one of my suits missing and I filed a report, I also then decided to lose that report."

"Who?" said Haig, sitting up. "Who told you to lose your report?"

"Dekker," said Retallick.

Like he had been summoned, Dekker marched in.

He said nothing but kneeled down and searched under Haig's bed, prodding at the foam. Finally, he stood up and glared at Haig. He ripped the blankets away, shook them viciously, then dumped them on the floor, leaving Haig exposed in a paper gown. Blankets deliberately out of reach.

He said, "Move your head," already reaching out to Haig's pillow. He held it in one hand and beat it with the other, waiting for something to fall out. When it didn't, he tossed the pillow to the other side of the room and grunted.

"No weapons," sneered Dekker.

Under his breath, Haig said, "Prick."

Dekker walked around to Retallick and began to wheel him out. "How're your hands?" he said, not unkindly. "Prendrick did mine, and they took months. Then I got Bethe to re-do them. I should have skipped the first doctor, like you."

Retallick said nothing, so Dekker nodded, muttered "Okay," to himself, then took Retallick out.

Haig heard Dekker say to Retallick, "Sile thought you'd be more comfortable somewhere else."

**

The Food Hall was quiet.

Gunport's staff had ceased being in here alone, regardless of shift patterns. Groups sat at opposite ends and tried very hard to make it look like they're weren't weighing each other up. Little glances over trays. A word from one making another two look up. Eye contact that ended too abruptly.

Haig's tray popped out, some food belched out, a protein block thudded out, a vitamin sachet slapped out, and a cup of water squirted out.

The food had tasted slightly different since Blatt had tried to crush his throat. There was slightly more life to it, perhaps sweeter. Something, Haig was sure of it. He used the greying spoon to slice it into small cubes, then scattered the cubes among the bowl of food paste, mixing thoroughly.

"Someone's being adventurous," said Wecht, sliding in next to him.

"Every day an adventure, Sarah," he said, smiling.

"Not if you keep using the same old lines."

"It tastes better than it did," he said. "Something's been added."

"You're not the only person to say that, you know. A few of my patients think the food has changed."

Haig mulled it over, took a spoonful of freshly seasoned glob into his mouth and mock-chewed, then smacked his lips. "Delicious."

Wecht rolled her eyes and sighed. "How's your throat?"

"Sore," he said, realising that he was massaging it, then realising that she'd asked because he was massaging it. "I tried eating like I did before, big mouthfuls, get it down, but it was too painful."

She pointed at his bowl. "So your culinary experiments have been forced upon you? Maybe that's why it tastes different. Because you're tasting it."

"We both know that's not true," he said, smiling wider. "There's a lot to be said for butter."

"Tobin could probably get some for you."

Haig pushed his fork into the bowl with a squelch, his face tightening in disgust. Tobin could get mostly anything. But you had to be prepared to pay the price, thought Haig.

Acaba entered, tentative, flanked by another Reactor technician. They stood inside the doorway for a long moment, scanning the Food Hall. The technician balled and unballed his fists. Acaba folded her arms and scratched at her elbows.

Haig stared at her until she looked at him. He didn't like this. It was provocative. Daring someone to approach her or challenge her. Acaba stared back.

He was about to stand up when Wecht placed her hand on his arm, and said, "She's not here to cause trouble. She doesn't feel safe." Wecht pointed at the technician, said, "Neither does he."

Haig looked at her, nodded, then picked his fork up again. Not provocation. Safety. Protection.

"Everything that's happened has everyone on edge," said Wecht.

Acaba's group walked to the dispensers and got their food, then sat at the end of another table. Their faces were hard, stony, their shoulders hunched, their arms close to their bodies.

"It's not going to take much for it to go wrong, Sarah," said Haig. "Some people go in groups for protection, but too often, it emboldens people. Makes them think they can do things they can't. Or shouldn't. You get two groups together like that, and it quickly goes to shit."

"Not her," said Wecht.

"Fear does things to people," said Haig.

Acaba's group didn't speak, and even across the length of this room, Haig could hear them eating as quickly as they could, breathing heavily through their noses to get the black blocks down at speed.

Haig was silent for a long time, then moved back into his food.

"I've brought you a gift," said Wecht. She took a tablet from her pocket. "Komarov's correspondence. There are some gaps. I can't tell if they've been deleted by her or someone else. Everything I could get."

He took the tablet gently, carefully. Held it in front of him with reverence. He tucked it into his pocket and gripped the top of Wecht's hand.

"You didn't think I was done?" he said.

"Are you?"

He shook his head and smiled. She finished the last of her food and left.

When he looked up again, it was into Acaba staring at him. She nodded slightly, almost imperceptibly, and tapped her wrist. Time for what? thought Haig, and shrugged. She did it again, deliberately, slowly, and he looked at his e-sleeve. A message from her. He nodded.

Attar strode in, glaring at Acaba. She stared intently at her tray. The technician didn't. He looked right at him. He puffed his chest out, brought his shoulders straight, and his mouth became a frozen, unhappy smile.

Haig slid to the end of the bench. His hand gripped his pistol.

Attar collected his food and sat on a bench opposite. His head was perfectly straight above his perfectly straight shoulders. Not hunched, not relaxed, but straight. As if measured to be at a perfect right angle to the bench.

He spent a few moments adjusting the contents of his tray. Identical distances between items. The spoon parallel to the top of the tray. The fork parallel to the side. He was careful, gentle.

And the entire time, he was looking at Acaba's technician.

There was a flicker of something in the jawline. A tension. Clenching and unclenching of muscles.

Only his arm moved to scoop up his food.

He and the technician only had eyes for each other now.

Attar radiated neutrality, blankness. The technician's mask slipped when Attar started to eat his food with robotic precision. The technician's stared with far-too-open eyes. They began to water. Every sweep of Attar's arm followed the same pattern, down to the bowl, a spoon of food, smoothly up to the mouth, deposit the food, down and up in time to find the mouth only just empty. Each spoonful contained the same amount of food, the same amount of time chewing.

He would crush the technician in an instant, thought Haig. And anybody else. He had the relaxed power of a predator, comfortable in the hierarchy, no thought of its place ever being threatened.

The technician's smile slipped, and he looked away. Attar's eyes glittered. The mechanical eating slowed down.

He's enjoying this, thought Haig.

The technician glued his eyes to the bowl, sped up, ate everything, scraped his spoon around the bowl, then vaulted up, slotted it into the Recycler, then marched out. Acaba watched him go, unsurprised. Moments later, she had finished too, and left with an exaggerated carelessness.

Attar had nothing to do when they'd finished, so he shovelled the rest of his meal in, slotted his tray into the Recycler, and was gone.

Haig checked his e-sleeve. The message from Acaba said, "Barnes is terrified. Won't talk to me. Need to be you."

**

The 7th Floor had been large concrete cubes for storage, but some years ago they had been cleared and painted. Now they were used for squash.

Galatea's algorithms regimented strenuous exercise for everyone, at least two hours each day. When the gravity dipped below Earth standard – it dipped often, but nearly imperceptible, a slight bounce in someone's walk, a dropped pen hanging an extra moment in the air – muscles wasted, atrophied. It didn't make any difference in a week or a month, but over a few years, it added up. Hence the exercise.

Haig told Galatea that he wanted to play squash. Galatea reminded him he was missing a leg, so he swore at it and told it to do it anyway.

This wasn't satisfactory, so Galatea further scheduled the bike and some strength training. Galatea wanted him to play squash in Gunport's evening. Wecht helped him find an in with Barnes. He couldn't be approached directly. After all, Haig was a hero now, and the Komarov matter was solved and over. Never mind all of the unanswered questions around the details, and the *why* of it.

Haig's general mood had darkened since Blatt's death, made into something more like a low-level anger. He could release his frustrations by battering a ball around, but what he wanted was what Barnes knew. If he was afraid, he might help.

The corridor was barely wider than Haig's shoulders. A dull plastic crack echoed into the corridor, so Barnes was already here, warming up. Changing rooms would be a luxurious use of space, so Haig simply stashed his bag under a maintenance hatch outside the court.

Harsh lights reflected against white walls, and the back corners in particular were spattered with purple squash ball marks and sweat stains from greasy hands slapping against them. The room was too small for squash by at least a metre on every side, the floor was much harder than it could have been, but they made it work. Giant air duct fans roared and swooshed overhead, some purple balls lodged in gaps and joints, unrecoverable. They would be stuck there until the gravity failed and it rained squash balls.

"Hello Anson," said Barnes, stopping to catch a ball he'd been warming up.

He was bouncing on his toes, lightly sweating, smiling. Bloodshot eyes flittered and revealed nervousness.

"Barnes," said Haig, nodding. He sat on the floor and started to change.

"So," said Barnes. "Are you any good?"

"I won't embarrass myself," said Haig, "But that doesn't mean you won't win."

He took care with his prosthetic as he pulled off his trousers and folded them neatly on top of his boots, pulled on some shorts and squash shoes, then jumped up. Finally he took the racquet out of the bag – a 3D-printed Kaneda special, made of recycled desk plastic, he was very proud – and took his place in the service box.

"Very well," said Barnes. "Do you need some time to warm up?"

"I'm ready," said Haig.

Kesh tossed him the ball. "After you."

Kaneda made mottled purple balls for Gunport's squash players, most often from disintegrated washers that Maseko plucked from spoiled water valves. Something about the recycling of rubber discoloured them.

Haig served, all ragged power and rage, a straight smash. Kesh lurched, flicked it back, too high. Haig stepped in and cracked it low to the back corner, watching it bounce and sit up close to both walls. A loud clunk was Kesh's racquet hitting wall rather than ball, and the first point was Haig's.

They smacked the ball around for half an hour. Haig prodded at Barnes with questions about gossip and rumour, surface chit-chat hiding real intent. Barnes wasn't stupid, thought Haig. He knows what I'm doing. Probably knows he needs to nibble before it can go anywhere. I need to be careful too. Let's circle each other some more and call it a game of squash.

"No-one's talking about Blatt? Or Komarov? Really? Everywhere else I've been, this would keep the mill grinding for a month at least."

Barnes became slightly withdrawn, the pomp sucked out of him. "Gunport is different, I suppose."

"My serve, then," said Haig.

They were evenly matched until the last ten points or so. Haig's technique was better but he struggled with bending low, especially in the back corners. Barnes was faster but struggled to get the ball low enough or deep enough to make Haig work for it. Finally, Haig stepped it up and reeled off a handful of points. The game was over. They shook clammy hands and shared a mutual look of post-exercise exhaustion. Barnes got two wetseal towels and they wiped themselves down, put them in a sealed plastic bag.

"You'll be able to drink part of yourself later," said Barnes, pointing to the bag. The towels would keep the moisture until dropped into a Recycling chute and it was squeezed out, fed back into the water supply.

Haig held his stomach. "Don't. It's disgusting."

"I think what happened to Komarov was awful," said Barnes. "Simply awful."

"She was bashed over the head then stuffed in that suit," said Haig.

Barnes lowered his voice and said carefully, "At least Blatt got what he deserved."

"I wish it had gone differently," said Haig. "But he was told to bait me. Set a trap."

Barnes stared intently at his hands, scraping dirt from under his fingernails.

Haig said, "I think you can help me, Barnes. I think you know who sent him. It's an open secret here. But I need proof. Blatt is dead. Sile has either threatened or bribed everyone. They either enjoy the perks of being in his pocket or they want out."

"And which do you think I am?"

"I'm here to find out."

Barnes was trying to decide. He looked at Haig. Looked at the wall. Crossed his arms into his chest. Tried to disappear into himself.

Finally, he said, "He told me that he'd have my arms pulled out."

"Sile?"

"Yes."

"Why?"

"I was performing my usual duties. Part of them is reconciling what we have on our screens with what we can see. Normally it's very easy, because there isn't anything in the sky. An occasional meteor shower takes us by surprise and we tell the AI about it, which then tracks it. Often there's a gap in the tracking gear. On this day, a shuttle launch appeared in the logs. And there certainly hadn't been a launch. It was clearly an error because we were having difficulties with radiation from Domiyat. Zero chance of a successful landing or launching. Gorgeous on the screens but anything caught in it got fried. I had to advise a week's delay for everything incoming and I remember Sile being particularly unhappy. We had to use alternative routes and so on. Hide behind moons and planets and all the other tricks Galatea and Aphelion's flight planners use. Anyway, I questioned this log. I can't simply delete it, so I sent a message up to Sile. I thought this might be an error from Tobin, perhaps, where he might have simply said that a shuttle had launched instead of being unpacked, something like that. So I logged it and thought nothing else about it untile Sile came to see me."

Haig started. "Sile himself?"

"With Blatt."

"What did Sile say?"

"Didn't say anything, really. Told me to stop interfering and concentrate on my job. That if I said any more about this launch, Blatt would crush me into a cube and slot me into a Recycler. Then they told me that if anyone asked, Komarov had left on this false shuttle."

"Acaba asked?"

"Yes," said Barnes, "Acaba, Mihalik and Komarov were friends," and then he began weeping. All of the tension and frustration and fear came tumbling out of him and he sobbed.

"Will you help me?" said Haig. "Knowing is nothing. I need proof. Aphelion will remove him if I can prove it."

"What will change?"

"What?"

"What will change if Aphelion remove him?"

Haig blinked. "He won't be in charge anymore."

"Yes," said Barnes, wiping his cheeks. "Yes, he will. You're assuming he'll just accept what they say. They're billions of fucking miles away. Sile isn't just going to go and sit in the Tank. He'll fight this and he'll fight you. Aphelion have had supply ships circling us the entire time you've been here. I've invented the most ridiculous fictions explaining their presence on the board. Some monitoring satellites, I said, straight-faced. Just waiting for this strike to end, one way or another. They all have too much invested in Gunport. They know Sile's soiled goods. That's why they sent him here in the first place. They expected him to fail miserably. Somehow, out of dust, he built them a castle."

"There's no mystery to it. He built it on a foundation of sand. Look too closely and it falls apart."

"That doesn't matter if you can't get close enough to tear it down. You're assuming Dekker and Holden and Attar and Janulis and Prendrick and everyone else will just fall into line. Even Acaba realised this. You can't win. They won't help you. They won't. And if they say they will, it's because he's told them to for some other purpose. He's got them wrapped around his little finger. They all owe him. Or they're fucked if he's fucked. It's in their interest to make sure that doesn't happen. I was honest, and he would have snapped me in half. And after he'd finished telling me how easily I could be broken apart, he gave me extra shower minutes. A reward for my bravery, he said. Not seconds, Anson. Minutes. I have the most glorious showers, Anson. I'm clean. I stand and I turn the heat up and I remember how I got those minutes and I scald myself."

"Then help me. Have an honest forty seconds instead."

"Oh, Anson. You don't realise what you're doing. He's told everyone you're a hero so that he can destroy you. He's going to clean house, and you're top of the list."

Haig stared limply at Barnes. He had nothing.

CHAPTER 12: COUNTER-OFFER

Haig listened to the voice hissing through the screen and bristled at its contortions.

"Please, everyone," said Sile. "Some of you may not have met IPRA's representative, Anson Haig. I want to take this opportunity to tell you that if you see him, he is to be congratulated. Thank him. He has helped resolve our dispute and made us safer. He has done more in a matter of weeks than some of us have done in lifetimes. Grab his shoulder. Shake his hand. He has become one of us. Well done Anson Haig."

When he turned the screen on, Sile had replaced the woman heading to Echion Alpha, and Haig missed her.

Mangan had messaged: 'I don't know what happened, but IPRA have changed their tune. My boss called. Congratulations, they said. Wary, but happy. Looks like you might get your housing after all.'

Olivia had messaged: 'Mangan's called again. He said you're coming home but he doesn't sound happy about it. He was very pleased to tell us we'll be going back to the old house when you get back. Additional air filtration, a different doctor. I thought they were giving you a new house, somewhere out of the dust? I thought that's why you took this on. Mangan didn't want to talk about it. Something's bothering him. Be careful.'

Sile had messaged: 'Dinner, to celebrate our guest's successes. All senior staff with our special guest. Tonight.'

Haig was restless and irritable. He was beginning to feel

trapped. Sile had been clever, in some respects. He knew that if Haig told everyone the truth now, after being declared a hero, that he would be ostracised. But I have been so generous, Sile would say. I have bestowed on him the keys to the city of Gunport. I have lauded the hero on a pedestal and commanded you to worship him. How good I am.

Haig paced his concrete box for ten minutes then collected his pistol and headed out.

***

Kaneda was hunched over a work table in the Workshop, wrestling with the drone that had crashed in the effort to rescue Retallick. A range of scuffs and dents decorated its shell, but all of the delicate equipment had been repaired, replaced. To his side were pieces of wiring that he'd cut away, some drops of solder, a few stray chips of plastic, a corner of a circuit board.

Haig watched him heave the corner of its shell into place, then struggle to bend it around enough to secure it. Haig watched him shift his feet for more purchase, shuffling around the table, then decided to step over, pushing his weight down onto the shell.

Hiro was surprised, relieved, and irritated, all at once. He took advantage of Haig's help and clacked it into place, bolted the shell down, then stood up, placed his tools onto the table, and stepped backwards, like Haig's help had tainted his repairs.

He couldn't meet Haig's eyes.

"Are you thinking about the Airlock?" said Haig. "It wasn't your fault."

"No," said Kaneda. "It was. In part. We convince ourselves that it isn't our fault when we're looking to abdicate ourselves of responsibility, Haig. To make ourselves feel better. Self-deception. There are rare times that we *know* – that there is no question of being anything else. The certainty of it is crushing. We know that we decided, that we executed, that the consequences are ours."

"How could it have been your fault?"

Kaneda walked over to another of his benches. Mihalik's ravaged tablet was carefully placed in the centre. He had pulled it apart, screws and circuit pieces placed in ever-widening patterns around it. The screws all pointing up. Anything with a straight edge placed parallel to another straight edge.

"I have deconstructed and reconstructed this tablet more than twenty times. Nothing she had done to it should have stopped me from locking her back in. Nothing. Not in the time I had. I recreated it, Haig."

"Recreated what?" said Haig slowly, frowning.

"Not on the Airlock, of course not," said Kaneda, waving his hand dismissively. "On a second lock. Without panic. Without fear, without shaking, sweating hands, it took me seconds."

"That kind of pressure, when you're unprepared, Hiro... No-one could have stopped her. She put herself in that position. She was clever, resourceful. And she was ill. She would have found another way to do it even if you had stopped her."

"This is precisely what I am saying. It is so easy to say that it wasn't my fault, it was hers. It wasn't your fault, it was hers. It is so easy to pretend that we have no part in it. A life, extinguished. And to what will be her great shame, is that it was suicide. Her name will linger here, reeking with the stench of cowardice. Will any lessons be learned? It isn't simply the equipment here that's sliced down to a lethal edge. It's the people. Does anyone stop to think that if going to a place requires you to give up parts of your body, people should never go there at all? If everything around you wants to kill you, that you should never go? But we are prideful. And vain. And all of these layers that Aphelion has make it so easy to do. The faceless 'They'. At the top? I'll tell them and they'll tell someone else and they'll follow orders. In the middle? Ah, they told me to tell you that you have to do it. At the bottom? Do it or you won't have a job. It should never have got that far. How many people has this place churned up? And you tell me it's not my fault. You, too, are to blame. Keeping things just the way they are."

Haig leaned against a table.

The majority of Gunport wanted to pretend the strike had never happened, that Blatt had never happened. It was why they had forgotten so quickly about Mihalik, except for those few. It was easier. The lies made things easier. Accepting the truth came with a responsibility to do something with that knowledge, and doing something always seemed to be so hard. The questions that came with it: what can be done? What can *I* do? And the answers overwhelming, distressing, until finally, beaten back and cowed, they retreated back into their base state. Of not knowing and not finding out and actively avoiding knowing.

"It's harder to do something than do nothing," said Haig.

"What will you do?"

"Before I killed Blatt, he told me who did it."

"Sile did it."

"You knew?"

"Have you heard of the ASC Dragonrunner?"

Haig shook his head. Kaneda sighed and picked up a small spring, rolling it in his fingers.

"I did not know this when I came here. I found out afterwards. My father did not want me to come here. He races the keirin, yes, but is an engineer too. When he found out that Sile runs Gunport, he sent me a series of new stories. Trying to get me home, I suppose. I dismissed it. My father interfering, prying. As he always has."

"Was he wrong?"

"He's never wrong, Anson. Simply irritating."

"What did he say?"

"Sile's father used to run a small robotics company. Space Hinge Robotics. Very heavily specialised. They made motors that turned different equipment on the outside of spacecraft. Guidance arrays, solar panels, comms, ion tracing, and so on. Anything outside a spacecraft that might need to point in a different direction. They needed to withstand heat, cold, and so on."

"They made hinges for space," said Haig.

Kaneda nodded. "Sile went to work for his father. His father was getting older, so he handed over the day-to-day running to his son. One day, my father told me, Sile's company undercuts his in a bidding war for a huge contract with Aphelion. Gunport is still under construction. Sile is very young. The Colony Race begins. Everyone needs robotics, Aphelion included. This is a shock because Space Hinge are known for making small quantities of the best. They've made countless small-batches for unique craft, or for experiments and so on. One-off ships. They never take mining contracts, for example, because the miners need millions of the same thing, cheaper, but Space Hinge make twenty, perhaps, at a time. But now they're saying they can make thousands. Millions. So they win the contract. They have a good reputation so this deal makes sense."

"What happened?"

"There were systematic failures on a fleet of Aphelion ships and shuttles. There was one craft that became lost entirely. The ASC Dragonrunner. Nobody knows what happened. It was performing research into some new guidance systems. Space Hinge's robotics failed and then it disappeared. Twenty three people presumed dead. Perhaps a year afterwards, Space Hinge was sued by Aphelion for the shuttle itself, sued by the families of the dead, sued by the WSA. And sued by all the others who suffered these failures. Space Hinge was obliterated. Sile's father died fighting to rebuild his company's reputation."

"How did Sile end up here?"

"Sile shorted out the stocks a month before the company's first lawsuit."

"Fuck."

"He's always been wealthy. His father left him property beyond Space Hinge. Beyond the reach of the law, tidied up into trust funds and everything else. His father left him all of the patents, the designs, the IP. All his. He used it to buy into Aphelion. Ran their Agriculture Research Laboratory on the Moon for a year. Ran it into the ground, Chiaki says. Then came here."

Kaneda put the spring down.

"I didn't believe the stories then. That someone could be so callous to profit from their father's death. To pull down their company to make more money, presumably. To compromise lives for their own gain. It's not even about the money. It's about being seen to be the best, or the winner, or not losing. Something."

"And that's what Sile's doing here?"

Kaneda said, "Sile will see every one of us dead if it means his bosses give him a pat on the back."

"You'll help me?"

"I will."

***

Sile's great table had lost its once brilliant sheen, the smooth timber's polish faded, thinly coated in concrete dust. The painting watched him and it took a surprising amount of effort to meet its eye. Fronds from the palm tree had yellowed and one balanced over the lip of the pot, undecided whether to stay or fall onto the concrete floor.

Haig ran a hand through the dust on the table and smeared the table with his dirty hands and looked at the paths he had made. When he brushed his hands together, the dust hung gently in the air, nowhere to go, the room close with the bodies of Gunport's senior staff.

He sat in the same place as last time. Sile at the head of the table; Haig, Tobin, Wecht on one side; Dekker, Kaneda, Barnes on the other. They were subdued, quiet. Conversation at a premium. Hostility offered generously.

They were eating the same food that they had had when Haig was last here. He listened to the clacking of their mouths and the clag of protein blocks and the hard swallowing as they forced the food down. He ate a corner of his own and recoiled. It had an ashen quality to it, bitter and brittle. The water did nothing to help.

Haig watched Sile eat. Watched the others eat. Barnes wouldn't look at him. Tobin did.

Finally Sile said, "This is supposed to be a celebration."

Tobin said, "Not everyone's here yet."

"Ah," said Sile. "Acaba sends her apologies. Prendrick his too. I wouldn't be surprised if we never see him here again."

"Well then," said Tobin. "What are we celebrating?"

"Getting back on track," said Sile, raising a cup of gunshine. "Sending ships to the stars and getting back to our vital role. We're humanity's best hope of a brighter future, all of you here. I hope you know that."

Janulis' lip curled and she scoffed. Sile glared.

"I'll toast to that," said Wecht suddenly. "I'd feared I might not get to Echion Alpha. With the strike." She swallowed. Looked at Haig. The implicit look: this is not the place to antagonise Sile. Do not bring up Komarov. Not in the way you want to. "Now it looks like I'll be able to get there sooner than I thought."

"The next shuttle is all yours, Sarah," said Sile.

"Congratulations," said Janulis flatly.

"Yes," said Tobin, looking from Barnes to Sile and back again. "I didn't realise the Masamune was ahead of schedule."

Sile waved a hand dismissively. "New routes are opening up all of the time," he said. "I reminded Aphelion how brittle we are here, how fragile their position is, and they have graciously expedited the first manned colony shuttle. Only a few months now and Sarah will be among the furthest living humans from Earth. A pioneer, Sarah. How wonderful."

"What did you say to Aphelion to get the shuttle moved up?" said Haig.

Tobin became interested. Dekker looked at Sile. Sile shook his head, almost imperceptible.

Sile opened his hands. "I simply reminded them that the strike could have gone much differently." Sile narrowed his eyes. "Imagine if your new friend Acaba hadn't been able to be persuaded."

"She had some help," said Haig.

The others felt it. Something amiss. Something that they didn't know about.

Barnes said, "When is our first new delivery due, Chris? You must be excited to get back to it."

"Delirious," said Tobin, draining his cup and shivering.

"The ships have arrived quickly," said Kaneda.

"Aphelion were very efficient at releasing them once they knew the strike was over," said Sile.

"They expected the strike to end," said Haig.

"A compliment to you, Anson," said Sile, his mouth stretched out, teeth gleaming, eyes burning. "To you and IPRA's faith in you. They knew you could deliver the right result."

"What are the Reactor techs getting?" said Kaneda.

"What do you mean?" said Sile.

"What agreement did you reach?"

Janulis leaned forward. "What did you promise them that you haven't promised us?"

"Nothing," said Sile.

"Nothing?" said Janulis.

Sile smiled. "Acaba saw the error of her ways and relented. Perhaps she realised that her course of action was not the best for all involved."

Janulis said to Haig, "What did you say to her? Did you offer her something?"

"I offered her nothing," said Haig.

Tobin cocked his head. He said, "Then what made her change her mind?"

Wecht was looking at the floor. She knew why Acaba changed her mind.

"That's a good question," said Haig.

"What negotiating did you actually do?" said Tobin.

"Very little," said Haig.

"Then why are you here?" said Tobin. "What have you actually achieved?"

Wecht said, "He stopped a murderer, Chris, you prick."

"Fuck you Sarah," said Tobin –

"Mind your tone," said Sile –

"Fuck off Chris," said Wecht –

Janulis leaned back and smiled. Kaneda stared fiercely at Haig.

Dekker said, "I came for the gunshine, not the bickering. Calm down and behave."

A small noise came out of Barnes. "What?" said Dekker.

"Komarov and Mihalik," said Barnes.

Sile shifted in his seat. "Is there something you'd like to add, Matthew?"

Barnes looked at Haig. Looked at the others. "Maybe she knew what they'd given and when she put it into perspective, she realised that other people had given up a lot more than air and water and everything else."

"Yes," said Sile slowly, warming to Barnes' theory. "Yes, I wonder if that's true. Acaba had finally seen how small her complaints seemed in the grand scheme of things and relented. She deserves credit for coming to her senses and admitting her fault."

Haig had had enough. Felt anger building.

"To Komarov then," said Haig. "And to Mihalik."

Sile glared at him. Dekker was straining in his chair, ready to burst forth and crush Haig. Haig met his eye.

"Murdered and driven to suicide. I didn't know them, but their deaths were unnecessary, cruel, callous."

Sile said, "A lot of people have made necessary sacrifices for Gunport."

Haig continued, "Abandoned out here in space. They didn't deserve it. They deserve some measure of justice."

"You have already provided it," said Sile.

"Not yet," said Haig, glaring at Sile.

Sile was rattled. "They've made, erm, necessary sacrifices. For Gunport."

"For you," said Haig.

"I am Gunport," said Sile.

"You're a fucking murderer," said Haig.

Silence. Blank faces –

Silence stretching –

Sile's face hardened. His lips tightened. He took out his tablet. He flattened his tone, made it perfunctory, formal.

This hadn't landed like Haig had expected. What had he expected? In a moment of anger, he had surrendered all initiative back to Sile. The others were stunned. Kaneda and Wecht looked at Haig with concern. Dekker had seemed like he wanted to pull Haig's head off but now he too was calm and composed. He smirked.

Haig sensed he had fallen into a trap –

"The body of Petra Komarov was discovered floating outside," said Sile. "I authorised a mission to recover her body, as requested by Anson Haig. The mission was a disaster, frankly. Conrad's life was nearly taken, he has life-altering injuries, and a vital drone was damaged."

"If you'd given him what you promised – "

Kaneda said, "The drone had been fully repaired. It performed its role well."

"Don't interrupt," hissed Sile, his tongue flashing across his teeth. "I'll get to you shortly."

Kaneda retreated, said, "My apologies."

"Secondly, Alice Mihalik falsely reported an attack on her by two of our best programmers."

Haig felt Wecht and Janulis bristle, for entirely opposing reasons.

"Her death – the last to see her alive were Anson Haig and Hiro Kaneda – and medical history, provided by Prendrick, shows a deeply troubled young woman. It is crushingly disappointing that you were not able to help her, Sarah, and that she did not seek out support when she needed it most."

Haig watched Wecht puff her cheeks out, glow molten with anger, her eyes full, barely containing tears of rage or shock or horror or disbelief. Her head wobbled on its neck, stunned, looked at her feet.

"Even more disappointing was the credence that a seasoned negotiator and military man would give to her evidence. Hearsay and nonsense ruled over reason and proven good character. And a better question is to ask is, why was Haig interfering at all? An agenda was forming."

The others looked at each other. Minds filled with spinning webs of Sile's shite, thought Haig. How can you know what is true and what is not?

"Anson Haig continued to defy the orders of his superiors. The autopsy of Petra Komarov revealed a tragic accident. A malfunction with her suit. Nothing more. Unfortunate of course, but a sacrifice that I am sure she would have been willing to make."

Haig said, "She was murdered. You've been calling me a hero for a week for solving her murder."

"Anson Haig pressed and pressed and pressed," said Sile, gathering pace. "Asking questions to which he already had the answers. Fabricating answers to questions no-one was asking. A fool's game. Harassment of key Gunport staff. Time and time again. The agenda coming more and more to the fore. Leading to the death of Felix Blatt. We have only Anson Haig's word that he did not murder Felix in cold blood. And clearly his word means nothing."

The room was momentarily silent. Sile wallowed in it. He was clearly enjoying this. Rehearsed, thought Haig.

Sile continued, his bland monotone rolling on.

"Let me be clear. Any threat to our work here must be dealt with in the most rigorous terms. Severe terms. I have judged your conduct to be severely lacking, Anson Haig. Never mind the strong possibility that you may have committed the offences which you claim to be investigating. And that you should not have been investigating to begin with. I do not need to find you culpable for these. I am more than convinced that you should be ejected from Gunport immediately for actions that I have a planet's worth of evidence for. I am remanding you to Gunport's jail cell, where you will be kept until the next available shuttle can take you to Able Base. I will recommend that you are summarily dismissed from IPRA's payroll, and your contract made null and void. You will lose any and all pay owed to you, and any medical or family benefits will cease immediately. Your family will be escorted from their premises immediately. Do you understand these consequences of your actions and my judgement?"

Haig was reeling in the chair. Had started to feel it coming, but it still hit like an asteroid. Disorientated. Tom would go into some thick-aired, grease-watered shithole, some rotten apartment fit for a corpse. His life expectancy would drop ten years in ten minutes. Olivia would never let him see him ever again.

He slowly became aware that he was being watched. The entire room.

Haig began to shake his head, gently at first, then with more violence.

"Fuck you," said Haig.

"Is that what you'd like added to your record?" said Sile.

"You've overestimated how much you can sweep under a fucking rug. Your brush isn't big enough, you smug fuck."

"Noted," said Sile. "And with that, Emilio, would you please escort Anson Haig to the Tank."

At some point, Dekker had drawn his gun. Held it two-handed, solid grip. Anything other than full surrender was getting Haig shot in the face.

"You'll preach until the end of days, John, but you're not any kind of human hope. You're a lightyear conman. You're on the edge of your nerves out here, out of your depth."

And then, an interlocking and clicking of gears and thoughts, coming together. Of course.

He turned to Janulis. "Komarov was investigating Galatea, Alison. Whatever she died for, he did it to Galatea. Galatea's not right, is she? She's sick? It was him. Komarov was trying to work it out and he killed her for it."

"Silence – " said Sile.

Janulis' eyes widened.

"When did the gravity start to fail? Water? Air? What did he do?"

Sile went white.

"Take him, Emilio!" he snapped.

"I'm going," said Haig. "Keep your concrete kingdom. Fill it with more bones. Dickhead."

Haig took out his gun – "Calm down, prick," he said to Dekker – and tossed it along the table, watching with pleasure as it gouged a scar in the wood and polish when it bounced and scratched its way to Sile.

Dekker shoved a gun under his ribs and marched him out.

***

Security was a large room on the 6th Floor.

There were ten desks, organised in a broad semi-circle that swept away from the door. Desks were cracked or greying. Conspicuously empty. Nothing on them or ever on them. No-one in here with him now. They could have been empty eternal. Some power cables poked out, never used. Dekker and Holden were the only two security officers, but it had been built for ten. Never filled. You don't need people to investigate wrongdoing if you pretend no wrongdoing has ever happened.

There was a separate office above the main desks, really just a differently configured concrete block room, with a glass screen to partition it. An off-white mug, real, chipped, and missing a handle sat on a ledge behind the glass. Haig recognised its SORG motto – 'Utrinque Paratus' – below a space shuttle with wings.

A few desks over, a small wooden carving of a tree, clumsily painted in a once-brilliant blue around the base. There was some lettering, long faded and indecipherable, running up the trunk. Whoever had carved it had decided against trying to carve leaves, the bare branches giving it an Autumnal feel, and it made Haig miss rain.

The desks surrounded Security's centrepiece – the Tank. Haig's new home.

It was a jail cell on a raised platform, four sides of thick metal bars that reached up the ceiling. It had been clumsily bolted in – Haig could tell that it was never supposed to be here – but it would hold a gene-edited person, even one up to their eyes on warpers. Every moonbase needed a place for people to cool off sometimes. Haig had briefly turned his thoughts to escape before concluding that not only would it not work, there was nowhere to go. The Tank was poorly designed, which made it difficult to escape from. It was metalwork at its simplest: concrete and bars. There were no locks he could be clever about, no leverage to be had in the door, no secret weaknesses.

There was a long metal bench, particularly uncomfortable. He tried shuffling his back into it, he tried straightening his back into it, he tried pushing his back into it, he tried slumping, he tried straightening legs, leaning elbows, splitting legs, locking ankles, locking knees, standing, sitting, sliding, slouching, and finally, he simply stood up, kicked it, then kicked it again. There were information screens high up on the walls around the Security Station that flashed the company logo and Echion

Alpha ticket adverts. Haig watched the advert until the woman in it touched the leaves, and then he swung around and lay down.

Haig was struggling for a coherent plan. The longer he was imprisoned here, the longer Sile could pour his poisons into the ears of the rest of Gunport's staff. He was fairly certain he could count on Acaba, Wecht, Kaneda, but that didn't mean it was fair to expect them to risk themselves to help him. Acaba wouldn't because she was afraid that what they did to Komarov and Mihalik would be done to her staff. Wecht wouldn't risk her trip to Echion Alpha. Brought forward by Sile. I have what you want, he seemed to be able to say. In exchange for loyalty in the face of everything I have done. Kaneda would help him, but Kaneda was only one person. He could be killed.

Escape was impossible. His shuttle was still grounded and Earth was months away. Without delays, and there was always a delay. Which meant that to Tom, he would have disappeared. Like his father had vanished, and left him. Abandoned him. And when Haig finally made it back to him, Tom would be someone else. All of those little moments that Haig saw when Tom was growing up, where Tom was a rotund child, pudding-wristed, and before Haig had realised what was going on, Tom was grabbing his knees, staggering around the house, moments from toppling. And then, thump. Tom was on his arse, baffled. 'How have I got here?' his face asked. A year had passed. Tom could walk, talk, play. The time was melting before him. Tom would be different when he returned. Secure a future for a child he would not see. Haig could not bear the idea of missing more.

Restlessness wrestled him back up. He paced the cell. There was nothing to be done but wait. He was too high profile now to kill. Sile would send him back to Earth in disgrace. There would be no appetite for investigating him as a murderer now that Blatt was dead, so Sile would brazenly wait this out. Rely on his enablers and deny everything until it went away.

Haig lay down again. He inhaled deeply. He exhaled until he felt his chest empty. He closed his eyes and willed himself calm.

Finally, he fell into a brittle sleep.

***

The man in the cell would not stop laughing and the wall burst and melted with molten concrete oozing bubbles and he observed his leg was missing and replaced by dirt and underneath a glowing bauble of rock burning through the floor and his father coming to him in flames and the man in the cell would not stop laughing –

***

"Haig," said the voice.

"Haig," said the voice. "Wake up."

Insistent. Barnes came into focus. "Barnes? What is it?"

He was in the Tank with him. The cell door was open. Security was empty. The lights were down.

"Come with me," said Barnes, whispering. "Quickly. We need to go. Prendrick will help us."

"Why?"

"I don't know," said Barnes, pulling Haig up. "He told me to bring you. He said he will put it in writing. For Aphelion."

Haig blinked. Woke up. Tugged at by Barnes.

In the Elevator, Haig said, "What did he say?"

"He said to bring you."

"He came to you?"

Barnes shuffled his feet. "Yes, he came to me."

"What did he tell you?"

"To bring you."

"How did you open the cell?"

"Dekker and Holden are dealing with something else."

"Dealing with what?"

"I said there were drunks."

"Drunks?"

"Come on, we don't have long."

"You said there were drunks and they just left?"

"Come on, quickly."

The Elevator opened at Medical and Barnes scurried out, quickly across to Prendrick's office. He opened the door and went in, letting the door swing behind him, Haig in the corridor.

It was dark, quiet. They hadn't seen anyone since leaving Security. The lights were out. No Wecht, no Bethe. Haig padded forward. Scalp itching. Throat dry. He stopped outside Prendrick's office and listened. Silence. Haig smelled gunshine, fumes seeping into the corridor.

He eased the door forward with a toe and stepped in.

Prendrick was dead. His head thrown back. Pale throat exposed. Hands on the desk, mottled blue and grey. Six empty bottles.

Barnes stood trying to hide in a corner whimpering and sobbing. Haig looked at Prendrick and then at Barnes and turned around and needed to leave, *now* –

A rapid scuttling of feet attacked him sideways. A blow glanced his head and sent him reeling. He put a hand down and tried to stand up, but only stumbled down again. Another blow put him down, another kept him down.

There was more shuffling. The lights clattered on. Haig saw motions and shapes and silhouettes blurring together. The back of his head was wet, pulsing with pain.

Barnes was being dangled in front of him by a shining hand, gripping his hair. Haig couldn't focus enough to see who held him.

Barnes had just enough time to say, "Haig – " before his throat was cut from ear to ear, and he was discarded, crumpling to the floor, his neck pumping blood. He lay gurgling and choking and coughing, dying in surprise.

Then black –

CHAPTER 13: SPACEWALK (PART 2)

Haig heard himself breathing.

Raspy, metallic, irregular. His mouth was dry. When he swallowed, a thick lump stuck in his throat. He felt like he was detached from his own body, floating above himself, languidly mimicking his own movements. His head was throbbing. There was something sticky his hair, matting it to the back of the helmet. A faint metallic smell. More breathing. Incredibly close, but muffled. Like being underwater.

Oh, fuck, thought Haig. Oh, fuck. Please no. He struggled to open his eyes. Part pain, part dread.

He knew what he would see when he opened his eyes.

He took a deep breath. Opened his eyes. His view was two rectangles. A grey one at the bottom, a black one at the top. A neat line punctuating them. Glittering dots shining in the black above. Razor dust below.

Haig was outside.

No sign of Gunport, of the Mine, of any tracks, of anything.

Endless grey.

Panic came on instantly. He was going to die, just like Komarov. Out here, alone. Without anyone to know what had happened to him. His son would never know. And he would never see him again.

He struggled to control the rising bile in his stomach. There was a commingling of panic and fear and anger that churned, his guts thrusting themselves up into his throat. He could taste the acid in his mouth, biting at the back of his throat.

The old Army instructor: "Don't panic. Never panic. Small things. Check what you've got. Inventory. Make lists. Do tests. Do it until you're calm and you know your situation. Radio it in. If your radio's fucked, radio it in to yourself. If you can't radio it in, you count everything again and check everything again until your head's back in the right space. What can you control?"

Okay, thought Haig. Okay.

I'm not dying out here. That fucker's not having the satisfaction. If only to prove a point.

First things first. Visual inspection of the arms. Both seemed intact. No obvious damage. He tensed and flexed both arms. They were warm, comfortable. No tears, no leaks. Haig was sweating profusely now. Whoever had stuffed him into the suit didn't see fit to give him a skullcap to keep sweat out of the eyes. His eyebrows were damp.

Next, his legs. There were some scuffs and grazes on the knees. They looked fresh. He'd been tossed out of the Airlock, and bounced his way out here. Thin strands of fabric floated around his knees, drifting lazily. He made fists with his toes, then unclenched them, then did it again. His head was still thudding but his limbs were fine.

There were two large pockets and a long tool holster in the trousers. Inside one pocket was an old mission guide – laminated cards with instructions on how to repair some kind of communications mast – but nothing to help guide him or provide directions. Haig tossed it to the dirt, watched it tumble lazily through the empty space and finally land. Another human mark in an alien land. In the other pocket was a meal ration. 'Just add water', said the silver foil. Haig tossed it.

In the holster was a multi-tool. A long handle with pliers,

screwdriver, wrench at one end, a crowbar at the other. Solid metal. One of the few things on Gunport that had to be metal rather than plastic. Haig thought it odd that he would be allowed to keep it, then wondered how quickly they had worked to get him outside. Rushed, perhaps? Panic made for poor decisions. Or, they figured that in the end, it would do him no good. A third reason might be the narrative. Make it look like he'd chosen to go out.

He took a deep breath. He'd been putting this off. Radio and locator. The suit had a gauntlet with all of the controls on it. The controls were intact. He pressed for the radio and got a bleep and then fuzz inside the helmet. The arm flashed red. Headphones and helmet were working fine, but the radio had been removed. Haig swore. Of course it had been removed. He checked the locator too – also gone.

He looked around. The suit was bulky but moved easily enough in the low gravity. He spun slowly through a complete circle. There was some dust kicked up where he stood, but it was near impossible to tell where he had come from. He could have been out here for hours.

He checked the air. The gauntlet told him he had three hours left. If the tank had been full, he'd been out here for an hour.

He could be anywhere.

Domiyat Outer was ahead, casting a long shadow behind him.

Let's summarise, thought Haig. I've been outside for an hour. They've not put the undersuit on, and I'm getting warm. Air will run out long before I broil – small mercies. The panic is subsiding. The warmth will settle. There's nothing I can do about the sweat in my eyes. Try to blink it out. I've no radio and no locator, but the suit is in good condition and I've got three hours of air.

What next?

Haig knew that if he went off in the wrong direction, it would doom him. Everything looked the same out here. Rolling stretches of grey, punctuated only by some chasm or pit. And what looked like a pothole could turn into the depths of a Vallis Adlivun, a Resnik Crater. Think this through, Anson. His head swelled with pain. Still throbbing.

You spent months reading about this place. You looked at the maps. You know the stars. You've seen the diagrams. It's in there. You've been in this situation before.

A beep. Air running down. He tried to blink the sweat out of his eyes and focus, feet planted in the dirt.

What's on the surface? The Skarian Mons. Anguta R-611's mountain, miles high. Can you see it? No. Line things up. Can you see Skarian Mons? No. Think about it. That narrows it down. Horizon distance here is about 12 miles. Narrows it down.

What else is on the surface? The Mine.

He'd seen the images. The Mine had been derelict for decades.

Towers of machinery, drilling equipment. Skeletal and frail, waiting for a strong breeze to collapse them, a whisper of a solar storm that would finally make planetfall and topple them. Their organs, nervous systems, every circuit and wire, gear and hinge, everything that didn't exhaust itself in the building of Gunport and could be repurposed, had been. Barnes' guidance equipment would have been from the rockets. Tobin's ceramic landing gear too. The robotics in Kaneda's drones would be from the drones that landed all of that time ago. Retallick's mesh tyres too.

The carcasses hung above the pits they had dug, wasted and useless.

Domiyat Outer is ahead of you now. Find your constellations. The Bucket and the Careless Reaper. If the Bucket is on the right and the Reaper on the left, you're facing North. Deep breaths, Haig. Get it right.

The Careless Reaper was a rough scythe of stars, a curved staff with stars that made a bent blade. The Bucket a square with a semi-circle of brilliant stars sweeping above it. Haig thought that if it was a real bucket, that semi-circle handle wouldn't hold up to much. He checked and rechecked. The constellations lined up.

He started to move. Don't think about what it means if you're wrong.

Two hours of air left.

Anguta R-611's gravity was weak enough to make Haig feel like he was floating, each step a bound. He had to be careful with planting each foot, had to be careful with deceptive shadows hiding deep craters, but he soon fell into a rhythm. Thinking about where he was made his stomach twitch, so he focused instead on what had happened.

The pain at the back of his head reminded him that he had been bludgeoned on every bound. As his foot came down, vibrations rocked through his body and into his skull, then receded as he went up, and started all over again when he landed.

Prendrick was dead. Impossible to know exactly how. Could be assisted suicide. Encouraged to take too many of his own pills with too much gunshine. Barnes was dead. Throat slashed in front of him. Haig would be blamed and sentenced in his absence, and when his dead, suffocated body crashed into Control they would say he was angry at Sile's judgment, escaped custody, threatened Prendrick – who he had driven to suicide – and murdered the good-intentioned Barnes who was only there to protect the defenceless doctor. And then, for reasons known only to himself – we can only speculate, Sile would say – he went onto the surface.

They had to make it ironclad. If he had gone back to the Moon, he would tell his story. At best, Sile would be brought home to answer questions. But now Haig was outside. And from there,

Sile would control the narrative. How quickly Haig had gone from hero to villain. How quickly Sile could flip the switch and tell another story.

Obvious questions – why go onto the surface? To do what? – would never be asked, because answers to them were tied up in whatever Sile was doing with Galatea.

Haig didn't have the answers to these questions either. Petra Komarov was killed because she had found something she shouldn't. That was clear. And Mihalik was killed because she would identify Komarov.

Haig skidded to a halt in the dirt, felt the boots vibrate, felt his landing rattle up through his teeth.

He saw the top of something – metallic, gleaming. A tower, but not Gunport. The Mine.

One hour of air left.

Adjust course. Head for the Mine. Or where the Mine should be, if you're where you think you are. Haig needed air. The corpsed ships would be useless, ravaged already and folded into Gunport. Some machinery, equipment, and perhaps other suits. Other suits meant tanks of air.

Keep moving. Find air.

Keep moving. Thud. Thud. Thud. Boots hitting the ground. And up –

Thud. And up –

Thud –

Thirty minutes of air left.

Finally, there lay a slope ahead of him that rose upwards. He stopped at the top. Then he saw it. He was wracked with great breaths of relief. It rushed over him. He was dizzy with it. He wasn't sure why, exactly, but he took out the multi-tool and wielded it like a club before pressing on.

The Mine.

There was no good way to approach from this direction. The vast majority of Anguta R-611 was flat, with the rare near-bottomless chasms and high-reaching mountains. Haig gripped and regripped the multi-tool and kneeled at the edge.

The Mine was a long and shallow trench that allowed the automated mining equipment to excavate their cubes and roll back up to the top before dumping them onto the conveyors. It had been abandoned for nearly thirty years, frozen in disuse. Still and gleaming, like all it would take is a button press to have it all rolling again.

Except it wasn't.

Haig peered over the edge.

The Mine was not as it once was. Not as it should have been.

At this end was now a vast cylindrical pit, robot-made. Flickering lights at the bottom betrayed robotics, working and scurrying. On the other side of the pit was a robot that worked like an enormous slug, sliding down the pit and leaving a concrete paste behind. Peering over the other side of the pit, a 3D printer was gently layering a cone-shaped building. It had completed at least twenty already. A small complex. None of them had doors or windows and therefore, thought Haig, air. One of the buildings had a scuffling of bootprints and wheel tracks in front of its opening.

Haig ground his teeth and squeezed the multi-tool and heard the creak of his gloves.

Sile was building another Gunport.

This was it, thought Haig. Sile had been using Gunport's meagre resources to start building another one. This was what Komarov had found. Somehow, Haig was certain, she had found out that Sile was diverting resources. Through her work on Galatea. And if Galatea had been told to build another Gunport, the AI would siphon resources away. Power, air, water. Chemicals for water. Hydrogen, oxygen. Used for blasting out the rock. Gravity would fail without power.

There wasn't enough here for one Gunport, but Sile was building another.

And he was willing to risk everyone on the first Gunport to do it.

He pushed it to the back of his mind. He couldn't do a single thing about it if he suffocated. The tracks suggested people, suggested air.

Twenty minutes of air left.

There was a flash of light on the other side of the pit, in-between two of the cone buildings. Haig caught a glint of a suit helmet behind it –

The ground shifted underneath him, and shimmering dust burst into his eye line. Shards of rock were plummeting upwards. Haig himself had been pushed gently to the left.

Lucky lucky lucky –

Another flash of light. Haig pushed everything into his thighs, leapt backwards, and a moment later, the rock exploded where he had been. Lumps of it pushed him away, and he rolled uselessly onto his back. He was breathing hard now.

Fifteen minutes of air left.

He shoved himself up and clipped the multi-tool to his gauntlet. He had no time for working his way cautiously around to his attacker, so he took a deep breath and run-shuffled forward, aimed for one of the cone buildings, tipped slightly at the edge of the pit, then pushed off and dove forwards, flying at the new Gunport.

The light flashing between the two cone buildings continued.

There was a deliberate pause between shots. Haig thought he was relatively safe in the air. The gunman had no landmarks to aim for, no way to know how close his shots were. Being accurate was hard work in these conditions, and the weapon he'd been shot at with was designed to breach airlocks, repurposed for mining. It should never hit moving targets.

The landing would be the problem.

He floated over the pit. The bottom was impossible to see. There was an occasional flicker of light, some sparks, some robotic guidelight blinking in the darkness.

And then Haig was across, and alive. The shots had ceased. Whoever was firing was probably guessing where he would land and preparing a kill shot.

Haig came in too high. He began flipping his body around to lead with his feet, then crashed into a cone, crunching the top of it off. It was weak, made from a paste farmed by the robotics, and it came away around him like a tangled rope. He caught up in it, then toppled down through the middle of it.

He lay there, breathing hard, getting bearings.

Five minutes of air left.

Inside were electronics, computers, machinery for humans, all wrapped in thick plastic. It was a half-finished surface building. This one looked like a workshop. No-one could survive in here until it was sealed properly, or it was properly set up for people wearing suits. He lurched up, looked for telltale air tank labels, or any kind of chemical symbol for –

The wall exploded. The paste stayed in thick ropes of mulched rock, became airborne, slapping his suit. He was thrown onto his back, could see the stars hanging high above through the hole in the ceiling.

He took a breath, gripped the multi-tool, and rolled himself up.

His attacker breached the hole they had made in the cone with a small pickaxe, raised high. They kicked through the broken cone's shell and leapt at Haig. Haig held the multi-tool up and batted the axe away, feeling the impact vibrate through his arm. The attacker toppled through and steadied themselves against the computers behind Haig. Both turned at the same time, weapons raised.

Haig caught the attacker with a glancing blow across the helmet visor and felt it crack. The attacker fell backwards and swung wildly, catching Haig's chestplate with the point of the pickaxe, ripping away the plastic shell, electronics tumbling out. The HUD in Haig's helmet went out.

The attacker began to slash blindly, one hand over their helmet. Haig left them to it, started to sift through the debris in the cone. There – an air tank – Haig seized it up, stepped out through the hole the attacker had made.

Stay calm, now. Slow down. Slower is smoother. Smoother is faster.

Three minutes of air left. Possibly. No HUD. No way to know.

Haig moved around the cone buildings and stood out of sight of the one he'd crashed into. He kneeled in the dirt and unclipped the backpack, taking care to keep the tubing into the helmet unobstructed. He opened the emergency valve, slotted the new tank in, sealed the valve, then breathed deeply. Haig's ears popped and he felt a tingle in the back of his nose.

The air was stale, metallic. It was glorious. He took another deep breath, replaced the backpack –

The attacker came at him from the side. Haig dropped to the ground and rolled away. Both were scrabbling in the dirt. Haig pushed himself up first, dust swirling all around him.

They were close together now.

Haig saw the crack in the visor. It was a long splinter, a knotted clump on one side that shot out and stretched to the other. Some sealant had been hastily applied to it, thick gobs of glue to keep it intact, airtight. The glareshielding inside had splintered and peeled away, revealing the face of his attacker.

Dekker.

He had blood around his nose and mouth, and he was deeply angry. He was breathing hard too. He was mouthing something. A string of obscenities, thought Haig. An unheard cascade of ways that he was going to fuck me up.

They stepped out of the complex of cones. Haig turned all the way around to look behind him. He was ten metres from the pit and Dekker was crouching to attack. Haig held up the multi-tool and side-stepped Dekker's leap, twisting around and swinging downwards, catching Dekker's backpack.

Haig saw metal and plastic come away, and Dekker fell down, trying to roll away from the pit. Dekker was on his back, five metres from the pit, feet slipping against the slope and the dirt. Haig stepped forward and brought the multi-tool down. Dekker batted it away with the pickaxe and tried to stand, feet not gripping, scuffing razor dust up.

Haig brought the multi-tool down again and again, blows glancing away from Dekker's gauntlet and pick-axe until one landed hard on the helmet. Dekker's face betrayed him. His eyes darted to the display on his gauntlet, panicked, then flashed back to something on his HUD. Dekker fumbled in one of his suit's pockets for more sealant.

His suit's ruptured, thought Haig.

He took advantage of Dekker's panic and shoved him. Dekker left the ground and suddenly, his feet were dangling above the pit. Gravity was weak here, but it was still gravity. The pit would be like a black hole, reaching out and taking him, never letting go, caressing him into its depths. Haig saw the panic in Dekker's eyes as he groped for some handhold, some grip above the pit, but he had already started his slow descent into the black.

Dekker started to throw his arms towards the walls of the pit, trying to move himself in mid-air. He kicked his legs out, too, at first in a controlled mid-air breaststroke, becoming more and more ragged. Finally, he stretched himself out, making his body as long as possible.

He'd done enough thrashing to move towards the concrete wall. He was greyed out now, the black of the pit beginning to eat at him. His hands scrabbled at the sides of the pit, but the smooth concrete offered nothing. When his shoulder hit the wall, it pushed him back out again, and he was back to floating and sinking in the centre of the pit.

His limbs stopped moving. Dekker's feet became black, and then his legs, his torso, his shoulders, his arms, his hands.

And then he was gone.

CHAPTER 14:
MORS MACHINA

Ten minutes left.

The Outer Door of the Airlock at the Ramp loomed large. He hadn't expected to get this far. Haig eased down the track and into the guidelights' glow. He looked at the camera above and waved with both arms, then headed to the side of the airlock, looking for the emergency release. As he took the first few steps, the Outer Door began to move. Yellow flashed inside.

He saw as Mihalik must have done.

He entered, tried to see who was inside the Ramp. Steeled himself for another fight.

The door rolled shut behind him, the vibration in the floor. The dust thrumming. It all-too-slowly closed. He was tapping his fingers against his suit, tapping his toes against the roof of the boot. When the amber light blazed green, he unsnapped the latches, yanked free the cords and piping, and threw the helmet to the ground.

He heaved in the new air, great greedy lungfuls.

It wasn't his own rancid stench and it was spectacular. He quickly worked his way down the suit, unclicking, unscrewing, unclasping, until finally the suit lay in a heavily discarded pile, slick with his sweat. He stood swaying for a moment, light-headed. Drunk with cool air.

The Inner Door still carried the scars of Retallick's buggy, scored with grinding metal tyres, and the concrete below scratched and mangled.

Haig waited at the Inner Door, listening. The Ramp was dimly lit, quiet.

He thought it was worth the risk. He took the multi-tool and used it to work the manual crank.

The door groaned until finally Haig could duck through. Haig used the manual crank to lower it back down and seal it behind him.

"You're alive," said Retallick, emerging from a shadow.

"You opened the Airlock?" said Haig. He swung a hand at the Inner Door.

Retallick held up a shaking implant. "I would've done more. My hands don't work."

Haig nodded. "Thank you, Conrad."

"Sile told us that you killed Prendrick," said Retallick. "Ripped Barnes' throat open."

"That's bullshit," said Haig, hands shaking, anger yet building. "They killed Barnes in front of me after I found Prendrick dead. They knocked me out and tossed me outside, Conrad. Like so much trash. No radio and no locator. Same as they did to Komarov."

"How did you get back?"

"Same way you would have done."

"Let the stars be your guide," said Retallick.

"I need to get to Sile."

"A lot's happened in the last few hours. Dekker led a briefing. Told us you had reacted angrily to being relieved of your role. After you'd been put in the Tank, you escaped and killed Barnes. Attar is Head of Security now."

"Where's Barnes?"

Retallick blinked. Said slowly, "He's dead."

"Fuck's sake, Conrad. Yes, I know he's dead. His body, Conrad, his fucking body. Where's his body?"

Retallick walked heavily to a plastic stool bolted to the wall, then sagged onto it. He was sleight, but seemed enormous, his limbs leaden, his weight settling, the stool creaking.

"They told us you'd taken him with you."

"Why would I do that? And people believed any of this? That I'd do any of that? No way Wecht was having any of it."

"Dekker locked Wecht in her room. Before the briefing. For helping you escape."

"Sile's building another Gunport in the ruins of the Mine," said Haig. "He killed Komarov to keep it quiet. I think she found out when she was writing water algorithms for the Core. I think Sile changed Galatea. Corrupted it somehow to get it to allow him to send power and material to the new one."

Retallick stared into the middle distance. He nodded. "Aphelion would never have approved it. Never wanted one Gunport, never mind two. If they knew he was reprogramming Galatea for that, he'd be sent home in disgrace."

"His disgrace weighed against Komarov's life. Mihalik's, Blatt's, Prendrick's, Barnes', Dekker's."

"Dekker's dead?"

"He shot at me with a mining cannon. We fought and he fell into the new Gunport with a crack in his helmet."

Retallick was in some sort of fugue. He looked grey. Sweat popped and ran down his nose. This was all too much too quickly, thought Haig.

"You have returned to martial law," said Retallick finally. "Acaba fought back with her crew. She rejected Sile's version of events. Attar and Holden subdued them. They've been rounded up and locked in the Food Hall or locked in their quarters." He lifted his hands up. "I think I've been forgotten about."

"Fuck," said Haig. The lines he had sensed being drawn had become concrete, real. "What about air, water, Galatea, everything else?"

"Galatea can run everything for a while," said Retallick. "But if it's corrupted – "

"We can't take that chance," said Haig. "Sile needs removing from command and Janulis needs to cleanse Galatea. Will the power hold?"

He held a gun out to Haig like it was a block of ancient sewage. "Take this," said Retallick.

His face had aged further still, new crevices forming into old skin. His eyes were half-closed and he said, "The Earth is round and blue. It's nice there. They have seas."

Retallick closed his eyes and exhaled. The gun started to fall and Haig took it as Retallick was dropping it. Retallick's hands began to jerk and twist while he was slipping into a clammy sleep.

Haig propped Retallick up and found a paper packet of immsups in his pocket. There was no water in the Ramp, no cups, no taps, so he crushed one into powder and rubbed it into Retallick's gums. Retallick moaned and muttered and mumbled but his breathing became steady and his heart-rate evened out. The jerking and twisting in his hands settled slowly and became an irregular twitch.

Haig took a tablet from a table in a corner and messaged Wecht: *Retallick needs medical help. SIRS. Immsups in gums. Stable for now. Help?*

Fired back: *Locked in quarters. Get me out and I'll help.*

Haig messaged: *En route.*

Haig pressed the button to call the elevator – I know it won't work, doesn't mean I can't hope – and nothing happened. The Ramp's Maintenance Doors were intact. He pushed his hand against the panel and it flashed red. He did it again and it flashed red again, except – Haig would swear – an angrier red. What are you doing? I'm locked. Fuck off.

Fortunately, the Ramp carried all kinds of interesting tools for manipulating metal. Haig took a blowtorch and melted the locks and hinges through the Maintenance Tunnel hatch, careful to step away as the last hinge tore before it melted away, landing with a dull thud and gouging a hole in the concrete floor.

The Maintenance Tunnels ran from the top to the bottom of Gunport, between Gunport proper and the shuttle tunnels. Down the spine of them were spiralling metal and plastic staircases that swayed and creaked underfoot. Miles of cabling and piping ran up the side of them.

He spent some time collecting equipment. He'd need to open the Maintenance Hatch on Wecht's floor, and Wecht's door would need wedging open too, so that keeping the multi-tool. The blowtorch was portable, so he slung that over his shoulder. The multi-tool he carried. The gun secure in a pocket.

In the Tunnel, Haig was hit by a wall of thick warmth and the stink of scorched electronics, concrete dust. Heat from the Reactor spilled into these tunnels and rose up, helping Gunport stay warm. The air was thinner too, waste gases hissing and pumping this way too. There was a dull echo of whirring machinery, the incessant whoosh of fans pumping air up. A change in pressure made him open and close his mouth. Thinner air meant he was struggling for breath. He grabbed an oxygen mask from a rack inside the Maintenance Tunnel and closed the door behind him, waiting for the solid clack to signal it closed.

Wecht was ten floors under him.

He moved deliberately, each foot landing solidly before

moving again to the next step. The stairs were narrow, the steps small. He passed the next few floors carefully, concentrating on breathing and stepping, and breathing and stepping, and creating a rhythm he could settle into. At least he was going down.

Somewhere far below, there was a distinctive hollow bang. The first echoing sounds of gunfire and shouting. He peered over the side, down half a mile of staircase and concrete. White noise of the tunnel was broken by different successive bangs. Someone was shooting at someone else.

He wiped his sweaty hands on his t-shirt and went faster. The stairs wobbled under him, the plastic absorbing his heavy footprints.

The Maintenance Door on '12' was already open, so he raised his pistol and crept through, locking it behind him. The door was pocked with dents and holes. Concrete at the next corner was speckled with shallow dents. Fragments of porcelain bullets crunched underfoot.

Indistinct voices moved quickly across a corridor somewhere up ahead. Haig paused and leaned into the wall, raising the gun. The voices faded as quickly as they had risen. Then it was quiet. Gentle hum of machinery. Not much else. This floor had seen fighting, thought Haig, but it was over now. It had had its turn.

He moved slowly to Wecht's room, taking his time to listen.

The blowtorch fired up and glowed in the dark. He melted through the first lock before the torch sputtered and gave out, so he discarded it and used the multi-tool to lever the door aside.

Her room was dark, the lights off. What little he could see was tidy, no upturned furniture or broken plastic.

"Sarah?"

"Anson?" she whispered.

He squinted and saw her shape in the gloom, a lump of concrete in her fist.

"You're alright?"

"Yes," she said, "Yes."

"What's happening?"

"I don't know," she said. "Dekker came to the Medical Bay. Said I was being put under house arrest, 'for my own safety'. They said people would be angry that I'd helped you escape. I didn't believe a word of it."

"None of its true, Sarah. They knocked me out. Put me outside in a suit."

"Oh, those wankers," she said. "What's this all about? Do you know what's going on?"

"Sile's been fucking about with Galatea so that he can build another Gunport. Where the Mine was, there's now a building site. I'm pretty sure Komarov was killed because she found out. I think she said something or questioned it, and Sile – or more likely Dekker – killed her. They dumped her into space and let her suffocate."

Wecht nodded, said, "If they've been changing Galatea's programming, that would explain all of the little glitches. All of the little things that keep going wrong."

Haig said, "If Aphelion had found out, they'd have sent him home."

"They'd take his fiefdom away."

"Right. And he couldn't have that."

"You think they argued?"

"Maybe she found out and he lashed out. Maybe he pushes her and she hits her head on something, then he panics. Retallick knew the suit was missing. Barnes knew there was no shuttle."

"Those wankers," said Wecht.

"Barnes is dead," said Haig. "Retallick's a fucking mess. Neither of them has done well out of this."

"I'll go to him now." She paused. "How did you get back?"

"Thank the Army for that. Reading maps and constellations. All that military training. Dekker was out there. Tried to kill me."

"What happened? Where is he?"

Haig sighed, suddenly exhausted. ""He tried to shoot me with a cannon. We fought. It's fucking awful, fighting in a spacesuit. He fell into the new Gunport with a crack in his helmet."

"He's dead?"

"Yes."

"This is awful, Haig. What now?"

"Fuck knows."

"Stop Sile and everything else stops."

"Can't without evidence. Need evidence Sile reprogrammed Galatea. Then get the evidence Earth-side. Attar's the new Security chief. So all without being bludgeoned to death by Attar's fists."

"Sile first. Evidence after."

"If Aphelion think their moonbase has been forcibly taken over by a group of striking Reactor techs and an IPRA negotiator, they'll send SORG. And SORG will kill everyone." Haig scratched his beard. "No, we need evidence. We need to counter Sile's stories."

Wecht sighed. "Retallick's got SIRS?"

"Fever, hallucinations, weakness, palsy."

She nodded. "That sounds like SIRS. I'll go now."

He offered her a gun. She pushed it away with disdain.

"I don't know enough about guns. And you need it."

"Attar doesn't stand a chance," he said, holding up his fists, swaying, sweating, bedraggled, exhausted.

"Attar doesn't stand a chance and you can barely stand," she said.

***

The tunnel that ran parallel to Wecht's was filled with more shouting, more gunfire, this time from where he wanted to be. Haig took a deep breath and started working his way up, one step at a time.

His entire body was raw. He thought about soaking himself in a cool bath. The water gently lapping at his stretched skin, the stinging patches at his joints where the skin had rubbed itself crimson. He would put his head under the water and blow small bubbles, becoming some sort of fish. He would feel revitalized, reinvigorated. Oh, for a bath.

A Maintenance Door opened above, bringing him back to Gunport. Haig cursed. There was a brief silence, quickly punctuated with shouting. One voice was pleading, panicked.

It was cut short by a gunshot. Then scraping, scuffling, moaning. Someone shot, writhing, thought Haig. Fuck. He leaned around and tried to look. A few floors above, he could see a shape lying prone, surrounded by the undersoles of boots. Far too many of them.

Haig waited, tucked himself against the column in the centre of the stairs. Silence. Silence that was too long.

Then scuffling, boots squeaking on the plastic flooring, a succession of thuds and cracks. The moaning began again, intensified, then panicked. The rails of the stairs vibrated and wobbled, heavy clanging, and a man's body fell from the stairs above and flashed past Haig. It clattered into a plastic rail and bounced away, wrenched some cabling from the wall, before being consumed by the dark.

He heard a voice shout, "Pay for your fucking water next time," then that same voice spitting down. Water wasted on petty hate.

Fuck, thought Haig. Is this what it's come to? Murder and score settling? He swallowed hard, pushed himself tighter against the column, gun partly raised.

The voices had a brief, heated discussion – two voices in particular shouting at each other – then went back onto their floor, and the Maintenance Door closed.

Haig exhaled, relieved despite himself, that he was alive, that he hadn't been found. He waited silently for another few minutes, then began to move.

***

The wall of heat pushed into the Maintenance Shaft from the Core, heavying his limbs, sapping at him. Haig stepped over tangled cables towards Galatea's centre, behind swirling tanks of coolants, atop the gantries. He pushed wiring aside and clambered up a ladder, listening to his footsteps clang.

The closest thing Galatea had to a centre was a table that Janulis had placed under a bank of screens in the middle of the central gantry. Thick steel beams had been welded at odd angles, reaching out from the central pillar of Galatea and piercing the concrete walls. Each beam carried thick cables, some hanging loose, some wrapped tightly in deliberate spirals, all leading somewhere else.

Underneath the bank of screens was a foamboard mattress. It carried a dark stain at its centre. Next to it was a tray, filled with circuit boards and offcuts of wires. He leaned down and ran his hand through it, listening to the gentle rattle of plastic and metal clinking against each other.

"Haig," said Janulis wearily, stood behind him. He stood up and turned to face her.

She had a ball-bearing attached to a chain around her neck, and she was rubbing at it. It was polished, gleaming, perpetually fondled. Janulis was exhausted, thought Haig. Somewhere far below, there was a clang, then some loud cursing.

"You're sleeping here?" said Haig.

"When I can sleep," she said. "What do you want?"

"Your help," said Haig.

She said nothing, looked at him numbly. Haig looked again at her face, hollowed out, now, dark circles around her eyes. A puff of air would knock her over.

"Sit down, Alison," said Haig.

She blinked. The fearsome Alison Janulis, an exhausted wreck. Haig helped her sit on the mattress.

"What's going on?" said Haig.

"She's dying," muttered Janulis. "She's dying and I can't save her. A sickness. Some sickness. And I can't find it. I don't know what it is. I've tried everything, Haig. I've tried everything."

"That's why I'm here," said Haig. "Did Sile ask you to change Galatea?"

Her eyes shone. "What do you mean?"

"Reprogram her. So that the safety protocols weren't as stringent."

She gripped the ball-bearing ever tighter. "He said he would take her away from me."

"Sile forced you to do it?"

"I made some small changes. At first."

"What did you do?"

"I told Galatea that we were all gene-edited," she said, in a small voice. "That's all."

Gene-edited blocks of muscle, twice as strong and half as needy. Lift twice as much with half the air. Less food for more power. Biological robots. Except they weren't all gene-edited.

Not even close. Bethe and Attar were left. Maybe another ten across the whole place. Ten out of one hundred.

"That was enough," said Haig. "Listen. Aphelion will come here and if they think you've corrupted Galatea – "

She lurched up and screamed, "NO, NO, I won't let them – "

Haig wrestled her back to her mattress, felt her hollow-boned and fragile in his arm. "If you help me, you can get ahead of it, you can make sure Sile is the one who gets what he deserves. You haven't killed anyone. You were following your orders. You did as you were told."

"I didn't kill anyone," she muttered, trying to convince herself.

"Komarov found out," said Haig. "And Sile killed her for it."

"Yes," said Janulis. "She wrote a water algorithm. Redistribution. To the Farm, and beyond. Reclamation. But Galatea rejected it. Said we didn't need to reclaim water from anywhere because it wasn't needed. Galatea didn't see why gene-edited crew should need more water. She didn't tell Komarov why because Komarov didn't ask the right questions. Not at first. Komarov thought it only made sense if Galatea had been corrupted somehow. We ignored her, but then she tried to tell Aphelion – "

"You knew?"

"Who cares about your showers?" said Janulis. "The water, the food, the air, the gravity. Galatea grants us these things, and now she will take them away."

"Why didn't you tell anyone?"

"Because *she* would be taken away from *me*."

"She will now," said Haig.

Janulis glared at him. "Corruptions, Haig. She has been tainted. Her purity taken from her."

"Galatea is a fucking failure," said Haig. "Gunport's dying

around you and it's because your overgrown calculator doesn't know what a human being looks like."

"FUCK YOU," she screamed, swiping a useless arm at him, collapsing backwards onto her filthy mattress. She sobbed.

"You're out of your fucking mind, Alison. Can you fix her?"

"A small change at first. But it escaped from me. She did it so well. She was so good at it. Like a daughter, growing up. She doesn't listen to me anymore."

"I said, 'Can you fix her?'"

"Galatea would never let me die," she said.

"You don't sound convinced."

Janulis blinked, swallowed.

"What about Attar? Where's Attar?"

"Who knows where he is," she said. "The traitorous slug."

Haig leaned down to her and said, "You gave Galatea away the moment you let Sile use her to tell his lies."

She rolled over so that her back was to him and she was facing the trunk of Galatea.

"Emergency Batteries," she said. "Galatea will need them. But she's been draining the batteries for the glorious regal vision that is Gunport the second."

The Emergency Battery was a phalanx of batteries in the heart of Gunport. Fully charged, they could power Gunport for up to eight months. In the worst case, it would allow for evacuation via shuttles that could be launched from the Moon. They were kept at a constant full charge, any excess power being filtered into them, and any time the Reactor needed maintenance, the power could be taken back.

"The Batteries aren't charged? Fuck me Alison. The Reactor's been taken right down. What happens if the Reactor isn't restarted? Have the batteries been drained during the strike?

The fuck – "

Janulis smiled. "Galatea will save herself above all else."

"What does that mean?"

"If Galatea fails, everything controlled by a computer fails. Which *is* everything. It will siphon power from the air pumps, the water filtration, from everything, everything, to make sure it is the last to go."

Fuck, thought Haig.

He turned away from her and sent a message to Kaneda: *Emergency Batteries intact?*

Fuck fuck fuck –

Janulis said, "Leave me. I want to be alone with her."

"Sile's killed you both," said Haig. "You're going to lie down and let him do it?"

Kaneda sent back: *You're alive. I'm glad. Emergency Batteries are Security's responsibility. Problem?*

"Fuck you," she muttered.

Haig: *G compromised. Batteries likely empty.*

Kaneda: *Locked in Food Hall. Manual door release in Security. Can bypass G physically to recharge EBs but need tools and need Reactor online.*

Haig scratched his beard and said, "There's still time to do something fucking useful. I hope you will."

He left Janulis mumbling to herself.

Haig: *En route.*

Kaneda: *If batteries die, so do we.*

CHAPTER 15: BARRELS OF THE GUN

Haig stepped out of the Maintenance Shaft, gun raised, and moved slowly towards Security. It wasn't far, perhaps a minute's walk. A handful of steps.

He peered around the corner and saw the remnants of fighting. A body bent at wrong angles. Scorch marks, gouges in the concrete. A crack in the door of Security. Some porcelain bullet shards shattered and underfoot. Quiet now.

Too quiet, thought Haig. A lot of control can be taken from here. Lots of doors, the communications systems. A handful of cameras. Where's Attar? Holden?

He picked his way through the debris and marched into Security, gun still raised.

Computer screens had splintered on hitting the floor. Plastic furniture had burst under fighting or gunfire or both. Everywhere Haig walked now, a story was told in the different cracking that he heard. Shallow and brittle? Bullet shards. Gunfights. Sharp and loud? Plastic. Furniture or equipment. What had happened here?

The Office was intact at the back of Security. The Tank was empty, the cell door hanging open. He looked inside. A spray of blood, dried and black, spattered the floor.

All of this in a matter of hours, thought Haig. How delicately it had all been held together. How easily it had unravelled.

The console in the office lit up when he prodded it, and he exhaled, realising he had been holding his breath.

Haig to Kaneda: *Access override how?*

Kaneda: *Plug tablet/e-sleeve in. Agree to share.*

"Anson, come in."

Sile.

"Come in Haig, damn you."

Haig ignored him. He groped under the desk and connected the tablet directly to the Security Station console. The tablet flashed and Kaneda took control.

Kaneda: *Need 5m. Sile will know.*

"Surrender, Anson. I know you're in Security. I won't have you letting your co-conspirators out."

Haig stepped over to the doors and yanked a plastic cover away from the Airseal Lever, then put his back into pulling the lever down, clamping the doors shut. The room was its own ecosystem now. No air would escape through the doors, and no-one could enter.

"Surrender. It's the only way that this can end well for you. Admit what you did and accept and the consequences. You'll be protected."

Prick, thought Haig. He jabbed the microphone symbol.

"You murdered a woman for your own gain – "

"I – "

"Then stuffed her in a spacesuit and dumped her outside – "

"Now – "

"Built another Gunport, doomed everyone on the first – "

"Progess – "

"Framed me for a murder you made me watch – "

"You'll say anything – "

"Sent your twirly-handed assassin after me – "

"Dekker was – "

"When this riot is over and everyone's safe, you're done."

A moment.

Sile's breathing heavy and angry. "I'll make sure you burn, I'll burn your – "

"Oh, fuck off, John," and he snapped the comms off.

Shadows moving outside Security. Bootsteps. He tucked himself under the desk and held the pistol.

The doors were tried. They beeped red. Then by hand. Clanking and rattling.

Then a pause before –

Gunfire ripped through the doors. Bullets punching through. The plastic screen above him exploded. Bullets raked the desk and blasted the tablet into shards. Porcelain bullet shrapnel tinkling onto the floor in front of him.

Silence.

Haig pushed away from the concrete, raised his gun, peered out.

The main door was hanging open, battle-scarred. Attar stood in the aisle, reloading a pistol. He saw Haig shifting his weight and ducked behind a desk.

Haig moved out of the office, staying low, listening for Attar moving. He circled around but Attar had moved away, and Haig lost sight of him.

Attar's gun clacked off to the right and Haig turned towards him into a shot that ripped a chunk of desk away. The plastic burst up and sprayed across Haig's cheek, drawing blood. Haig cursed and fired back, wild, hitting the wall with a succession of weak crunches.

Attar was fast, striding around and taking aim, only Haig's scramble stopping him from being cut down. Haig tumbled through a gap under the desks and crawled towards the Tank, hoping to get around it, when a chair landed and buckled in front of him, forced him to turn.

Attar stood on top of a desk now, firing intermittently, a steady stream of deliberate bullets.

Haig realised that he was being mocked, Attar enjoying himself. He turned and began to crawl to Security's main door. The desk in front of him collapsed under another lobbed chair so he stopped and waited. Attar would have to come to him.

There was quiet for a moment.

"You dare to shoot me, you speck, you mote, you fucking mote of dust. You're so fucking little, with your useless leg and your tiny mind, you don't understand how insignificant you are. When lives are unequal, when mine is worth more than so many others."

Attar leapt down and grabbed the desk above Haig, started ripping it up.

Haig turned his face away and covered his eyes, then emptied a clip into the bottom of the desk. Attar roared. The desk sheared away in a blizzard of plastic and Attar sank through it, his hand speckled with blood and shards. Some of the shots had landed. The bulk of the desk cracked and sagged, plastic bursting across the room.

When Haig looked up, Attar was clutching his face and stumbling out.

Haig let him, shook himself clean, plastic tinkling onto the floor, plucking the sharpest shards out of his clothes and skin. Then he lurched up, taking a moment to balance and breathe, leaning against one of the chairs. The Tank wobbled, his vision unsteady, then cleared. Exhaustion was creeping in around the edges, taking hold.

The corridors were empty, lights on. In some corners, it was like nothing was happening at all. In others, like the battle would spring to life at any moment. Softer emergency lighting in places, harsh strip lights in others. Some UV, some not. Power fluctuating.

The tablet had exploded before it could do its work, which meant Kaneda was still trapped in the Food Hall. He had to try to restore power to the Emergency Batteries himself. He needed to try. The Food Hall was locked up tight and would be guarded by Attar, Holden, whoever, so getting Kaneda out was not going to happen, not yet.

Haig was on his own.

***

The Emergency Batteries were monolithic slabs of smooth black plastic and metal, featureless and imposing, each about the size of a large person. Each had its own bay, its own palm-sized screen. They were in countless rows and columns, the low ceiling imposing, the darkness and heat trying to reject Gunport's crew.

Haig crouched and listened. There was the gentle hum of electronics, the dry stink of circuit boards. A computer clicked and whirred. He felt his lips pucker in the dry. Haig caught sight of the skin around his nails, cracked and receding. All of him was dry. Too dry.

He went to look for a control panel. Each of the phalanx of batteries displayed a number in red. Eight percent, six percent, three. Of course they were low, thought Haig. They're Emergency Batteries. They should be at ninety-five and above but it's siphoned off for the new Gunport. The batteries have never been allowed to fully recharge. Which begs the question: why didn't this get flagged before? And returns the answer: it has been flagged.

Sile knows all about it.

He knew about it when the strike happened. If the Reactor was online, it could be contained. But the strike meant it was draining and draining. If Haig hadn't come, Acaba would have met the same fate as Komarov. A duet in zero-gravity. Floating bodies and no-one to find them. Humanity's base instincts transported. Wherever in the galaxy, greed had power.

The main door to the Battery opened, and Holden entered with two men. All three carried pistols. Holden carried a long black bag, something heavy inside.

Haig stepped away from the panel and into an alcove, out of Tobin's sight.

Holden turned. Had heard Haig's feet and their slightly out-of-sync steps.

"Anson? Is that you?"

He peered round and saw Holden motioning for the men to surround him. The Maintenance Tunnel was too far for Haig to reach without being shot at.

"Would you like to know what Excalibur brought for me, Anson?" said Holden.

The men had separated. They crept along their separate walls, guns raised. Haig breathed. Waited.

"Two things," said Holden, setting himself against one of the blocks.

Along Haig's wall, the man crept forward. Gun raised. Not practised. Not checking the shadows. Not professional.

Haig waited for him to step past. Let him walk alone in silence. Thought he knew where Haig was. Haig stepped in behind him. Raised his gun.

"Gun down," said Haig.

This man was isolated, alone. No line of sight to the others. Haig heard Holden and the other man's feet shuffle, readjusting.

"So it is you," said Holden, his voice changed. Sound echoed from the blocks of batteries. He was further away now. Some whispering. More scuffs of boots. "Do as he says, Jensen."

"Place it at your feet," said Haig.

Jensen did, and Haig backed him up, collected the gun, then hit him hard in the forehead with the butt of the gun. Jensen fell and thudded out into the corridor.

Holden sighed. "Anson, you need to give yourself up. Should never have come back."

"Give up so that I can be thrown over the side of a railing, eh, Holden? Policework in action?"

Holden's tone hardened, darkened.

"The first thing was a Tobin special," he said. "Vacuum packed beef. Real, too, not protein-farmed. Crawling in bacteria, most likely. It's only now that I'm thinking about how I would actually cook it. Butter and oil and salt."

Haig heard zips and toggles being untied. Something being slotted into something else. Holden's bag.

Holden grunted. "The other is simple enough. It's a gun. But it's perfect for using out here. It doesn't need ammunition. Just needs regassing every so often. Uses compressed gas to launch whatever you load into it. Right now it's full of crushed desks and chairs. Razor sharp plastic. Shred someone through to their guts in a single shot. If I put concrete in it I can take down whole fucking doors."

"That's a lot of effort to get into someone's bedroom," said Haig. Glib, thought Haig. Try and make him move. Try to get him where I want him, even if I have to blurt out stupid shite.

Footsteps began again in earnest. Haig moved to the end of the column of batteries and peered around.

Holden was holding what looked like a rifle with a bucket slapped to the side. A gas cylinder rested underneath the barrel.

Holden saw Haig duck back, said, "Surrender."

The other man was easing around the opposite block of batteries, aiming for a pincer movement. Haig breathed deeply, then raised the pistol and stepped around the battery, fired two shots at Tobin's feet, and marched across the centre of the room. Tobin jerked backwards, surprised, fired a shot of his plastic-musket into the ceiling, obliterating a striplight.

Haig came upon the other man, dazed by the broken light. He tried to raise his gun before Haig cracked him across the temple, the gun skittering away. He fell down, clutching his blooded head, trying to stand, falling. Haig kicked him hard in the back, and he scuttled back to Holden. Jensen was staggering to his feet too.

"Are you going to rip my throat out as well?" said Holden.

"You knew this riot was coming," said Haig.

"Not this," said Holden. "Not exactly. But the anger's been rising, rising."

Haig heard the fumble of a gun being reloaded and stepped out, levelled his pistol at Holden's chest.

"You two, fuck off," said Haig, and the two men with Holden did exactly that, holding their heads, wiping blood out of their eyes, escaping through the main door.

Holden was wild-eyed, dishevelled, shards of plastic sprinkled liberally through his hair. He was desperately trying to stuff some pieces of a keyboard into the bucket, detached at his feet. A pistol dangled loosely on a length of electrical wire at his side.

"You know I didn't kill Barnes," said Haig. "You know Sile's twisted everything. It amazes me what people choose to believe. That's why there's riots. People don't believe him. People are starting to realise that he won't keep them safe. "

"This place is a box. A concrete coffin. Everyone can sense it. We're out here, at the end of the universe. We can all feel it, like anything can happen here. You can do anything."

"Listen to me." Haig shook his hand at the slabs of battery next to him. "These batteries are at nearly at zero. Do the fucking math. The Reactor goes down, any rescue will take far too long to get here. And the Reactor will go down if this rioting carries on much longer. Sile's going to kill us all."

"There's a chance here, Anson. To get out. To get out from under the company. To make this place our own. We just need leverage. Some control back. Something that they want."

Now Holden gestured to the batteries.

"Power," he said. "This place needs power. Everything else comes from it, like the stars. Everything grows from it. You control the power, you control Gunport. Aphelion would never let this place go. Sile needs leverage. A way to make them surrender it to him."

"If you do that, the company will cut you off. Like a gangrenous limb. They're building another one. At the Mine. They've turned the Mine into another Gunport. They'll just build around you. They'll take both. This place is already borderline ceremonial."

"You can do anything here," said Holden quietly, and tightened his grip around his pistol.

Haig watched his hand, watched his finger curl. Saw his eyebrows pinch, watched him hold his breath. "I'll shoot you," said Haig, wiping sweat out of his eyebrows. Haig's exhaustion crept in around the edges. Exhausted with people making poor choices.

"I don't think you will," said Holden. "No, you won't."

He – very slowly, almost imperceptibly – began to raise the gun. He looked at Haig and then at the gun and then back at Haig, like it wasn't within his control anymore.

Haig exhaled. If he raises it beyond his hip, I'll shoot him. Holden was getting more brazen. It came up beyond his hip. If it passes his stomach, thought Haig. It passed his stomach. There was something approaching a smirk on Holden's face. His composure was wavering. At chest height he jerked his arm forward –

Haig shot him.

Holden blinked a few times. His chest heaved, trying to find vital oxygen, desperately unsuccessful, each attempt at a deep breath getting stuck in his throat. There was a flower-shaped hole in his chest, blood oozing into his clothes.

He scowled at Haig, and tried to shoot him, a feral groan escaping a dying chest, bullets cracking harmlessly into the ceiling.

He sank down, disbelieving, and then he was dead.

Holden's gun was sticky with his blood, so Haig left it and collected the other. It was one of the Security Station's, the clip missing a handful of bullets. He had only been outside for a few hours. How much shooting had they done? He plucked the gun up with thumb and forefinger. Emptied the pistol, took the clip, dismantled it, hands slick with blood. He tossed the firing pin. No-one else was firing this gun now, he thought.

Holden was lying on his front with his arms by his sides. The blood had seeped from under him, a gored circle forming. The gun would still fire, covered in blood, mud, or whatever else could possibly stop it.

There was a momentary pull of guilt for Holden. Haig's negotiator's mind pressed and prodded at him. Could you have talked him down? No, thought Haig. No, there was no time. Are you justifying shooting someone you didn't like very much? No, I'm not. He was Sile's lackey and he was trying to consolidate power. What happens when people realise that the people in charge are only in charge because they are allowed to be? Those people wreak violence. Seize and grab and clutch and rip for control. The last desperations of a rocket-riddled shuttle, sinking into a well of gravity, trying to escape and failing, taking everything down with it.

Haig touched his e-sleeve before looking again at Holden's body. He could have Kaneda walk him through it via e-sleeve but there was a way to get Kaneda down here.

He stood over Holden and when he realised what he would have to do to him to be able to unlock the Food Hall, he felt his stomach lurch.

***

They were waiting for him.

He opened the Food Hall and met his welcoming committee. They had feet planted, hands raised with lumps of concrete, plastic blocks. They had chosen terrible weapons. Either too heavy or too brittle. None of them moved. They were waiting for someone else to cast the first block. Acaba stepped out.

He was standing in the doorway with the bloody strings of Holden's commstem in one hand and the pistol in the other. Haggard and hunched.

Acaba whispered among them, told them to calm, then turned to Haig and said, "What the fuck, Anson?"

"You tell me," he said, lowering his gun.

"I found out you'd been taken and I told Sile we weren't having it. It didn't make sense. You looking into Komarov and Mihalik and then being hung up for murder. You were trying to make it right. I told him that. There was no proof of what he said. Barnes' body got ejected before anyone else saw it, and we're supposed to take Sile's word for it? It stank, Haig, like it was a greasy film that stank, you could feel it coating you. Made me feel dirty. So I said we wouldn't work. The strike was back on. And this time it wasn't just us. Chiaki said she couldn't work without water. Tobin stood his guys down. Sile fucking lost it. I've seen flashes of it. He couldn't believe it. I think he just expected us to roll over again. It's like the film has been lifted from people's eyes. Like now, they know he isn't on our side."

"What happened?"

Haig felt a large and sudden need to sit down. Acaba pulled him by the shoulder to a bench where a crumpled corpse lay. It was Choudhury, Haig realised, broken and bloody, face pummelled to wet meat. His wrists had been broken, his palms pointing outwards, fingers cracked, arms with extra right angles, twisted near elbows.

Haig fell heavily onto the bench next to Choudhury and scratched his beard, rubbed his eyes, yawned.

"Attar grabbed him when they piled out of the elevator. Broke his hands and then his face. No warning, nothing."

Haig said quietly, "He deserved better."

Kaneda pushed through the crowd and said, "Haig? The Batteries? If it's as you say – "

Haig held up Holden's commstem and said, "Path to the Batteries is safe. Take this."

Kaneda stared at him for a long moment, then nodded, took the bloody commstem, frowned, went to the Elevator.

Acaba said, "Why is he going to the Batteries?"

"What state is the Reactor in?"

"Is that all you give a fuck about?"

"Come on, Sunita," he said, suddenly conscious of another twenty pairs of eyes looking at him. Hands clenching, brows tightening, nostrils flaring. Adrenaline and cortisol still high.

"If the Reactor fails, we're all dead," he said.

"The Batteries are – " she started to say, but stopped when he shook his head. "What did they do?"

Haig grimaced, nodded. "Sile's building another Gunport on top of the Mine. He's been siphoning power to do it. When you went on strike, they drained even quicker. Komarov found out, and it got her killed. Dekker tried to kill me. Dekker's dead. Holden was in the Batteries. Holden's dead." He closed his eyes. "I'm tired, Sunita."

She was wide-eyed, afraid. Quietly, she said, "Haig, that's what'll keep us alive. They'll have to send a shuttle now, won't they? Rescue us?"

"We need to fix it now. On our own. They might send a shuttle but if the Reactor's off and there's no battery power, there'll be no-one here to save. That's plan A. There's no plan B."

"We need Galatea," said Acaba. "Sile always kept it all separate. Said that compartmentalised would help us to focus on doing the best we could. I made the power but Engineering distributed it. I never really knew where it went. Only he knew all of that. We need Janulis. Then I can stop it."

"There's bad blood here," he said, a little louder, for everyone to hear. "But we've one thing in common. All of us. We all want to get out of this alive. That means you all need to keep the Reactor working, and the programmers need to get Galatea working. And you need to let each other do it. You need to help each other."

There was some muttering. As Haig felt it was about to subside, a woman stepped forward, slapped him, then spat on him, and before he could speak, they –

He was shoved roughly to the floor, stood on, kicked. The mob surged as he tried to stand, and he was thrown back onto the concrete, scraping elbows and knee. They carried him violently between legs and boots, his head knocked down by wayward knees time and time again, the mob feeding itself, angrier and angrier.

He reached a hand out for a bench before his fingers were stamped on. His chest was crushed, air pushed out of it, and he was fading. He could feel it, blood thumping against his temples, the fake blue sky like the gentle death of a dream.

He pointed his gun up and shot at the clouds.

The mob hissed and made a hole, like a wound, Haig at the centre.

He got to his feet. Swung his pistol in a rough circle. Saw them baring teeth. Raising fists. Low growl. He shot at feet.

He pulled himself onto a bench.

"For fuck's sake. What the fuck are you doing? You know what I'm saying is true. Of course you do. You're not fucking stupid. So what are you doing? Do you feel better? For crushing the messenger half to death? You need them and they need you. It's that simple. There's no Emergency Battery power." He waited, let that hit home. "No rescue shuttle is getting here before we freeze. Or suffocate. Power goes, so does the heat, so do the air recyclers. You all know this better than I do."

Acaba rose from among the crowd, cradling her jaw.

He slowed down, lowered his voice.

"So what will you do? Die for what? For Aphelion? To settle a few scores? Don't be fucking stupid."

"They need to pay," said a voice, but it was a half-hearted attempt at defiance now. The crowd was coming round.

"I'll open the elevator," said Haig, to Acaba, "If you take your team down to the Reactor."

Acaba nodded, led the way. Her team squashed in together, and she stared at Haig, the elevator packed with technicians, brooding, silent, while the doors closed.

There was silence. Haig lay down on the bench, alone,

watching clouds move and reverberate that he knew should have been still. When he tried to blink the clouds into oblivion, there was a dull thudding behind his eyes. When he moved his eyes quickly from side to side, his stomach went with them. Only when he centred and stilled his eyes did his stomach settle.

When he got up, he went to the water machine and held a cup under it, then pressed the button. Rattling and hissing pre-empted a flickering red light and unnerving silence. Haig fought back a wave of nausea, stepped backwards, watched the machine's flickering light turn into something solid. Somewhere down below, the water was giving out. The Chemical Line had ceased. All of the splitting of fuel or the smashing together of gases to create oxygen and water had halted. Never mind less water in shortened showers. There was no water at all.

He realised he was still holding the cup. He tossed it on the bench and went to the comms panel.

"Haig for Kaneda," he said.

"Haig," said a voice, swollen with relief. "I've locked myself in the Batteries. I've had to mangle the wiring to keep Galatea out, but the Batteries will recharge as soon as the Reactor restarts."

"Good," said Haig. "I'm still in the Food Hall. Acaba's taken her team down. Water's finished up here. When you've secured the Batteries, can you get down to the Chemical Line?"

"I can try," said Kaneda. "You sound unwell."

Haig rubbed at the various bruising and swellings Gunport's crew had given him. "Nothing a few years of rest and relaxation won't solve," he said, smiling despite himself. "They should behave now. Watch out for Attar. He won't be happy."

"I will," said Kaneda.

"Get the water and air going again. And if you can't, then – "

"Stop them from exploding."

"Please."

"What will you do?"

"I need to have another crack at Janulis. If power is back on track, then she needs to right Galatea."

There was hesitant optimism in Hiro's voice. "If the Core and Reactor are working, then we may be alright. What will happen afterwards? After everything returns to normal? If everything returns to normal?"

"Fuck knows," said Haig.

"And Sile?"

"We're going to have a conversation he won't like."

***

Haig began sweating as soon as the elevator doors opened, hit in the face by a wall of sickly warmth. Heat rose from pipes, walls, wires, and he felt like he was wading through sand, each step sinking into a mess of cables. Bile rose in his throat.

He picked his way through the corridors, through the humming and whirring circuits, past exposed wiring and hanging cabling, around the carcasses of computers and electronics, catching the dry stink of burned electronics.

Message from Acaba: *Reactor live. Kaneda confirms Batteries charging.*

Typing and muttering greeted him in Galatea's centre from high up. A shadow working on the screens above.

"Janulis," he said, making for a ladder. "The Batteries are charging. We need Galatea working."

He clambered onto the first gantry, a hollow clank reverberating through the chamber. There should be more people here, he thought. More noise, more working. Busier.

"Janulis," he said again.

The next gantry carried a shattered tablet, cracked plastic. Haig's stomach knotted and he drew his pistol.

Attar's head appeared at the top of the ladder. "There's no need for that."

Haig stepped backwards, surprised, awkwardly raised his pistol.

Attar sighed and showed his open hands. "I've come to tend to Galatea. Her mother is nowhere to be seen." His voice was heavy with resignation, and he turned back to the screens, ignoring Haig.

Haig lay on the gantry a moment longer, pistol raised, before getting to his feet. Attar was speaking before he'd even started climbing the first rung of the ladder.

"It's staggering," said Attar. "I am staggered."

Haig climbed up onto the central gantry. The screens flashed with some lines of code, some other technical information. Attar was looking up at them, his back to Haig.

"Alison has nurtured Galatea through her entire life," said Attar. "A great achievement, truly. But something is wrong."

Attar turned around. Half of his face was scratched and bloody, his eye closed. Like a slab of raw meat.

Attar sighed. "She told Galatea lies. But not as a mother protecting a daughter from a cruel world. This was toxic. Like a microbe at Galatea's heart. A small germ, allowed to grow. Each microbe multiplying, eating at something in Galatea's mind. The beginning of a slow and certain reaction. The inevitability of it. Every time a shower ended early. Every time the gravity failed. Every time a door wouldn't open or wouldn't close."

"She told Galatea that everyone on Gunport was gene-edited. Can you fix it? Can you reprogram it?"

"No," said Attar. "This was not the only change made. After Alison told Galatea her lies, Galatea made countless small changes. I have tried to tell her that we are not all edited, but she cannot reconcile such a change. No, her decline is confirmed. I can slow it, but not cure her. Janulis was the master of her code. She kept secrets, Haig. Even now, I don't know how much she rewrote, how much she changed."

"Could Janulis do it?"

"No. At least, I believe not. She has written and rewritten programs. Some are missing entirely. Others serve no obvious function. I believe she was trying to repair her own mistakes, unsuccessfully. Galatea was altered by Janulis, but then altered by Sile too. And when Janulis tried to fix Sile's 'additions', it only made things worse. Galatea is dying, Anson. Cancerous."

"There's not a back-up?"

"Do *you* have a back-up?" Attar spat. "Galatea is a living entity, Haig. She evolves and processes and she will die."

"You can't reset her?"

"Have you not been listening? It would be a simplistic solution to a problem you cannot begin to comprehend."

"Then make me comprehend."

"At its simplest, after Galatea was born, she began to learn. Since she became mother she has learned to look after us. A reset, as you crudely put it, would not bring back the Galatea we need. It would kill our Galatea and birth a child who knows nothing of the problems we have."

"I need to find Janulis."

"Go," said Attar, turning back to the screens, waving a hand. "It will do us no good."

Then, Sile's voice through Gunport's base-wide comms: "This is John Sile, Executive Officer. This violence will end now. Some of you have seen fit to side with the murderer Anson Haig. I have tried to get him to surrender, but he refused. So you have an hour to turn him over to me before extreme measures are enforced. I will preserve Gunport first and you second. You've been warned. You have an hour."

Fuck, thought Haig. There's all kinds of things Sile could do. The fire suppression systems could be activated, sucking the air out. Doors closed. Water kept from them. Sile would get the ringleaders in a room then suffocate them. Or look at who he needed then remove the rest –

He could use this as a way to get to Acaba. Replace her. Find someone else, someone more pliable. Someone who might even send power to the second Gunport in exchange for certain favours. More water. Months shaved off their contract. A bigger bonus at the end. The promise of a cool breeze and clean water on Earth.

Attar had turned away from his screens and was looking at Haig with dark curiosity.

"Don't worry," said Haig, patting his gun. "I'm going."

CHAPTER 16: I'M HERE TO TALK

Sile's floor had taken the brunt of the fighting. The lights overhead had been broken, swinging into the corridor, flickering, shadows lengthening and shortening and twisting into corners. Shallow bullet dents in concrete became bottomless chasms as the swinging light contorted itself around its cable.

Haig stepped over a body immediately on exiting the elevator. Not someone he recognised. He picked his way through lumps of concrete and dust, gun raised. He peered around the door of Sile's office and saw him sat behind his desk, scratching his chin with the barrel of a polymer pistol.

"Don't let these people suffer any more because of you," said Sile. "I've a handful of environmental controls prepared here, Anson. The first will override the fire safety protocols in the Reactor. A minute after that, the oxygen is gone. The Reactor's too far from the surface to be voided into space so it's an argon system instead. Every single one of them would suffocate, cursing your name on blue lips. If you've got a gun, throw it on the table and come in. Sit down."

Haig figured he had no choice. He tossed the gun onto the oaken monstrosity and watched it scrape a line parallel to the other he had made, then sat at the end of the table nearest the door. The gun was well out of reach, settled at the other end.

"I came to talk, John," said Haig. "The two of us. Calmly and sensibly. Thinking before we do anything else."

Sile nodded. "I ran my father's company," he began. He spoke easily, practised, looked from chair to chair as though performing for a larger audience.

"Profit margins soared until they used cheap materials. I was the scapegoat, you see. My father blamed me. I deserved better. A few weeks before he died, he said to me, 'We all make mistakes.' And he looked at me. Right in my eyes. This phlegmy old carcass rotting in his bed. Those yellow eyes. Enormous bloody tangerines. Staring at me. I knew what he wanted. He wanted me to say sorry. Well, it wasn't my place to say sorry. I did nothing wrong. The apology he wanted was from the plant. Or the factory. Or the designer. They all blamed me, you see. When it started to go wrong. It was their designs, their materials. The company went under and I took what I could. Aphelion was only too happy to hoover up the plans, the patents, the IP – rubbing their fat hands with glee. And gave me a failing department, infested with losers and wasters. 'Turn it around,' they said. It was unfair, Anson. A bombed-out husk. Of course I couldn't rescue it. Of course it sank. I was persona non grata. Dumped somewhere unbecoming. But I started to sense a shift in Aphelion's priorities. They wanted to send people into space, so I volunteered. After I gave them so much, too. Sent me here to fail. Outpost at the end of the universe. And then, I made it a success. Beyond all expectations. I think they hoped I would die on the way. I would have taken a warrior's death, exploding in a ball of rattling fire, soaring across the stars. Spectacular, futile, everything and nothing. But I survived the BD-C. And I made this place work. Made it make money. Got more out of this lot than they ever thought possible. Getting more out of them than they ever wanted to give. Sometimes you just need to know what motivates them. What they need and what they want. Sometimes they want to earn your loyalty. Sometimes they need a reminder of who they work for. Aphelion never took this place seriously. Like a black sheep. A black sheep compounded by a black sheep. They sent me here so that when it failed, they could pull the plug. Have all the ammunition they needed to shut it down forever. They wanted to replace us with robots, Haig. More and more robots. Safer, they said. Unscrew Galatea and pick its bones clean. Instead of sending ships here, they'd bypass us. Well, Gunport was too successful. Made too much money. And so to save everyone here, to save Gunport, I started building another. Make this moon into the only way ships could get to Echion Alpha. The premier mid-route port. So big that they couldn't ignore us. Would need to use us. I knew they wouldn't say yes, so I went ahead without them. Without Aphelion's permission. I was very clever, you see. I had Dekker lay the cables and Alison told Galatea to send the power. Acaba was with them. With Aphelion. She never wanted this place to be successful. She was Aphelion's spy, working against me, working against Gunport. Against humanity. I had her cut out of the loop. Reminded her that power and power alone was her remit, and that I controlled where it went. Alison reprogrammed Galatea. Emilio went out to the Mine and brought it back to life. Glorious industry, in silence, only a mile away. It could have been billions of miles away, but we made it here. We built something new. Made what was better. Invested in our future. And then your bitch Komarov came along. Knew that Galatea was helping me. Wouldn't listen to what she was told. Janulis told her. She wouldn't listen. She pushed me, Haig, and I pushed back, and, well, I was forced to do it. She wanted to tell Aphelion, but it wasn't ready yet. If she hadn't interfered, she wouldn't have been hurt. She had her finger in my face, and I shoved her, and, well, her head didn't like the concrete. I didn't deal with that well, let me tell you. Emilio cleaned up for us. Hid in her in the biggest empty space we had. But then your Acaba, she decided to go on strike. 'Conditions,' she says. Water, air, gravity. I knew she wouldn't understand if I told her what it was in aid of, so I didn't. She went on strike with her moron crew and Aphelion sent you. You, goddamn you. Emilio didn't clean up as well as he should have. He could have taken her out of that suit and put her into the Chemical Line. Or Holden should have told him to keep her at the Mine, just until our new project was complete. Anyway. Your Komarov hit the Tower and everyone lost their minds. It is just a body, for goodness' sake. We're in space, Anson! People die here. All of the time. And she gave herself up for progress, for humanity. A worthy death, if ever there could be one. But you, Anson, you wouldn't let it lie. Conrad, and this girl Mihalik, and Felix, and Prendrick and Barnes, and Emilio and Dominic. They're all on you. Conrad wouldn't have lost his hands if not for your desperation to bring a dead body inside. She was already dead! Mihalik killing herself because you unsettled her. Felix being confronted in his own home. Barnes chose the wrong side, Anson. Emilio and Dominic desperately trying to repair your mistakes. Everything that has happened here is because of you, Anson. You should have done your job. Now Aphelion and their kangaroo courts will be trying to lay this around my neck. After everything I have done for them, for humanity. Well, I won't have it. You'll surrender and confess the truth."

"The truth is simpler than all of that," said Haig. "And it's shorter because the truth doesn't need your steaming bullshit to justify itself."

Sile scoffed.

Haig said, "You wanted more power and more control. I don't think even you know why. But Komarov found out. She was going to tell Aphelion what you'd done, and you couldn't have that. They'd bring you home. And everything they said about you, how fucking useless you are, it'd all be true, wouldn't it?"

Sile ground his teeth and said, "You're a fucking liar!"

"So you murdered her. And then you panicked and put her in a spacesuit and dumped her outside. You threatened Barnes, bribed Retallick. You cajoled and intimidated and had Dekker and Blatt act as your thugs. When Komarov reappeared, you didn't want anyone to know what you'd done. You lied and lied and lied. First there was no body. Then there was an accident. Then you said I murdered her. You couldn't have Mihalik telling me who she was, so you had Blatt threaten and rape her. *You* murdered her by driving her to suicide. I confronted Blatt about it and *he* tried to murder *me*. Then, you said Blatt murdered her. You murdered Prendrick because he told me about the non-autopsy. Missed him out of your grandstanding shite, didn't you? And you murdered Barnes because he told me how he'd been threatened. You had me thrown out of a fucking Airlock, John!"

"And how magnificently you responded," said Sile, a weary pride creeping into his voice. "If only you had seen the bigger picture too. What I could do with someone like you. So right. So sure. So unbending."

Haig spoke over him, determined to get to the end of his rebuttal, "Dekker tried to shoot me with a mining cannon. A fucking cannon. Attar murdered Choudhury because you've lost control. This isn't yours anymore, John. Acaba showed how brittle your power is. You've lost it. You murdered and lied and cheated and now you've been found out. And you don't even know why you've done it."

"I've been outside, Anson. I've been to the next step. And you can't smell it, can you, but your mind tells you what it smells like. It smelled of wet dirt and rust, to me, Anson. The dirt paste being used to create those shells of buildings. The stink of it. When the new Gunport was ready, we would have used both. Space there and space here. Automated systems, run by Galatea. Really push to the stars. Commit fully. Suffer now to thrive later."

"Bullshit," said Haig. "Make them suffer to help you thrive. You're a liar and a killer and Aphelion are going to bring you back and hand you over to the WSA who will dump you in a hole."

Sile was shaking violently now.

"You have your version of events," he stuttered, standing up on unsteady feet, using both hands to pick up the gun, "And I have mine. An outsider, interfering in things he does not understand. When you're dead, all that will remain is my version."

Haig pushed his chair back, the wood screeching against the concrete.

Sile raised the gun. Pointed it at Haig. And held it, his hand shaking.

And held it. And swallowed. And blinked.

And raised it to his own temple –

Haig lurched forward, too far away, not having this prick kill himself –

Sile sobbed, moaned, roared at the ceiling –

Pointed it back at Haig –

"You useless jelly," said Sile, "You've done this to me."

Pulled the trigger –

Haig dropped to the side of the table, splinters ripping the air around him, shredding at his back, rolled underneath –

Sile fired into the table, bullets spracking, ricocheting, ripping up ancient wood –

Haig saw a new set of boots enter the room, new gunfire meeting old –

Sile went down, so did the new boots –

Janulis' face crashed to the floor, shoulder pumping blood, panting –

Sile, clutching his stomach, groaning –

Janulis standing, firing wildly –

Haig reached up, groping for his gun, Sile noticing –

Sile blasting a chunk of table into Haig's hand, Haig snatching his hand back, bloody and spiked with blood –

Janulis landing another shot, Sile going down –

Sile under the table, Janulis shooting the table legs –

"You fucking killed her!" she screamed –

Haig scrambling to get out from under it –

Sile hitting Janulis in the legs, groin –

Groaning wood –

Haig out –

Splintering, cracking, *going* –

Sile under –

Janulis down –

The table cracked and splintered and collapsed, boomed thunderous, sagged at the centre and thudded, vibrated through the floor, shook the lights, threw concrete powder into the air.

Haig staggered to the door, eardrums burst. He leaned against the door and reeled.

The concrete dust hissed down, like gentle rain, and much of it remained in the air. Haig coughed and choked and lurched out into the corridor, sank to his knees, bent double, deep breaths, gulping.

It took a long time before he felt he could stand, climbed up the door frame. He looked into the room –

Janulis was lying prone, body full of black red blood. Dust coagulated as it came down, stuck to her clothes, her face, matted in her hairline. Haig checked her pulse and she was dead. The lines around her face had smoothed out, her hair unspooling out around her head. All of her determination to be the mother of Galatea, all of the plotting and scheming and everything else, had gone out of her. She was younger in death.

Sile's legs stuck out unnaturally angled from under the collapsed table. The rest of him was a bloodied pulp. Haig wobbled over to him and tapped his foot.

In a moment, it washed over Haig, like rancid sewage, like Gunport's recycling plants. His stomach rolled one way and he felt dizzy, felt his brain going opposite to his stomach. It was over.

Sile was dead.

EPILOGUE (PART 1)

Kaneda had spent two days with a 3D-printed saw – he made three, because why make one good one when you can make three shite ones? – to cut the table into rough planks, now piled in the centre of the room. The dust had settled onto chairs so that when they sat down, a puff of concrete escaped.

Haig had contacted Aphelion and IPRA and the WSA in the hours after Sile had died. He had told them everything that he knew, from start to finish, and evidenced it where he could. While they waited for Aphelion's reply, they got to work bringing Gunport back up to a condition in which they would be safe. The Reactor was restored, and the Chemical Line resumed making fuel, water. Kaneda and Retallick made repairs to doors and walls damaged in the fighting. Chiaki was able to rescue the bulk of her crops, and the protein blocks were back to their disgusting but vital selves. They stayed busy because what else was there to do? The supply ships continued their orbits. The Tower pinged them to circle indefinitely.

Bags of concrete debris made their way up and down the elevator. Piles of concrete dust were everywhere, swept into corners or ducts, the gentle spattering sounds echoing down the maintenance tunnels where people could not find the energy to put them in the right place.

The bodies were wrapped in plastic and stored in the oxygenless Pit.

An uneasy peace was brokered with Attar, who arrested Galatea's decline. He took it down to its base functions, buying them two years or so of coherent Galatean thought. In the event, they wouldn't need two years.

Over the next few days, adrenaline coursed out of Haig and he spent most of it sleeping.

He was exhausted. There was a patchwork of bruising of all shapes and sizes, colours and creeds that decorated his chest and back. The join between his leg and prosthetic was so swollen and tender that the prosthetic had been off for most of it. Haig had near peeled it away, the skin throbbing and then roaring as he did so, reminding him never to undertake quite so much physical activity quite so quickly again.

"I won't be going to Echion Alpha, then," said Wecht.

She sat with Haig and Tobin and Acaba in the Spacewalk. All gunshine fuelled.

"This won't be the end of the colony programs," said Haig. "Gunport was always like a glorified decoration. A castle built on sand. Sile made sure everyone forgot to look at the foundations. But Aphelion will turn to robots and the rest of it. The B-DCs will be revamped. You'll get there. Might just take a bit longer."

"I just want to get out of here," said Acaba. "Some air. Some trees. Trees, Sarah. Some trees."

"I want to get back to my boy," said Haig. "Growing old without me."

"Are you sure about going?" said Acaba. "To Echion Alpha?"

"Just because Sile fucked up Gunport doesn't mean we shouldn't still try. That the universe is just waiting for us."

Tobin raised his cup. "I wouldn't go anywhere near that shite. But I wish you all the best, Sarah."

They raised cups, sipped.

Retallick came and sat. "Any word from Aphelion?"

"None, Conrad. Takes time for the message to land. And they'll likely be scrambling to decide what to do. I sent the same message to IPRA and the WSA too. I think they'll bring us all home. Pay us off."

"I don't want their fucking money," said Acaba.

"No, but I'd take it. Give it to someone else, if you like. Make them feel good about it. Make Aphelion leave you alone."

They sipped at their gunshine. Retallick and Tobin looked at each other.

"Fill in the gaps, then, Anson," said Retallick.

Haig looked at each of them in turn, all expectant. "Sile was sent here as a punishment," said Haig. "He bankrupted his father's company, scavenged what he could from it and bought his way into Aphelion, then fucked up again. Aphelion built Gunport as a tax write-off or whatever."

"They were just getting into the space business," said Retallick. "They wanted to make a statement."

"That too," said Haig. "Tax write-off or white elephant. Point is, they didn't expect it to be successful. It was symbolic. A legacy holdover from their founder. The new board wanted it to fail and they wanted to get Sile out of the way. In their eyes, failure plus failure equalled opportunity. Get rid of both. When he got here, he made it successful, despite Aphelion's efforts. Profits up. Cut costs. Raised productivity. For Aphelion, it became a surprisingly viable way of getting stuff to Echion Alpha. They started getting paid to get payload there. Started making a profit for them. And they didn't ask questions about how he'd made it succeed. If they'd asked any questions at all, they'd know something was amiss. They gave him no resources and no help, so he must have done something off the books. But if they don't ask and he doesn't tell, then everyone can pretend they didn't know. He was emboldened, I think. Or scared. I'm not sure. Emboldened by Gunport's success but scared they'd see how successful it could be. Scared they'd send someone with real nous to take over and really drive it. He was paranoid about losing it. So he started building the second Gunport."

"He was taking things from the supply ships," said Tobin. "Draining my power," said Acaba.

"Yes. With Janulis' help. She told Galatea that we were all gene-edited. Meant it thought it could send spare power and resources to this new Gunport. They changed the safety protocols too, so that the new Gunport would have more power, materials. Let the Emergency Batteries run down. Putting this Gunport at risk. Komarov found out and he killed her, panicked, hid her in a suit. Dekker tried to cover it up for him. Fast forward and you went on strike, Sunita. And then I was sent here. Komarov's body hit the side of the Tower and Sile was on the defensive immediately. Mihalik tried to talk to me, and Attar raped her to try to silence her. She killed herself because of them. Sile had Prendrick pretend there was no body in the suit, but we'd already seen it. If he could control the narrative, he could beat this, he thought. But then everything began to topple out. They forged shuttle logs to make it look like Komarov had left. Prendrick was honest and he was killed for it. Barnes was coerced but when he was honest he was killed too. They tried to frame me by murdering him."

"He lied about everything," said Acaba.

"He was brazen," said Haig. "Thought he could bend the narrative by saying it was something else. Repetition of the lie gave it a life of its own. And I think it worked most of the time."

"I followed along for years," said Tobin.

"We all did," said Wecht.

They sat silently and stared into their cups until the gunshine was gone, and one-by-one, they got and left.

***

Aphelion responded. A reluctant appreciation. Back-handed gratitude.

You're all coming back to the Moon before we redeploy you, they said. Shuttles and experts en route. Co-operate fully and you'll be home in a year.

Hostility and aggression mostly dissipated. Knowing that they were leaving meant that there was no territory to fight for, nothing to hold on to. They settled into their rhythms, waiting on their flights.

The only surprise, Tobin had said, was that it was a small fleet of shuttles and an ORC, one of Aphelion's Orbital Rescue Craft. It'd park in orbit and they'd ferry people to it. He'd expected them to cram into the smallest of spaces. Haig didn't know how lucky he had been to have a shuttle to himself, said Tobin. Retallick and Kaneda repaired the Excalibur and Haig would be among the first to go, his purpose for being there exhausted. Tobin suspected that the ORC was not just to take the people, but to take assets. Aphelion would want Galatea, would want the Reactor. Might even send a team of poor bastards to try and fix it. Would certainly never admit that it had failed. Aphelion would want them out before any hint of failure hit Earth.

Their redeployments scattered them far and wide.

Wecht was going to the Moon for a year for research into the effects of isolation on a person's ability to operate at high capacity for long periods, before then, finally going on to Echion Alpha. Retallick and Kaneda to a space station off of Neptune. Part of Aphelion's Extra-Universal program. Fuel cell engineering. Kaneda spent a disproportionate amount of time packing his keirin equipment, and Haig wondered if it was to avoid thinking about what was next. Bethe's medical facility was copied and rebuilt – larger – in another Aphelion facility above the tertiary moon of Anacilius Delta, a mere month from Earth. Bethe's facility was going to be bigger than the one he had now, purpose built for his particular skills. Wecht was with him when he saw his posting. He had been near silent now for several days, she said. Attar was going back to Earth, programming drones to monitor crop rotations. He seemed neither pleased nor disappointed, and unlike everyone else, no-one asked him about it. One of the few pleased with their new duty was Acaba, being sent to build reactors for Aphelion's research into colony ships. All being well, she said, they would be able to send humanity somewhere they had never been before, somewhere pure and clean.

Haig was a sticking point. He wasn't Aphelion's and IPRA weren't keen on having him back but couldn't fire him because he had not only completed his assigned mission, he had brought murderers to justice. So, with more than a tinge of embarrassment, he was being outsourced. Back to Earth, to AWSE-S, All-World Space Elevator – Urban Police, a small force that policed the town around an enormous Space Elevator. Back into uniform proper.

Haig sent a message to Tom, smiling as he typed: 'I'm coming home.'

EPILOGUE (PART 2)

A lone body is floating across the Plains of Clarity.

Its arms are frozen into place, the body curling at the spine and rigid. The arms reach out for something that might help, that could keep it alive, but nothing is coming, nothing will come, and nothing has ever been coming.

Stars pierce the blackness above and the hard crystals of ice at the body's lips and ears shimmer and glisten. It stares coldly at the surface, coarse dust rolling by. The body crosses a track of silver, the faintest waft of glittering dust still hanging in the air, and as if in solidarity, it sinks momentarily to offer a perpendicular scar, to bring itself across what it has seen.

The body rolls slowly in the air, and without realising, crosses the lip of the Vallis Adlivun, the depths of the canyon sinking and warping out below. It sees two of its colleagues hanging in the open space, neither sinking nor ascending, half in light and half in shadow. One wears the frayed costume of a moon-going explorer, an open visor aimed upwards, the petrified face bleached pale in the light of Domiyat Outer. The other has been ravaged by the whizzing of micro-meteors tearing through it again and again until it was punched and wrenched into this pit, where it sags, shredded and defiled.

Where it passes its former colleagues it simply drifts by, watching them sink or be pulled apart, battered to dust by the moon. It will take centuries for them to become as one with Anguta R-611, for them to be subsumed into it. The moon will not host them kindly.

The body continues its journey. It floats amongst the ruined paste-buildings of Gunport 2, brushing a frozen toe against a hardened cone, scraping a shoulder into abandoned mining equipment. There is a rumble below, lights flickering up from the pit.

Perhaps this circuit will become the same as the others.

Printed in Great Britain
by Amazon